Suzanne & Bill Becker

March 2003

Finished 4.12.03
on flight to Houston
en Route to Mexico City

Green Grass Grace

A Novel

Shawn McBride

A TOUCHSTONE BOOK
Published by Simon & Schuster
NEW YORK   LONDON   TORONTO   SYDNEY   SINGAPORE

TOUCHSTONE
Simon & Schuster, Inc.
Rockefeller Center
1230 Avenue of the Americas
New York, NY 10020

TOUCHSTONE and colophon are registered trademarks
of Simon & Schuster, Inc.

For information about special discounts for bulk purchases,
please contact Simon & Schuster Special Sales: 1-800-456-6798 or
business@simonandschuster.com

Designed by Colin Joh
Text set in Goudy OldStyle

Manufactured in the United States of America

1   3   5   7   9   10   8   6   4   2

Library of Congress Cataloging-in-Publication Data is available.

ISBN 0-7432-2311-X

For Chloe, Alyssa, and Aislinn

Green Grass
Grace

Because, my dear sir, there are so many different kinds of boob. There is the apple boob, the pear boob, the lewd boob, the bashful boob, and God knows what besides.

—Gustave Flaubert, letter to Louis Bouilhet, 1851

1

Hellfire hallelujah and halitosis. Mike Schmidt sits to pee.

How you doing, fuckface? My name's Henry Tobias Toohey. I love Jesus, rock and roll, and Grace McClain but not in that order. Can I get an amen? Can I get a witness? I come to you in the Holy Name of God, Yahweh, the Big Finger, the Eye in the Sky, He Be Who Be. He came to me in a vision and gave me a mission of love. He said: Henry, make Grace your wife. Sing to her and propose marriage in front of a wedding reception crowd. Do it for her love, for your parents to fall back in love, and for your depressed older brother to snap out of his sad sleep. Is that all, Big Fella? Not a problem. Your Will Be Done.

Good morning, St. Patrick Street. Good morning, Philadelphia. City of brotherly love. City of dead-end and one-way streets. A blossoming metropolis, center of commerce, magnet of opportunity for criminals both organized and unorganized. Home of the Phillies, Flyers, Sixers, and Eagles, in that fucking order. Good morning, Americas North, South, Latin, and Central. Good morning, Canada. Good morning, Russia, Czechoslovakia, Honduras, Zimbabwe, Brazil, Puerto Rico, Nicaragua, Australia, Ireland, Japan, China, Appalachia, Chile, Mexico,

Upper Mongolia, Outer Mongolia, Lower Mongolia, Inner Mongolia, Inside-Out Mongolia, Upside-Down Mongolia. I leave anybody out? Tough break, fuckheads.

It's a perfect Friday morning on the last weekend of summer vacation, 1984. The sun punches through the NFL curtains on the window of the bedroom I share with my older brother, Stephen Joseph Toohey, who's eighteen and a drunk. Stephen sleeps below me on the bottom bunk. He's snoring loud, has puke on his pillow, and most likely doesn't remember last night's fistfight with our dad, Francis Nathaniel Toohey Junior.

Stephen and Francis Junior have made late-night fights a family tradition. Fight Night with the Tooheys, every night. In this corner, standing five-nine, weighing a buck fifty, looking lost to everybody, is the underdog, Stephen Toohey. The Pug with the Lonely Mug. In the opposite corner, standing five-seven, weighing a buck eighty, and having more hair on his back than on his head is our champion, Francis Nathaniel Toohey Junior. Francis the Fighting Mailman.

I want a clean fight, fellas. No rabbit punches no clinches. Keep quiet so the neighbors don't call the cops again, so Cecilia Regina Toohey Senior and Cecilia Regina Toohey Junior, AKA Cece, don't cry. Please refrain from punching Francis Nathaniel Toohey III when he comes inside the living room from his house next door to break up the brawl. Most important, keep the action away from the television, which has recently been equipped with cable. Knocking over a cable television is more of a mortal sin than pissing in a priest's chalice, so if you have to knock over furniture try a coffee table or armchair.

My Philadelphia Phillies alarm clock says ten-thirty. Damn. I'm supposed to meet my best pal Bobby James now. I'm not worried, though. I'll be down there in an hour after I get dressed and comb my hair. Before I do anything, though, I have to deal with Mike Schmidt. I guess I should explain who he is in case you are either A) a broad or B) a fella who plays with dollies.

Mike Schmidt plays third for the Phillies and is my mortal enemy for reasons I don't care to discuss right now due to personal inner pain. I'm trying to get on with my life since the Incident. Bull's-eye. The spitball I shoot at his poster hits him square in his big honker, the fucker, next to hundreds of other spitballs. I do this every morning. It's therapy. I'm already feeling better.

I walk down the hallway toward my parents' bedroom straight ahead, past Cece's bedroom and the bathroom, heading for Cecilia Toohey's records. Her collection, like my hair, is spectacular. She owns every album made between 1950 and 1979. Stacks of LPs line the walls, and 45s are stuffed in spilling cabinets. I go to the 45s—won't be time to hear an album. What do I feel like? Here we go: "Let It Hang Out (Let It All Hang Out)" by the Hombres. Good tune. I pull it out of the sleeve and walk to the record player in Cece's room, where our band, Phillies Alarm Clock, practices. I drop the needle. The song starts with a sermon. It also has handclaps. I dance and sing along in my white underwear. Tell me the truth: have you ever seen such rhythm in a honky? Say yeah. Make me laugh.

"Henry, shut the fuck up and turn that down," yells Stephen from his bed.

I lower the volume, stop singing, and do the hustle backwards to the bathroom. I'm at the mirror as the Hombres keep singing. A quick check for armpit hair reveals none. No stubble on the face either. Fuck a duck, I'm thinking, as Stephen staggers into the bathroom, kneels in front of the bowl, and pukes.

"Yo. Henry, there's something wrong with you. You know that, don't you?"

Stephen has bright green eyes, even when he pukes in the bowl after a bender. His black hair is a wet, spiked mess. He's five-nine, handsome, but not like I am. Far as handsome goes, I'm in my own freaking league. Ask any broad, or me.

"Yo. How do you figure?" I ask, as I soak my head under the sink faucet.

"Where would I start? The music. The hair combing. The preaching." He pukes.

"I wasn't preaching. That was part of the record. I was singing along, jerk-off."

"Maybe so," he says, "but I have heard you repeating stuff TV preachers say."

"So what?" I ask. "They're funny. Don't you think so?"

I watch preachers on cable and dig their clothes and hair-styles. If I'm not watching preachers, it's stand-up comedians. Same thing, really, except comedians have bad hair or bald heads and can't dress for shit, the fucks.

"I wouldn't know," he says. "I don't watch them." Puke.

"Don't know what you're missing," I tell him.

"If you say so," he says. "I like it better when you imitate the stand-up comedy."

"I don't imitate nobody, you fucking fuckball. Stay here," I say, then walk pissed to our bedroom and open my top dresser drawer, where a box protects Big Green, my comb. Once I open the lid, remove a brown bag, unzip a sandwich bag, and unroll a wad of tissue, Big Green, a bad unbreakable motherfucker, appears. "What's up, pal?" I say. Yeah, I talk to my comb. Fuck you. Big Green, a man of action, says nothing. I walk him to the bathroom, where Stephen now sleeps on the rim of the bowl. He put on fifteen pounds since he left high school last June with a diploma he'll need to cover his head when he's sleeping on the street in the rain, which is what Francis Junior has been threatening him with.

Stephen started drinking a year ago after his girlfriend Megan died in a car crash up the block. Then he quit football a month later, for his senior year. His grades dropped. His personality disappeared. He was always funny before. He made everybody laugh, he made everybody feel better about themselves, about life, especially me. He was my hero. He always stepped in to stop a bullshit fight with a couple jokes. He was never not smiling. A room buzzed when he showed up. Then Megan died and the bottom dropped out on him. Francis Junior got involved, and it's been downhill from there. Stephen drinks, comes home, throws hands with Francis Junior, and passes out. He wakes up the next day, pukes in the toilet, falls asleep on the toilet, wakes up, and asks me questions about the night before, which he doesn't remember.

"Henry, you seen Daddy this morning?" asks Stephen.

"No," I say. "Ain't seen him since you two fought last night."

"What?" he asks. "When did we fight?"

"You're kidding, right?"

"No. I remember coming in and having a hard time climbing the stairs."

I rub two globs of gel into my hair. Next, I comb the hair straight back. I'm ready to make a part in the middle, but I want to tell Stephen what the fuck happened last night. I can only do one at a time. It wouldn't be fair to Stephen or the hair otherwise.

"You *did* have trouble getting up the stairs," I say.

"Yeah, see, I told you," he says, relieved.

"Daddy and Frannie *carried* you upstairs. You were out cold. So you could say you had a hard or easy time, depending on how you look at it."

"Seriously?"

"Seriously."

"Daddy go after me or I go after him?" he asks.

"I don't know," I tell him. "I was on the top step, filling out a fight card, eating jujubees and malty balls."

"Shut up. What I say to him?"

"Don't really remember. Fuck you, fuck off, jerk-off, cock-sucker. The usual."

"I mention Daddy porking Mrs. Cooney behind Mommy's back?" asks Stephen.

Francis Junior is cheating on his wife, our mom, Cecilia Regina Toohey Senior, with Mrs. Cooney, who lives across St. Patrick Street, the last house at the other end of the block.

We're the last house on this side. If St. Patrick Street was a rectangle, a straight path from the Tooheys' to the Cooneys' would cut it in half into two triangles.

"No, nothing like that," I say.

"Did Mommy cry?"

"Yup."

"Shit. What else happen?"

All of a sudden I'm not up for telling him more. First off, I still haven't parted the hair. Second, I still haven't parted the hair. So I let him off easy. Mentioning the police visit or his sobbing won't do any good right now. Have to get to the hair here.

"It wasn't that bad," I say. "You knocked over some shit is about all."

"So that was it? You sure I didn't say nothing stupid in front of Mommy?"

"I'm sure. She knows anyway, don't she?"

"That don't mean you spell it out for her. There's a thing called class." He pukes.

"Look, this has been real," I say, "but I gotta fix the hair, buddy. Go back to bed."

"Yeah, I'm gonna right after this," he says, then dry heaves. "There, that's better. Have a good day, young Henry. Put some clothes on. You go out like that, broads will run from everywhere to shove dollar bills in your BVDs."

He walks back to our bedroom, moaning and muttering that life blows, in a scary-nervous voice. The idea of broads shoving bucks in my trunks excites me. Now I have a boner, standing at the bathroom mirror in my white underwear. Look at this fucking thing. I wish I knew how to get rid of them. I need to hit the library. Time to get my mind off the boner and back to the hair.

It (the hair) stiffened enough that I consider showering and shampooing so I can start from scratch, but I'm not that desperate. I'm not what you'd call a bather. I part and feather the hair—piece of cake—then spray. Here's a tip: when you spray your hair, don't pay attention to instructions on the can. Let it rip for three minutes straight. You want the bathroom in a cloud of haze so thick that you fart and mistake it for a foghorn. Done and done. Now that the hair's complete it's time to dress.

But first a quick review of my hair and fashion tips. Showering every day is overrated. There's no need. I stick to Mondays, Wednesdays, and Saturdays. Sundays are Days of the Lord, and it should be noted that vain exercises like bathing are sins. However, hair care and not bathing are only two steps to looking and feeling great.

Step three is picking an outfit that separates you from the herd. How? Simple. Avoid sports team T-shirts unless you work under cars or feed slop to pigs. Try a collared shirt with buttons like the one I'm putting on now. No one will find one as cool as mine, what with all the moose on the shirt, but the point is to find one that says you like a shirt full of moose says me. Ignore those gurgling and snorting noises Stephen makes. Choosing shorts is simple. With a moose shirt it only makes sense to wear plaid shorts. No way a broad like Grace can resist. For shoes I'll wear black sneakers with yellow racing stripes. They throw off the color scheme I got going, but it doesn't kill you if the shoes don't match the rest. Next, I tuck Big Green inside a tube sock for quick-draw access.

Finally, no outfit is complete without some article of clothing that praises Jehovah somewhere. I go low-key with scapulars, which are like two cloth stamps with pictures of saints attached to shoestrings. You wear scapulars like a double necklace, half in front, half in back. And here's the beautiful thing: scapulars are a get-out-of-Hell-free card, guaranteed. You die wearing scapulars, you go straight to Heaven, no questions asked.

For instance, say today I go outside, hijack a bus, and, I don't know, run over old ladies with walkers. Then I get off the bus and empty the change out of their purses. I take that money, go to the bar, get drunk. At the bar, I start an argument with a fella about who's better looking, me or Bobby Redford. He says me by a little. I say me by a lot. I go back outside, get behind the bus wheel, come through the bar wall, and run him over. I take money out of his wallet, walk over to the juke, and punch up the song "Old Time Rock & Roll" by Bob Seger and the Silver Bullet Band. I sit back down, order another drink, and start another argument with another fella about who's tougher, me or Bobby De Niro. He says De Niro by a little. I say De Niro by a lot. I end that argument also by running him the fuck over with the bus.

I settle in for another drink. De Niro walks in the bar, sits down next to me, orders a shot, and knocks it back like the badass he is. He squints and asks, *You talking about me? Were you talking about me?* I tell him *Yeah, but I was saying good things, Bobby.* He isn't buying that shit. He pulls out a big-ass Mob gun, blows me full of holes. I'm dead but wearing scapulars. After all that, the question is, do scapulars save me from Hell? Yes and no. Ordinarily I'd go straight to Heaven, even if I passed through the Pearly Gates holding the bus steering wheel and a cold beer.

But we forgot the worst sin of all. Worse than murder, or missing Mass even. I played Bob Seger on a juke. Even God can't forgive that shit.

The living room is a mess. A lamp lays on the floor next to the overturned coffee table and spilt magazines. Plastic covers on the sofa and love seat aren't fastened firmly. At least the television and cable box are safe. I grab the remote off the cable box and push the power button. It's the usual shit heap: talk shows that'd be funnier if folks fistfought, music videos with German jerk-offs playing pianos like guitars, cooking shows hosted by fat broads, black-and-white reruns, soap operas, and game shows. Finally I find a Jesus channel, where a preacher with high Elvis hair, ruffled shirt, and powder blue tuxedo holds the fat hands of a whale woman with tits like two waterbeds. The whale woman with the waterbed tits blubbers. She lost Jesus somewhere but found Him again, praise God. The preacher smiles and sweats. The audience applauds and shouts shit. I flick off the TV. Then back on. Then back off. On once more. Off again. I love this remote.

Outside, a dog growls, and a man yells in pain. I run to the front porch, where my dog Gwen Flaggart is biting the mailman, who's also my dad, Francis Nathaniel Toohey Junior. Francis Junior calls Flaggart a fat bitch as she chomps his ankle.

"Yo, Dad," I say. "Got a package for me today?"

Me and Bobby James placed an order in the back of MAD Magazine for a ton of shit including, but not limited to, plastic dog doo, trick gum, smoke pellets, and a hovercraft. We're going to ride the hovercraft to school. Hovercrafts get chicks.

"Yo, Henry," he says. "What? You talking about this?"

He pulls a small brown box out of his stuffed mailbag and hands it to me while Flaggart growls and bites. He points his dog spray at her and lets go with the juice. Bam. Flaggart, one ugly bitch, rolls on her back, runs her paws over her eyes, and sneezes, her yellow fangs looking almost like a smile.

"Get her in the house before I kill her, Henry," he says.

I open the door and he kicks her in the ass. Inside, she bitch-strolls over to Gene, our other dog, who's sleeping. Gene wakes up, spots Flaggart, and moves. Flaggart sits down in his warm lost place. Me and Francis Junior stay outside on the porch.

"Henry, is Stephen still asleep upstairs?" he asks.

"Nah," I say, "he was awake."

"How's he doing?"

"Not too good. He's puking."

"I figured that. I meant did he seem upset? Sad?"

"Yeah, but he's always that," I say.

"I know," replies Francis Junior, who looks exactly like Stephen with a gut, less hair, a fatter face, and dark circles under his eyes.

"He mentioned going down to Community College today," I lie.

"Did he? Wow," says Francis Junior. "Maybe something I said sunk in."

"Yeah, OK, Dad," I say, patient, although he's dumb to think that.

"You understand my point about school and shit, don't you?"

"Sure."

Up the street, Bobby James pokes his fat head out his door and looks toward my house but is too blind to spot me from this far. This is good because if he saw me he'd throw a hissy fit. Once he goes back inside, the phone rings behind me.

"I gotta stay on his shit now, Henry," says Francis Junior. "He's drifting. Can't let one heartbreak break you, goddammit. Life blows, that's a fact, but it moves on and you have to too. He should play ball and go to college. You too. I don't want you lugging junk mail and running from dogs. You're both too smart for that."

"I hear you, brother," I say.

"Stop being funny. I'm serious now. This job ain't easy," he answers, a faraway look in his eyes. This means he's launching into a speech, which he has to stop here and there to answer questions about the mail from the neighbors. "Henry, I just want to see you get more than I got out of life—*Hello, Mildred, yes your* Reader's Digest *came in, I'll be right there*—I was working at the Post Office when I was sixteen, Henry, I only got a break from that to go to Vietnam—*Harry, that insurance check didn't come today, I'll keep looking for it, I promise*—your brother ain't thinking straight and will kick himself later for bad decisions he makes now—*Eunice, I'll be there in two minutes, for crying out loud, you toothless old coot*—you're even smarter than Stephen; I won't let you refill water glasses at catering halls when you could be reading important books at college, chasing skirts, away from all this noise and nonsense. I can't let Stephen throw everything away because his high school sweetheart died. I carried my baby brother dead out of my own house when I was seventeen and he was seven. I had work the next day. I went. Life was waiting. If I gotta fight your brother to keep him on this planet, I will, goddammit—*Yes, my own dog bit me, Mike*—look, I have to go before these people light torches and chase me down for the mail. Your hair looks fine; you can put that thing away. Listen, what are you doing with yourself today?"

"The usual," I say. "Hanging with Bobby James. Looking for chicks and loose change. Professing my love for Yahweh out loud."

I always say shit like this because he doesn't listen.

"Write your mom a note, OK?" he says. "And behave. You got any money?"

"Do I ever?"

He pulls out his wallet, which has three ripped one-dollar bills. He hands me two, looks at the last bill, then hands me that too. "Here," he says.

"Thanks, pal."

"Don't mention it."

"Dad," I say, switching gears, "why would a fella pork another broad behind his wife's back?"

"What?" he asks, almost jumping out of his sneaks before dropping his bag to bend down and retie them and not look at me. "Why do you ask?"

"No reason," I say. "Somebody mentioned it the other day up at the playground."

"Who were they talking about?"

"I forget. Not you."

"I wasn't thinking me," he says, standing up, putting his bag back on his shoulder.

"I know," I say. "But you'd be a punk to do that, right?"

"Yeah, something like that. Look, I gotta move. Be good today."

"You too."

Francis Junior leaves to finish the street, climbing porch railings with his legs windmilling like he's a gymnast. I watch him for a minute, then walk back in the house, find a pen and paper, and write, "Ma, I went out. I'll be back. Yours in Christ, Henry." Cecilia will laugh at that. She likes Jesus jokes. I click off the television with the remote, then turn it on and off again. Remote controls. Wow. It's five minutes to noon. The phone rings in the kitchen. Stephen pukes and moans upstairs. The needle scratches at the 45 I never turned off. I step out into the sweet summer air. The sunshine hits me with the warmth of Yahweh's infinite love.

2

Sister Edwina Immaculata, my seventh-grade homeroom nun last year, got sick in May, right in front of class one morning while screaming at Daniel McDaniel, whose hair was a lumpy bedhead mop, for putting erasers up his nose. I thought it was a pretty funny bit myself, but nuns are a different breed. They laugh at corny jokes told by creepy priests and don't recognize rubber erasers up the nose as the kind of comedy that separates the pros from the hacks. I was jealous of Daniel for the bit. Physical comedy isn't a strong suit of mine. I got a laugh or two in my day by walking into this street pole or tripping over that park bench, but it was always an accident. Not Daniel McDaniel. Those erasers were up his nose because he put them there.

We all laughed so hard that Sister Edwina Immaculata, who only has one hard tiny tit as a result of jug cancer, turned around from writing the Seven Deadly Sins on the blackboard and found one of her students acting not Catholic. Sister, who had a short fuse, flew off the handle and accused Daniel McDaniel of sloth to incorporate the lesson into real life. That is, she broke a fucking pointer over her knee and shouted *sloth sloth sloth* until she turned red and hit the floor. She dropped like somebody shot her and didn't get back up either, unless you count when paramedics lifted her twitching carcass onto a stretcher. Legend has it she sits on a porch rocker at the Sisters of the Immaculate Heart vacation home in Cape May, New Jersey, drinks tomato soup through a straw, and mutters *sloth sloth sloth* until someone bends her over and puts a needleful of horse downers in her spotted ass.

All this has nothing to do with anything other than the substitute teacher we got to finish the year for Sister, a young small-boobed fox named Mizz Jenkins, who was tall with long brown hair and brown eyes. She wore short flowered skirts with sleeveless shirts. She bent over to help you at your desk and you could see her bra. She had a dark freckle on her dancer calf I wanted to eat like a chocolate chip. She made fun of Catholics, designated Fridays as creative days, showed us paintings by great painters, and introduced us to her favorite kind of art, minimalism.

Which leads me to my point. If you, like Mizz Jenkins with the flat tits and ballerina calf muscles, are a fan of minimalism, St. Patrick Street isn't for you. Narrow row homes line either side of the street. The front doors—all white, with black eagles—open on concrete porches enclosed by black iron railings. The porches are littered with barbecue grills, Big Wheels, roller skates, toy boxes, hubcaps, car parts, Phillies and Flyers pennants, headless dolls, dog shits, and trashcans full of empty beer bottles. Every two houses share a cement path, with two sets of steps, that leads to the sidewalks at the bottom of the steep, skinny, grass-hill front yards.

The yards are the cappers. Despite the fact that each yard is a foot wide and a mile steep, the neighbors on St. Patrick Street go all out in decorating with MONDALE-FERRARO FOR PRESIDENT AND VP signs, flowerbeds, cardboard farm animals, KEEP OFF THE GRASS warnings, American flags, and saint statues. Everybody owns a saint statue. St. Patrick Street has seventy-eight row homes, seventy-eight hills for lawns, and seventy-eight cement statues of dead saints. Wait, seventy-seven saints and one Virgin Mary. My bad.

Now add people. The roller skates and Big Wheels not sitting on porches are under the asses of little kids zooming everywhere. Their moms got short Bride of Frankenstein hairdos, wear fake gold earrings and purple velour sweats, smoke Virginia Slims, and shout at the top of their lungs for the kids to slow down, speed up, zip up, come back, or stay out. Their dads wear Jeff hats—which is what we call those wool hats that the newsies wore—and strut to Paul Donohue's, the corner bar up the block, while their wives warn them not to come home drunk again. Older teens stand in packs of five and six and hover around cars with the hoods up and their shirts off. Old bags cross their arms, frown at anything anyone under thirty does, and wonder out loud to each other, the Lord, and their husbands in Heaven how kids today behave like disrespectful monsters. St. Patrick Street is Irish Catholic, period. Anybody who isn't is a dirtball or a heathen or both, doesn't live here, doesn't belong here, and isn't welcome, even to stroll the sidewalk, unless they like taking beer bottles off the head.

Today on St. Patrick Street, things look pretty ordinary. Bobby James's dad, Mr. James, who has short neat hair parted on the side, stands in his cop uniform, responding to a call at the Mahon house. Mrs. Mahon, who has torpedo tits, locked Mr. Mahon (bald with a greasy combover on top) out of the house because he's returning from an all-nighter at Paul Donohue's. Mrs. Mahon drops full bottles of Budweiser on Mr. Mahon from an upstairs window in an attempt to crack open his head.

"Here," she screams, "you like these goddamn things so much."

"Why are you doing this, Peg?" asks Mr. Mahon, calm and clumsy, as he tries to catch his babies. He was saving them at a high percentage until he decided to open one and drink it. Now, his attempts to one-hand the falling bottles while drinking another has led to foam and broken glass. Mr. James, a gentle guy, keeps calm and tries to talk sense.

"Peg, this solves nothing. Dan, do you have to drink another right now?" he asks.

"Yo, Mr. James," I say. "How you doing?"

"Yo, Henry," he answers. "All right until I had to come see these two."

"Hi, Mrs. Mahon. Hi, Mr. Mahon."

"Hi, Henry, tell your mother I said hello," says Mrs. Mahon.

"Henry, help me catch some of these bottles," answers Mr. Mahon.

"Don't say that to the kid. Stay where you're at, Henry," Mr. James tells me.

Damn. It looks fun catching beer bottles falling from a window. I could catch more than Mr. Mahon, who probably dreams about Bud bottles falling from the sky, only not aimed at his head by his wife from the upstairs window of the house he calls home. In his dreams, they float down with parachutes and land right in his full red cooler, and his wife isn't in the dream unless her head's packed in the ice with the Buds.

"Henry, what would you do if you were in my shoes?" asks Mr. James.

"Shoot them both," I say. "Then go back to the doughnut shop."

"Not funny, Henry. I'm telling your mom you said that," scolds Mrs. Mahon.

"Less jokes, more help catching these bottles," says a now frantic Mr. Mahon.

"Shoot them," laughs Mr. James. "It's probably better you come from mailmen than cops with that strategy. If you pick one as a profession, go with mailman."

"I'd like to be a mailman-cop," I say. "Deliver the mail, and if I see somebody climbing through a window, fucking spray him with Mace, then mail him to prison."

"You think this fella would fit in a mailbox?" asks Mr. James, pointing to Mr. Mahon, whose faded Phillies shirt never covers his belly.

Francis Junior walks up to the Mahon house with their mail. He nods to Mr. James and Mr. Mahon, then calls up to Mrs. Mahon. "Peg, you need a change of address card for this boob? I can put one in the box with the mail."

"Yeah, do that for me, Fran," she says. "Can you forward mail to Siberia?"

"Beats me. Only thing I know about mail is how to misdeliver my own route."

"And you do that well," says Mr. Mahon.

The men laugh and work together to catch the falling bottles.

"You boys watch the Phils last night?" my dad asks, his bag held out for a bottle.

"Carlton didn't pitch so hot," says Mr. James, snagging a bottle that hits the porch awning without breaking before rolling down and racing for the cement. "His fastball had no bite. His curve hung high."

"Supposedly he has a chip floating in his elbow," Mr. Mahon tells them while catching a bottle without taking his eyes off either of them.

"Don't matter. The docs can zap that shit right out in a half-hour operation and have a pitcher back on the mound in a couple weeks," says Mr. James, who misses one that breaks before catching the next.

"Carlton should get it done before the pennant drive. Can't expect Schmidt to hit a homer in the ninth every game," says Francis Junior, who catches one, twists the cap off, and hands it to Mr. Mahon.

"Thanks, Fran," says Mr. Mahon.

"No problem."

"Fuck Mike Schmidt," I tell them.

Everybody besides Francis Junior looks at me funny.

"He don't like Schmidt," Francis Junior explains, shrugging.

"Yeah, I can't stand him," I say. "Gotta knock for Bobby James. So long, folks."

They say so long, then return to their fun, Mrs. Mahon dropping bottles and yelling about changing locks, all four of them laughing about marriage and kids and how the whole deal blows.

Folks are like that around here. They fight, but they're friendly at the same time somehow. Similar shit happens every two houses the rest of the way to Bobby James's. Three-hundred-pound Mr. Mulligan (Elvis hair and sideburns) bends three-hundred-pound son Tubby (same deal hairwise) over a clothesline with his pants down and smacks his bare ass for pulling the fire alarm on a telephone pole. Three-hundred-pound blimp-titted Mrs. Mulligan tells Tubby it hurts them worse than him to beat his big bare ass in public. The fire chief, Mr. O'Malley, who wears a piece and lives on the block, hides his eyes in his hands as the fat fucks fight. Jimmy Kilpatrick and Jimmy Mulaney, two crewcutted five-year-old punks, run down the street with a diaper they stole off the ass of two-year-old Denise McKeever. Mrs. Kilpatrick and Mrs. Mulaney, who are both young with cantaloupe tits and no bras (hallelujah!), chase after them screaming and laughing to each other about their monsters. An old bat, nice-titted Mrs. Farber, squirts old-bat best friend and worst enemy, no-titted Mrs. Wilson, in the face with a garden hose in a flowerbed beef gone bad. Tennis balls hit front doors and parents shout Yo from inside. Bottle rockets and firecrackers whiz past three-year-olds on tricycles. Dogs chase cats and squirrels. Televisions blast from inside the houses of the deaf and dumb. Francis Junior hands everybody their electric bills and boxes of checks.

I'm combing my hair and close to the James house when Ralph Cooney and Gerald Wilson call me from across the street.

"Yo, Henry the comb-o-sexual," says Gerald. "Get over here."

I cross the street and meet them at Gerald's car, which sits on four cinder blocks and has no windows. Gerald, whose hair is bushy and parted on the side like a chess club fuck, is grandson of the Mrs. Wilson coughing up hose water. He lives with her because his parents are dead. Ralph, who has a dry boxy army cut, is the son of Mrs. Cooney, the lady my dad is porking. He hates my whole family, like we're all porking her. Gerald and Ralph are both military weapons buffs. They wear camouflage shirts, burn ants, build bombs, all that cool shit chicks love. Gerald is tall and skinny. Ralph is short and stocky.

"Yo," I say. "You two are tank-sexuals."

Gerald laughs. "The tank-sexual statement shows how little you know about sex and military equipment, Henry. A tank only has one orifice and it's far too wide to accommodate any kind of enjoyable friction during penetration."

"You're losing me with all this military jargon, General," I say.

Ralph laughs, angry, moving closer. "Military jargon. How old are you now?"

"Thirteen," I tell him.

"Thirteen. *The mailman* knows all about those words, don't he, Toohey?" says Ralph, who calls Francis Junior *the mailman* like it's more spit than job description.

"What?" I ask. "Maybe. He was in the army in Vietnam."

"You think he ever came close to being killed by a gook? Probably not, since he's sneaky like a gook. Look, your sneaky gook dad is sneaking up to my house right now. Ma. *Yo, Ma,*" Ralph shouts to his mom, like a broad, as she smiles and takes the mail off my dad on the porch of their house, the last one he delivers on our street before heading up the Ave and elsewhere.

"What, Ralph?" she asks, impatient, lighting a smoke, Francis Junior standing next to her, looking like the guilty bastard he is.

"Where's Daddy?" asks Ralph.

"He's working at the prison, Ralph," she says. "You know that."

Mr. Cooney is a guard at Holmesburg Prison, which is five blocks east of St. Patrick Street, near I-95 and the Delaware River. Living near a prison is cool. Sometimes you see a jerk-off in a jumpsuit and handcuffs sprint up the street after busting out. A lot of neighborhood dads are guards at Holmesburg. Either that or mailmen, cops, firemen, construction workers, roofers, truck drivers, or gas or electric men. Around here, nobody's dad leaves for work in a tie or comes home clean. And, with jobs like that, nobody goes to bed hungry but nobody has money in the bank either. Paycheck to paycheck is the name of the game.

"Maybe you should let the *mailman* deliver his *mail* and finish his *mail* route."

"Maybe you should mind your goddamn business, Ralph," says Mrs. Cooney, who has C cups and is short with short hair, dark features, and olive skin. She's cute but can't touch Cecilia Toohey by a mile. "Henry, how you doing?" she asks me, smiling. She's always nice to me, so I talk to her polite, not shooting her static but not letting her think I like her either.

"You know," I say, "can't complain."

"My son bothering you?" she asks.

"No, we're just talking down here, trading recipes and shit. The usual girl stuff."

She laughs. "Well, let me know if he does bother you, and I'll straighten his ass out. Ralph, I'm going in the house to use the phone and watch some TV. That OK?"

Ralph says nothing back to her, instead staring at the ground with his mouth clamped shut, his jawbones showing through his skin. His mom says something we can't hear to Francis Junior, who nods before climbing over their porch rail and hopping down into the alley next to the Cooney house to head up to the Ave.

"When you getting windows on this heap so I can see what I'm doing?" I ask Gerald as I comb my hair without a mirror. Not that I need one. I just prefer one.

"You and your jokes, Toohey," sneers Ralph. "The Tooheys. You're all pussies."

"This is true, Ralph," I agree, still combing my hair, not bothered. I feel bad for him for the most part. Not a happy home, his.

"There you go again," he says. "Shut the fuck up for once."

"Ease up, Ralph," Gerald tells him before turning to me. "Henry, what are you doing tonight? Going up Tack Park?"

"Doubt it," I answer. "We're playing Freedom on the street. Oh, and Seamus O'Shaunnesy is hosting a bra-removal seminar. I'm going to that."

"What does Seamus know about bras?"asks Gerald.

"What do you know about bras?" I say.

Gerald clears his throat, points to the car. "I'm getting flames painted on there."

"And why so interested in what I'm doing tonight?" I ask. "We ain't pals."

"No shit," says Gerald. "Still, you might be needed at the park tonight."

"Huh?"

"Some Fishtown dirtballs might show up at the park tonight."

Fishtown is a white neighborhood located mostly under the El, near all-black North Philly. Fishtown is poorer and meaner than our poor and mean neighborhood, which is called Holmesburg, just like the prison.

"So?" I say. "How do you know?"

"I heard at the park last night," says Gerald. "Some kid said his sister met a Fishtown kid at a dance last week, and that he's coming up to the park with a couple buddies to see her and maybe play some hoops."

"So what?" I ask. "Always fellas up there. What do you need me for?"

"We need anybody and everybody, and it's not for basketball," says Ralph, staring at me hard, his eyes darting and shrinking, fear in there with the anger.

"My bad. You wanna beat them up, twenty kids on three. That's fair."

"Look, this ain't about fairness," says Gerald, scowling. "It's about teaching dirtballs from a dirtball neighborhood that coming here ain't allowed." He arches one eyebrow. "Your brother Stephen will be there."

"Least we're *hoping* that," smiles Ralph. "I mean, all Tooheys are pussies, everyone knows that, but maybe you two add up to one real man."

"Easy on the math. You got smoke shooting out your big ears," I say, finally annoyed. Turns out to be a bad move, because Ralph, who's been waiting for a chance to step shit up, makes like he's going to pop me. I hop back, trip on the curb, and land on my ass. I get up quick but they laugh at me anyways.

"Fucking pussy Tooheys," says Ralph. "You need to toughen up, kid. Look, we'll be up the playground tonight with the men. You stay here on the street and play Freedom with the little girls. What do we care? Now you better go before your girlfriend over there has a stroke." He points to Bobby James, who stands on his front porch, talking into his dad's police bullhorn. HENRY TOOHEY, PLEASE REPORT TO MY FRONT PORCH PRONTO. HENRY TOOHEY, MY FRONT PORCH PRONTO. THAT IS ALL.

Bobby James needs fucking help. The kid isn't all there.

3

"Yo," says Bobby James. "You're late, Henrietta."

"Yo," I reply. "All this unnecessary worry will give you an ulcer, Roberta."

"All this unnecessary combing will make you bald."

"What kinda sick fucking joke is that?"

"Who's joking, Kojak?"

There are several keys to understanding Bobby James. He's not giving you any Bazooka bubble gum. Not regular, not cherry, not grape. He's not giving you any potato chips. Not ruffled, not barbecued, not sour cream and onions. He's not giving you any soda. Not Pepsi-Cola, not Coca-Cola, and especially not RC Cola. Why he won't is a mystery. His mom Mrs. James has the house stocked with candy like a fucking A-bomb might drop.

Couple other James facts. He always wears a Phils cap and Sixers shirt. He has blond hair like me, except his is more red and mine more white. He feathers it nice but then crushes it with the cap, the asshole. He calls his shits bowel movements. He French kisses his Chinese pug Beauregard, scoops Beauregard's poops off the lawn for dough, and likes doing both. He's a closet Cowboys fan and walks with the weight of that shame.

He's a neat freak. He polishes his sneaks, combs his leg hair, irons his tube socks, and Windexes his wristwatch. He jumps like a bitch when you got something for him.

"You get the doggy doody and smoke pellets?" he asks. "The hovercraft come?"

"Calm down, girl," I say. "Here's the pellets. The hovercraft is on back order."

"What'd those two want?" he asks, pointing to Gerald and Ralph playing guitar with wrenches to "Crazy Train" by Ozzy Osbourne on the car radio they got to work somehow. I'm not the biggest Ozzy fan but that song's all right.

"They want us to help beat up Fishtown kids tonight at Tack Park," I say.

"What?" he asks, scared. Bobby James objects to playground war on the deeply religious grounds he can't fight for shit. Not that I can. No one's called either of us tough since slaps and hair pulls went out of fashion with fellas in fights.

"You heard me, fuckball," I say.

"Fuckball?" he asks. "There's class. You ain't going up there, are you?"

"Why would I? My face is my livelihood."

"Seriously, Henry."

"I seriously ain't going up there. I got no beef with Fishtown kids."

"Plus you can't fight," he says, as he feeds himself a piece of gum.

"Exactly. Got another piece?" I ask.

"No, I don't. None at all. Listen, we still knocking for Margie and Grace today?"

"Definitely." We slap five.

"Cool. They better let us feel their tits soon. We're all eighth graders now. It's time to give up the goods," he tells me, stuffing more gum he doesn't have in his yap.

"True and true," I agree, even though I still never even kissed a broad yet.

"Bobby James, you got a phone call," interrupts his big-titted big sister Jeannie James, who's getting married tomorrow at St. Ignatius. Standing inside the doorway and holding the phone, Jeannie spots me and smiles, like most broads do. "Henry Toohey, what's up? What are you doing today?"

"What's up, Jeannie? The usual. Styling and profiling. Looking for babes."

Jeannie laughs and her tits jiggle, reason enough to tell jokes.

"Can't hurt to look," she says. "You still coming to see me married tomorrow?"

"Yeah I'm coming," I say. "The real question is will you show up?"

"I'll be there, partner. It's Ace I'm worried about."

Ace is the almost-husband. He's cool. He takes us to Phillies games and yells with us at Mike Schmidt even though he doesn't give a fuck.

"You think he's seeing another man?" I ask.

"Whatever," she says. "I'd like to hear you say that to him. He's just nervous. The man hasn't eaten since last week. Not a pea, not a potato chip."

"What's he afraid of?" I say. "You stand up there. Have a small exchange with the priest. Say yeah, then you kiss. What the fuck's to that?"

"You should talk to him," she says. "Every other man tells him not to do it."

Up walks Francis Junior, everybody's favorite mailman.

"Jeannie, how you doing? I forgot this letter when I passed your house."

"So what else is new?" She laughs. "I'm good, Mr. Toohey. How about yourself?"

"When did you start calling me *Mister* Toohey?" he asks.

"About the same time you started going bald," she says.

"What?"

"I'm kidding. You almost dropped your mail purse when I said that."

"No, I almost swung it, doll. Can't tell an old lady she's going bald."

"Your hair's fine. Henry's the Toohey who'll go bald."

"Can we stop with the bald talk? Christ. Dad, hit her with your purse now," I say.

"No can do, Henry. You ready for tomorrow, Jeannie? Any second thoughts?"

"Hell yes. And no," she says. "You trying to tell me something? This a warning?"

"Nah, nothing like that," he tells her. "Just asking."

"How long have you been married?" she says.

"Since the day I found out Cecilia was pregnant, more or less." He smiles, embarrassed. "We're coming up on twenty-five years."

"Damn. Good job. How did you propose?"

"Long time ago. I forget," he tells her.

"Oh, come on. You're lying. Tomorrow's my wedding day. Tell me."

"Yeah Dad, tell her," I say, because it's about my parents in love and happy, two things they don't seem much anymore.

Francis Junior looks around, as if to make sure no one else listens. "All right, fine. I had a buddy drive us out of the city one night, like he was our chauffeur, in his dad's big Olds. We went north to the river by New Hope, near Washington's Crossing. When we were dating, we used to talk about leaving the city, getting a place in the suburbs with some space between the houses. Someplace the kids could play Wiffle ball in the yard. Someplace you could see the stars at night. Anyhow, I got dressed up in a tux with a white jacket. We drove up there. It was the end of August, nighttime, and it was still hot. I was sweating my balls off. Maybe I was just nervous, though. We parked by the river. I sat on a big rock. She sat on my lap. We talked about the things I just told you about, the house, the trees, the grass, the whole nine. Then I stood up, sang 'Beyond the Sea' to her, and proposed." Francis Junior clears his throat, his face red.

"Can you even sing?" she asks.

"Not a note," he says, laughing now.

"Why 'Beyond the Sea'?"

"It was the only song we ever both liked."

"Mr. Toohey, I didn't know you had it in you." Jeannie beams.

"There you go with that mister shit. Stop that. How did Ace propose?"

"He asked me over burgers at McDonald's," says Jeannie, her eyes rolling.

Francis Junior laughs. "You're shitting me."

"I shit you not," she answers.

"Quite a romantic bastard," he says.

"No, he's not. But he loves me. So is it all worth it? You've been hitched a quarter century. Impart some wisdom."

"Wisdom? I deliver the mail. Poorly. Look, here's another letter for your house," he says, spotting it in his bag, handing it to her. They laugh. "Some days it's worth it."

"How about today?"

"Ask me tomorrow. Gotta move."

Off he goes, up the street toward the Ave. He walks in the side door of Paul Donohue's—the door everybody uses—under a big neon sign with an arrow that reads LADIES' ENTRANCE.

"Henry, we got a crisis here," says Bobby James, who stood on the porch and mumbled on the phone while Francis Junior and Jeannie shot the shit. He's holding the mouthpiece against his chest.

"Is it Harry Curran?" I ask, already knowing the answer.

"Yeah," says Bobby. "He wants to know what we're doing today."

"So tell him we're hanging out," I say. "See if he wants to come."

Harry's a physical fitness freak. He jogs to Tack Park at 6 A.M. with a basketball and a notebook to record shots made and missed. He cuts most of the lawns on St. Patrick Street. When he's not doing these things, he talks about them.

"No chance. I know how to get rid of him. Hold on. Har," he says into the phone, "you can come if you want, but I should warn you we're going to the art museum then an outdoor classical concert. What? Jesus Christ. Hold on. Henry," he tells me, "Harry said he loves art and the symphony. What now?"

I laugh. Bobby James walked into that one. Harry does love the symphony. He told this to twenty kids standing outside the 7-Eleven last night, broads too.

"Well, Roberta," I say, "it looks like we're off to the symphony." I jump on a wooden porch table and conduct an invisible orchestra. Bump ba ba bump ba ba bump ba ba bump *ba* bump! "Let's strap on ankle weights and jog to the symphony. Places, everyone. We must have silence. Tuba section, begin with the elephant farts."

Jeannie, holding the phone base from inside the door for Bobby James, laughs.

"Don't encourage him, Jeannie. He ain't funny," he tells her. "Henry, get off my mom's new table," he says to me, then, to Harry on the phone, "All right, you can come. Leave the fucking ankle weights and jump rope in the house. Hurry up or we're leaving without you. Good-bye."

He hands the phone to Jeannie, who disappears inside. Harry, who lives next door to Bobby James, steps out of his house, hops over the railing, and now stands on the James porch. Harry has poorly feathered brown hair parted in what he thinks is the middle, freckles, and five inches on five-foot-tall me and Jamesy. He wears red and blue knee-high tube socks and a matching red T-shirt and gym shorts that both read FATHER JUDGE BASKETBALL CAMP 1984. He's also wearing his trademark Kareem Abdul-Jabbar goggles, complete with the strap on the back.

"Yo," he says.

"Yo," I say, friendly.

"Yo," says Bobby James, not friendly, through all the gum.

I should stop here to point out that *yo* is the most important word in Philly language. You can use it to call somebody, to say hello, to point something out, to express pleasure or disgust. Say for example I see Jeannie James's bare tits and want Bobby James and Harry, both standing across the street, also to see them. Now say Harry loves them, Bobby doesn't and gets mad, and I have to calm him down. Here's how the conversation would sound.

HT: Yo. Yo.
HC: Yo.
BJ: Yo.
HT: Yo!
HC: Yo!
BJ: Yo!
HT: Yo.

But since Jeannie's bare tits aren't in plain view, I ask Harry if he's buying lunch today. Harry's rich from all the lawn cutting. He owns a fleet of lawnmowers, retains a personal accountant and attorney, and sports the best basketball sneakers money can buy. These would be the Dr. J. Converse. Any fucking how, Harry tells people he has four hundred grand in the bank. I've got no problem swallowing such bullshit so long as it comes with a hoagie, soda, and bag of chips.

"I'll buy," says Harry, "if you say a prayer before we start, Minister Toohey."

"You asking me to offer a blessing before we begin today's journey to Jericho?" I ask, already talking like a preacher, and Harry, an easy audience, is already laughing.

"Yes please," he says.

"I have nothing ready on index cards. I'll have to let the Lord work within me."

"Amen. Let Him work within you," Harry urges.

"Yes, amen is right!" I shout. "Let us go forth unto this neighborhood," I say, making a sweeping gesture toward the row homes with my left arm. I can see Mrs. McKeever's tits as she bends over to refasten her daughter's diaper. Praise Jesus! "We shall search high and low to find and admire the big-chested chicks of St. Ignatius and their big chests."

"That's right," Harry shouts.

"Amen," says Bobby James, finally joining the fun.

"Their beautiful breasteseses are gifts from God," I say.

"Uh-huh," testifies Jamesy, arms above his head, eyes closed.

"That's the truth," testifies Curran, in the same pose as Bobby James.

The Spirit has made its way inside them. Or they're just thinking about tits. Hard to say, but who gives a fuck? Either way works. I climb on the wooden table.

"Can I get a witness to thank Jesus for mammary protuberances?" I ask.

"What are they?" asks Harry, putting his arms down.

"Tits, fool," I tell him. "I need a witness to stand on the table with me."

Harry steps up. "I love the Lord and tits."

"But in that order, right? The Lord, then breasts. Is that correct, Brother Curran?"

Harry opens one eye and fixes it on me. "Yeah?"

Jubilation!

"Yes, Brother Curran, you must love the Lord more than tits. Brother Bobby James, come forward and testify."

"Can't I do it here? If this table breaks, my mom'll punch the shit out of me."

"Even more reason. Come up here with your brothers and shout it to the hills."

"No, man. She just bought it."

"You Godless pussy," I call him, quieter, to make a serious point. Also because some crybaby fucking neighbors are yelling *Shut up, Toohey*. "Brother Bobby James refuses to join us. His mind and heart are clouded. He's more concerned with bubble gum than Jesus Christ. Yes, Bazooka bubble gum, people," I say, shouting again, ignoring the heathen neighbors who now call me asshole. "It is written that whosoever don't share his bubble gum, the fires of Hell shall tickle his ass like a feather. Bobby James will clean dog shit off your lawn for cash!"

Crash. The table collapses. Me and Harry fall to the cement, me laughing, him crying. Bobby James panics and, like always when stressed, says the Hail Mary real fast.

"Quit praying. I didn't mean it. Harry, take the goggles off to wipe the tears."

"That's just it. You never mean it, Toohey," complains Jamesy. "You didn't mean to hurt Archie when you hooked up those firecrackers to his wheelchair. You didn't mean to embarrass your mom when you put her underwear on your head and did that parachute bit. Am I getting through here? You remember this shit?"

"No I don't," I lie. Of course I do. Neither was a big fucking deal. Archie, my little sister Cece's crippled boyfriend, *wanted* to do the firecracker stunt. I used Cecilia's old *maternity* panties as a parachute, not her regular ones. "I'll pay you money for a new table. Harry, give him ten bucks." Harry, still crying, reaches for his bill wad (one hundred, one twenty, and twenty singles) and asks Bobby if he has change for a twenty.

"Put your money away. Let's just take the table to the curb," says Bobby.

Me and him carry the table down his steps while Harry stays on the porch doing toe touches and sniffling. When we get back, Bobby James asks, "Now can we start knocking for these broads already?"

"What broads?" asks Harry, who's scared of broads, turning white. "I thought we were going to the art museum and the symphony."

We leave the porch and hit the street. A billion girls and two billion tits await us. I'm only interested in one and two.

4

Me and Bobby James debate which girl we visit first—Grace McClain or Margie Murphy—while Harry does one-armed pushups. James, that fuck, says Margie lives closer. I say Grace does. The argument is stupid, I admit. Margie lives next door to Bobby James, and Grace lives next door to Margie.

Mr. Murphy sits outside his house on a metal lawn chair and reads the sports section. He's wearing cut-off jeans and no shirt—his gut hanging over his waist—and just finished mowing his lawn. Harry walks right up to him. Mr. Murphy stands between Harry and a lawn monopoly. Him and Harry also attend the same Wednesday night St. Ignatius church group, which Harry uses to woo new customers and keep present ones happy. The boy networks.

"Yo, Mike," says Har. "How's things? How's Cheryl?"

Mr. Murphy, a handsome dude with decent hair, smiles. "Yo, Harry. Fellas."

"Yo," Bobby says.

"Yo," I say.

Harry scans the yard in such a way as to let Mr. Murphy know he's scanning the yard. He isn't subtle, but no millionaire is.

"Not a bad job. You took out some of Cheryl's flowers over there with your trimmer. You missed spots around St. Peter and under those cows."

"I ain't real delicate doing it," says Mr. Murph. "Can't get under the farm animals with the trimmer, and I'm not up to bending down and pulling weeds out by hand."

"Back still slipped?" asks Harry.

"Yep. Ain't getting any better either."

"Still, Cheryl can't be pleased. Look at that high grass by St. Peter. He humping through rice paddies? Christ, Mike."

Mr. Murphy looks down, ashamed. "I hear you, Har, but what can I do?"

"For starters," says Harry, "get a good pair of long manual weed clippers. You won't be hunched over then and can sit in the grass and keep your back straight while you trim under those lawn animals. My mom got the same ones last week, by the way."

"Really?" asks Murphy. "Even the cow with the sunglasses and umbrella drink?"

"You bet," says Harry. "And the hippo on the tractor and the pig on the lawn chair. You try the cow's udder yet?"

"What?"

"Watch."

Harry reaches under the lawn cow and squeezes its udder. The cow says *Do I know you? We laugh. I comb my hair. Bobby James changes pieces of gum. Harry squeezes the udder again. Aren't you supposed to say cough? And where's your white coat?* Another squeeze. *I love you, marry me.*

"Besides stopping back pain," Harry continues, "the clippers help you get around those flowers and animals without massacring them, which'll make Cheryl happier. Now about the back. I got these new ankle weights I think might help. I use them when I jog."

"Jogging?" asks Mr. Murphy. "I haven't been running in years."

"You *walk* in them. They strengthen your back. And also tone your buttocks."

Bobby James shoots me a look, not believing Harry said *buttocks* to an adult.

"Really? I'll try them, Har. Thanks. You coming to church group this week?"

"Wouldn't miss it, Mike," says Harry, who points and winks.

"Great. See you then. I suppose you boys are here for Margie. I'll get her."

"OK, Mr. Murphy," answers Bobby.

"Bye, Mr. Murphy," I tell him.

"So long, Mike. Heat then ice on that back," says Harry.

"Harry, you're an asshole," says Bobby, once Murphy's out of earshot.

"Why, because I offered advice about back pain to a church group friend?"

To answer yes, Bobby James hops around making siren and bell noises. *Woo woo, ding ding ding, we got a winner,* he shouts. At this time, out comes Margie Murphy, owner of Bobby James's small black heart, in time to see him acting like a fucking fire truck. Not a good start. A bright red Jamesy senses this and quiets down.

"Yo, guys," says Margie, a tomboy with palm-size tits, nervous and biting her lip, standing in her doorway, her deep blue eyes checking us out real quick. Margie knows we're here on a romantic mission but isn't sure who's Romeo. Slim pickings.

"Yo," says Harry, deep-knee-bending. "Tell your dad I cut lawns for a low fee."

"Hello, hallelujah," I say, or some shit like that, smiling like a lying senator.

"Yo, Margie," says Bobby James, lifting his hat to smooth a cowlick and talking through twelve pieces of gum before he thinks better and spits out the gum, which lands on St. Pete's head.

"Hi, Bobby James," Margie answers, smiling, all braces.

"Margie, you have a nice tan," he tells her in a voice half horny, half robot.

Margie grins. "What a sweetheart you are. I got it at summer camp. We swam and canoed every day. I wore a bikini the whole time."

Groans, boners, until mean titless Mrs. Murphy comes out her door in a foul mood, like always, maybe because of the no tits. She scopes the lawn and calls inside.

"Michael, come out here please," she commands in a calm, cold voice.

"Yes, honey?" asks Mr. Murphy, like a skirt, making clear she wears the pants.

"Michael, I just went to the flower shop for these begonias last week, remember?"

"Of course I do," he says.

"Of course you do," she mimics. "Were they expensive or cheap?"

"They were expensive."

"Did we buy them for you to shred with the mower?" she asks.

"No, honey, we didn't," he says. "Right?"

"Right. So why are they lying on the lawn instead of standing in a flowerbed?"

"Beg pardon. Cheryl," Harry interrupts. "Mike has back pain and can't reach tough spots. I offered some solutions, but a better one would be to call me at this number," he tells her as he hands her his card, which reads HARRY CURRAN CO. WE CUT THE GRASS, YOU SIT ON YOUR ASS.

"It's Mrs. Murphy," she answers, scowling. "My husband cuts the lawn."

"I'm sorry, I was just saying I cut most of the lawns—"

"I know you do. No thank you," she snaps, handing back his card.

"C'mon, Cheryl, lighten up," Mr. Murphy says, scared. "The kid's just being nice."

"I'm sorry, did you tell me to lighten up?" she asks.

"No, I, uh, didn't," he mumbles.

"Good. Come inside. You can help me with lunch and cut the sandwiches."

"Right away, dear. You like triangle halves, right?" he asks, as they disappear.

Margie stares far away, her face bright red.

"Margie," says Bobby, "you want to hang out with us today?"

She smiles, grateful. "Maybe. What are you doing?"

"Riding bikes," he answers, winking at me and Harry. "Right, boys?"

"Oh yeah. Bike riding," I say, playing along. Bike riding works. I'm in.

"How 'bout it, Margie?" asks Harry, also understanding and cool with it.

"I'd love to," she says.

"Cool. We'll pick you up after we eat and make bowel movements," Bobby says.

"OK then, Bobby," she says, smiling, before she goes in to God knows what.

"Now let's see if you can sweet-talk your girl like I just did mine," Bobby James tells me when she's gone, his pointy elbow in my ribs, fifteen pieces of gum in his hole.

Grace McClain has straight brown hair, pale skin, and freckles from forehead to toenails. Cigarette smoke stains her big bunny teeth. Her eyes are green as grass and tree leaves. She is, for now, titless. I'm patient, though. The tits will come. Grace doesn't take shit off anybody. She'll put her smoke out on your forehead if you fuck with her, so don't. She has three stickball pitches: curveball, fastball, slider, and says two others—forkball and knuckleball—will be ready by spring training 1985. Believe her. I fell in love with her three weeks ago, when she let me touch her legs under a blanket.

On that night, we sat alone on her porch under a half moon after a game of Freedom. It was chilly, and most of the kids went in for the night. Grace dared anybody to stay outside with her and eat an ice cream cone. I said fuck it and accepted, and we moved to her porch. She made the cones, three-scoop fuckers. We ate them, talked, and watched across the street as a neighbor named Mr. O'Toole (receding hairline, gray hair pulled back in ponytail) left his wife, Mrs. O'Toole (very boring B cups). He went in and out of the house a couple times, throwing trash bags full of stuff in his truck. It was a quiet breakup. Mrs. O'Toole held the door for him as he went back and forth. They kissed good-bye when he was done. Their five-year-old son Julian (bad bowl cut) watched them from their front window, his fists under his chin.

"John Lennon had a son named Julian who went through a divorce when John left Cynthia, Julian's mom, for that smaller-titted sea hag Yoko Ono," I told Grace. "Paul McCartney wrote the song 'Hey Jude' to comfort Julian."

"I don't like the Beatles," Grace said.

"Huh? What's not to like?" I asked, annoyed.

"All their songs sound the same," she answered.

"You got funny smokes there," I told her, pointing to the pack she smacked with her palm, "if you can't hear the difference between *Meet the Beatles* and *Sgt. Pepper.*"

"*Meet the* Fucking *Beatles, Sgt.* Fucking *Pepper,* same fucking difference," she said, her lips clamped on a smoke she lit.

I got mad until she threw a blanket over us and put her legs in my lap. I got a boner then. I can't be mad with a boner. I touched her legs with my fingertips from her ankles to her shorts. Grace didn't try to stop me. She smiled and smoked. We talked about something while all this happened, but I can't remember what. I was on autopilot. We might as well have been talking stock options and shit.

Mrs. McClain came outside then to interrupt us, drunk and cross-eyed.

"I hope you kids got clothes on under there," she said, chucking an empty beer in a blue trash bucket, which killed the mood, even though she went back inside.

"I should probably put her to bed," Grace sighed before she took her legs and blanket in for the night and I walked home in pain with my boner pointing the way.

Right now, my boner is pointing at the McClain house as we stand in front of their door and knock. Mrs. McClain, who wears an Eagles sweatshirt in the heat over her navel-orange-size tits, answers and smiles, holding a beer can wrapped in blue foam.

"Yo, Henry. Yo, Harry." She pauses. "Good afternoon, Robert."

Last week, Bobby James ran across the McClain lawn during Freedom and trampled flowers first planted by Mr. McClain, who died fighting a fire three years ago. Since he died and until they got trampled, Mrs. McClain kept the flowers real nice in his memory, so she's mad at Bobby James.

"Yo, Mrs. McC," I say.

"Yo, Shirley," says Harry.

"Yes, good afternoon, Mrs. McClain," answers Bobby James, real cold.

"Come in, fellas."

"Grace around?" I ask, getting right to business.

"She's upstairs in the shower," she says.

We grunt like mutts or faint like bitches, take your pick.

"Sit down and take a load off, boys. I'll get some drinks."

We plop down on the plastic sofa cover. The TV, on at a low volume, shows *The Price Is Right*. A titless biker broad runs and hugs the host, who grabs her ass and kisses her. Mrs. McClain returns with two tall drinks with lemons and umbrellas, hands one to me and one to Harry, and sits next to Bobby James, who gets nothing and frowns.

"Harry, we square for my lawn?" asks Mrs. McClain.

"I think so, Shirley," answers Harry, pulling a fat notebook from his underwear waistband. "Yeah. I cut your lawn Tuesday, and you paid cash—five ones and a five."

"Wow," she says. "You got that businessman thing down to a science."

"This notebook is nothing. I keep files on computer in my home office."

"Computer files," laughs Mrs. McClain, who likes to talk and listen. You could tell her about foot fungus and she'd say "No shit."

"Tell you what, I'll pay you in advance for the rest of the season. Fifty dollars OK? Here, hold this beer," she says to Bobby James. "I'll get Harry's money from the kitchen."

Upstairs, the shower stops, and I shiver, picturing Grace stepping out of the tub in a towel. Downstairs, Bobby James tilts his head back and chugs Mrs. McC's beer.

"You crazy? Put that down," begs Harry.

Bobby James grins and chugs more. A squeak on the stairs scares us. It's Grace McClain, who just slid down the railing wearing only a towel. I would stand to clap but I got a boner. What do I do with these? I get ten an hour. *That's one every six minutes.*

"Yo, girls, what's up?" she asks us, biting her nails and looking beautiful.

"Yo," answers Bobby.

"Yo," says Harry.

"Yo. I love what you're wearing," I say before gulping.

"You should see what's underneath," Grace laughs.

"You're probably naked under that," Harry tells her, dead serious, hoping to help.

"Correct. I am naked under that. Asshole. Roberto, you drinking my mom's beer?"

Bobby burps. "Nah. This one is mine."

Mrs. McClain returns to the living room, hands Harry two twenties and a ten.

"Ma, you seen my smokes?" asks Grace.

"Not since I smoked them," her mom answers.

"Again?" says Grace. "You wench."

"Calm down," says Mrs. McClain. "Here, you can have some of mine."

"But these are *lights*," complains Grace.

"I'll buy you more regulars today, OK?"

"Fine then, but try to keep your mitts off my smokes in the future."

Don't be alarmed. This is normal talk at the McClains'. Least they like each other.

"You hear this, Henry? My own daughter scolding me. Ain't she something?"

"Yeah, she is," I answer, my eyes never leaving Grace's legs.

"What does Hank know? He likes the Beatles," Grace tells her.

"I'm into heavy metal. Sabbath. AC/DC. Satan-type shit," says Bobby James.

"Figures," Mrs. McClain tells him. "I like early rock and roll. Fifties stuff."

"I like classical more than rock," says Harry, "but I do manage Henry's band."

"A band?" asks Mrs. McC, surprised.

"Yeah, a band. Phillies Alarm Clock," I answer.

"They're not a band, Ma, and Harry don't manage them. They hang out in Cece Toohey's room, use pretend instruments, lip-sync to Mrs. Toohey's records, and smoke bubble gum smokes Harry bought."

"You're there with us, Grace. You do it too," Bobby tells her, before burping.

"Yeah, but I don't smoke fake shit, fucker, plus I know it's pretend," says Grace.

"That's your problem," I laugh. Duh. "We'll be a real band at some point."

"Right," says Grace, "the only things holding you up is instruments and lessons."

Mrs. McClain sits down next to Bobby James, takes the empty can from him, and shakes it, puzzled, as he burps. Me and Grace laugh. Harry clutches his chest like an old broad with rosary beads at early Mass. Mrs. McClain walks to the kitchen for another.

"Grace, what kind of hair products do you use?" I ask, staring at her hair.

"Shampoo. I use shampoo, Hank," she tells me.

"But what kind? How often do you condition? Are gel or hairspray involved?"

"I just wash and rinse, dude," she says.

"Ever consider herbal shit? I can see split ends here and here." I point with Big Green without touching her hair. No need to get her involved with Big Green yet. My comb, my hair. Plus I don't see split ends anywhere. I just want to get close and smell her.

"Split ends?" asks Grace, pretending to care. "You serious? Look, Hank. I see cootie colonies here and here," she says, before cuffing me in a headlock and rubbing knuckle noogies in my head, hard. As she does this, my face presses against her tiny tits, and I can see the streaks of water that slide over the freckles on her thighs. God is great, God is good. Grace pushes me on all fours and climbs on my back. Oh my. Bobby James and Harry cheer until Mrs. McClain returns with a fresh beer.

"Grace, what are you doing? Get off him, go upstairs, and get dressed," she scolds, before she hands Bobby James her beer and says, "Hold this while I go to the basement."

"OK, Ma, take it easy," Grace answers, hopping off me and starting up the steps, so far away from me. There is no God. "Hank, what are you sissies doing today?"

"Riding bikes," I say. "Margie Murphy's going. Want to come?"

"Only if you take the flower baskets off your bikes," she says, half up the steps.

"Flower baskets? Please," snorts Bobby James. "I got a five-speed with a gear shift," he tells her before crushing the can he just chugged on his forehead and burping.

Mrs. McC returns, puts a lamp with no shade on an end table, and takes the crushed can from James. "I should slow down," she mutters, heading for the kitchen.

"This beer is making me hungry, Henry," says Bobby James. "I need a ham hoagie before we ride or run your errands. Grace, go get me another beer."

"Fight me and I will," she threatens.

"Never mind. Let's get a move on, boys," Bobby says, scared.

Grace laughs. "Hold on, sissy. I'll get you a beer. Watch me, Hank. Here I come."

She climbs to the top of the stairs. I move to the bottom. She slides down the railing again and lands in my arms. "What kind of errand you have to run, Hank?"

"Nothing big," I say. "Just stuff related to us getting married."

We fall. Grace straddles me, laughing and rubbing her wet hair in my face. I see God in all things and am too shocked to spring a boner. Maybe I hit my head and died, and this is Heaven. If so, sweet!

"*Us* getting *married?*" she asks, smiling and looking right in my eyes.

"Did I say us? I meant Jeannie and Ace getting married," I tell her.

"Us getting married. That'd be something," she laughs, before smacking my cheek twice and standing, leaving me alone on the floor of a huge godless universe while she grabs a beer for Bobby James.

"Here you go, Miss James," says Grace, back from the kitchen, smoking, and shoving the can down his shirt.

"Jesus, these are cold," he yipes. "Your mom got another blue foam thing?"

"No," she tells him. "Get out."

"Fine," says Bobby. "I got my beer. Let's roll, fellas."

"Hold on a second," I say. "Grace, can I ask a favor before we go?"

"Anything, Hank, what is it?"

"Can you slide down that railing one more time?"

"I sure can." She smiles, and ten thousand miles away, glaciers big as mountains melt like ice cubes on frying pans. She blows out smoke and flicks her lit smoke at Harry, who stands half in, half out of the house. Staring at me the whole time, Grace walks backward up the steps, then slides down. At the bottom, I close my eyes and open my arms. Wham. We're on the floor again, her on top, her wet hair in my face, a loving God above us, His whole universe smelling like coconut shampoo.

"I'll get my dirt bike ready while you're gone. Don't forget me after lunch, Hank."

"Not a chance," I tell her.

"Cool."

Footsteps from the basement. Grace jumps off me and runs upstairs. Bobby James thanks her for the beers as we split. She tells us, *Yeah, yeah, get lost, you skirts.*

5

A skinny bastard named Matt Mungiole, who everybody calls
Fat Matt, owns Fat Matt's Deli at St. Patrick and Frankford Ave.
A few blocks north of the deli, past St. Ignatius on the other side
of the Ave, Fat Matt also owns Mungiole's, the banquet hall
where Stephen works, where I'll sing to Grace. Fat Matt, who
slicks back his short gray-black hair, says he's connected to the
Mafia if you ask him, so don't. He fills the walls with famous
dago pictures: popes, saints, and singers and with thank-you
cards from dago families whose dago parties he catered. He
makes hoagies and tells the same whoppers about wiseguys who
got whacked back in the day.

"Fat Matt, tell us a story about a Mob hit," says Bobby James,
as a soundless TV behind the counter shows Mike Schmidt hit a
homer and a stereo blares Blue Eyes singing "Making Whoopee"
off *Songs for Swingin' Lovers*. Good tune, good album.

"Always the gangsters," complains Fat Matt, not serious. "Why
don't you fellas ever ask me about somebody on my walls, like Leo
the Twenty-third or Tony Bennett?"

"We got priests to tell us about popes. Fuck Tony Bennett,"
Bobby tells him.

"Fuck Tony Bennett? I danced with my wife to Tony Bennett

at our wedding. Hold your tongue or I'll cut it off on this meat slicer," warns Fat Matt, who claims to know where Jimmy Hoffa's body's buried, as he drops a block of bologna on the slicer, his white fingers wrapped in gold rings.

"What Tony Bennett song?" I ask.

"'Let There Be Love,'" he tells me, smiling, stretching out the word *love*.

"From *The Beat of My Heart*, right?" I say.

"Yeah, that's right. Look at you knowing that," answers Fat Matt, impressed.

"Ain't that song kind of fast for a wedding dance?" I ask.

"We didn't dance slow to it, Henry," says Fat Matt. "We fast-danced."

"Right in front of everybody?"

"Yeah, Henry, right in front of everybody. We were the bride and groom."

"You *fast*-danced. Interesting," I say.

"I hate to bug you old-timers," bellyaches James, "but Matt owes us a Mob story."

"So I do," says Matt. "I got one for you. Happened at this cocktail joint called the Taboo Tiki Bamboo Lounge, which was located in the middle of South Philly. Francis the Dancer ran the place. He was a made neighborhood guy who got his nickname because he could dance like a fruit even though he was the toughest guy I ever seen. Now this Irish fella—Danny Cleary—walked in and started bossing all the help around."

"Why was he bossing the help around?" asks Bobby James, nudging me and winking, because, like me and Harry, he heard this one twenty times.

"Danny Cleary was an Irish asshole—all Irish are assholes, no offense—who knew how to work a hustle and keep his mouth shut," says Fat Matt. "This got him Mob work, but he thought it meant more than it did. It went to his head. He felt entitled to act like a prick. He'd park his Olds right in front of a joint, then gamble, eat, and drink without paying debts."

"So what happened to Danny Cleary?" asks Bobby James, his eyes big.

"He got whacked inside the restaurant, in front of everybody. He was grabbing waiters by their ties and pinching waitresses' asses, many of whom were dating other Mob guys, *Italian* Mob guys, *Sicilian* Mob guys. Something had to be done, you understand," Fat Matt tells us as he makes hoagies so fast you see gold streaks from his watch and rings.

"How did he get whacked?" asks Harry.

Fat Matt looks right at us while neatly wrapping a hoagie. "He drowned."

"How did he drown inside a restaurant?" I ask.

"Let's just say the restaurant had big water pitchers, and Danny Cleary's head ended up inside one too long." Fat Matt laughs, his gold tooth shining in the store lights.

"You the one who whacked him?" asks Bobby James, despite knowing Matt will tell us, like he told the Feds, he don't remember nothing.

"It's like I told the Feds, fellas. I don't remember nothing." Another gold tooth grin. He rings up our grub. "Six bucks even, Harry."

"Got change for a hundred?" asks Harry, taking the hundred off his wad.

Fat Matt ignores Harry, pulls six singles from the wad of cash, and puts them in his drawer. The deli doorbell rings. Eight-year-old Archie O'Drain, a wheelchair cripple, and my mom, Cecilia Toohey, his chauffeur, crash to the floor after she tries and fails to carry him in his chair up the steps into the store. Cece Toohey, my little sister, also eight like Archie, enters behind them, wearing a PHILLIES BALL GIRL T-shirt, her blond hair pulled into a ponytail. She steps over them, spots me, beams, and jumps in my arms as I try to move toward Cecilia to help her, but not Archie, up from the floor.

"Yo, Henry," says Cece, grinning, tickled to find me here.

"Yo. What's up? You push them over?" I ask her, pointing to Cecilia and Archie.

"No, but I thought about it," she whispers, dangling from my neck as I comb my hair, Harry stretches his groin, Bobby James shoplifts a beer off a six-pack, Fat Matt puts Archie back in his chair, and Cecilia Toohey lights a smoke and picks up prescription pills that spilled out of her purse.

"No smoking in here," scolds Fat Matt, back behind the counter.

"I'll stop smoking in here when you build a wheelchair ramp outside," snaps Cecilia, who is tall, wears a short summer dress, and has perfect C-cup tits. I'd touch them, I'm not proud. Blowing smoke straight up, she looks at me playfully. "Hank Toohey and his two best pals. What a happy coincidence. Yo, Mr. Curran, no lawns to cut?"

"Yo, Cecilia," says Harry. "I took off this weekend."

"OK, fair enough," she says. "Jamesy boy, is that a beer can in your pocket or you just happy to see a store full of bubble gum?"

Bobby James, who's afraid of Cecilia Toohey's tall beauty and quick wit, reaches into his pocket, pulls out a smoke pellet, and chucks it on the floor. Boom. Smoke. He runs away like a bad magician.

"What was that thing?" asks Cecilia, laughing, as he hides behind a chips display.

"A smoke pellet," he tells her, peeking out.

"What are they for?" she asks.

"My sister's wedding reception, for use when cornered by a relative."

"No shit?"

"Yeah, no shit," he says.

"Can I see one?" she asks.

"I guess," he says, annoyed now more than scared, handing her a pellet.

"Cool," she says, like a kid, holding it between her thumb and finger, checking it out close. "Hank, come here and ask me what I'm making for dinner."

"OK," I say, walking over, feeling game. "Ma, what are you making for dinner?"

She chucks a pellet on the floor—poof—then darts behind the chips display.

"I love that," she giggles. "Give me another, Bobby."

"What? Seriously?"

"Yeah, cough it up," she says. "Thanks. Matt, tell me I owe you ten bucks."

"Mrs. Toohey, please. Haven't you shot enough smoke in here?" he begs.

"Do it," she tells him.

"Fine," he sighs, then claps his hands together. "Your bill will be ten dollars."

She drops one—whoosh—runs out the door, and comes back in laughing.

"Are we done now, Mrs. Toohey?" asks Bobby. "Can I keep the rest?"

"Fine," she says before she takes a drag, blows it in his face, and he coughs.

"Time-out. Here comes my commercial on channel eleven," says Fat Matt, turning down Sinatra on the stereo, turning up the TV, squinting at his remote, and pressing 1-1. A great thing about cable TV is homemade commercials by local stores. Turn on MTV, and in between Michael Jackson videos, you see somebody from the neighborhood advertising the schnook store they own. "Here it is. Quiet, please."

On the tube, a slick-haired Italian guy walks into Fat Matt's. He holds a pop bottle and strokes his chin, looking at the lunch specials, before smiling and nodding at Matt.

"How you doing?" he asks.

Fat Matt smiles just a little. "I am fine today. How can I help you?"

"Yeah, I'll take this soda here," says the fella, sliding a sixteen-ouncer on the counter.

"What will you have with the drink?" asks Matt.

"Nothing," he tells Matt, "just the pop."

"But it's lunchtime, my friend," Matt tells him. "Do you not eat a lunch?"

"Well, yeah," says the fella, confused, "but I already ate a hoagie."

"You already ate a hoagie?"

"Yeah, that's what I said," the fella tells him.

"From where did you purchase the hoagie?" Matt asks, squinting.

"What do you care? Down the Ave, at another deli."

"Another deli?" says Matt, not happy.

"Yeah. You hard of hearing?"

"A non-Sicilian deli? A nonunion deli?"

"I don't know. Same difference. You going to ring me out or what, Pops?"

The lights darken, just a spotlight on Matt and the jerk-off.

"Pops." Matt laughs. "I could almost like you, had you not betrayed me, this deli."

"What?" asks the dumbass, totally confused, starting to worry.

Matt pulls him in and kisses him. When he lets go, a few goons with Gatling guns step out of the shadows from different places—the pickle bucket, the bread rack, the cooler cases, the cold cuts display—and fill the guy full of holes. Soon as he lays still and dead, the goons disappear, the lights come back up. A woman walks in the front door, spots the jerk on the floor.

"Vinny," she cries, running to the stiff. "My husband! Father of my thirteen children! He's dead! You killed him!" she shouts, running at Fat Matt, throwing her fists into his chest. "Why why why?" she sobs.

"Because," Matt says, grabbing her wrists, staring into her

eyes, "he bought his hoagie from a non-Sicilian competitor," he explains.

"He did what?" she asks, startled, angry, no longer crying.

"He bought a hoagie elsewhere, outside the neighborhood."

"Then damn him, the traitor, I spit on him, puh," she says, making the sound but not really spitting, before she turns back to Matt. "Can I get a pound of turkey, a pound of cheese, and a half pound of liverwurst? Do you need any lime for the body?"

Dago classical music swells. A narrator says, *Fat Matt's Deli at St. Patrick and Frankford. Fat Matt's Deli is not connected with La Cosa Nostra.* The commercial ends. We clap and whoop for Fat Matt, who takes a bow, then turns off the TV and puts Tony Bennett's *The Beat of My Heart* on the stereo after smiling to me and showing me the album cover.

"Yo, what's up, ladies?" Archie O'Drain asks, cool as a cucumber, rolling over to us as we stand by the register at the counter. His wheelchair—with its fuzzy leopard-skin seat, horn Super Glued to one armrest, fuzzy dice swinging from the other armrest, bumper sticker on the back that says I BREAK FOR DAMES, and truck flaps behind his wheels—is a cross between a Hell's Angel's hog, an eighteen-wheeler, and a rock star tour bus. Archie, whose hair is feathered nicely on top but long and stringy in the back, is the only brother, the only sibling, of Stephen's dead girlfriend, Megan O'Drain. I love the kid, even though I'd never tell him. That'd be too easy. Plus, since he's crippled, it's important that we torture him just like we do non-cripples. A fun way to do this is to call him Archibald and compliment him with big words he assumes are busts. Example:

"Yo, Archibald. You are a sagacious and loquacious motherfucker," I tell him.

"I know you are, but what am I? Don't call me Archibald," he warns.

"Archibald," says Harry, "your intellectual capacity has an Einsteinian rapacity."

"I know yours does, but what does mine? The name is Archie, Mary."

"Archibald, you are the negative reciprocal of an infantile imbecile," says Bobby.

"I know you are, but what am I? Next punk who calls me Archibald dies."

Cecilia leads Fat Matt to the lunchmeat display. She bends and points to something. Two gas company fellas, both with poodle rocker hairdos, walk into the deli. They watch her bend down and elbow each other. Cecilia gets up, sees them looking, and smiles big and friendly. She takes a hardhat off one fella and puts it on her head, then says all I need now is a jackhammer. The men stare at her, then each other, and smile. Tony Bennett sings "Love for Sale." Fat Matt's hands slice meat at the speed of light. The deli doorbell rings again. Francis Junior walks in with the mail and spots a surprised Cecilia wearing the hardhat and standing between the gas assholes. He smiles, knowing this drill.

"Cecilia, you gonna introduce me to your boyfriends?" he asks.

"Sure. This is Biff and Brent. They're male strippers. And you already know those four studs over there," she says, pointing to us four boys. "Where's your girlfriend?"

"Right here," replies Francis Junior, picking Cece up out of my arms.

"Ain't you a sweetheart," says Cecilia.

They both smile, even though she doesn't mean it and he knows it. Despite this, when they smile at each other, you can still see love. Weirdos, man.

"*Archie's* my boyfriend. Tell him, Archie," Cece says. There's a pause. "Tell him now or suffer later."

"Uh, I'm Cece's boyfriend, Mr. Toohey," says Archie.

"Guess I better put her down then," says Francis Junior, sitting her on the counter and taking a free soda off Fat Matt, who gives him one every day. "Thanks, Matt. Cecilia, I'll be home regular time today. Didn't get no overtime." Overtime—the difference between steak and meatloaf—is a big conversational topic with parents on St. Patrick Street.

"Will you be eating with us or elsewhere?" she asks.

"I'll be home like I always am," he tells her.

"Right." She snorts.

"What's that supposed to mean?" he asks. "When have I ever missed dinner?"

"Oh, that's right. You're always around for the fucking food," she says.

"Mrs. Toohey, please," begs Fat Matt.

Cece slides off the counter and heads for the pickle buckets over by the corner. The two gas men sneak out after the F-bomb. As they leave, my oldest brother, Francis Nathaniel Toohey III, AKA Frannie Toohey, enters in his mailman uniform. Better families can brag about generations of doctors. Not Tooheys. We come from a long line of striped shorts, dog bites, and tomato Mace. Frannie, who lives next door to us, is twenty-four, balding, and funny looking. He looks sixteen besides the balding part but is wise beyond his years, like an oldest, ugliest child sometimes has to be.

"Everybody behaving in here?" he asks, casing the joint, smelling trouble.

"Yeah, not counting your mother," answers Francis Junior.

"That's a lie, Frannie," argues Cecilia. Her and Francis Junior fall in line a little when Frannie's around. They'll bicker, but they answer him like they owe him answers.

"Lie? I came in here, hard at work, to find her dancing with the Village People."

"Oh, so I'm lying?" she asks no one. "He came in from ringing twice at the Cooney house, then got upset because I was talking to two strapping gas company studs."

Frannie watches them both carefully, like a principal trying to decide which jerk-off threw a ball through a window. "I'll get to the bottom of this. Cece, what happened?"

"Don't even know what they mean by Village People and ringing twice," reports Cece. "It was mainly the usual: they talked to each other like assholes."

Ring. Stephen Toohey walks into Fat Matt's, spots the entire family, and walks out.

"See, you scared Stephen away," says Frannie, sounding again like a principal, a tired one, and taking his free soda off Fat Matt. "Let's just try to get along, OK?"

"I'll just leave," says Francis Junior. "That way we don't have to try—and fail. You heading home to hide until punch-out time, Frannie?"

"Yup."

"I'll go with you. Thanks for the soda, Matt. See you tonight, Cecilia. Can't wait."

"Yeah, me neither. Fuck you," she shouts as he walks out, bells ringing. "Cece, get off the floor. Get your feet out of the pickle bucket."

"Her feet are in the pickle bucket?" gasps Matt. "Oh dear."

"They're on the bucket, not in it," Cece tells Fat Matt, annoyed, laying on the floor on her back, her flip-flops off, her bare feet on the bucket. "You done yelling, Ma?"

"For now."

"Good, then I'll get up," she says, cool, walking over to us, throwing her arm around Archie, who winces. "Were you fellas messing with my boyfriend earlier?"

"I ain't your boyfriend," sulks Archie.

"You just told my dad you were," she tells him.

"You threatened me."

"So I did. Shut the hell up. You'll speak when spoken to, mister."

"Yes, dear." Archie sighs. "Henry, what are you fellas doing today?"

"Riding bikes," I say.

"Can we come?" he asks.

"What are we gonna do with you and your chair?" I ask.

"I can keep up," says Archie.

"I'll push Archie and wear roller skates," offers Harry.

"Twelve dollars even, Mrs. Toohey," says Fat Matt.

"Here," says Harry, handing him his twenty, then telling us "I just got new skates. Pushing a cripple in a chair'll be a great workout. What do you think, Archibald?"

"Name ain't Archibald," says Archie, "but that's cool with me."

"OK, it's settled then," I tell everybody. "Archie and Cece go home with my mom, and we'll catch up after lunch. Sound good?"

The third-graders say yeah. Fat Matt flashes his gold teeth. Cecilia grabs her brown bag. We help her lower Archie from the store steps to the sidewalk.

"You OK?" I ask Cecilia, who stares and watches traffic on the Ave.

"What?" she asks.

"Are you OK?"

"I'm fine," she says, snapping back from sleep, placing the grocery bag on Archie's lap, and taking Cece by the hand. "Are you ever gonna treat a wife that way?"

"Nope," I say, telling the truth.

"You gonna get yourself a girlfriend, leave the wife feeling stuck with no money and no place to go even if she wanted to leave you?"

"Nope."

"You gonna be faithful? Treat her nice? Respect her? Love her more every day?"

"Yeah, yeah, yeah, and yeah," I reply, grinning.

"Beautiful." She smiles. "You keep that goodness and optimism. Don't let nobody ever take those qualities from you."

"Not a chance, doll," I promise her.

"Doll," she repeats, snorting and lighting a smoke. "You still need work on how to talk to broads, though. We'll fix that later. You got the important stuff down. All right, kid, gotta roll. Be good today. Oh, one more thing. Jesus loves you, but I don't."

I laugh. We first heard a woman say this to her cheating minister ex-husband on a live, late-night religious show, and it made us cry laughing for days afterwards. So now it's a running joke. Cecilia smiles and winks at me before she lets Cece stand on Archie's chair. Cece makes motorboat noises, Cecilia twists the handles, and Archie shouts in a British accent, *On your marks, get set, go.* Then they're off, racing down St. Patrick Street: my hot mom, my strange sister, and a cripple with a chip on his shoulder.

Me, Harry, and Bobby James eat our hoagies on a train trestle that sits maybe thirty feet above Frankford Ave, which we call the Ave and which is the main street in our lives besides St. Patrick. Frankford Ave travels through most of Philly, from the city line north, to the Kensington neighborhood south, where it becomes Kensington Ave. The neighborhoods run down the whole way south on the Ave. You can start at an old-fashioned drive-in movie theater under the stars, then end at a tattoo parlor under the El.

St. Patrick Street sits almost exactly in the middle, both in distance and appearance. The Ave at St. Patrick is decent, but on the way downhill probably. Kids break windows and write graffiti on walls and shit like that here, but it still pisses the neighbors off, know what I'm saying? There's fights at the playground all the time, like tonight, supposedly, but it's usually fistfights, sometimes punks bring bats, two-by-fours, or screwdrivers to stick somebody or make like they will. Murders around here are usually inside houses, family bullshit, drugs and booze involved, a twenty-year-old son strangling his mom for money, waking up the next day not remembering a thing.

So it's rough, but not that rough, and the people who find trouble here usually have to look for it. Even tonight, maybe that's the case. Maybe the kids are assholes and want a scrap. Philly is a divided fucking town, and not just based on race. Even the white kids don't go to different white neighborhoods. That's what tonight's fight is about—what the fuck are *they* doing here—and why I never go much farther than four blocks either way on the Ave. I'm too pretty. Don't need to, anyway. The neighborhood already has anything you need. The dads work jobs maybe five blocks tops from the houses. The moms stay home with the kids. Any kind of service you need, if you ask a neighbor, is on the Ave around the corner. You name it: beer distributor, pizza place, corner bar, dry cleaner, jeweler, seafood take-out, delicatessen, travel agent, funeral home, used-car dealer, free library, fire-house, post office, bank, five-and-dime, Catholic Church. It's on the Ave around the corner. The neighborhood looks old-fashioned, and judging by the homes and storefronts, it could just as easily be 1963 as 1984. The only way to know the real year here is to look at the cars and add a decade.

From where we eat on the trestle, we're four blocks south of St. Patrick, which sits to our right as we face it. Also on our right, on that side, stores—including Fat Matt's deli—run in a row, broken only by streets parallel to St. Patrick and by Tack Park, the playground, which covers three blocks. Across the Ave, on our left, sits St. Ignatius Church, which stretches eight blocks total counting the cemetery, the schoolyard, the rectory, the convent, and the two school buildings. The church grounds are between the bike path and Nickleback Park, directly on our left, and Mungiole's, the catering hall, also on our left but so far down it's almost out of sight.

We're not supposed to sit up here on the trestle, but it's hard to obey a bullshit order like that. A slow train used to move on these tracks and cross this trestle, but no more, not since a kid named Danny Doyle lost his leg trying to hop it a couple sum-mers back. Right after that, the parents got together with the priests to put a stop to the train, and that was it. Even still, train or not, they bug us constantly to keep off the tracks and the tres-tle in particular. The wood boards up here are wobbly, and wide enough apart that skinny bastards like me could fall through and land on a windshield. But that won't happen. None of us three is brave or daring, so we're happy enough to find a sturdy plank and sit the fuck down to just enjoy the view, which I love, because it feels maybe like being dead.

Not that I'm into deadness. It's just that I can see my whole world from up here, from above it, and it looks prettier than from the ground floor. Like on my right, on the store side, the sun makes the windows glow, the same windows that I know have crud caked all over them when my feet are on the sidewalk. The left side is even better. The park runs behind the church property, and when you're up on the trestle, you can see the first couple bends of the bike path and creek, and the tops of the green trees that drop shade and leaves down on them. Even the church property looks pretty and peaceful instead of scary and crawling with corpses, priests, and penguins, which are nuns for you heathens keeping score at home. It all looks so quiet from here, the stores on the right no louder than the park and cemetery on the left. The only sound we hear from the trestle is from underneath us, the whoosh of cars and the clang of the trolley, which runs on electricity. The trolley squeaks to a stop every block, letting old farts on and off, sparks shooting from the two poles that stick out the top like bug antennas, connected to wires above. It's a nice noise and has a calm rhythm to it, and all this together makes me feel something perfect, something that feels like love as big as it gets, for this place I call home. If I let my eyes go out of focus, I stop seeing the park and cemetery side as all green, and the store and street side as all concrete. Instead it's all green, like grass.

"Henry, who you think has better tits, your mom or my sister?" asks Bobby James, sipping the beer he stole off Fat Matt as we stare at funeral procession cars turning right out of the cemetery and rolling toward us, their lights on in the lunchtime sunshine, orange flags that say FUNERAL inside a cross suction-cupped to the car hoods.

"Tough call," I say. "Your sister's are bigger but I'd rather squeeze my mom's."

"I disagree. What else is there to tits besides bigness?" he asks.

"Perkiness," I answer, annoyed. "Roundness, firmness." I hold up a finger for each of these important items. "You never want more than a handful, like a cantaloupe. Your sister has watermelons. I love them and all. I'm just saying you could get a black eye fiddling with that. You could get killed," I say.

"*Killed?*" he says. "*Maimed* maybe but not killed. Bigness beats everything in my book. I'd rather feel my sister's. Harry, whose would you rather squeeze?"

Harry, who has been sitting silent, hoping he wouldn't get asked this, spits out his sports drink at the question. It lands on the windshield of a station wagon in the funeral line. The driver, a big-haired man with a B-cupped wife in the passenger seat, looks right and left confused, but not up, so he doesn't see us.

"Damn, you just spit on that funeral car," says Bobby. "Whose tits, my sister, Henry's mom?"

"I don't know," answers Harry, embarrassed.

"What do you mean you don't know? Pick one," demands Bobby.

"No," says Harry, looking straight ahead, scared and stubborn.

"Just say a name. Jeannie James. Mrs. Toohey."

"No, I won't."

"You disgust me. I hate saying that, but you do. I need to sit a little further from you than I already am," says Jamesy, getting up quick. His right leg slips into a space between two track planks. Me and Harry yell *Shit* and *Jesus Christ* and grab his shirt. He lands on his balls on a board but doesn't fall through. Below us, his beer hits another procession car roof. The Beaver Cleaver–headed fella driving that car looks out the window and spots us above and behind him, and frowns, but he doesn't say anything, maybe out of respect for his dead pal.

"Henry," says Harry, changing the subject as James rubs his

balls, "where should we go first today? Jewelry store, music shop, or funeral home?"

Tomorrow night I'm singing Bobby Darin's "Beyond the Sea"—like my dad did to my mom—then proposing to Grace at Mungiole's, during Jeannie James's wedding reception, probably after dinner. We're going to the jewelry store to buy the ring, which is fake and costs a hundred bucks. Last year, Stephen bought it to propose to Megan O'Drain, then she died, and he sold it back, along with his heart and head. We're stopping at the music store to confirm with Mouse McGinley, the owner, that his big band will show up and play behind me—free, thanks to Harry and his grass-cutting connections in the adult world— as I sing. Then the funeral home is to arrange for the hearse to drive me and Grace around the town afterwards. A hearse isn't my first choice but it's free, again thanks to Harry. Far as Grace goes, I don't really expect to get engaged or married. I just want to tell her I love her in a big way in front of a big crowd.

"Let's wait to do the funeral home tonight," I say, "when it's dark."

"Yeah," agrees Jamesy. "When it's dark."

"No, let's do the funeral home in daylight," says Harry, who feels the same about funeral homes as tits. "There's coffins in there. I'll be scared."

"That clinches it. Funeral home tonight," says Bobby James, slapping five with me.

"Besides," I say, "the music shop closes early today and ain't open tomorrow."

"Fine." Harry pouts.

"Right, there you go, Har, who cares?" says Bobby, before turning to me. "Here's what I want to know, Henry: will all this be worth it? I still can't see you going through with it, singing and proposing to Grace. Not that you're not fool enough to do it. I just want to know *why* you're doing it. You're both thirteen. Do you think she'll say yes?"

"She probably won't, but it don't matter. I got other reasons. Stephen, my parents."

"OK, now it all makes sense," he says, sarcastic.

"Henry's buying the ring Stephen bought for Megan the day she died," says Harry, who's always been smarter and more in tune to me. "He's singing the song his dad sang to his mom. He wants to help his parents fall back in love. He wants to reach Stephen. Can you grasp all that?" snaps Harry, who usually backs down to Bobby but not when it counts, another reason to love the kid despite the ankle weights.

"Oh," says Bobby, looking over at me. "Then what are we waiting for?" he asks quietly.

"Exactly," says Harry, collecting the trash from our hoagies and sodas in a brown bag. He spots me looking toward the woods. "What are you staring at, Henry?"

"All those trees over there," I say, pointing. "They'll start to change colors soon. We sit up here next week, we'll see yellow and red spots on the leaves."

"Yeah," agrees Harry, "but they're still all green today, though."

"Yeah, all green," I repeat, smiling, but only a little, like Mona Lisa.

We stand up to get down for the short walk home.

6

You'd think getting seven same-block-living kids together to ride bikes would be easy and quick. Ten minutes tops. Not so. It takes one hour, seven minutes. I'll break it down:

1:10 P.M. James, Curran, and Toohey walk home—James to make a BM, Curran to count his millions, Toohey to get his little sister and her crippled sidekick.

1:13 Toohey delivers street-corner sermon. Topics include 1) Yahweh's love for all people except Bobby James, 2) high hot dog prices at Phillies games, 3) how Jesus kept his long hair wavy in Jerusalem's humidity, and 4) a call for an investigation to see what's hidden inside Mike Schmidt's mustache.

1:20 Curran and Toohey drag James away from Paul Donohue's doorway.

1:30 Curran suffers a charley horse doing squat-thrusts. James refuses to touch him. Toohey squeezes Curran's calf until crying stops. Carful of teens yells *Homos*.

1:40 Toohey arrives home. Stephen, Cece, Archie, and Frannie sit silent watching *Leave It to Beaver*. Ward and June Cleaver discuss Beaver as Francis Junior and Cecilia, upstairs in their bedroom, knock shit around and yell each other's names over and over. Toohey goes to basement to get his no-speed sissy bike with homemade silver paint job and chewed seat. Rides bike from back alley to front of house.

1:45 Toohey, back inside, rescues Archie from Frannie, who is holding Archie by the waist and swinging him like a clock. He takes Cece and Archie outside as Cecilia dances around singing "Everything's Coming Up Roses," Francis Junior devours a bag of chips, Gwen Flaggart growls at Francis Junior, Frannie picks cheese out of his toes and sings along with Cecilia, and Stephen walks out the door.

1:50 Toohey pushes wheelchair down Toohey front lawn. Archie falls out of his chair, doesn't cry. Cece asks to see it again. Toohey complies, with Archie's blessing.

1:52 Curran comes out of his house wearing matching purple helmet and skates. He loses balance, flips over porch railing, knocks on James's front door with his wheels.

2:07 James steps out of house with wet head and beer can. His orange bike with the five-speed gear shift that everybody wants shines brighter than the summer sun.

2:10 Mr. Murphy fusses over Margie's brand-new baby blue bike. Mrs. Murphy tells him to stop treating Margie like a china doll. Mr. Murphy warns Toohey, Curran, and James against marriage.

2:14 Grace McClain busts out her door on a dirt bike, bunny-hops off her front porch, jumps a Mondale-Ferrarro sign, skids in front of her St. Francis of Assisi statue, and puts out cigarette on his bald wise head. Praise God.

2:14:30 Without saying why, Toohey makes buddies wait thirty seconds until his boner disappears.

2:15 Crew leaves St. Patrick Street.

The seven of us cross the Ave in front of the church. We ride single file, Harry and Archie first. Margie Murphy rides quietly behind them. Bobby James rides behind her and stares at her ass, I'm sure. Grace rides behind Bobby James, smoking a smoke and not staring at his ass, far as I can tell. I ride behind Grace and of course stare at her ass. Cece rides behind me and doesn't stare at my ass, I hope. We cross the Ave and enter the cemetery, which we always lap on our bikes before we hit the bike trail.

A wide cement path circles the huge cemetery's edges in a U shape, slicing through the neat, green grounds, letting folks visit their dead loved ones without leaving the comfort of their air-conditioned cars until they're ten steps from the target tombstones. You see one parked car every ten rows of tombstones, while somebody near the car drops flowers on a grave or maybe lights a red candle and clips weeds near the stones. There are no trees here, so the sun beats down on the grass, but it's always bright green, watered by the cemetery crew, fertilized by the stiffs in the ground. We whiz past the tombstone rows, calling to each other, chattering, laughing, not meaning disrespect, not being noticed by the scattered folks standing over graves, probably because they're lost in fogs despite the sunshine. The names run past you in a blur. Venziale, Murtha, Kane, Ginter, McCann, McCloskey, Sullivan, Foody. The bottoms of the stones have inscriptions like GOD'S LIGHT AND LOVE, LOVED BY ALL, IN LOVING MEMORY. You see the word *love* every five feet in a cemetery, a hundred more times than you see or hear it in real life, and I wonder why the fuck people wait until somebody is dead before they tell the world they loved them.

After five minutes of fast pedaling west, away from the Ave, where we can't hear the traffic anymore, we make a left turn on the loop into the deepest part of the cemetery. Things get scarier back here. We can still see the Ave, and the church buildings, including the grade school and surrounding playground, both of which sit inside the cemetery and this path, but we're in a different world. The tombstones back here are older and creepier. Up front, near the Ave, most of the birth and death dates fall in areas like 1910 to 1978, 1915 to 1981, shit like that. Glass protects the smooth gray stones, always decorated with fresh flowers. Back here though, you see mausoleums almost as big as our houses with names like McManus spelled out wide over the door. They smell funny inside, if you have balls enough to stick your head in between the bars covering the openings that pass for windows. Today we don't and keep moving like good soldiers on bad bikes with bells on the bars, flags on the seats, and baseball cards in the spokes.

Besides the mausoleums, the stones, more brown than gray, have years like 1808–1848 on them and oval mug shots of stiffs who look like Old West outlaws. Sometimes there aren't even stones at all, just silver crosses sticking sideways out of the dirt, faded statues that look more like Hell's Angels than saints, and broken beer bottles from the kids who smoke pot and drink beers here until the cops come. The only recent burials back here are for folks who can't afford better plots closer to the Ave, the neighborhood, and life.

Megan O'Drain's tombstone is back here, in the corner of the cemetery, right at the point where you turn left in the loop to ride back to the Ave and the angry sounds of life. Stephen is here, like he is every day, sitting cross-legged on the grass of her grave next to Father S. Thomas Alminde, OSFS, a young priest with short neat hair who beats parish kids and coaches the altar boys. Father Alminde, who squats like a baseball catcher next to Stephen, was saying some shit into Stephen's right ear until they both heard the bikes coming close. Now they watch us approach. Archie blows a kiss to his sister's grave but otherwise doesn't show emotion. Father nods and stares at us without saying anything. Stephen watches me and Cece in the back of the pack with his big hurt eyes. He almost smiles, then turns his eyes back to Megan's stone right before we turn left to the Ave.

"Hey, beautiful," I call to Cece, who stares ahead, sad but swallowing it, pumping her little legs like she's climbing a Tour de France hill. I slow down so she catches me.

"That's me, how can I help you?" she asks, still staring straight ahead.

"Not you, me," I say. "I caught my reflection in your handlebar mirror."

"Oh, right," she says, her serious face about to crack a smile, the gap in her teeth so big I could chuck a tennis ball through them. "Did the mirror break?"

"Not a fucking chance," I tell her. "Cec, how much you want to bet I can do a handstand on my bike, backflip to yours, somersault on top of Jamesy's head, then land on Archie's lap, all while we're moving?"

"I'd bet you a hundred billion trillion bucks," she giggles, "but you don't got it, and neither do I. So just stay right where you are, buddy. I like when you're close to me and not hurt."

"Yeah, me too with you," I answer, wanting to hug her, both of us smiling, bike tires spinning toward the Ave, toward Nickleback Park, away from the cemetery and all its dead depressed things.

The park starts just past the cemetery. The bike path meets the sidewalk and rockets you down a fifty-foot hill into the woods, which widen behind the cemetery. When we get to the path, Harry stops, holds his hand up, and points to the creek, which runs to our left down the first hill.

"Check out the sun reflecting off that shopping cart in the water," he says.

We're all impressed by the cart, which shines like a diamond.

"Look at those car tires to the left of the cart," says Archie. "I bet they're ten years old but the water makes them look brand new. Wouldn't mind them on my chair."

We ooh and ah.

"Gotta love nature," says Grace, flicking her smoke to the sidewalk. "Everybody sure they wouldn't rather hang out on St. Patrick Street?"

We look back to the block between the honking cars and spark-shooting trolleys, then laugh and blast off. The path is noisy and dangerous at first. Puerto Ricans hang out by a waterfall at the first bend. They smoke pot, write graffiti on trees, barbecue ribs, and blare fast music full of drums and horns. They jump in the water wearing all their clothes and sometimes knock honkies off bikes with broomsticks to steal wheels. You have to move quick past the Ricans, staring straight ahead but looking everywhere, always ready to turn around if you see one with a stick duck behind a tree. Zoom past them, cross a wooden bridge over the creek, your inner ears tickling from the bikes vibrating on the bridge.

Sun and shade hit your face as you ride under trees. The path turns all honkies here. Hard-ons wearing Harley T-shirts walk big dogs without leashes. Skinny bald pussies jog in short shorts and no shirts, and if you're lucky you see a German shepherd attack one, which is always fun.

You climb a long incline, pedaling harder. Then a sharp right turn, down a hill, past a big stage, where bad folk singers sing Woody Guthrie and Pete Seeger songs to weak applause from thirty no-job burnouts sitting in the grass. Past there is a sunny straightaway, then you cross another ear-tickling bridge, make a left turn, and pass a second waterfall, where there's more rib-cooking pot-smoking bike-stealing tree-painting Puerto Ricans, who you fly past to where the path grows shady, all turns and trees. You ride under a concrete arch and shout words like *yo* and *asshole* to hear the echo and laugh.

The woods thicken past the arch, with less people, then no people. It's just you, your six best buddies, and Mother Nature. Here the tree bark is brown and strong and not painted with hearts that say JULIO LOVES MARIA. The air tastes like honeysuckle. Yellow and purple wildflowers poke through the wide fields of green grass on both sides of the path. The trees open up, the sun beats on our backs and heads, then trees crowd the path again, hanging over us like weeping willows, like dancers. Deer munch on berries and run toward the water when they hear the gears click on our bikes. We call to them, gently, with love. We tell them don't be scared. There's nothing to be scared of here today. Cece says, *Look at me, Henry, I'm riding my bike with one hand, and a leaf landed in my basket.* Margie Murphy makes left- and right-turn signals with her arms for safety reasons. Bobby James picks berries off bushes and throws them at the helmeted head of Harry, who ignores the attack to steer Archie safe. Archie raises his arms in the air when his chair plunges down hills. Grace rides without hands and lights smokes, tilts her head back to blow the smoke straight into the air, and stares at the blue sky.

I watch it all, feel love everywhere and love it back. I wish it could always be like this. Tall trees, fresh air, space, and quiet. Peace. No broken bottles and beat-up cars. No dollar stores and corner bars. Just me, my family, my friends, out of the crowded city. Everybody I love happy and in love with somebody sitting next to them, in the woods—on a farm maybe—with flowers, trees, green grass, and Grace McClain Toohey, next to me, in love with me. It's all right in front of me as I ride through the park. I can see it, taste it, feel it everywhere, even fingertips and toes. Nothing's strong enough to interrupt the feeling.

Nothing except the Hill, which waits like a mugger for bike riders six miles deep on the path. The Hill is about forty miles high and so steep so quick it's like riding up the side of St. Ignatius to reach the steeple. Us kids on bikes can make it with a struggle, but Harry and Archie are going to have problems. We pull over, fifty yards from the Hill bottom, to discuss. Harry is optimistic.

"Why can't I make it?" he asks. "I had carbohydrates for lunch. I can do this."

"We all believe you can," says Margie Murphy, frowning. She's the most responsible kid here. By which I mean she's the only responsible kid here. "So why try, right? Let's just turn around."

"Hold on a second," says Bobby James. "This is America. If he wants to roller-skate up a hill pushing a wheelchair, that's his right. Who are we to stop that? Are we *commies* here?" he asks, caring less about democracy than a possible crash.

"Henry, talk to your idiot friends," says Margie, pointing to Bobby and Harry.

"I'm with them," I tell her. "Harry wants to try, why not?"

"Thanks, Henry," says Harry.

"No problem, Har, we're friends," I answer.

"I can't believe this," complains Margie. "Cece, don't you think this is stupid?"

"Hell no," says Cece. "I believe in America just like Bobby James."

"Grace, back me up here," begs Margie, almost out of options.

"Get the fuck outta here." Grace laughs. "I wish I had my camera."

"Unbelievable. I'm surrounded by idiots," says Margie, sounding like her mom.

"Anybody care what I think?" asks Archie, chewing a tooth-pick, the group's small reflection in his shades, all of us quiet, waiting for what he'll say. "Let's do it."

We clap and shout, except for Margie, who slaps her fore-head. Harry tells us to pedal up the Hill and wait. We grunt and sweat up the Hill, except for Grace, who burned right up there and waits for us at the top, smiling, smoking, and calling us sissies. Once we all get there, we move to the side to look back at Harry and Archie, the creek on our left down a fifty-foot cliff. In the creek, a tubby older fella with a fat mustache, floppy hat, and hip boots fly-fishes, chews a cigar, drinks out of a shiny flask, and talks out loud to Jesus about the lack of fish in the water, not seeming to notice us.

"Lord, you shoulda seen the strings I had to pull at work to get off today," he says. "All so I could come out here to relax. First I had to switch days with Mike Patterson, who's an *asshole*, as you probably know. That was like pulling teeth. It was an overtime day, too. My boss looked at me like I was nuts for giving that up to fish in this no-fish-having puddle. Then when my wife found out, well, you saw that scene. Don't mind telling you that wasn't pretty."

His line back on the pole, he takes a swig from the flask, then recasts his line.

"She called me lazy of all things," he says. "Thirty years climbing poles in all kinds of weather to make sure everybody's phone works. I even got zapped once. I think we almost met after that one. It was close anyway. I remember that."

Harry and Archie steam toward the Hill. Archie whoops, loving life.

"She caught me buying good frozen corn at the supermarket for the fish today. The brand-name stuff. You'd think that buying it was a mortal sin the way she acted. I haven't eaten anything besides no-frills food in thirty years. All my friends get Cheerios in a bright yellow box for breakfast. I get toasted oats spelled out real big in black on a white box. I ever complain? No. And she has the nerve to yip at me like a poodle because I spent thirty extra cents on a bag of corn with a picture of a big green giant jerk-off in short pants and a scarf on the front."

Archie and Harry hit the Hill's bottom. Archie raises his arms over his empty head. Harry's face is all business. They're halfway up the Hill when Harry loses steam.

"What I'm asking for, Lord, is simple. Let me catch a fish before I go home to that screaming banshee today. Just one. A sucker, a sunny, I don't care."

Harry and Archie move forward in slow mo, Harry struggling like he's lifting a car. Three-quarters up, they stop dead.

"Here we go," says Archie, smiling at us.

"Oh dear," says Harry, like a broad, looking at us in terror as we all laugh, wave, and say bon voyage. They roll backward real fast. Funny fucking stuff.

"I don't care if it's a guppy, Lord. Or drop down a goddamn whale from the sky."

Harry and Archie break the speed of sound, hit a huge rock, and fly into the water ten feet from the fisherman, who jumps like a bean on a hot plate and drops his cigar and fishing rod. The cigar floats away, the rod sticks out of the water on an angle, a couple feet from Archie, who sits in his chair in the creek, laughing like a loon. Harry, who landed face first three feet from Archie, stands up and wobbles to the fisherman. He pulls his goggles away from his face to let out water, takes his money roll from his underwear waistband, and peels a wet bill off the wad.

"Here's ten bucks. Let's keep this shit quiet," he says, falling into the knee-high water like a drunk waiting for Jesus to baptize him with beer on the banks of the Jordan.

Archie's wheelchair survived the death plunge with scrapes and a wobbly wheel. Now we sit in the shade under a fat tree with big leaves, across a curvy road from the bike path's end, eight miles from the neighborhood, watching cows stand around and fucking moo inside a huge fenced farm. Archie and Harry are stripped to their white underwear while their clothes dry on a big rock. Harry pulls a bag from his waistband.

"Anybody hungry? I got sunflower seeds," he says.

We groan.

"What's wrong with sunflower seeds?" asks Harry, offended.

"No sugar," says Cece.

"No fat," says Archie.

"No icing," says Bobby James.

"Put your seeds away, Slim," says Grace, reaching into her backpack. "I got Tastykakes and milk," she tells us, lighting a smoke, pulling out a box of the cakes and a quart of milk, passing each around. Life is good. We all lean back with our treats—us the cakes, Grace her smokes—and relax, lazy and sleepy, while the cows swat bugs with their tails and chew grass slow, looking dumb as doorknobs.

"Henry, what's that thing under a cow called?" asks Cece.

"That's a testicle sack," answers Grace, who takes my head with both hands and puts it on her lap before I can correct her for telling Cece about testicles. Holy holy. Now what the fuck were we talking about again? Oh right, cows and nut sacks.

"It's an udder, Cece," I tell her, with difficulty, my mind clouded by a sky full of flying boners. "Harry, chuck me your helmet," I say, resting it on my lap when he does.

"You wanna see a testicle sack, look over there," says Bobby James, pointing to Harry, who picks a wedgie as he examines his drying clothes. When he bends over, the word DEFENSE, written on the ass of his Villanova Wildcats undies, expands. After we laugh at him, Margie Murphy puts Bobby James's head on her lap.

"Henry, what's a testicle sack?" asks Cece.

"Never mind that," I answer Cece, wiping coconut off her face with my shirt. "You remember the other day when I said how farmers got milk from udders?"

"You said they *squeeze* them," smiles Cece, looking like a hockey player with pigtails. "Can you fellas lift Archie out of his chair so he can put his head on my lap?"

Me and Harry lower Archie, his face red behind his shades, to Cece's lap. Then I slide right back to Grace, put my head back in her lap, and put the helmet back over my boner, which is doing something like the cha-cha: bump bump bump bump bump, ba!

"Nice to get out of my chair once in a while," says Archie, swatting at a bug in the air.

"Henry, does all this land belong to one family?" asks Cece, staring at the farm.

"Yeah, most likely," I answer.

"Like all the grass inside the fences is their yard?"

"Yeah."

"All of it?"

"Yup. All theirs."

"And it's quiet and peaceful like this all the time?" she asks.

"I'm sure it is," I say.

"So why doesn't everybody live on a farm?" she says, which makes me laugh.

"Farms are weird," says Grace, playing with my hair.

"What do you mean weird?" I ask quickly, worried.

"Weird like somebody *lives here*. It's so open and quiet. I'd be scared at night."

"No you wouldn't," I tell her. "You'd be right there with your husband. You could sit outside and hold hands. You could fall asleep on his shoulder with his arm around you, and he could feel your soft hair on his cheek and smell your shampoo. The stars would make the night bright, and the quiet would mean no fights. You wouldn't feel nothing but love. No fear, not weird," I say, real emphatic.

"Jesus, Hank," says Grace, "almost sounds like you're talking about me and you."

"What if I was?" I ask, smiling, looking right up at her, not blinking.

"Oh, OK, I'll play," she says, smiling big back. "So if we get married and live on a farm and I get scared at night, you'll protect me? Is that right?"

"Yeah, that's right, doll." I beam. "Me. Hank Toohey. Your protector."

"Oh, boy. We should get a dog too," she says but grins, her eyes dancing on me.

"Done," I say. Whatever Grace wants, Grace gets.

"And some security guards."

"Done."

"Maybe a tank and some hand grenades. A tiger too."

"Done, done, and done."

"All righty." She laughs. "Anytime you want to propose then, Hank."

"Cool, I'll have to think up something special," I say.

"Like what?" she asks, watching me close, smoke floating out of her mouth.

"I don't know. Maybe I'll sing a song, dance a dance, all in front of a crowd."

"Sweet." She laughs. "Let me know when so I can dress up and look nice."

"Can't help you there, honey," I say. "Has to be a surprise. Besides, you look nice in anything. Rags, trash bags. Don't matter."

"Trash bags," repeats Grace, a huge grin on her face staring down at mine, still on her lap. "You're too much, Hank Toohey." She flashes an even bigger smile, warmer than the sun above us, and it feels like it lasts forever until finally Cece says something.

"Archie, how are you going to propose to me?" she asks.

"I won't," he answers. She pulls his ear. "Ouch."

"Oh, I'll tell you how you'll propose. You'll rent a boat by a lake. On the lake there will be rows of lit, floating candles that make a path to the middle. You'll paddle me out there, through the candles, then hand me a dozen roses, then tell me I'm the most beautiful woman in the world, then ask me to give you the privilege of marrying me. And ask slow, don't rush, got it?"

"Got it." He sighs.

"Good boy," she says, pleased.

"I want to propose to my future wife while we jump out of a plane," says Harry.

"Don't you mean future husband?" asks Bobby James.

"I don't care how I get asked. I just want to stay in love," says Margie, "and be happy. I wanna be married and happy, not just married."

She looks far off, toward the house inside the farm, maybe trying to picture future life and love not like she sees it through her parents; we're probably all doing that a little. Nobody says anything for a while. The broads play with the fellas' hair. Harry performs martial arts poses. Nobody breaks his visible balls for it. Every once in a while, a cow moos and we giggle. A warm wind blows the grass and leaves. The sun bakes us like brownies. Quiet station wagons mosey down the road loaded with happy families going for tall sundaes at restaurants that require shoes and shirts. Grace leans her face above me. She smiles. Her brown hair tickles my cheeks and turns red from the sun, which shadows her face and lights her head like a halo. An hour passes maybe, then another. We lay there, thrilled by love, loving life, saying nothing. Finally, still not talking, we get up to head back to the city, to St. Patrick Street. There are no big hills to climb to return. The hard part's leaving. You can kill yourself trying.

We ride the eight miles back in sad silence as the sounds and sights of city life reappear. Grass and crickets surrender to cars, shouts, shopping carts, and spray-painted trees. Then, just like that, we're back. We pass the cemetery, where Stephen is twenty yards back, finally walking out toward the Ave to return home. We wait on the light at St. Patrick. A fella on a ten-speed bike punches the passenger-side door of a car that almost hit him. We cross as they fight and curse. Back on St. Patrick Street, the row homes on the hills throw shade on the street. Riding your bike and looking straight ahead, it almost seems like the saints on the lawns hold the Mondale-Ferraro signs like angry union fellas at an ugly picket.

7

Two fellas and two broads walk up to the counter of Mouse McGinley's Music Store, located on Frankford Ave right off St. Patrick Street in the heart of Holmesburg. The fellas are young, maybe twenty-five, and dressed like thin-haired accountants who read the Bible before bed. Both broads—one blonde, one brunette—have big tits, definite D cups; wear plain blouses and skirts below the knees (yawn); and approach owner Mouse McGinley, a skinny fella, early forties, also a neat-haired accountant type.

"Hi," says the blond broad, like a zombie, to Mouse. "We want to buy musical instruments to form a rock band so that we can rock. But you look more like a librarian, how can you help us?"

"Honey, looks can be deceiving," says Mouse, snapping his fingers. His clothes change from button-down shirt, sweater vest, and khaki slacks to a sleeveless silver sequined jumpsuit with matching cape, sunglasses, and platform boots. Mouse holds a red V guitar with flames painted to spell MOUSE and launches into Jimi Hendrix's "Purple Haze," jerking his body all over the place. Then he stops and smiles at the impressed customers.

"Wow," says the brunette, dumb as the blonde, "can you do that for us?"

Mouse snaps his fingers again, and the four twits are onstage in tight purple unitards, three with guitars, one with drums. They rip through "Purple Haze" like Mouse did while Mouse holds a lighter in the air and pumps a fist. The music fades and a narrator says, *Mouse McGinley's Music Store, St. Patrick and Frankford, arrive in a square daze, leave in a purple haze.*

"You fellas like the commercial?" asks Mouse to me, Harry, Archie, and Bobby James, who dropped the other kids off on the block before heading to the Ave and my marriage errands. "Or do you think it's too much?" he worries, his hand on top of the TV behind the counter. Mouse, who plays every instrument and loves Jimi Hendrix, John Lennon, Charlie Pride, and Charlie Parker all the same, wears the same accountant clothes that he did in his commercial.

"It's great," I tell him.

"I should have known you'd like it, Henry. What did you other fellas think?"

"I liked it, but maybe for the next one you could plug my landscaping company," Harry says.

"The big tits on the chicks was a plus. But they coulda been bigger, the tits," Bobby James says.

"It needs some wheelchair stunts. I can do those, you know," Archie says.

"Landscaping company plug, bigger boobs, wheelchair jumps. Got it. Here, Henry, I want to show you something," says Mouse, reaching under the counter and pulling up four albums. The first is called *Pan, Amor y Cha Cha* by a Spanish broad—Abbe Lane—with C cups, brown hair, and a great ass. In the picture, Abbe stands sideways, wears a gold gown, and pulls her dark hair up so you can see her neck and shoulder blades as she stares at the camera in a French-me-Henry way. I can almost hear her purr. Downstairs in my skivvies, my boner motor does just that.

"Hello, honey," I say, real friendly. "Good stuff, Mouse, not bad."

"How about this one?" he asks.

Mouse sits the next album, *Hawaiian Paradise* by The Hawaiian Islanders, on top of the first. Wow, this one's even better. A Hawaiian chick in a grass skirt holds her hands behind her head, and the only thing hiding her D cups is one of those flowered wreaths they give everybody who gets off a plane. And for this right now I hate all Hawaiians. But you can still see the inside of her jugs, so it's not a total loss, and my boner grows some more.

Mouse flips to the next album, and we gasp. The facts: band, Dick Shorkey's Percussion Pops Orchestra; album, *Holiday for Percussion*; picture: one naked broad. Yeah, you heard me right, a naked fucking broad, visible from the waist up, standing sideways, leaning back, a big perfect mouth. Long straight hair covers her tits. And for this right now I hate long hair, but not enough to not clap with the three other fellas. I have a full perfect painful boner. My head feels hot.

"I saved the best for last," says Mouse. "Check this out."

Slowly, Mouse shows the final album. *Music of the African Arab*, performed by a band called Mohammed-Al Bakker and his Oriental Ensemble, who look like donkey salesmen. On the cover, the donkey dealers hoot at a broad dancing on a table. From the feet up, she wears baggy belly dancer pants. Her belly shows. So does her, oh Christ, left tit and nipple. Her left tit and nipple. Left tit. Nipple. I see a darkness.

Next thing I see after the darkness is a ceiling fan spinning inside four shadows. I blink, then make out Mouse, Harry, Bobby James, and Archie above me, watching me concerned, the weak air from the fan feeling cool on my hot face.

"What happened?" I ask.

"You fainted," says Harry.

"Fainted. Jesus," I say. "Don't I feel like a jerk-off?"

"You did better than Harry," says Bobby James. "He cried and covered his face."

"I did not," argues Harry, still sniffling, his hands still over his face.

"Shut up, yes you did. You still are," says Jamesy.

"Oh. So what? Shut up."

Jamesy reaches over me for Harry, and I watch him strangle Harry from the floor, which feels as soft as a bed right now, until Mouse breaks them up.

"All right, all right, knock it off," he says. "Let's help Henry up."

Harry, Jamesy, and Mouse pull me up by the arms and sit me on a stool. Archie rolls over with a soda can, opens it with a hiss, and hands it to me.

"Thanks. How's my hair?" I ask them, worried, needing a straight answer.

"Fine," says Mouse. "It never even moved. Still, I don't think I'll be showing you any more album covers soon."

"Then I want to buy them," I say. "I'll lay down in bed before I look at them."

"Henry, I can't be responsible for you blacking out," Mouse argues.

"First-time thing, I swear. Please let me have them. I'm begging you."

"First time? You passed out *last week* when I showed you those *other* covers. Besides, they're collector's items. Probably worth a fortune," says buck-hungry Mouse, shifing gears to salesman, in a way that means "make me an offer."

"I'll give you two bucks for all four," I say.

Mouse laughs. "Try sixteen bucks for all four."

"Four bucks," I tell him.

"Eight," says Mouse.

"Six."

"Seven."

"Done. Curran, pay the man," I say.

"Let me show you boys something else," says Mouse, taking Harry's money. He leads us to the store back corner, where electric guitars line the wall. "I just got these babies. This here's a cherry Fender, used, restrung, with several chips in the back. It's a lead guitar, thirty bucks. Right here is a violin bass, like Paul McCartney used, but not a real Hofner. Also used, also restrung and chipped, also thirty bucks. Here's a rhythm guitar signed by Tiny Tim's second wife's brother: forty bucks. With these three guitars, you're a drum set away from being a legitimate band. Together they cost a hundred bucks, but I'll give them to you for ninety-five, tax-free."

"No thanks, not today," says Harry. "We came to check about the band for Henry tomorrow night. They still gonna show up and play?"

Mouse plays sax in a big band that does Tommy Dorsey horseshit, show tunes, Sinatra ballads. As a favor to Harry, he got them to play for me tomorrow.

"We'll be there," he says. "Henry still singing 'Beyond the Sea'?"

"Yeah, he is," says Harry. "Your band ready to play it?"

"We can play that shit in our sleep," brags Mouse.

"Excellent," says Harry. "What time'll you be there?"

"We'll be there by eight-forty and set up by nine. That OK?"

"You got that, Henry? Nine P.M. all right?" asks Harry.

"Yeah, whenever's fine," I tell him.

Mouse folds his arms and squints at me as I comb my hair.

"Admiring my beauty?" I ask. "You want to take my picture?"

"No and no. So you got your dance steps all worked out for the song?"

"Yup. Been practicing that shit every night," I say.

"You really going to propose to that chick tomorrow?"

"Yeah."

"What's her name again?" he asks, smiling.

"Grace McClain."

"Reminds me of when I proposed," says Mouse, who picks up an acoustic guitar with no strings. His cat Dizzy jumps out meowing. "There you are, Dizzy."

"You proposed? I never even seen your wife," I say.

"That's because she left me ten years ago, which would make you what, three, four?"

"Three," I tell him. "Sorry for asking."

"No, it's cool," he says. "We were together for ten before she left. They were a good ten. Maybe a good nine is more accurate." He smiles—sad, maybe happy—and picks up a strung acoustic. He sits next to Dizzy on the counter and sings the Beatles' "Eight Days a Week" to her, soft and quiet, while we all watch, feeling happy.

"Mouse, how did you propose to her?" asks Harry, after the song.

"I played the entire John Coltrane album *A Love Supreme* on my saxophone under her window," says Mouse, looking out the store window like the scene where he proposed is a movie, and the window is the screen. "I must have played it ten straight times, and she just leaned out her window the whole time and watched."

"So how'd you get past the playing part to the proposal?" asks Bobby.

"Her dad shoved a grapefruit in the sax, then I asked her. He said *Oh no*, she said *Oh yes*, we got married three months later and spent nine good years together."

"What went wrong?" asks Harry, who never met a question he wouldn't ask.

"Everything. Nothing. I don't know. Love's a mystery. That's today's lesson."

He puts the guitar down and picks up Dizzy, who lets out a half meow, half purr, sounding almost like a bird she'd eat in two bites.

"Sorry it didn't work out, Mouse," I tell him.

"Thanks. I'm fine. It's all good. You wanna hear me play some Hendrix?"

We all shout yeah.

"Cool. Wait here, I'll be right back," he says.

Mouse disappears into the back room, then returns in the Superman getup from the commercial, his hair still parted on the side. He walks to a small stage at the back of the store, where a wood wall draped in black velvet holds a neon sign that reads MOUSE. He flips a switch to light his name, then in a fake accent that sounds exactly like Hendrix, he asks in his mike, "How's everybody doing tonight?" like we're forty thousand kids, not four. We go nuts, and Mouse says "all right" like Jimi. He picks up the V guitar leaning against the velvet wall and plugs it in as it hums. He straps it on, picks at the strings, and twists the knobs at the top.

Then he's off, pounding on the guitar, making it sound like a monster truck is crashing in the store playing pretty blues through a spaceship muffler. Mouse barks the lyrics out like his supper depends on it, never hitting a note, never caring. He plays the solos on his knees and ends the song on his back, never once looking at us. With the guitar noise still coming through the amps, he drops the guitar on the stage, then walks off the stage into the back as we riot, making noise, going nuts.

Mouse returns—back in his accountant clothes—and wipes sweat off his forehead with an MM hanky. He unplugs his guitar, sets it back on its stand, and walks to the storefront to look out the door, where no customers wait to enter, which doesn't bother him. A smile on his face, Mouse walks to a small fridge behind the counter, pulls out a quart of milk, and pours it into a bowl for Dizzy, who dives for the sweet treat. He puts the milk back and picks up his sax, which is as gold as hubcaps on a muscle car.

"You boys need anything else?" he asks.

We tell him nah.

"Then if you'll excuse me and the Dizz, we'd like some time alone."

Mouse starts into John Coltrane's most famous album, *A Love Supreme,* the one he played for his wife under her window when he asked her to marry him ten years before they split. But he's right. It is still all good, love. As we leave the store, the sad saxophone notes leave with us, pick us up, and carry us back to St. Patrick Street like ski lifts, like clouds, like magic carpets with footrests and heated seats.

Cecilia Toohey took me and Cece to the Philadelphia Museum of Art last year on a Sunday morning, because it's free then. While I was there, I saw the most beautiful thing ever. It wasn't the art, which is all bullshit that bores me. Portraits of boneheads with muttonchops making googly eyes at the young fellas who painted them. Chinese vases you aren't allowed to touch. Long murals of seven hundred naked knuckleheads, bleeding and dying and reaching up to God, who sits on a cloud above and scratches His Golden Ass with an ivory wand. Fucking ridiculous.

So anyway, we were standing outside the art museum, afterwards. Me and Cece ran up and down the steps like Rocky Balboa about a hundred times while Cecilia smoked and smiled and talked to some dick with chick hair who said he went to grad school at Penn. I noticed a broad in a bikini tying her sneaks ten feet from where I stood. She'd just finished jogging. Her tits, dotted with dew like fresh produce, drooped peacefully as she tied her shoes. What a pair of tits! Good God! I wanted to walk over and hold them for her, to take the weight off her back, as she fastened her laces.

I love tits. There are so many kinds. There's the beach ball tit, the watermelon tit, the blimp tit, the tennis ball tit. There's the kind created for the thirteen-year-old comedian, the tit that makes you laugh and cry at the same time, it's so big and bouncy and full of love and doughnut cream. There's the train titty, the pointed kind with bright lights that hauls ass right at you, daring you to open your mouth like a baby bird and stand in its path.

There's the kangaroo tit, the one you straddle and ride one bounce at a time until you reach the sunny fucking shores of Australia. There's the tit like planet Earth, the spinning center of all life, the very fucking source of the air you breathe to live, the tit that's dry and wet and safe and dangerous at once, the tit that erupts in volcano explosions and earthquakes, leaving you shaking in your boots loving it more, your boner big enough to hit a softball to center, while sweat pours off your forehead and you beg God to strike you dead before you explode like a cherry bomb dropped in the hopper. Oh, mother. That's the tit a fella has in mind when he calls for take-out at the tit shop and says, "Bring me a dim-witted sophomore lass with huge tits." That's the one that appeals to a horny bastard like me.

All this was on my mind as I showed up for the bra-removal seminar at Seamus O'Shaunnesy's house, which got bumped from after dinner to before dinner for reasons I don't know and don't care to fucking know. *Sooner the better,* Seamus, who's my age, told me twenty minutes ago, decked out in a shirt and tie, setting up folding chairs on his lawn around the statue of St. Blaise, who's bald and holds two candles as a symbol of his status as patron saint of sore throats. Seamus is charging five bucks a head for today's event to start saving for seminary school so he can become a priest. He lives two doors down from me, next to Frannie Toohey, who lives next door to us. Soon as Seamus told me about the time change, I yelled up the street to Bobby James, who was washing his bike on his porch. Now he's at my door, showered, wearing a collar shirt and pleated shorts, and holding a brown leather binder and a Phillies pen. I got a Sixers pen and the same kind of binder but, unlike James, I didn't shower or change. Doesn't matter; I still look better.

We walk to Seamus's front lawn, where twenty fellas—all our age, maybe a year younger or older—from the block are already here, wearing casual dress clothes and holding leather binders and Flyers pens. Seamus, who spikes his hair and mousses it wet, greets each fella, writes his name on a HELLO MY NAME IS sticker, and slaps it on his shirt. We approach the sign-in table, which is from the O'Shaunnesy dining room.

"Yo, Henry, Bobby James. How's things, fellas?" asks Seamus as he writes BOBBY JAMES on one nametag and REVEREND MINISTER TOOHEY on another. We all shake hands—even me and Bobby James—and laugh.

"Yo," Bobby says.

"Yo," I say. "The setup here looks nice."

Besides the table, there are folding chairs, a blackboard, a buffet spread (water pitchers and a fruit salad bowl on the table), a podium (which is wood with a cross on the front), and a chick mannequin in a Catholic schoolgirl uniform.

"Thanks, Henry," says Seamus. "You're the first to notice. Look at those animals."

Raymond McAfee, a big-haired horny bastard, takes the mannequin, puts her inside St. Blaise's arms like they're making out, and responds to our cheers by sticking his tongue through two fingers.

The crowd is boiling already. McAfee stands on a chair and leads a *Breasts, breasts, breasts* chant. If anybody was fooled by the collar shirts and nametags into thinking this'd be a calm event, those dreams went right the fuck out the window.

"Yeah, well, you know how tits get us all crazy," I say.

"We all been there," agrees Bobby James.

"I understand. I just want some furniture left when we're done. Everybody's been going nuts since I told them my sister's coming out for a demonstration," says Seamus.

"You're kidding me," I gasp, delighted.

Sheila O'Shaunnesy has double-D cow tits. Correction. Triple-D.

"No, I'm not," he says.

"How'd you pull that one off?" I ask. "You pay her?"

"No. I told her twenty fellas would watch her take her bra off."

"That makes sense," says Bobby. "I heard she's a slut."

"Watch your fucking mouth about my sister," says Seamus. "She agreed to take off her top for science, as a public service."

"Public service. Maybe we can get a crew to film it for PBS," I joke.

"Nah, I already called them and offered. They said no," says Seamus, glum.

"That's a goddamn shame," says James, sad. "Look, Henry, let's find seats."

"Wait," says Seamus, "where's Harry? He paid me for all three of you last week."

"I don't think he's coming," I tell him.

"He's passing up a chance to see my sister's tits? He a homo?"

"Hard to say." Bobby James shrugs.

"Well, he can't have a refund. I'm saving this money to become a priest."

We sit down, greet a few fellas with yos and handshakes, and agree the seminar should be super. Seamus approaches the podium. Let the 1984 Tit Expo begin.

"I'd like to thank everybody for coming," he says.

Applause. Raymond McAfee stands up, whistles, and throws his pelvis.

"There's too many unhappy broads out there," continues Seamus. "And not just on St. Patrick Street. It's everywhere. And why are they unhappy? Because the boys who try to get into their bras are clumsy amateurs. We'll correct that problem today."

More applause. McAfee runs around and slaps everyone five.

"Thanks for the enthusiasm, Raymond," says Seamus. "It's very contagious. I planned an informative, informal, interactive program today. We'll talk about bras. We'll talk about tits. But we won't just talk. We'll learn by doing."

The crowd goes nuts. McAfee cartwheels.

"And like I told you earlier, my sister Sheila will be out for a live demo."

The cheers hurt my ears.

"But let's start with a Q and A," says Seamus. "All right, you first, Raymond."

"When is your sister coming out to show us her tits?" he asks.

"She'll be out soon enough. Any more questions? You in the back."

"Your sister in the house right now?"

"Yeah," says Seamus. "Anybody else? Go ahead."

"She in her underwear already?"

"I'm not sure. Another question. You, sir."

"Can I help her undo her bra when she comes out?"

"Let's move to the mannequin," sighs Seamus, who looks tired already. "Can someone please pass her up here," he asks, pointing to her as she kneels with her face near the boner area of St. Blaise, who stares up happy at Heaven. We pass the mannequin up to the front, each fella either squeezing her tits or reaching up her skirt as she passes hands. Once Seamus has her, he frowns and smooths her blouse like a mom would.

"This is the Catholic schoolgirl uniform," he announces, urgent. "This item is the enemy, its design masterminded by priests and nuns whose *existence* is dedicated to keeping you from the treasures inside." Seamus stares at us hard. The silliness disappears. Everybody knows this is a serious fucking problem needing a serious fucking solution. "The design's brilliance is simple: one long zipper in the back, nothing else. What that means is that it's either on or off. There ain't room for your hand to wander in the tit area, even if you're in the basement with a broad while her parents are upstairs mixing drinks, unless you take the thing completely off. Only a fool or a madman'd do that."

"So what's the secret?" someone asks.

"The secret is there ain't no secret," says Seamus, disgusted as much at the question as the problem. "The Catholic schoolgirl uniform is impenetrable. You're with a broad wearing her school uniform, you might as well go home and kiss your dog." Seamus works the uniform off the mannequin. We whistle. Two kids, neither one me, pass out. Seamus tosses the uniform onto St. Blaise's bald head. We cheer. He slips T-shirts and shorts on her—we boo—and writes PATIENCE and SMOOTHNESS on the board. "There's two keys to getting a bra off. It takes patience. And you gotta be smooth."

Now it's almost dinnertime, and dads too tired to notice us carry thermoses and rolled newspapers and walk down the block past tired cars parallel-parked on the crowded curbs. Moms poke their heads out doors to call kids in for dinner. Francis Junior and Frannie greet each other without smiles and walk up the Toohey steps they share, never once looking my way. The seminar noise rises above Seamus's voice.

"I spoke to neighborhood broads. They're sick of the way we go after tits like cavemen. This is 1984. They want respect," says Seamus, trying without success to shout over our *Breasts, breasts, breasts* chant. Then it changes to *Bring out Sheila, Bring out Sheila, Tits now, talk later, Tits now talk later.* "Feel around her back. Give her a muscle rub. It loosens her up and shows you ain't afraid to work for the prize." *Cleavage or our money back, Cleavage or our money back.* Bobby James hands his dad's police megaphone to McAfee, to lead us louder in cheers. *Two scoops in every bra, Two scoops in every bra.* "Say something nice to her. Get her in the mood slow." Seamus whispers in the mannequin's ear, his eyes closed. I think he slipped her ear tongue. Is he sweating? *Come on out and take it off, Come on out and take it off.* "When you think she's ready, move your hand around to the front." Seamus's voice cracks. He sweats like a pig man in a meat freezer. He *wants* that mannequin. *No shirts allowed, Sheila, No shirts allowed, Sheila.* Most of us stand on chairs. Seamus loses it with his hand half up the mannequin's shirt.

"Fuck it. Sheila, get out here, please. *Sheila, show us your tits, Sheila, show us your tits,*" he shouts with everybody.

The door opens, Sheila appears. The shouts stop like a needle ripped off a record. After that, there's a good minute of sincere, nervous, excited applause. The main attraction(s) has (have) arrived. Proper respect is paid.

"Yo, fellas," says Sheila, who's fifteen, brown-haired, and wearing a tank top and jean shorts despite being a little fat. But that's OK; she's tan, and her tits, well, I already told you about those. We are in paradise, my friend. Welcome to Fantasy Island.

"Yo, Sheila, how you doing, may we please see your tits?"

"Seamus, I thought we were gonna teach them how to undo a bra strap," she says.

"Plans changed," says Seamus, trembling. "We just wanna see the tits. Let me help you with that shirt," he says, pulling her shirt over her head the way hockey players do in fights. The tits—still snug inside the bra—pop out into the Philly air, two pure pale balloons floating lost in a cold polluted town. *Buh-yoink.* Allelujah, allelujah. Couple fellas behind me weep. My knees buckle and I let out some kind of noise but otherwise hang tough and stay conscious. Bobby James says, *Hold me, Henry.* I do.

All of a sudden, Mrs. O'Shaunnesy (same wonderful tits as Sheila) flies out of the house. She's got a beer can, a spatula, and a look on her face like you'd expect from a half-lit broad who walked out of her house to see the following things, in this order: her own son squeezing the tits of her own daughter; twenty fellas standing on chairs cheering; St. Blaise wearing a schoolgirl uniform. She runs for the statue.

"Who put this girl's uniform on St. Blaise?" she gasps. "That's sick."

She rips the uniform off St. Blaise and kisses a ring on his hand for forgiveness. Mr. O'Shaunnesy, who has Brillo pad hair, comes to the door and looks around.

"Is that one of my beers?" he asks his wife. "What time's dinner ready?"

Ah, life on St. Patrick Street. *Fuck the tit seminar on our lawn; who put the dress on the saint, is that my beer, and what time's dinner ready?*

8

"Fran, how much cash you got left in your wallet?" asks Cecilia Regina (Fitzpatrick) Toohey, who was born April 1, 1945, the youngest of five girls, to a dad who drank and cheated and finally left her suicidal mother. The Fitzpatricks lived on St. Dominic Street in St. Bernard's Parish, which isn't far from us, maybe ten blocks south. Cecilia spent her childhood angry, pulling her mom's head out of the oven, shaking down classmates for loose change, using that dough and the money her dad sent her in the mail to buy rock-and-roll records, which she played loudly in her locked room.

"I don't know, maybe five bucks," says Francis Junior, who was born on April 1, 1944, the oldest of fifteen children. His dad, who spent two years in the seminary before dropping out, delivered mail in the daytime and hung around parish nuns and priests in the nighttime. His mom was either spitting out kids or recovering on the sofa of their home on St. Ignatius Street in St. Patrick Parish, not far from here, maybe fifteen blocks south. All this left Francis Junior default dad to his little brothers and sisters all his life. He never met a day that wasn't full of duty, especially if you ask him, so don't.

"Five bucks? You just got paid," complains Cecilia, dropping her pen on the table and rubbing her eyes in disgust. She met Francis Junior on March 25, 1960, on a blind date. She was fifteen at the time and not allowed to date, so her friend arranged for them to meet in secret on a corner a couple blocks from her house. Cecilia stood and waited for Francis Junior, who was late, and fumed. *Where is this fucking asshole? He'll probably show up with booze on his breath, a dent in his fender, a bra swinging from a finger.*

"Cecilia, I bought the pizzas, kept five bucks, and gave you the rest," says Francis Junior, who had parked and waited for her at a different corner. *Broads are always late,* he thought, *unlike me. I'm always on time. I can be counted on. All day long I'm expected to pull my weight and then some, and do. Not other people, though, no, the lazy assholes.*

"Something's not adding up, Fran. I can't cover all the bills with this," says Cecilia, who had circled the neighborhood in a flowered dress and flaming rage, hunting for her date, who was now an hour late. She found him in his car, in a collar shirt, asleep.

"So pay some this week and the others the next," says Francis Junior, who had jumped awake when Cecilia pounded on his car door to startle him. He rolled down his window.

"I did that last pay, remember, Fran? Or were you up the street then?" says Cecilia, who had punched out one of his front teeth when he rolled the window down, in the first second of their first date, before they ever even said anything to each other.

"Cecilia, leave me alone," says Francis Junior, not looking away from the TV.

"Fuck you," she says, looking right at him.

Good evening and welcome to Action News at 5. Tonight's top stories: fifteen cops open fire on an unarmed black teen, now clinging to life at Temple University Hospital, in North Philadelphia. Two toddlers die in a row home blaze in West

Philadelphia. President Reagan survives a bomb threat at the White House. It's payday and pizza night at the Toohey house, where tonight's guests—Archie O'Drain, Harry Curran, Bobby James, and the lovely Grace McClain, along with Frannie, Stephen, Henry, and Cece Toohey—eat pizza slices over paper plates, watch the always entertaining fireworks between Francis Junior and Cecilia, and create their own sparks as well.

"Bobby James," says Frannie, "that a wad of gum on your plate?"

"Yeah," says Jamesy, who sits on the sofa next to me, between the Francises.

"What, are you saving it?" asks Frannie.

"Yeah," says Bobby, looking up from his book (*Shout!*, a Beatles biography), "for after dinner."

"Why not just throw it out and get a new piece?"

"He can't," I say, looking up from my book (*Hellfire!*, a Jerry Lee Lewis biography), "he's running low."

Frannie, who picks Bobby up by his ankles and shakes him while dozens of Bazookas fall out of his pockets, was born December 25, 1960, exactly nine months after Francis Junior and Cecilia's first date. He scored straight Cs in school, poured water for ball teams, and never got near a broad except when her cooler boyfriend dumped her and she needed a supportive shoulder to blow snot on. His two biggest triumphs in life are acing the postal test and generally pleasing his parents. Other than that, he's pretty much an asshole, like Jamesy says.

"Asshole? Everyone hear that? Bobby James called me an asshole," says Frannie.

"You are one," mumbles Stephen, who is sitting at the dining room table and was born June 25, 1966. Stephen was everything Frannie wasn't: handsome, charming, funny, smart, and good at sports. My parents paid more attention to him. They'd clap in the living room as three-year-old Stephen threw a Nerf football with a spiral while Frannie pulled weeds outside.

"Frannie ain't an asshole. He's an ugly virgin lass," says I, who was born August 15, 1971. I came out of Cecilia asking the doctor if afterbirth held hair like gel. I was a lot like Stephen, except stranger. I did song and dance shit at pharmacies while Cecilia waited on prescriptions. I told jokes and burned like a furnace. My hair inspired respect that kept me safe from bully types. I longed to rock, and if not to rock then to save souls, and if not to rock or save souls then to make people laugh.

"Why the argument, fellas? Frannie's all these things and more," says Cece, standing behind Archie, her hands wrapped around his throat. Cecilia Regina Toohey Junior was born August 15, 1976, during a thunderstorm blackout, after Cecilia Senior's water broke. From the tub, she told me to find an adult and a car. The first person I found was Francis Junior, delivering on the street, but he refused to leave duty, so I grabbed Mr. James, who was asking Mrs. Mahon to unlock the door for Mr. Mahon. He drove us to the hospital in his squad car, siren screaming, while me and Bobby, both five, shouted *Mayday, Mayday, pregnant leaking broad.* Ten minutes after we got there, Cecilia gave birth to Cece. I was the first man in the family to see her. I loved her like crazy right away and still do. She goes where I go in life.

"Can you quit strangling me?" asks Archie, with a red face and funny voice.

"Not until you tell me I'm beautiful, asshole," she orders.

"OK," he gasps, "you're beautiful, asshole. Now can you stop?"

"All right. It's Grace's turn anyway," she tells him.

"Hey, asshole," says Grace to Cece, "you want me to strangle this asshole?"

"Yeah, asshole," laughs Cece, as Grace strangles Archie, "that asshole."

"OK, why don't we stop fucking cursing?" says Cecilia. "Fran, say something."

"I'm eating, Cecilia. Frannie, what time you get out on the street today?"

"Ten," says Frannie.

"Light day?" asks Francis Junior.

"No, heavy. We had cable guides."

"You get a lot of those?"

"I get enough."

"How many?"

"Total number?" asks Frannie.

"No, house-to-guide ratio," says Francis Junior.

"Three to one."

"Damn. What time did you finish delivering?"

"Twelve-thirty."

"Where'd you hide?"

"Here, remember? You were, uh, upstairs."

"Oh, right."

"That a bite on your leg?"

"Yep."

"Happen today?"

"Yep."

"Where at?"

Francis Junior points to Flaggart, who growls at him through the porch door.

"Fran, can you let the dog in?" asks Cecilia from the table.

"No," he says. "Stephen, what time you done working tonight?"

"Leave Stephen alone and let the dog in, Fran," says Cecilia.

"Screw the dog. Stephen, I asked what time you're done working tonight."

"Can't you leave him alone for once?" asks Cecilia, angry.

"Don't answer me then, Stephen," says Francis Junior. "I know when you're done. Eleven. Be in the house five after."

"Fran, shut the fuck up and leave him alone," snaps Cecilia.

"Five after, Stephen. You got that?" Francis Junior repeats.

Cece beats Archie's head with a brush. Grace takes the brush off Cece and whacks him too. Bobby James and Frannie slap-fight. Harry frowns at *Forbes*. Flaggart growls outside. I comb.

Stephen pushes back his chair. Cecilia tells him, don't be so rough, ain't it bad enough you two fuck up all the furniture after midnight? The news spits out war pictures from foreign countries, interviews with bikini chicks, home run highlights, and apartment fires, followed by the weather, which'll be this today and that tomorrow, who gives a fuck?

Stephen, says Francis Junior, don't you slam that front door when you walk outta here. *Slam.* Goddamn it, Stephen, he says. Five after eleven or I change the locks.

Leave him alone, Fran, you don't mean that anyway, says Cecilia.

The hell I don't mean that, Cecilia.

What about these bills, Fran? Can we talk money here?

What's to talk about, Cecilia? You piss it all away. I work overtime and don't buy nothing and you blame me. Why don't you get a job?

A job? I raised four kids. Two are still in grade school. No, five kids. I inherited one in a wheelchair because his parents can't fucking do it themselves.

Cecilia, shut the hell up. What kind of thing is that to say in front of the kid?

Oh, give me a break, asshole. He knows the score. I take good care of him.

You got no class to say shit like that, no class at all.

Fuck you, I don't got class. I'm all class.

Right, you got class, Cecilia, slithering around in a short dress like a whore.

You're the whore, Fran, you and that Cooney cunt up the street.

Don't call her that.

Oh, you're gonna defend her now? What, do you think she loves you?

I don't even know what you're talking about. You stop taking the Valiums?

No I stopped the Lithiums, asshole, but I took some Valium

today and I'll take more too if you want. You want me to take them all so you can move in with the cunt?

There you go again with that word, Cecilia. You're a sick bitch, I hope you know.

I'm sick? You punch your son practically every night.

We're losing him, Cecilia.

So you punch him?

I gotta be tough with him.

Right.

I wasn't out drinking when I was eighteen, I was married and raising kids, I wasn't pissing money away on booze standing behind a Dumpster like a goddamn bum getting drunk and feeling sorry for myself. I wasn't having fun.

Boo fucking hoo for you, Fran? Is that the problem?

Fuck you.

No, fuck you.

Go to hell.

Go up the street and cry to your cunt, you piece of shit.

Fuck you, pill popper.

At this point, I call an emergency Phillies Alarm Clock rehearsal upstairs.

First thing I do is pass out bubblegum smokes to everybody in the band. Cece gets two because she drums and don't sing much. Grace gets none because she's already smoking her own here in Cece's room. After I pass out smokes I walk to Cecilia's room. First I grab some of her records. After that I go into her bureau top drawer to get the banana shaped vibrating muscle massager hid under her panties. Archie, who sings lead, uses it as microphone and harmonica.

Cece's drum kit is a cardboard box and two dog bones. To warm up, she beats the box with the bones half as hard as she does when we play for real. Bobby James tunes his bass, a yardstick, hands me my twelve-string (also a yardstick), and says, "Here, pal" through his dangling smoke. Archie test-blows the harmonica, twists it on, picks his nose with it, and complains out loud to nobody that it smells funny. I tune my twelve-string and play a couple Byrds melodies.

The room turns from color to black-and-white. Instead of regular clothes we now wear matching gray suits with white shirts and skinny black ties, even Cece. Her room turns into the Ed Fucking Sullivan Show. Onstage, Ed tells two hundred screaming broads to calm the fuck down. He says about to perform is a band that makes the Beatles look like the Kingston Trio, who blow as we all know. Their first album, *Never Mind the Fuckheads, Here's the Phillies Alarm Clock,* sold six more records than there are people on the planet. Their second record, *Comb! Comb! Comb!,* sold ten more than the first. Tonight they're here to promote their latest LP, *Damn Straight It's All Killer What the Fuck Is Filler?* All the way from Philadelphia, PA, here's the Phillies Alarm Clock. The curtains rise. Chicks scream and rip off their angora sweaters and poodle skirts. I get a boner.

First song is "So What?" by the Lyrics, except right now it's not their song, it's ours. We play loud, fast, and mad as hell. Rock and roll isn't about making friends, Fred. We play to drown out the sound downstairs. Archie barks into the buzzing banana. Bobby James blows bubbles and slaps his bass. Cece chucks and catches her dog bones, then beats the snot out of the box. I smile and wink at broads. A couple bras land on my head. Harry stands sidestage in a black suit and black cowboy hat. He claps and shouts *Smile* and *Stand up straight.* Grace laughs and smokes. The tune ends. Bobby James throws Archie out of his chair at the drum kit. Broads rush the stage and stomp Ed Sully to tear our clothes off. Before they get us we change venues.

Sold-out Philly Spectrum. Bobby James sings lead on the AC/DC song "Have a Drink on Me," except right now it's our song, not theirs. They can have it back when we're done, the assholes. We wear black leather now, not suits. Everybody's hair (besides mine) is short and teased on top and long in the back.

Fireworks explode onstage every ten seconds. A giant inflatable Satan floats over our heads as we play. Dudes in the audience hold lit lighters. Broads throw panties at me. The song ends. Bobby James bites the head off a stuffed puppy from Cece's doll shelf and beats it with his V guitar. Then he dumps Archie out of his chair onto the puppy corpse. This pisses off the cops, who rush the stage and start a riot, the pigs.

Grand Ole Opry. Archie Possum Jones and Cece Wynette sing "Two-Story House." Archie has fat muttonchop sideburns and wears an orange tuxedo with a ruffled shirt. Cece's ballgown and eyeshadow match the tux. Bobby James wears overalls and plays the stand-up bass. I wear overalls and play the fiddle. Cece and Archie hold hands as the song ends. Folks in the audience swill moonshine, shoot off rifles, and shout *Yeehah* until a fight starts. Fellas break chairs over the heads of toothless girlfriends with great asses. Colonel Harry tells us to play something happy to calm the crowd, but it doesn't work and we take off.

Next song, me and Grace sing "Solid" by Ashford and Simpson on *Soul Train*. Cece, Archie, and Bobby James wear parachute pants and sleeveless hooded shirts, play instruments, and move in time side to side in the background. Me and Grace make up our own moves and pass the mike back and forth as folks dance on platforms and two kids unscramble the name FREDDIE JACKSON on the *Soul Train* scramble board.

Last song: "C'mon, Get Happy," Partridge Family. For this, we're cartoon characters. We wear striped bellbottoms and suede vests and dance matching steps in the clouds while rainbows and birds shine and whistle. We laugh and clap and can't hear the fight downstairs. The song ends. We hug and high-five, sweaty and satisfied, and carry Archie downstairs.

The living room is quiet. The Francises watch TV, Francis Junior eating a chocolate bar, Frannie chewing sunflower seeds. Francis Junior flips channels with the remote from M*A*S*H to game shows to *Happy Days* before stopping at the Phils game.

Cecilia blows her nose and cries at the dining room table. Cece runs over, jumps in her lap, and strokes her hair.

Me, Bobby, and Harry watch without saying anything, like soldiers in a boat floating past a burned village in Vietnam. Nothing we can do will make it better. Fighting adults have no time for kids. We fall out of the house into the street to have fun, to laugh, to play Freedom. There's nothing fun inside the Toohey house once the sun sets. It's all channel changing and nose blowing.

9

Last week, Bobby James got the idea to sneak around St. Patrick Street changing people's channels from outside their houses with a remote control. He came up with the plan while me, him, and Harry played Suicide off the back wall of St. Ignatius School. Suicide, which we call Suey, is a game where two or more fellas take turns chucking one tennis ball off a wall. If you throw the ball off the wall and somebody catches it in the air, you have to run to the wall, tag it, and say, "Suey." Until then, everybody's allowed to throw the ball at your ass or head, whichever they fucking prefer. Same deal if you drop a ground ball somebody threw off the wall. Run for the wall, say Suey, and take twenty tennis balls off your ass in the meantime.

On this particular day, it was just us three, throwing the ball off the wall, surrounded on three sides by the cemetery. The back wall has twelve big classroom windows, six on each floor, so we chucked it off the brick between the windows. Me and Bobby threw the ball and talked about our love for cable TV and remotes. Harry, who can't catch, spent his time dropping ground balls, sprinting for the wall, and ball-boxing when Bobby James beaned his head. This went on until Harry dropped another ball, then kicked it in the grass to buy time to run for the wall, which is against the rules in that only a pussy would do it. The penalty for that is a free shot, which means Harry had to stand still, facing the wall and weeping while Bobby James threw one at his ass with all his might. Bobby got the remote control idea right before the throw. While Harry begged for his life, Bobby James looked around the cemetery, first at a family right behind us visiting a stiff, then farther away at Stephen standing over Megan's grave.

"You know, Henry," he said as Harry whimpered, "everybody has the same remote. We could take one around and change channels through doors and windows."

"James," I told him, grinning, "you should win the Nobel Fucking Prize. Now break his ass with that ball and then let's go home to make plans."

Instead the asshole missed Harry and chucked it through a window, and we sprinted out the cemetery past a pack of power-walking penguins as Bobby James prayed the Hail Mary and Harry cried. We didn't get caught and swore by blood oath to forget everything that happened there—besides the channel-changing idea. Now here we are, a week later, with the crew and one remote, ready to cause confused conniptions inside living rooms.

Between six and seven P.M. is the best time to pull it off. The sun's still out, but it's the only time of day when nobody's outside, since folks are finishing dinner, watching TV, and waiting until it cools off later to sit outside, drink beers, play cards, and listen to the Phils until the mosquitos bite. Then they go in and watch.

Our crew includes me, Harry, Bobby, Margie, Grace, and Cece. Archie's not here because he can't go over railings and shit, so he's stuck at my house, waiting for us to show up and change the channels there. We got the remote and a *TV Guide* so we can make informed channel-changing choices. We figure it'll be funniest if we change whatever someone watches to the program most opposite it.

Grace holds the remote. Bobby James stands behind her with *TV Guide*. I'm next, then Cece, holding my shirt and giggling nonstop. Margie and Harry bring up the rear, Harry hanging on to her shirt and begging us to back out of the prank. We don't have a map of houses worked out or anything. We figure it's best to start small, with places where we're pretty sure there's no guns inside, but most screen doors have stickers with hands holding smoking guns next to warnings that say THIS HOME PRO-TECTED BY MISTERS SMITH & WESSON.

First house we stop at is the Murphys', even though Margie whines. Only weapon there is Mrs. Murphy's whip, and the only target is Mr. Murphy's bare ass. As we walk to the porch, we hear Mrs. Murphy upstairs, singing along with opera, which blows, period. Grace tiptoes to the open screen door, then waves us up. Inside, Mr. Murphy stares closely at a TV talk show where all the broads shout about their ape husbands. Bobby James flips through the *TV Guide*.

"*All in the Family* looks like the best bet," he says. "Channel five."

Grace changes the channel and we all crack up quietly. Archie Bunker tells Edith, *No wife tells me what to do*. Mr. Mur-phy says "what?" out loud, grabs his remote, and changes back to the broads, still screaming about men. Grace flips it back to Bunker. Archie says, *Broads belong in the kitchen*. Murphy laughs and leaves it on. When he leans back to settle in, Grace turns the talk show back and we bolt, giggling.

Next stop is Mrs. McC, who watches the national evening news, a Wall Street story. After Bobby James consults *TV Guide*, Grace changes to a sports channel where muscle dudes in Speedos sprint on the beach. Mrs. McC leaps out of her seat and looks around her house, more guilty than confused. She flips to Wall Street. Grace flips to Speedo World. Mrs. McC stares at the

TV as the muscle punks run in slow mo. She opens a can of beer that shoots foam. Grace changes back to Wall Street and we laugh and run.

At Harry's house, where his folks watch little kid shit with Harry's four little sisters, Grace changes to a bedroom makeout movie scene, and everybody runs but me, because I got a boner. I catch up with them at the Mullen house, where Mr. and Mrs. Mullen watch a nun talk to the camera from a desk. Grace changes that to a Mötley Crüe video before we bolt.

Next, we creep up to the Cooney house. This time, I'm the one who isn't real happy about this stop, but I don't say anything. Inside, Mr. Cooney, a big bear with hair so curly it might be a perm, watches the Phils and drinks a beer. Ralph sits next to his dad. Phils pitcher John Denny walks a batter. Mr. Cooney calls him a no-talent, and Ralph agrees out loud. Denny gives up a double off the wall. Mr. Cooney calls Denny a bum, and Ralph calls him a bum. Mrs. Cooney comes out of the kitchen with a plate of food, which she puts on a coffee table in front of Mr. Cooney.

"How was work?" she asks, flat, like she doesn't care.

"The game's on," he answers, annoyed.

Grace changes to a PBS ballet.

"What happened?" he asks, flipping back.

"Oh, right," says Mrs. Cooney. "Sorry, Bernie. God forbid you miss a touchdown."

"A *touchdown*? Donna, what we get in the mail today? I'm waiting on a check."

"Probably someone else's shit," says Ralph. "The *mailman*," he says, staring at his mom, "has a hard time with numbers and letters."

On a 3–2 count, Denny pitching, bases loaded, Grace changes to ballet.

"What is with this goddamn TV?" shouts Mr. Cooney, flipping back in time to see Denny slapping fives and walking back to the dugout. "I missed a big strikeout. Now what were you babbling about, Ralph?"

"I was saying how the *mailman* can't read," says Ralph, still looking at his mom. "But he's good at other things, though."

"Shut up, Ralph," says Mrs. Cooney, mad, not scared.

"Donna," asks Mr. Cooney, "is Fran Toohey still our mail guy?"

"What? Oh, OK, yeah. He's still our guy. He didn't bring a check."

"His son Stephen quarterbacked the high school team couple years ago, right?" asks Mr. Cooney, who, like a lot of dads, is either at work or home drinking and doesn't know most of the other seventy-seven families and row homes on his small block that well. The only people who do are the moms, the kids, and my dad, the mailman.

"Yeah, but he went crazy and quit," says Ralph, fast and happy to remind himself of this. "Now he just drinks all the time. He's an asshole."

"How dare you, Ralph," shouts Mrs. Cooney. "He's a nice boy."

"Oh, yeah, all the Tooheys are nice guys, ain't they, Ma?"

"Watch your mouth," she says, squinting. "Don't forget I'm your mother."

"Yeah, ain't I lucky?"

The Phils are back on the TV but Grace doesn't change it. Instead, we all stare, frozen, at this family fight, which gets uglier when Mrs. Cooney slaps Ralph on his face. He chokes back tears. The slap snaps Mr. Cooney out of his drool stare at the Phils.

"What the fuck you slap him for, Donna?" he asks.

"Because she's a bitch," Ralph shrieks. In one quick scary move, Mr. Cooney gets up off his fat ass and punches Ralph in the mouth. Ralph falls.

"Only I call your mother a bitch," he says, sitting back down, Ralph crying.

"Real nice, Bernie. What a wonderful father and husband," says Mrs. Cooney.

"See, this is where he gets the mouth. Can't you leave me alone? Ain't it punishment enough I married you and had a loser son who makes fun of kids who captained football teams? Donna, go to the kitchen, do the crossword, call your girlfriends, whatever it is you do." Mrs. Cooney stomps to the kitchen, picks up the phone, and dials a number. "Quit crying, Ralph. I let you off easy. Talk like that again you won't have teeth left. Now get the fuck out of the house, and if you see a kid like Stephen Toohey out there, stay close, maybe some of him'll rub off on you."

Ralph rushes for the door. We jump over their railing to the house next door and duck behind a barbecue grill. Crying, Ralph hustles down the steps and up St. Patrick Street to the Ave. When he's out of sight, we cross the street to my house, where Cecilia leans back on the sofa in the living room, her hot long legs up on the coffee table. On TV is a show where losers with bad hair and snow white teeth ask asshole movie stars asshole questions outside an asshole movie premiere. Archie sits near Cecilia in his chair, watching the show while she watches Francis Junior, who stands in the kitchen doorway, talking on the phone and twirling the cord, his face red. After giving twenty thousand one-word answers, he hangs up, walks to the living room, and sits in his chair.

"Who was that on the phone, Fran?" asks Cecilia.

"Nobody. A guy from work," he tells her, staring at the boob tube.

Grace changes the channel to a show where some kind of foreigners dance to a creepy tune played by a toothless bearded bastard on a bamboo fucking kazoo.

"What's with the cable?" says Cecilia, changing back to her show, with Americans and teeth. "Who'd you say was on the phone, Fran?"

"Danny Dollar from work," he says, squirming in his chair.

Grace clicks, and we're back to jigging camel jockeys, no teeth, not America.

"Christ, this cable," says Cecilia. Zip. Back to her show. "What did he want?"

"What's with all the questions?" asks Francis Junior, already too mad.

"Easy, buddy," says Cecilia, who notices the overreaction. "What did he want?"

"He, uh, wanted to switch days with me next week."

Zap. Grace strikes. Foreigners hokey-pokey and smack forehead flies.

"Oh, fuck this cable bullshit," yells Cecilia, chucking the remote off the TV. I almost gasp out loud. "Archie, what's so goddamn funny?"

"Nothing, Mrs. Toohey, nothing." Archie laughs, looking for us out the window.

"Is this an official investigation, Cecilia? Should I get a lawyer?" asks Francis Junior. "Have I been read my rights or charged with anything? Any more questions?"

"Just one," she says. "How come every time I answer the phone at night, somebody hangs up on me, then when you answer, it's somebody from work who isn't even smart enough to dial?"

"Are we gonna do this again already, Cecilia?" he asks.

"No, I just wanted to know if you could answer that question. I see you can't." Grace turns back to the Hollywood show. "Look at that. My show came back. This TV is like you, Fran. It strays and pisses me off, then comes back like nothing happened."

Francis Junior stands up and heads toward the stairs. "I'm getting a shower."

"Got a hot date tonight?" she asks.

Francis Junior mumbles something like "whatever" and disappears upstairs.

"Something else you'd rather watch?" asks Cecilia, now smoking, to Archie.

"Yeah," he says, "*Laverne and Shirley*'s on channel fifteen."

Grace punches it up before Cecilia can grab the remote. On TV, Laverne and Shirley hide under a desk while the boss makes phone calls and the audience laughs.

"Thanks," says Archie.

"No problem, thing changes itself. I think we got a ghost in here." She laughs.

"I mean thanks for letting me be here all the time," says Archie, serious.

She smiles. "You're welcome. I don't know how you put up with the noise."

"I like the noise," he tells her. "There's lots of life in here. And no ghosts."

She plays with his hair. "Yeah, I guess you're right. You want some iced tea?"

"Yeah, OK," he says.

"Watch your show. I'll be right back with the drink."

She walks to the kitchen, at which point we hop the railing to Frannie's house.

"Henry, Frannie don't even have cable," groans Grace, looking in the window.

"Oh, that's right, he don't," I say.

"Fuck it then," she says. "Kids are coming out for Freedom. Let's roll, troops."

Grace, Margie, Harry, and Bobby go down to the street to play. I stay.

"Cece, time to come inside," says Cecilia, now out on our patio.

"OK, Ma, be right there." She hugs me. "Play nice, see you later, kid."

Before I go down to the street for Freedom, I peek my head inside Frannie's house, which has no furniture except for a big black-and-white TV, a sofa, and *The Last Supper* hanging over the TV, where Frannie and Stephen play Atari Space Invaders. They stare at the screen as aliens sink closer to their ground guns, making blip-blip-blip noises that can put you to sleep. Both drink beers as they play. Stephen wears his work tux.

"Stephen, this is the last time you hide here after you call out," says Frannie.

"OK," answers Stephen, flat.

"I don't feel right about it anymore, know what I'm saying?"

"Yeah, all right, Frannie, I heard you. You want me to leave right now?"

"That's not what I'm saying. I like having you here. You're my brother. I want you to know I'm here for you. In case you want to talk. I'll listen."

"Thanks," says Stephen evenly, but nothing more, not biting any bait.

"Or, if you don't want to talk to me, maybe you could talk to somebody else."

"Like who, a fucking shrink?" says Stephen, finally with emotion. "No thanks."

"You can't keep on like this," says Frannie. "You have to forget about her."

"*Forget* about her?" asks Stephen, offended, almost ready to fistfight.

"I just want to help," sighs Frannie.

"So tell Daddy to stop fucking Mrs. Cooney and get off my back."

"Him and Mrs. Cooney ain't your business."

"How do you figure?" asks Stephen. "He's hurting Mommy."

"You don't even know if all that bullshit is true," says Frannie.

"Oh, come on, everybody knows it."

"Even so, you got other problems. You think if Daddy and Mommy make nice you'll be happy? You got a bad job you never go to. You drink too much and spend hours every day at the cemetery. It ain't healthy."

"Fuck you it ain't healthy," says Stephen. "Megan is there. That's why I go."

"She's gone, Stephen," says Frannie. "There'll be other girl-friends."

"What the fuck do you know about girlfriends? You've never even had one, you live next door to your parents, and you want to tell me how to handle the girlfriend situation?"

Frannie rubs his forehead with his fingertips. "Fine. Maybe you should leave."

"No problem. Thanks for the beer."

Stephen moves quietly for the door. Frannie stares at the TV as the aliens land on the planet to take everything that should be his from him. I climb over the railing to our porch. Stephen walks down the steps and heads right up St. Patrick Street for the Ave. Inside the Toohey house, I hear Francis Junior call downstairs and ask Cecilia, "What time Stephen say he's done working again?" Right then, Grace, who came back, kicks me in my knees and punches me in the chest.

"C'mon, let's go have some fun, handsome," she says, smoking, smiling.

I wobble and hurt. Love is grand but it fucking blows too.

Pokey Jones best not pick his nose. That's rule one when you play Freedom on St. Patrick Street. There are others. Don't cut across Mrs. Mahaffey's lawn or she'll shoot you with a BB gun. Don't hide under a car unless you want to get run over. Don't kick over full beer cans on porches. Don't let a broad tag you, ever. Then there are the less important rules of Freedom. Two teams, even sides, one team chases, the other hides. You chase people and tag them, then take them to the prison (the blue mailbox at St. Patrick and Erdrick Street, right in front of my house). The hiding team has to break through untagged to the mailbox, touch it, and yell *Freedom* to set everybody loose. If everybody gets caught before that happens, the teams switch sides, the chasers hiding, the hiders chasing. The boundaries are the alleys that surround the backs and sides of St. Patrick Street's houses. All of those rules are important, but the most important remains: Pokey must not pick. If Pokey Jones picks his nose, something long and green'll come out, and Bobby James will throw up and go home. This summer, Pokey already cost us three games of Freedom; two hoops, three stickball, and two Wiffle ball games; and two movies. Plus a 9:30 Mass got ugly too.

So far so good, though. Me, Bobby James, Harry, Grace, Pokey, and Margie are all on the same team, the one hiding. There are four other kids on our side. Big game tonight: ten on ten. The sun's almost down in the sky. I don't know where Bobby James, Harry, and Margie are. Don't care either; I'm hiding with Grace. We're laying flat on our backs underneath reclining lawn chairs on the overdecorated front porch of Mr. James T. Clark, who owns the end house closest to Frankford Ave on my side of St. Patrick Street. Mr. Clark is sixty, silver-haired (short, parted on side), and unmarried. He talks like a broad. Mean teenage fellas egg his house and write FAGGOT on his front door twice a week. Mr. Clark suffers this bullshit with class. He scrubs the word off the door, hoses yolk off the cement, sits down in his wicker chair, and sips suds out of his beer can—never mad or sad—and listens to Barry Manilow, Bette Midler, and Judy Garland records. They all blow, but whatever, I like him so I cut him some slack. Right now we're listening to Esquivel through Clark's front window as he sits with his beer in the wicker chair between the recliners where we hide. Esquivel music is crazy shit. Cross Bugs Bunny music with bird calls, jungle drums, a rocket ride, and a headful of cough syrup, and you're halfway there.

Potted plants hang and stand everywhere on Clark's porch, along with white shelves with skinny wagon wheels that hold flowerpots and painted ceramic elves. Chimes and windsocks sing and whisper in the wind. A big-ass bug zapper with four purple light tubes and a cage hangs from the porch awning over the chairs. When a bug hits the zapper with a *zipppp*, Mr. Clark, who hates bugs, unless they're dead, expresses delight. All this bullshit—the potted plants, wicker chairs, scented candles, Esquivel tunes, and bug zapper—adds up to a savage jungle vibe on this city row home porch. I wouldn't even blink if I saw a monkey swing past. *Zap.* Two bugs hit the zapper. Clark says *Hot damn, bug barbecue.* A couple of apes go nuts on the Esquivel record. Grace, smoking on her back under the recliner, laughs. I have a huge boner, yes.

"I love this porch, Hank," she says. "How we looking out there, Clarkie?"

"Let's see," says Mr. Clark in a whisper voice to not blow our cover. He sits up and rests his beer on the wicker table that matches his chair. "OK, I see two boys across the street tiptoeing toward the St. Basil statue on the Conners' front lawn."

"Which two boys?" asks Grace, since we can't see the street.

"I can't tell," he says. *Zap, zap, zap.* "Yes! Three bugs! Die, you little bastards! Let me put my glasses on. Oh dear."

"What is it?" she says.

"It's Jeremy Finn and James Mulaney," he tells her. "God, they're homely."

"Mean, too," I say. "They grab anything to make a capture: ball sacks, underwear waistbands. Best to go quiet if they spot you unless you wanna talk like Mickey Mouse."

"Hank," says Grace. "James Mulaney tried to kiss me two weeks ago."

"He did?" I ask, startled, annoyed. "What did you do?"

"I punched his face," she says. "Popped a couple fucking zits too." *Zipppppp.*

"Wow, that bug must have been a blimp. Miss McClain, why the language? Mr. Toohey asked a straightforward question," says Clark, who calls kids Mister and Miss. He's old-fashioned, except for the fact that he kisses men.

"Sorry," says Grace. "What are they doing now?"

"Still creeping up on St. Basil." *Zap.* "Good night, bug boy. I love that zapper. There's a husky boy hiding behind Basil with a finger up his nose. Oh, yuck. The husky boy wiped a booger on Basil. That's not right. Who is that?"

"Pokey Jones," we both say at the same time, looking at each other, laughing.

"Pokey. How'd he get that name? Hold that thought. He's about to make a break."

"Yo yo yo yo yo," a kid shouts. "Get his fat ass."

"Get off my lawn, you little bastards," yells a mom.

"They trampled Mrs. Conner's flowers," says Clark. "They're headed this way."

Footsteps, then a fall on the concrete.

"Whoa," says Clark. "The husky boy fell. Oh dear, he's weeping."

"Why did you tackle me? This ain't football," whines Pokey, who I can't now see but know has a fat baby face and short brown hair and wears a black baseball shirt that reads GRIM REAPER, a band that blows. He always wears a Reaper shirt.

"Stop whining, Pokey," says Finn, who has dirty curly nerd hair. "Nobody tackled you. You fell because you were running with your fucking finger up your nose."

"My finger wasn't up my nose," says Pokey.

"It still is, asshole," says Mulaney, a soup-bowl-cut victim.

"Oh," he says, probably pulling it out, checking for boogs. "You still tackled me."

"Whatever, Pokey," says Finn. "Just go to the prison, you fat fuck."

Pokey heads for the blue mailbox prison, out to which Francis Junior will walk three times a night to warn us that it's federal property and that we could get hard time in Holmesburg for sitting on it.

"All right, Misters Finn and Mulaney," says Clark. "Clean up the language and take it away from my house, please."

"Are you talking to us?" asks Finn.

"Of course I am," says Clark.

"And you're serious?"

"Sure. I don't wanna hear language like that."

"Don't tell me what to say and where," says Finn. "You ain't my dad. Or my *mom*," he sneers, smiling at Mulaney, I bet.

"I'm not trying to be either. I'm just asking you to show some respect and move."

"Bet you'd *like* to be my mom, wouldn't you?"

"Not really," says Clark. "Then I'd feel guilty for your being here on the planet."

"Ha ha, look at this, a funny fairy," says Finn.

Mr. Clark sits calm in his chair, wearing an Eagles T-shirt and faded yellow shorts. He puts his left leg over his right thigh and traces a line through the sweat on his beer can with a finger. "Just take it away from the house, boys. A simple request."

"Go fuck yourself, faggot," shoots Finn. "Also a simple request."

Grace starts up from under her recliner, but Mr. Clark puts his foot in her way.

"It's nice out tonight, boys," he says. "There's a warm breeze blowing. That breeze'll be cold in two weeks. I won't be able to sit out here, drink beers, and listen to insults from boys who don't even understand the words they throw around like manure. I'll miss that. Now I'm asking again. Can you please take it away from the house?"

"Sure thing, faggot," says Finn as they laugh like assholes but move. Clark takes a long pull on his beer, sighs, then whistles along to an Esquivel melody.

"Dammit, Clarkie," complains Grace. "Don't stop me next time. I could beat both their skinny asses at the same time."

"I'm sure you could, Miss McClain, but there's no violence and anger welcome at my house. No violence and anger," he says slow, like the two words weigh two tons.

"Oh, come on. How many times has your house been vandalized?" asks Grace, annoyed, not understanding. To her, if somebody hits you, you hit him back.

"What, this week, this month, or this year?" he asks, laughing softly.

"You should maybe move then," I say. "Lot of angry people around here."

"No, I won't move. This is my home. I've lived here all my life. Besides, I won't move for angry people. They're everywhere. We witness it here because we live here."

"What planet are you from?" asks Grace. "You won't fight but you won't run?"

"Exactly," he tells her. "I won't fight. I won't run. There you go."

"I'm gonna move far from here," I say. "Get a farm, more trees, less people."

Grace snorts. "Less people. What would you do without an audience, Hank?"

I'd read books under trees. I'd walk barefoot in the grass. I'd kiss you under twenty billion stars and a fat full moon. I'd give you so much love. "I'd manage."

"I doubt that," says Grace, stubbing out her smoke, flicking it into a butt bucket ten feet away, and lighting another before the first butt hits the bucket.

"Mr. Toohey, I have to confess I'm as baffled and surprised as Miss McClain," says Mr. Clark. "You seem far too energetic for farm life. The quiet would kill you."

"Maybe," I answer quickly, sounding almost mad, "but I'd like to try."

"Fair enough," he says. "I wish you luck with your dream. It's simple enough."

The evening breeze turns chilly, and the porch cement is cold through my clothes. Mr. Clark lights a bug candle that gives off a sick, sweet smell. Grace stares at me from under her recliner. Her eyes narrow as she pulls smoke into her lungs.

"You and your farm," she says. "You getting chilly over there, Hankster?"

"A little," I answer, pouting some for pity.

"Maybe we should move somewhere where we can both get warmer," she says.

Oh, man. Boner alert. Grace laughs. Did she notice my boner? Hear it grow?

"You should see how big your eyes got when I said that." Grace smiles. "Clarkie, give me a streetside report," she requests, as Mr. Clark pops open another beer can, the Esquivel record attacks our ears like B-52 bombers blaring bird calls, and the zapper fries four straight bugs. *Zip, zap, zip, zap.*

"Good night. See you bugs in Hell," says Clark. "All seems well, Miss McClain. Those two ugly spuds made another pass, then headed down the alley behind my house." Since he lives on the end of the block, Mr. Clark has alley on two sides of his house. "I should also mention there's a boy blowing bubbles and throwing things at my porch from behind the seafood store Dumpster."

Something big and wet hits the porch. Clark laughs.

"A squid. There's a new one," he says, almost delighted.

An oyster shell lands next. Then a fish head. Then a crab.

"All right," Clark says. "Go see what this kid wants before he throws a whale."

Me and Grace scoot out of our spots and spot Bobby James, crouched behind the Dumpster, standing next to Margie Murphy, his hands cupped over his mouth.

"Sorry about the dead fish, Mr. Clark," he whisper-yells. "Henry, Grace, c'mere."

"Will you be all right cleaning this up?" I ask Mr. Clark.

"I'll be fine," he says. "I'm a pro. Go play and have fun with your friends and leave the dirty messes to the adults."

"OK if we hop the railing instead of going down the steps?" asks Grace.

"Sure," he says.

"Cool. C'mon, Hank," says Grace, throwing one leg over the

porch railing. I do the same. Grace flicks her smoke into the butt bucket as we face each other and smile.

"Say good night to Mr. Clark, Hank," she tells me.

"Good night to Mr. Clark, Hank," I say.

We laugh. Grace asks me if I'm ready to take a scary plunge. I say hell yeah. We jump off the porch like paratroopers in love, falling, falling.

Jesus Christ: Bobby James and Margie Murphy are making out, pressed against the seafood store Dumpster, stopping only to greet us.

"We figured you two might want more privacy," says Jamesy, before he offers Margie gum with his tongue and she takes it with hers, which makes Grace flinch.

"Oh, gross," she says.

"You'll get used to the Dumpster smell," he tells her.

"My sense of sight, not smell, is the problem," says Grace. "By the way, how'd you see us under Mr. Clark's chairs?"

"The lit tip of your smoke," says Margie.

"Oh."

A hairy bastard walks out of the seafood joint and chucks trash in the Dumpster. Used slimy seafood spills out of the top and lands near our feet.

"Henry," says Bobby James, his arms wrapped tightly but awkwardly around Margie, "why don't you and Grace go to the other side of the Dumpster? We'll stay here."

Oh shit, make-out time. I liked it when Grace straddled me after she got out of the shower, but kissing's different. It requires skill. Bad-kissing fellas get pink slips from bored girls. She must be scared some too, though, because we both walk to the Dumpster's other side with our heads down and stand there forever, not saying anything. My stomach spins and my heart beats so loudly I swear they sound like a clothes dryer and a kick drum. The seafood door swings open and slams closed. Creak. Thump.

The dude chucks another bag in the dump. Thud. It falls at our feet. Squish. Grace moves closer, drops her smoke, steps on it, and stares at me real soft. I have never seen such a green.

"You know you're a real jerk, Hank Toohey," she says.

"How come?" I ask.

"You just are."

"OK."

"Anyhow, I tell you what a dick you were?"

"No, you said jerk."

"You're both." She smiles.

Her green eyes dart all over my face. My blue eyes do the same to hers. Brown hair falls from the side of her head into her mouth. I reach out and put the hair behind her ear gentle, gentle. Do it soft. Don't stick your finger in her eye and blow the deal. Feel her cheek with the back of your hand. I smell smoke on her breath but it doesn't bother me. Up close, her freckles turn more tan than brown. Her earlobes remind me of cauliflower. She throws her arms around my neck, and I wait for a headlock that doesn't come. Then I pull her in and boom, we kiss, warm and wet. Wow. I see fireworks, flowers, flying bags of seafood falling out of Dumpsters. My boner does backflips, and some funny feeling starts in my feet and makes it up to the knees before somebody yells *Ha* and pushes us. Fuck, busted: Jeremy Finn and James Mulaney. When they giggle and tag us to make the capture legal and binding, Finn's hand brushes Grace's right tit. She smacks him hard.

"Get your hands off me, fucker," she says.

"Oooh, I love it when you call me names," he answers.

"Quit talking shit or else," warns Grace.

"Or else what? You gonna sic Henry on me? Will he beat me with his comb?"

Grace lights a smoke and punches Finn in his face. He falls and cries.

"Fuck with Hank, fuck with me. Let's go to jail," she says, dipping ash on Finn.

Grace hauls me down St. Patrick Street in a headlock like I'm used to, but not hard, and it doesn't hurt like usual. As we walk, I watch her freckled legs and children's sidewalk chalk drawings that pass in a pink blur of hearts that say LOVE inside.

"My older brother Frannie is an interesting fella. He's twenty-four, works at the post office, and moved into the house next door." Pause. "That guy ain't getting a girlfriend anytime soon." Wait for laughs. "He *carries dog spray*. That always seems to scare off broads. They're funny like that."

I'm doing stand-up for the mailbox prisoners to keep morale high. Mailbox jail is tough on the spirit. It does strange things to a man. A few jokes can go a long way. I'm also telling jokes because Harry Curran is sneaking down the street to free us. The funnier I am, the more everybody pays attention to me. This includes kids on the other team. If Harry frees us, I can kiss Grace again behind the Dumpster.

Not everybody's laughing, though. Bobby James and Margie Murphy make out. They need to get a room. Little Jim Jardine, who's bald, isn't laughing either, but that's because he watches them make out and looks like he'll hump something soon. I'm hoping it'll be the mailbox, not another kid. Mailbox humping's a federal offense. Geoffrey Garry, a fat brush-cutted jerk-off who hates me, isn't laughing either, but fuck him, the punk. Everybody besides that, though—Grace, Holly Hallowell (no tits whatsoever), Heather Hennessy (mediums, I'd pay to see them), and Pokey Jones—laughs. Even fellas on the chase team make their way back to the box to hear my stuff instead of look for Harry, who I spot falling over a porch railing. He gets up quickly, like a ferret, looks around, and disappears again.

"And what's the deal with dollar stores?" I ask. "What happened to five-and-dimes? It's the same shit. They just want ninety-five more cents. If they're gonna charge me more money for a paddle and a ball on a string, I want a cedar or oak fucking paddle. Am I right or what, folks?"

"You ain't right, Fruit Loop Toohey," says Geoffrey. "Eddie Murphy told that joke on *Saturday Night Live* last week."

"Who brought the retard?" I ask. "Where's your hockey helmet, Geoffrey? You're supposed to wear it all the time, not just on the yellow school bus."

Laughs. Steam rises off Geoffrey's fat empty head. Smoke blows out of Grace's nostrils. Bobby James and Margie Murphy neck. Jim Jardine stares. Harry Curran climbs one porch closer. My boner shakes pom-poms and cheers. It's nighttime now on St. Patrick Street. Humming telly pole lights drown out the bugs that buzz around them. Parents sit on porches sipping beers and smoking. Broads hose their lawns in the evening cool. Car stereos blare bad music like Journey and Styx on the Ave. Bottles clink and men shout inside Paul Donohue's, which keeps its side door open all summer. At the Toohey front windowsill, Cecilia Toohey paints Cece's fingernails. Yellow lightbulbs pop on and off in upstairs windows as black shadows pass. TV lights turn window screens pale purple. Radios on porches crackle as Harry Kalas and Richie Ashburn call the ball game. Laughs here, a shout there. A phone rings. Beer cans are crushed and chucked. See-through drapes float out open windows like ghosts of skinny broads wearing long summer dresses. A rowdy cheer goes up from Paul Donohue's and a couple of houses, which means the Phils did something good.

"Gotta love the fact that broads shave their legs once they get to eighth grade," I say. "I can't wait to go back to school just to look at legs in navy socks and plaid skirts. Broads tell you whether or not they tongue kiss by the way they wear their socks. Yeah. You know that? Chicks who pull their socks up to their kneecaps should be avoided. They're saying they'd rather say the rosary than make out. A chick who yanks her socks up is half a nun already. No, you want the girls who push their socks down to the ankles. They got issues. Maybe they don't like their parents or authority figures. Either way you got a green light. Chicks like that will suck face forever."

A porchful of adults, and Harry—holding a tall iced tea with an umbrella—bursts into laughs.

"There he is!" somebody shouts. "Get him!"

Ten kids book for Harry, who puts his drink on a coaster and runs like a nut for the prison to free us. It's going to be a straight sprint down St. Patrick Street, one man versus ten. Let's go to the play-by-play in Harry's head:

Curran weaves around John the Baptist and hops a Mondale-Ferrarro sign. He darts past St. Francis of Assisi—oh my, Curran even took a second to pet the bird on St. Francis's shoulder. He floats over a second Mondale-Ferraro sign, stiff-arms Our Lady of Guadeloupe, and jumps another Mondale-Ferraro sign. Harry Curran's on pace to set the world record for leaping campaign signs of hopeless Democrats and weaving past dead bald stone saints in dresses. Curran's way out in front of his chasers. But what's this? He spots Old Mrs. Shappel, who struggles with a shopping cart up the steps leading to her porch. Curran slows to a trot. Oh dear. He's gonna help Shappel lug her cat food up the steps, fuck the world record, not to mention his buddy Henry Toohey, who wants to suck face with Grace. Curran yanks the groceries from Mrs. Shappel. She looks at him like a turtle on her twelfth shot of booze. Curran runs to the porch with the cart and trips. The cart falls out of his hands. Cat food cans fly everywhere. He tries to clean the cans. He looks back. His chasers close the gap. Oh my, Curran takes off again. He runs past Shappel and promises to clean the mess. She has no idea what happened anyway. Was she mugged? Struck by lightning? The ten chasing fellas run past her and spin her around. Mrs. Shappel cries, *Help me, St. Peter, is it time?*

Curran's twenty-five feet from the prison, then fifteen. Tommy McRae breaks free from the chasing pack, just out of reach. Ten feet. Come on, Harry. I need more kissing practice. Five feet. It's close. Oh my! Bam! Freedom! Woohoo! I sprint straight for the Dumpster but hear no footsteps besides mine and stop. Where's Grace? What the fuck happened?

Everybody's still by the mailbox. I walk back, annoyed, and

see Billy Burke and Christian Crump, two older ugly crew-cut football fucks, with Ralph Cooney and Gerald Wilson. Burke wears a Sixers jersey, Crump a sleeveless TEMPLE OWLS T-shirt. The four of them look drunk, and when I come closer, I smell scotch and schnapps.

"Hoc Toohey," says Billy Burke with a Marlboro Man smile. "That was some sprint. You should try out for the football team next year."

"What, do you need a water boy?" asks Ralph.

They laugh while us younger kids stay quiet.

"Grace McClain," says Burke, "you should be up Tack Park with the older kids, not here. Ain't you fifteen?" he asks, looking her up and down.

"I'm fourteen. I just look fifteen," smiles Grace, who has a weak spot for older assholes that annoys me. "What's going on up there tonight? Anything interesting?" she asks, popping the gum I just tasted four or five times, each pop hitting me like a slap.

"Couple of Fishtown fucks might show up," he says. "We came to see if Henry and the other fellas wanted to help. Got a quarter keg up there too. How about it, Henry Boy?"

"I can't," I say. "Got some shit to do. Going in after that."

The older fellas laugh. Ralph says *Pussy* under his breath.

"Henry," says Grace, annoyed. She can't believe I said no to this offer, this test. "They just said they need you up there. You're going, right?"

"No, I'm not," I tell her, calm-sounding but angry.

"I understand, Henry," says Burke, smiling, all fangs and blood. "I would have been scared when I was your age too. Don't worry. You youngsters stay here. C'mon, Grace. Henry, we'll tell Stephen you said hello."

"Yeah, you do that, Billy," I say, followed by "fucking fuckball" under my breath.

"Sure thing. Stephen will represent your family just fine. He can bring that bottle down on a head. He's almost done drinking it. Let's go."

They laugh like pirates and start up St. Patrick Street.

Grace hops from one foot to the other, all nerves.

"You going, Hank? You really not going? I wanna go. Fuck it, I'm going," she says, tossing a smoke to the ground that lands on my heart. Holly and Heather call out *Wait for us Grace, wait for us.* Geoffrey Garry says *Shit,* shakes his head, and follows them. Now it's me, the French kissers, Nose Picking Pokey Jones, Peeping Jimmy Jardine, and Good Samaritan Harry. Pokey works his pinkie near a nostril. Jardine watches the kissing. Harry walks over, holding up a coin.

"See? I made a quarter. Money's everywhere. You just have to look," he says.

"Yeah, that's great," I mutter.

"What's wrong?" he asks. "What did I miss?"

"Those Fishtown fellas will be up at Tack Park soon," I say. "Billy Burke and Christian Crump came by and asked me to go up and play. Grace went with them."

"Do they want me to play?" he asks.

"She went right up there with them," I say.

"Why wouldn't they ask me? I'm the best player in the city, not counting Sixers."

"She's trying to make me jealous," I say. "That must be it."

"So are we going? We still have to hit the rectory and funeral home, right?"

"*Yo, check this out,*" yells Pokey, a footlong booger hanging out of his nose.

Bobby James stops kissing Margie. He stares at Pokey's booger almost like it's a broad he loves, then pukes. Pokey flicks the booger. It hits the mailbox like a metal bolt would a cookie tray. Radios on porches blast the ball game. *Long fly ball deep center field, that ball is outta here. Home run Michael Jack Schmidt.* Cheers from houses and the bar.

"We'll go to those first," I say, "then the park. C'mon. You too, Bobby James."

We walk up St. Patrick Street to the rectory, the funeral home, the playground, a ball game, a fight, to Stephen and Grace. As we start, Cece spots me out the window and flashes a peace sign. I flash one back. Saints on either side of us stare at the sky, looking for a sign from God and getting no reply, seeing nothing but black outer space and feeling inside like the empty million miles between Heaven and here.

10

"Look, quit breaking my balls and just pay me my money," I tell Father S. Thomas Alminde, OSFS, the young parish priest who talks to Stephen and Cecilia Toohey separately about our fucked-up family. In addition to counseling Tooheys, Father Alminde coaches the altar boys, punches grade-school kids, smokes cigars, drinks Wild Turkey, brings broads up to his room, and plays dumb because he's a cheap bastard when it's time to pay me for answering the phone three nights a week at St. Ignatius Rectory.

The rectory is a big, white, boxy Colonial home that stands next to the church. You walk in the front door to a long dark hallway with red carpets and paintings of archbishops on the walls, and two offices apiece on your left and right. Past the hallway is the kitchen and a staircase on the right, and a door that leads to the sacristy and the church on the left. Right now I'm arguing with Father in the office where I answer the phone, second on the right from the front door. This office, the rattiest, is a closet really with an old desk, a metal chair, a black-and-white TV with an aluminum foil antenna, three walls of old file cabinets, and a four-line phone, which rings the whole time I shake

Father down for my fucking pay. Harry stands afraid next to me, and Bobby James waits afraid outside.

"Settle down," he says. "I'll pay up. How many hours you work this week? Six?"

"No, ten," I tell him.

"Wait, I thought you worked three hours a night three times a week."

"Right, I do, and that's nine right there, Father," I say, pissed. "Plus I was here an extra hour last time while you were upstairs with Mrs. McKeown."

"Oh, right," he says, thoughtfully. "She had a serious Bible question."

"Sure, she did, Father," I tell him. "Buck up."

"Okay, ten hours, fifteen bucks, right?"

"No, twenty bucks. I get *two* bucks an hour," I say, flashing two fingers in a V.

"Two bucks an hour? You're robbing us," smiles Father, who has short thin brown hair parted on the side, and a high forehead that throws shadows over his face. His choppers are yellow and fanged, like Gwen Flaggart's. Anytime he opens his fucking yap I want to throw a dog bone in there. "Here's your money," he says, handing me a torn, taped twenty.

"Thanks. Was that so hard?" I ask.

"Honestly, yes. What's wrong, Mr. Curran? Cat got your tongue?"

"Yes, Father," says Harry.

"Are you afraid of me, Mr. Curran?" asks Father.

"Yes, Father."

"Is that Bobby James waiting outside, Mr. Curran?"

"Yes, Father."

"He afraid of me too?"

"Yes, Father."

"Sissies," says Father. "Would you get that phone, Mr. Toohey?"

"No way," I tell him. "I'm off the clock."

"Come on, I got somebody in my office," he says.

"Make them wait, buddy," I answer.

"It's your brother Stephen, dumbass," says Father.

"Oh."

"So you'll get it?"

"Yeah, all right."

"Thanks." He leaves for the office and my brother. I pick up the phone.

"St. Ignatius Rectory, can I help you?" I say, very professional.

"I got something for you," a weird whispering voice tells me.

"Oh yeah, what is it?" I ask.

"A big fat cock," he says.

"Great." Click. We get lots of cranks here. All part of the gig. Ring.

"St. Ignatius Rectory, can I help you?" I ask.

"Religion is for the weak and stupid," says another lonely putz.

"Tell me about it." I laugh. "What can I do you for?"

"It's no more than mythology, no different than Greek gods or Aesop's fables."

"You don't say. That all?"

"If there's a hell, then priests and nuns will be the ones who burn there."

"Can't argue with that. Have a good night." Click. Ring.

"St. Ignatius Rectory, can I help you?"

"I'm Steve Smith from the *Daily News*. Care to respond to charges that your parish turns away bums without so much as giving them a drink of water?"

"On the advice of counsel I have no comment," I say (Father taught me this).

"So you're not denying the charge?" he asks.

"Guess not. Have a good night, buddy." Click. Ring.

"St. Ignatius Rectory, how can I help you?"

"Hi," answers a sniffing broad. "Father Alminde there?"

"Ma?"

"Hank?"

"You OK?" I ask.

"Yeah, I'm OK," she says. "Same old bullshit with your dad."

"Why don't you just leave him?" I ask, not meaning it.

"And go where?"

"Kick him out then."

"Then who pays for shit?" she asks.

"So it's about money, Ma?"

"No, Hank. It's way more complicated than that. I got Stephen and Cece to think about. Archie too. I can't chuck more trauma on top of the pile right now. I'm just hoping your father quits playing grab ass and keeps his pecker in his pants."

"You should do something, Ma. He has a *girlfriend*," I tell her.

"She ain't his girlfriend," answers Cecilia, sharp, before blowing smoke on her end. "Besides, marriage is a long ride, buddy. What he's doing ain't all that unusual."

"Seriously?" I ask, totally surprised in a sad, disappointed way.

"Seriously," she tells me.

"Yeah, but you never did that." Pause. "Right? Right, Ma?"

"Remember that kid last year after the art museum? He gave me his number."

"You cheated on Daddy with him?" I ask.

"No, Hank," she says, "but I almost did. Cece, climb down off Archie's chair."

"But you didn't, right?"

"Right, but I lost his number. I might have done it. You get what I'm saying? Cece, you punch Archie one more time and I'm rolling him right the fuck home."

"No, I don't get it," I say. "You marry somebody, you love them forever, period."

"In a perfect world, kid," she says, her voice quiet.

"Yeah, in a perfect world. There you go," I tell her, annoyed.

"You're such a romantic, Hank," she says, and I can tell she is smiling now, which warms and relieves me. "Listen, is Father around?"

"He has, uh, somebody in his office," I say.

"Oh. What you doing there, by the way? Did he ask you to work tonight?"

"Nah, just getting my pay. He asked me to man the phone for a couple minutes."

"He pay you what he owes you?" she asks. "You worked that extra hour, right?"

"Yeah, he paid me," I say. "Broke my balls, though."

"He always does that. What you doing tonight? Weren't you just on the street?"

"Uh-huh. We were playing Freedom but the game ended. I came up to get my pay, then I think we're going to Tack Park. To shoot hoops," I say, careful.

"Behave up there. No fights or anything like that. Be the man you are," she says.

"Got it," I tell her, and I do. No fights, and I'll be the man I am.

"Good."

The front door opens and closes. Father Alminde walks in the office frustrated.

"That kid is a piece of work," he says. "Can't reach him yet. The phone for me?"

"Yeah," I say, holding it out to him.

"Who is it?" he asks.

"My mom," I say, almost in a guilty way, though I'm not sure why I feel that.

He laughs. "More Tooheys, those lovable wack jobs."

"Who you calling lovable, Father?"

He laughs again. "Oh, I *apologize*. Certainly not you."

"Father, can I ask you something? How come you're so interested in my family?"

"That bother you?" he asks, concerned, not mad, like a shrink doctor.

"Nah, just curious," I say.

"Well, for one, your mom is hot," he says.

"C'mon, quit kidding."

"Who's kidding? I also had an older brother like Stephen when I was your age."

"His girlfriend died, then he drank and fought with your dad?" I ask.

"Just the last two," says Father.

"Oh. How'd he turn out?"

Father looks far away, upset, and I get my answer.

"We'll do better with Stephen. Now get lost and go watch over him out there."

"Got it. Later."

We leave, me steering a stiff-shouldered Harry out the door, pick up Bobby James on the rectory porch, and spill onto the Ave sidewalk, surprised to see it deserted right now, no cars, people, or noises. We watch Stephen stumble north toward Tack Park. A trolley zips by from nowhere, also heading north, blocking our view of Stephen for half a second. Once it passes, he's somewhere inside the playground, gone from sight.

The Charles McFadden Funeral Home sits by itself on a high hill on the store side of Frankford Ave, right across from where the bike path starts. It looks like the rectory except it's twice the size, and the fact that it sits on a hill next to a crowded row of tiny city stores makes it look like the Bates Motel misplaced on a 1960s Mob movie set.

Me and Bobby are both psyched for this visit. Harry, on the other hand, is terrified, his knees knocking so fast they sound like Ping-Pong balls in a popcorn popper. We approach the carved white double doors, which have gold stained-glass ovals for windows. I ring the bell. *Bing, bong, bing.* Me and Jamesy slap five as Harry mutters, *Please don't answer, please don't answer.*

The door swings open. Kevin McFadden, a classmate, stands there in a dark suit. Kev is short, maybe four-five, with nice feathered hair. He's the eighth and youngest son of the home's owner, Charles McFadden, who's also short, maybe five-three.

All the sons in between Kev and his dad range from six-two to six-six. Like Grace said earlier about Nickleback Park, you have to love nature. Kev, who's a crybaby about his height, doesn't share this view.

"Yo," says Kevin.

"Yo."

"Yo."

"Yo."

"What are you fellas doing here?" he asks.

"We got business with your old man," I tell him.

"What, you kill somebody?" asks Kev, laughing.

"Not today, not yet," answers Bobby James. "What's with the suit? Midget convention in town?"

"Funny. Look at you guys," says Kev. "You and Henry ain't tall either."

"Yeah, but we both hit the five-foot mark," says Bobby, way too proud.

"I'm almost four-ten," Kev tells us, also way too proud.

"Yeah, six more inches and you're there, brother," says Bobby.

Kev slams the door. James rings the bell. *Bing, bong, bing.*

Kev opens the door. "What?"

"Hey there, short stuff," says Bobby. "Your dad around?"

Slam. *Bing, bong, bing.*

The door opens. "Keep it up, jerk-off," warns Kev.

"You're right, I'm sorry," says Bobby James. "Now can you go tug on your dad's pant leg and say we're here?"

Slam. *Bing, bong, bing.*

Once more, the door: Mr. McFadden (combover). "What's going on, kids?"

Mr. McFadden is a real nice guy but weird like you'd expect from a funeral director. He's proud of what he does and loves getting a scared rise out of people. There's a good chance that if we get in the door, we'll see some stiffs.

"Nothing, Dad, nothing," says Kev. "We're just messing around."

"You can't do that at a funeral home. Show the dead some respect," he says, pointing to three caskets off to the side of the entrance lobby, in a little room. Harry whimpers while me and James hug each other like grandmas who just won at bingo.

"There stiffs in those coffins, Mr. McFadden?" asks Bobby James.

"No, but I knew that would shut you up. Come in," he says, smiling.

The home reminds me of something you'd see in an old Civil War movie, except smaller and uglier, but not small and not ugly, and full of formaldehyded dead seniors in their final pairs of adult diapers. The first thing you see when you walk in is a grand staircase that leads to where the McFaddens live, except for the mom—she's dead. The first floor is reserved for business. On the near left is a coat closet and an oak stand where they lay out a sign-in book and a pile of holy cards for folks to swipe when they walk in for a viewing. On the near right is Mr. McFadden's office, a dark room, all oak, velvet, and leather. The far right is a storage room where they keep different model coffins and bigger flower arrangements and shit. On the far left is the viewing room, where they put a kneeler, a coffin, and ten rows of ten folding chairs for mourners. In case you're a Hellbound non-Catholic, I'll give you the rundown of what happens at a viewing. Immediate family stands next to the coffin. Folks form a line from outside the home, waiting to kneel down and say a prayer in front of the corpse and coffin before they say something to the survivors one bawling mess at a time. Crazy shit. I've been to nine McFadden Home viewings: four grandparents, two aunts, one uncle, one second cousin, and Megan O'Drain. Megan's was the worst. The line to get in was three blocks long. Folks threw themselves on the ground, screaming, crying, kicking. Her parents bawled, her mom through so many face bandages she looked like a mummy who just dunked her head in a pool. Archie wasn't there, because of his age and the fact that he just turned cripple.

Stephen Toohey, who stood near the closed coffin with the O'Drains, didn't cry. His face never changed its stony expression, except his eyes were frantic. He shook hands and looked over respect payers' heads at the door like he expected Megan to walk in, but she was in the coffin, and after that day, that look never left his face, at least not when he was sober.

"Henry, you in there?" asks Mr. McFadden.

"What?" I ask, startled.

"Come on upstairs so we can talk about tomorrow night," he tells me.

"Right, tomorrow night. OK," I say.

We walk up to the fancy living room, where there are straightback chairs, china closets, and bookcases that'd collapse if a snowflake fell on them. We sit down.

"Harry," says Mr. McFadden, "you also don't look so hot. You OK?"

"There any dead people up here?" asks Harry.

"Not unless you drop over," he says. "What time is it?"

"Nine-sixteen," says Harry.

"Jesus. I almost forgot," says Mr. McFadden, grabbing his remote, flicking on the TV, and flipping to a channel. "Kevin, here comes our commercial. Watch this, kids."

On TV, the first thing we see is the viewing room with no people but nine coffins, seven big ones, two small ones on either end. Mr. McFadden pops up out of a small one.

"Hi, I'm Charles McFadden."

His big oldest son pops up out of the next coffin. *Boing.* "And I'm Charles Jr."

Boing. "And I'm James McFadden."

Boing. "Michael McFadden."

Boing. "Timothy McFadden."

Boing. "Thomas McFadden."

Boing. "David McFadden."

Boing. "John Paul McFadden."

Boing. "Kevin McFadden."

The McFaddens, all bald or balding except Kev, climb out of their coffins. Kev struggles around, unable to get out of his. While he wiggles, the seven older brothers join their dad, who says, "I've been in the funeral business thirty years. Here at the Charles McFadden Funeral Home, we provide the best accommodations in the worst possible times, to lighten your load and allow you to grieve."

Kev still struggles to get out of his coffin.

"The Charles McFadden Funeral Home offers you affordable coffins in pine, mahogany, oak, and ivory, even specialty coffins in Eagles green with the team logo tastefully stenciled on both sides. We make the arrangements for you, with caterers, churches, and cemeteries, so that you can concentrate on grief and support."

Kev McFadden shakes his coffin, still stuck.

"Our goal is a proper, low-key service, free from hassle, full of dignity."

Kev McFadden falls out of his coffin onto the floor.

"Give us a call at the number on the screen. We'll do the rest, here at Charles McFadden's Funeral Home in Holmesburg on Frankford Avenue."

The commercial ends, and we rib Kev McFadden for his fall.

"Don't listen to them, Kevin," says his father. "You did fine. Besides, it would have cost too much money to reshoot the whole thing. Harry, the color's back in your face."

"Yeah," says Harry. "I feel much better."

"Good. Who wants to go down to the cold room?" asks Mr. McFadden.

Me and Jamesy whoop *We do, we do.* Harry sinks into his seat.

"Come on, let's go then," says Mr. McFadden, who takes us downstairs into the storage room, which is unlit, past a couple coffins and giant stand-up wreaths that look like shit you'd see at the fucking Kentucky Derby. In the back corner of the room is a silver metal door with a handle like on a fridge, which I guess makes sense. He pops it open and smiles at us as cold smoke floats out into the room.

"Two in here on tables," he says. "You ready?"

"Yeah," I say.

"Hell yeah," says Bobby.

"God no," whispers Harry.

"You wanna wait outside?" Mr. McFadden asks Harry.

"Can I?"

"Suit yourself," says Mr. McFadden, as me and Bobby chant *Stiffs, stiffs.*

"Listen, Henry, Bobby," says Mr. McFadden, serious now. "These are deceased people in here, not stiffs. I don't mind showing them to you—I have an important job here that I love and will share—but it's important that you behave with respect, OK?"

We both nod, trying real hard to pull our shit together in adult fashion.

"That's better," he says. "Come on. Kevin, close the door."

Soon as it clicks closed we hear a knock.

"I'm scared out here," says Harry. "Can I come in?"

The cold room is maybe fifteen feet long, ten wide, and full of bright yellow lights. I can already feel my nose numbing and running. The walls are plain white, nothing really in here except the two stiffs—deceased people, I mean—under blue blankets on rolling metal tables, and another metal table full of tools against a wall. Mr. McFadden walks to the bodies while we lean back toward the door we came in.

"Don't just stand there," he says. "Come closer. Have a look."

We approach the table slowly. Mr. McFadden pulls the blanket back and says *Ta-da* like a magician who just put a hot sawed broad back together. Except this broad isn't hot, she's fat, and dead. Her face is white and purple, her eyes closed, her mouth clamped weird, like she died biting down on something in a dentist's chair. Her short permed hair looks like steel wool. Can't see her tits, still covered with the blanket. If I had to guess, though, I'd say single Ds. Looking at her, I'm a little scared but not quaking and shit like Harry, who covers his eyes. Bobby James is quiet and I can't read his thoughts but figure he feels about the same as me.

"Boys," says Mr. McFadden, "meet Martha Mooney, wife and mother of four."

"Hello, Martha, what's up?" says Bobby James.

"Martha, how you doing, doll?" I ask.

"Martha came here two nights ago from Nazareth Hospital," says Mr. McFadden. "Her big night is tomorrow."

"How'd she die?" asks Bobby James.

"Won the slots down in Atlantic City and dropped dead," Mr. McFadden tells us.

"No way," says Bobby.

"Come on, be serious," I add.

"I am," he says. "She was pumping quarters in a slot machine. She hit for a grand, had a heart attack, and died on the floor next to her money."

"Yuck," says Bobby, blowing into his hands. "Glad I don't have your job."

"It isn't so bad," he says. "Only have to worry about their faces really. I drain the fluids, replace them with formaldehyde, do the makeup, she's ready to rock."

"Who's that one over there?" I ask, pointing to the other person.

He covers Martha Mooney and pulls back the sheet on a bald Nosferatu fuck who weighs no more than eighty pounds and has marks like banana bruises in a couple spots.

"Henry, let's guess how old this dude is," says Bobby James.

"All right, he's ninety," I say.

"I'm gonna go lower: eighty," says Bobby. "Who's closest, Mr. McFadden?"

"Neither. This is Joseph McCalister, age of death: forty-eight."

"Get the fuck outta here," says Bobby, before I can.

"I'm serious," he tells us. "Mr. McCalister had cancer, which doesn't take prisoners. I lost Mrs. McFadden to cancer ten years ago, when Kevin here was potty training."

We say we're sorry, blowing smoke over Joe McCalister.

"Thanks, boys. I'm OK. I only mentioned her to illustrate my point. When she got it, she weighed maybe a hundred twenty pounds. When she died two years later, she was seventy-five pounds."

"Jesus," I say. "Isn't it hard to work with dead people and not think about her?"

"Not really," he says. "It's my job. I think about her more when I'm doing fun stuff, like eating soft pretzels at a parade. Now, speaking of the missus, what time do you want me to take you around tomorrow night, Henry?"

"How about nine-thirty?" says Harry, the nuts and bolts behind my big dreams.

"That's fine," he says. "Henry, do your folks know about all this?"

"Nah," I say. "I want it to be a surprise."

Mr. McFadden laughs hard. "It will be, trust me."

"How'd you propose to Mrs. McFadden?" I ask.

He looks up to the ceiling and laughs again, smoke shooting from his mouth like a face on the wall at a carnival ride. "Falling down on my ass at a roller rink."

"What? Did you plan that?" asks Bobby.

"No, jackass. The roller rink part was, but not the fall. I started dating Mrs. McFadden—Denise—who was Denise McBride at the time, when we were both seventeen. There was a roller rink at Cottman and Brouse that held doo-wop nights once a week. It was still there when you kids were little. Remember it? Probably not. Anyhow, we'd been going together six months, and I knew she was the one. Just knew it. I waited until we both graduated that year, bought a ring, and brought it to the roller rink. She was really good on skates, and I was really bad. That's why we started going to the rink in the first place. She wanted to teach me. I got pretty good except I could never go backwards during guy-gal slow skates, when we held hands and listened to 'Earth Angel,' which was a big hit she loved at the time. She was crazy for it."

"I love that song too," I tell him.

"Right. Me too, Henry," he says. "I decided that I'd pop the question skating backwards while that song played. I practiced every day for two months in alleys between houses. I got a concussion and a billion cuts, but I finally felt good enough to try. Then when the night came, and the song played, I took her hands, skated backwards, pulled out the ring, and fell right on my ass. The ring flew out of my hand. I lost the thing. And she ran me over and fell too. It took an hour to find the ring, and she was the one who found it. I was on my knees, crying, my head in a trash can. She touched my shoulder, held it out, and said yes. We got married a month later."

"Wow" is all I can say.

"Yeah, it worked out. Harry, when you gonna take your hands from your face?"

"Soon as we leave your establishment," says Harry. "No offense."

"None taken," says Mr. McFadden, winking at me and Bobby James and reaching in a drawer, where he pulls out a wolfman mask and puts it over his head. "I covered the bodies, Harry. You can open your eyes."

Harry lowers his hands and looks.

BOO!

Harry shrieks, runs out of the cold room, then out the front door. Me and Bobby James laugh and cry, doubled over, pushing into each other with our shoulders. Jamesy bumps me too hard, and my hand lands on Mrs. Mooney. I scream, then Bobby screams, and we run the Harry route out the door, both McFaddens laughing.

"See you tomorrow, Henry," yells Mr. McFadden. "I'll bring Martha Mooney here. We'll double-date."

11

Tack Park smells like three dollars' worth of cologne and perfume, but not because each of the sixty kids here wears three-dollar cologne and perfume. I'm saying the price of each kid's fragrance totaled together equals three bucks. Nickel a pop, tops. The playground stinks on Saturday night.

Tack Park's not the same kind as Nickleback Park. In Philly, playgrounds are called parks too: Tackawanna Park, Russo Park, Shark Park. Playground parks have basketball courts, sometimes tennis courts, some grass maybe, full of dog shits and beer cans. Philly folks also call real parks parks. Nickleback Park, Fairmount Park, places with trees and streams, bike paths, horse trails, ecologic life. Tack Park has none of that, unless you count weeds growing through cement cracks as gardens or the wood backboards with faded 76ers logos as trees. Tack Park is split into four equal parts: basketball court, parking lot (for cars), parking lot (for stickball), and two tennis courts with no nets or players. The basketball court, which always has nets, thanks to Harry and Mr. Curran, sits on the Ave, across the street and diagonal from Mungiole's. A concrete clubhouse stands next to the basketball court, and a giant Megan O'Drain painting faces the court from one clubhouse wall. In the painting, Megan, who had C cups and red hair, wears a yellow uniform and stands, holding a soccer ball at her side, smiling wide, looking right at you, her big blue eyes dancing and following you everywhere. The painting went up right after she died, and there was also talk about renaming the playground after her, but that fizzled. Instead, the park stayed Tack Park and got a giant painting with a plain plaque underneath that simply reads MEGAN O'DRAIN 1966–1983.

The photo that this painting was done from hangs in my room, on the wall above Stephen's bunk bed, underneath mine. I like the painting better. In the daytime, the sun hits the wall hard, and Megan fucking blazes, bright and alive. At night, her red hair, yellow uniform, and blue eyes almost glow in the dark, like they soaked in the sun's rays all day. She looks happy and holy, not dead, and watches the neighborhood kids she left behind with peace and love. The picture at home is a different story. Since it hangs on a wall between bunks, it never gets any light, always covered with a shadow. Its frame is dark and too big and makes her look trapped in a box, far from the sun. It makes Megan look too much like what she really is, beautiful and dead.

Tonight, Tack Park is pumped with life, with electricity. Sixty kids, dolled up and smelling nice, stand around the court and sip beers out of plastic cups. They make time with each other—fellas telling loud jokes or acting tough, girls giggling and blowing big bubbles that pop—waiting for later, when they can fight and make out. The summer's over. The half keg's full. The chicks look hot. School starts Monday. The chilly air promises something.

The five Fishtown fellas shoot baskets on their end of the court. They have short crew cuts, angry faces, cut-off sweatpants, low-top black Adidas soccer sneaks, skinny legs, and fat sweat socks.

Stephen's drunk, near the keg in front of Megan's painting.

He ignores it (he doesn't look at it ever), pumps the tap, and fills drinks for chicks. Drunk, he makes broads laugh, and they eat up the charm that comes from him even when he's depressed, but they don't get close. All the broads know that later on his head'll be in a beer and they'll be in somebody else's arms.

Also at the playground off the court, Bobby James and Margie Murphy make out, don't pay attention to anybody, and don't get any back, except from Jim Jardine, who stares. Grace smokes smokes and tells jokes with tough older broads who like her and smiles as I shoot a jump shot that gets nothing but net. I'm fucking good. Can't say the same for the rest of my team. Crump and Burke are built but not tall. They move on the court like football fucks, like big robots trying ballet. Big Georgie O'Keefe's also on our team. Georgie's six-seven and weighs a hundred pounds, counting the twenty-pound braces in his mouth. He's seventeen with greasy black hair, has seminarian written all over him, and is the kind of fella who comes to the court to let off steam after reading boring bullshit books all day. Georgie has no coordination, grabs no rebounds, and puny punks like me could push him off the court. I like him, though, even if he does blow. He's not a cheap shot or a crybaby; most fellas on a court are one or the other or both. Harry, who rounds out the team after paying Crump and Burke ten bucks apiece to play, runs full-court sprints. Everybody laughs at him but he doesn't give a fuck.

Despite the fact that our team blows except for me, we should do good enough. None of the Fishtown kids is taller than five-ten or weighs more than a hundred-fifty. Besides, they're not even hitting the backboard with shots, let alone the rim. Fishtown's a soccer neighborhood. They play games on a gravel field called Newts, under the El, and their parents throw bottles on the field if the ref makes bad calls.

"Yous dudes ready to run?" asks a Fishtown fella, walking over to Crump.

"We been ready," says Crump.

"Those two little guys playing?" he asks, pointing to me and Harry.

"Yo, that's our center and power forward there, pal," says Crump.

The Fishtown dude smiles and flashes missing teeth. "Whose ball we using?"

"Ours," says Crump, showing him a brown leather ball, the kind used by kids whose dads make overtime, unlike the red-white-and-blue Sixers freebie bullshit they brought.

"What do you wanna play to?" asks the kid.

"Eleven, by two," says Crump.

"Cool. Make it take it?"

"Nah, losers out."

"All right. You fellas got any special home court rules we should know about?"

I see a chance for jokes. Jokes cause laughs. Laughs prevent beatings.

"Yeah, we got a couple. Come over here, Harry," I say.

Harry obeys, the moron. I'm about to use him as Daffy Duck to my Bugs Bunny.

"There's none of this," I say, karate-chopping Harry in the gut. He yells *Ow.* "Or this." I step on his toe. He groans *Ugh.* "Or this." I kick him in the ass. He shouts *Yo.* "Or this." I pull his goggles from his face and let them go. He says *Jesus, Henry, stop it, we're on the same team.* Players on both teams laugh. One of the Fishtown boys asks me, "What about this or this or this or this?" as he smacks around a buddy, who yells *Ouch, hey, what the, quit it.* More laughs.

"OK, everyone got that? No beating each other up. *During the game,*" says Burke, grinning, then glancing at ten fellas lurking near the keg. This group, which includes Ralph and Gerald, is definitely on for the fight. Stephen stands with them at the moment but I don't know if he's in on the plans. He wouldn't be, sober, but he's not sober. Wobbling, he notices I'm at the playground.

"Henry! Is that my little brother? It is," he slurs, running on the court, sweating and clutching a bottle neck in a brown bag.

"Watch this shit, Henry," he says.

He steals the ball and runs around dribbling sloppy and whistling "Sweet Georgia Brown." He botches a couple of fancy lay-ups. Everybody laughs, except Burke.

"All right, Toohey," he says. "Back to the sidelines. Give us athletes the ball."

Stephen flashes a fuck-you grin at Burke and walks toward him until Ralph Cooney calls, *Get off the court, you drunk asshole.* Then he turns sharply to Ralph and walks right up to his face.

"What you say, Ralph?" he asks.

"I said, get off the court, you drunk asshole," says Ralph.

"Got a problem?"

"Maybe."

"Either you do or don't. Which is it?"

Ralph looks to the ground and reaches to sneak in a push, but Stephen's ready. He pulls Ralph's shirt over his head and kicks him in the ass while everybody laughs.

"Now leave me the fuck alone," says Stephen.

Ralph pulls his shirt down, face red, eyes watering and watching the girls laugh.

"They won't think you're so funny if I get my dad's gun and shoot you," he says.

"You always say that," says Stephen. "Get it and shoot me or shut the fuck up."

Ralph shuts up, his face flushing again.

"Good dog," says Stephen, turning to the broads by the keg. "Now where were we, gals? I believe I was tending bar for your beautiful selves."

They giggle. Stephen fills their drinks, already forgetting Ralph, who fumes alone.

The game starts. We play man to man. I check the ball to the kid I guard, a fella named Stan with no left hand. He pounds the ball with his right hand. I force him to go left. Soon as he puts the ball on his south side, I pick him clean and take it all the way for a lay-up. One nothing, us. Grace clamps down on a smoke with her lips and claps hard with both hands. Stephen pumps the keg. Neighborhood thugs work on their beers. Bobby James French-kisses Margie Murphy. Across the Ave, the big round stained glass window above the steps of St. Ignatius Church watches us like Yahweh peeking through a walleye at the sinning kids who stink up his planet with beer farts and fake French toilet water. The Fishtown fellas bring the ball down after my bucket. Pass it three or four times, sloppy. A fella chucks some bullshit from the corner, but it drops after hitting the rim twelve times. We're not exactly playing the Celtics here.

The game gets even sloppier. Georgie O'Keefe and Harry chuck up three ugly airballs apiece. The Fishtown fellas make ten-step moves to the basket before they put holes in the backboard with bricks. We stay tied at four for twenty minutes. The sideline crowd works the keg and ignores the game, except for Grace, who cheers or boos everything I do. Beer flows, fellas hit on the gals. Stephen drops his scotch bottle—smash—and switches to paper cup cold beers. Shots drop. I hit two bombs. Burke and Crump barrel to the basket for ugly lay-ups. Georgie banks a hook shot from the top of the key. The Fishtown fellas match us the whole way, finding holes in our defense when Crump and Burke leave the court to refill their beers. We go up 10–9 when a loose ball hits Harry in the head and finds its way into the basket. Harry jumps up and down like he won the lottery (which is sorta true) and loses a lens from his goggles. The game stops so he can crawl and look for the lost lens.

The Fishtown fellas huddle together on the court. Crump and Burke slither over to their boys at the keg to make plans for the beating, the fucks. Stephen stumbles as he jokes with two broads. They look at each other uneasily. James and Murphy make out. Grace smacks a cigarette from the back of her palm to her mouth as a small crowd watches and claps. Harry crawls on the cement, weaving around the kids drinking beer and talking loudly. I make my way over to the Fishtown fellas. I got a plan for their salvation but I gotta be slick.

"Yo," I say, to Stan, my man.

"Yo," he says.

"See all those fellas standing by the keg over there?" I say, nodding, not pointing.

"Yeah?" he says, meaning *so what?*

"They're gonna pound you after the game," I tell him.

"What?" Stan asks, mad but not surprised. Now they're all listening to me.

"They want to jump you after the game."

"Why should I believe you?" asks Stan. "Who the fuck are you anyway?"

"I'm Henry, Stan."

"Don't call me Stan, Henry. We ain't friends."

"Sorry. I'm trying to help."

His face relaxes some. "Why you telling us now? Just so we know ahead of time?" he asks, as fellas by the keg now notice me talking to the Fishtown dudes and point in our direction and Harry yells, "I found the lens! I got it! Time in!"

"Look, I got an idea to save you," I say.

I'll save them by preaching God's Word or by making an ass out of myself. It all really depends on how you want to look at it.

"What? How?" he asks me.

"Look, just throw the ball away when you bring it down. I'll do my thing. Then wait for a sign from me. Then run. You got it?" I ask, all business.

Stan nods and looks at his buddies as players stroll back to the court. Billy Burke puts his hands on my shoulders and flashes his cowboy grin. Right at this minute, I see him fifteen years from now, beating his son on a ball field for dropping a pass.

"Henry, are you consorting with the enemy?" he asks.

"Just telling them they're gonna lose," I lie.

"That's right." He hands Stan the ball and smiles. "You ready?"

"Yeah, what the fuck," says Stan, sullen but not scared.

The Fishtown fellas move the ball back and forth but don't try to work it inside. Good. They're following the plan. Kids on the sideline make more noise now and pay attention. The ball swings to the side near the crowd and keg. Grace yells at me to play defense, goddammit. Stephen falls on his ass, gets up laughing but not happy, his dead girlfriend over his shoulder. James and Murphy French. The crowd hums, their faces dark and staring with hate at five boys from a neighborhood like ours except poorer. The ball flies out of bounds when Stan chucks it ten feet over a teammate's head. They did their part. Now comes mine. I touch my scapulars for luck; this crowd will be the biggest I've preached to thus far. Burke inbounds the ball to me. I dribble twice to the foul line, then pick up the ball, run for a bench, and jump on, the ball on my hip. I don't have anything prepared to say. I praise the Lord, of course, to start. Can't go wrong with that. Sometimes you just say shit to stall for time when you preach, it's not rocket science. I call God something like Jesus Jehova or the Potato Sack–Wearing Potentate, one or the other.

"Shut the fuck up, you little asshole," says somebody from the crowd.

"Shut *up?*" I ask. "I'm praising God, you jerk-off."

"I know you are. Shut up," he says, getting more laughs than I have so far.

"Fuck God then, I'll praise tits," I say, changing gears, getting desperate. "I love tits more than life itself. I love your tits and your tits and your tits and yours," I say, pointing to broads here and there. "I'd adopt and raise them all if I could. I'd push them around in baby carriages. I'd feed them the milk everybody's always drinking from them, then burp them, tuck them into bed, sing them songs, sit over them as they sleep. I'd bathe them in bathtubs, sit them on shelves, stroke them, squeeze them, love them."

I stop for half a second to look at the crowd, which is now at least kind of quiet with a couple folks chuckling, but not Grace, who looks pissed that I professed my love for every pair of tits on this big planet. Oh well, fuck a duck. She'll have to come to terms with that sooner or later in our relationship.

"Yes, tits, people! Nipples! Bras! Or no bras! Even better! Who will come up on this bench with me and tell the world that they also love tits like I do? Be not afraid, boys! Girls, too! You can love tits too! What is not to love? Get up here, people, pro-fess your love. Who here has love in them?" I ask, spit flying out my mouth, the crowd again mumbling, kids here and there call-ing me asshole and pussy. Fuck them.

I'm looking right at Stephen Toohey, remembering a time four years ago when I was nine and he was fourteen and playing in a peewee football championship game. Two players got in a fistfight that erupted into a brawl, both team benches clearing, then the stands, everybody on the field, like a Civil War battle minus the beards and blue coats. Stephen made his way over to the loudspeaker on the sidelines and sang "Why Can't We Be Friends?" and danced like a douche bag until the fight stopped. Fellas froze holding heads in headlocks, mouths open and about to bite legs like sandwiches, shit like that. And Stephen sang for at least half an hour, until everybody was laughing and nobody was fighting.

I want that Stephen back now, so as I'm shouting that I'm looking for folks full of love, I'm looking at him, I'm only asking him, challenging him to answer me. Come the fuck back. You be the funny guy again. Tell me you're still in there, that your heart's still alive. Be my hero again, please. Look, I'm almost cry-ing in front of all these assholes. Help me save these kids from taking a beating in front of your dead girlfriend on the wall.

Stephen leaps on the bench. He kisses both my cheeks and almost falls off the bench but catches himself after flapping the wings. Beer spills out of his cup and baptizes the cracked con-crete. He testifies that he loves tits and Jesus almost as much as beer. I frown. He says he loves them all the same. I make another face. He changes his mind to loving Jesus, beer, and tits in that order, then I frown and tell him the correct order is tits first then the next two, either way, who gives a fuck past tits? Stephen picks tits, beer, and Jesus, and I say fine. We laugh. I look right at Stan and mouth *Run*. They take off, running from the crowd toward the gate at the other end of the playground across the Ave almost diagonal from the church. Someone spots them and yells *They're splitting!*

First, twenty fellas chase after, then the whole mob follows. Everybody shouts. The crowd moves under me on the bench like a fucking current. Stephen jumps off the bench and runs to the action. Fellas catch the Fishtown kids at the gate. Stan's first. Somebody pulls his shirt off from behind. He disappears. The other four kids turn around and get swallowed up. They throw punches on their backs. Kicking and punching. Kids screaming. *Motherfucker motherfucker. Yo yo yo.* Girls screaming. *Get them. Get the motherfuckers.* Stephen pushes in. He pulls kids off the pile by their shirts. Somebody shoves him. He falls and gets up. He punches somebody holding a bat. Ralph Cooney. The bat falls to the cement, ringing like a schoolyard bell through a thunderstorm. Grace, near the fight, yells *Stop it stop it.* Sneakers kick at faces. Blood spills out of the noses and mouths of faces that look sleepy from drugs. Heads bleed. Shouts. The Fishtown kids lay still on the ground. Neighborhood fucks kick them in the face, the ribs, the neck. They stomp on their stomachs. *How you like that, motherfuckers?* Behind the fight the church looks like a vampire spreading his cape. Ralph Cooney stands up, picks up his bat. He walks toward the bloody pile, raising the bat. Then cop sirens scream, and he drops the bat. *Cops cops cops. Run!* The mob moves back to me, still standing on the bench. I don't see Stephen. It sweeps past. I feel hands tugging at my arms, and voices—Grace, Bobby, Harry—shouting *C'mon Henry, run,* but I don't look at them, yank my arm from their grips, and listen to them run as the squad cars show up. I can't move, I won't move, until I see those boys get into an ambulance. I won't run either. I didn't beat their faces in like those other fucks, who can go fuck themselves.

Red lights flash on the brown brick church. The five boys lay on the concrete steps of the playground. Only one kid—it's Stan—moves. He looks at his hands as he lays on his back and lets his head hit the pavement. His chest rises and falls in choking breaths. Two red paramedic trucks arrive. The drivers load the boys into the back. The trucks scream down the Ave and fade. It's quiet. Three cop cars remain near the playground gate, their lights still flashing. The cops stand around the gate. A nosy old man says something to the cops, who throw their heads back and laugh. Mr. James is with them, not laughing, looking at me, a hundred yards away, standing on the bench. He walks over, his hair messy tonight.

"Henry, you all right?" he asks.

I think I nod.

"Where's Bobby James? He OK?"

I nod again.

"He wasn't involved, was he?"

I won't fucking answer that. He knows the answer.

"You see what happened?" he asks.

More people, more nosy fucks, gather at the gate. They talk, loud and excited. They love this shit, the fucking pricks.

"Henry, do you know who did that to those boys?"

A cold wind blows. A fall wind. It smells like rain and throws trash around the playground. I stare across the Ave at the cemetery.

"OK. You don't have to tell. Can you get down from that bench at least?"

I look at him, then at my feet on the bench. My shoelaces are untied. I get down.

"I'll ride you home," he offers.

I don't say anything.

"All right. Here comes your brother Frannie anyway," he says.

"Hi," says Frannie, face worried. "I heard the sirens. What happened?"

"Playground bullshit. Five fellas got rushed to the hospital," says Mr. James.

"Jesus," says Frannie, scared. "Was Stephen one of them?"

"No, they were all Fishtown boys," says Mr. James.

"Henry, was Stephen here?" asks Frannie.

I can't answer him even though he's worried.

"Well, are you all right?" he asks.

"I don't know," I say, looking right at him, not sad, just confused.

"Let's get you home," he says, putting his arm around me, which makes me feel safe. "I'll see you tomorrow at the wedding, Mr. James. Tell Jeannie I said hello, OK?"

"I'll do that," replies Mr. James. "It'll be a nice change of pace from tonight."

"Definitely," says Frannie.

We walk home the same way the mob ran, Frannie's arm still around me, me still feeling safe in there, but only there. Everywhere else is either black sky or bloody ground, except for the bright Tack Park lights, which shine on us. We leave the playground and disappear down the dark streets off the Ave, noticing no one, saying nothing.

12

Music is my best friend, not counting people. It makes me feel better, helps me sort shit out, keeps love in my heart. I'm in my parents' bedroom, alone, sitting in a chair facing their big window, which looks out on St. Patrick Street. The bedroom lights are off. I use the soft white-purple light from the telly poles outside as a night-light while I look through Cecilia Toohey's record collection. I love to hold these albums. Listen to them creak when I open them. Run my fingertips on the record grooves. Laugh at the haircuts and clothes. Read the titles and song lengths. Wonder what the young faces on the album look like now, twenty and thirty years later.

The house is quiet, no lights on except from the bathroom and the TV downstairs. Cecilia and Cece sleep together in Cece's tiny bed, Cecilia's long thin arm around Cece. They lay there like different-size twin dolls who stir when you kiss their foreheads, all blond hair, long eyelashes, and deep sighs. Francis Junior sleeps downstairs, snoring on his La-Z-Boy, his hands clutching the armrests like an astronaut bracing for takeoff, the remote control lodged in his right hand. I took it from him when I came in from the beating and flipped past the Phillies postgame

(Mike Schmidt, that fuck, won the game with a late homer), hospital dramas, and redneck Texas soap operas before I found a stand-up comedian. He was a bald fuck in a bad sport coat who told jokes about his wife stealing the covers and sitting in church near people whose nostrils whistle. Safe bullshit. Nothing dirty. If I left it on I'd be snoring next to Francis Junior, so I flipped again and found a preacher with gold teeth that matched his rings and wristwatch. He smiled like Satan, sweated a lot, and kept saying *Sinful fornication*, whatever the fuck that means. I wasn't into it, though. I needed to think. God and TV can't help me there. Only music. I slipped the remote back into Junior's jumpy hand and headed upstairs.

The stereo in my parents' bedroom is an oak monster Cecilia got from my grandpop when he died. The turntable's in the middle, deep inside the fucker, under a heavy lid. Your arms disappear to the elbows when you drop the needle on a record. Big speakers bookend both sides and sound like love or a kiss on the ear. You don't miss a noise: fingertips tiptoeing across guitar strings, tambourines ringing like church bells, drum brushes brushing past drum kits like a mime dusting library bookshelves, snaps, claps, coughs, and laughs.

When I was little, the stereo stayed downstairs and played all the time as Cecilia hopped around cleaning, changing records nonstop, while I slept with my head near a speaker. I remember mostly soul and disco during this time: the Spinners and Bee Gees, "Rubber Band Man," "Jive Talking." I love disco, I'm not ashamed to say it loud and proud. All that's a memory now anyhow. A couple of years back, when we all got bigger, and Francis and Cecilia started arguing, Cecilia stopped playing the records, stopped singing and dancing, and she ordered it carried upstairs by the Francises.

As far as albums go, Cecilia Toohey has everything you need. Ernest Tubbs, Clancy Brothers, Miles Davis, Mel Tormé, Tom

Jones, Janis Joplin, Jefferson Airplane, ABBA, Aerosmith, Smothers Brothers, Isley Brothers. Old country, R and B, rock and roll, big bands, swing bands, jug bands, jazz bands, classic rock, you name it. It's all here, lining the small bedroom walls, making it look like a radio station storage closet with a broken bed in the middle. Cecilia alphabetizes by artist in each decade. Take the letter B. In the 1950s, we've got Hank Ballader and the Midnighters, Harry Belafonte, Freddie Bell and the Bell Boys, Chuck Berry, Pat Boone, James Brown and His Famous Flames, Johnny Burnette. The 1960s: Joan Baez, the Band, Barbarians, Beach Boys, Beatles, Jeff Beck Group, Bee Gees, Archie Bell and the Drells, Big Brother and the Holding Company, Booker T and the MGs, James Brown again, Buffalo Springfield, the Byrds. The 1970s: Bachman Turner Overdrive, Badfinger, Badger, Jeff Beck again, the Bee Gees again (this time with cooler, whiter clothes), Black Sabbath, Blue Öyster Cult, Jackson Browne (no relation to James or his Flames), Rocky Burnette. Pickings are slim for the '80s, when the stereo and albums got banished, forgotten by the broad who collected them. I should mention that we do have the '80s album *Thriller* by Michael Jackson. I insisted. But besides that, since then, we got jack-shit.

I can't decide what to play. This happens all the time: lot of choices. I never get frustrated looking, though, because I love the covers. In the '50s, they're funny without trying to be. Almost all have head shots of pretty boys with blush painted on their cheeks, standing next to sports cars, sport coats thrown over one shoulder, twenty broads on the other. Hairstyles are out of hand. I respect the fact they combed so thoroughly, but the slick look makes me sick. Too much gel spells amateur. Shame on them, the pussies. My favorite '50s cover, fellas division, is *Chet Atkins' Workshop*, where Chet wears a bobo sweater and holds an electric guitar in front of a mad scientist lab full of amps. I'm not sure why I like that one so much, but I do.

Broads dressed way too nunlike on '50s covers, often wearing skirts below the knees. There's no fucking reason for that. One wonderful exception is Julie London's *Calendar Girl:* twelve perfect pictures of Julie wearing short shorts and bikinis, beautiful stuff that always gives me a boner. I got one right now, in fact. Another boner inducer is *Swingin' Easy with Bill Doggitt,* where a broad in a bikini and high heels leans against a rock. All of a sudden, I want to rub this album against my boner. Fuck that. Cecilia'd walk in the minute I tried that shit, and I'd be off to a priest by my ear.

Things get better and weirder on '60s covers. Letters fatten like inflated tires. Rainbow mushrooms, trees, flowers, farms, and animals show up on them. Men's hair is less wet but longer and frizzier (one step forward, two back). Folks wear purple sunglasses, beads, Indian jackets, and pinstripe bellbottoms. The skirt-length problem disappears—Thank You, Fucking Jesus— plus all the broads wear hair long and straight. I never understood short hair on women, like curly perms. What the fuck is that bullshit?

I can't even pick out a favorite from the '60s because there's too much to choose. We've got *Are You Experienced, Mr. Tambourine Man, Rubber Soul, Bringing It All Back Home, Psychotic Reaction, Psychedelic Sounds of the 13th Floor Elevators, The Who by Numbers, Disraeli Gears, Music from Big Pink.* And that's just the bands with fellas. The broads are even better: the Shirelles, Ronettes, Angels, Shangri-Las, Supremes. Wow. I'd kiss them all against a fucking Dumpster. Best one, though, by far: *Sugar,* Nancy Sinatra. Nancy's tits pop out of her pink bikini top to say, "Henry, take a nap right between us." Also, more important, Nancy's pulling down her bikini bottoms. Holy shit. I *will* rub my boner against *this* one later.

In the '70s, covers are best fucking forgotten. They combine the worst parts of the '60s—pirate clothes and hippie hair— with the worst of the '50s—no nature backgrounds outside.

Besides, of course, Roxy Music's *Country Life*. This one excites me too much, then confuses me too much, to describe. Anyone who hasn't seen it should look it up—but don't buy it, because it blows.

After looking at about a billion covers, I finally make a choice: Beatles. *The White Album*, a double album, which has no cover, just plain and white. But when you're the Beatles, the tunes are good enough that I forgive you for no tits on the cover. Wouldn't have killed them, though, but what the fuck are you going to do? I pull the side two vinyl out of the sleeve and, holding its sides careful, lower it onto the turntable. I flick the On switch. The arm rises, pauses, moves sideways, and drops. I grab it and help it to "Good Night," the album's last song, my favorite Beatles song. The needle scratches the grooves, the music starts, and I lean back in my chair.

Outside, rain starts, first in heavy drops that hit the window like birdshit every ten seconds and leave streaks. Street lamps make the streaks glow like lights on Christmas trees. Now the rain changes and falls in a quiet, heavy mist. Water washes down the window. I stare at it, my stomach spinning, heart beating, head lost in a fog. I think about those boys, laying there on the pavement, bleeding, maybe dying, I don't even fucking know. I think about their moms, sitting beside hospital beds, looking out windows like this one. Are they praying? Do they ask God to forgive the fucks who kicked their sons' faces? Maybe they demand revenge, tell God to fuck off. It could have been Grace or Stephen, Bobby James or Harry. They were all there. Maybe if something like that happened to one of them, I'd turn angry. Maybe angry people have stories like this to explain the anger: midnight rides to hospital beds where your kid's attached to tubes that replace blood that now stains a playground. A mountain of bills on a busted table, a small house squeezed on a street with seventy-seven others, a broken-down car, a bum knee, bad jobs humping mail, pounding beats, jackhammering streets.

Empty bank accounts. Too much concrete, not enough green in wallets or out windows. Shit like this shapes life on St. Patrick Street, but not mine, fuck that.

I got plans to get off of this street with my family, with Grace McClain. Grace. I hope she loves me half as much as I love her. I hope our kiss made her feel like I did. I'll be honest, I had no idea what the fuck I was doing. I tilted my head, opened my mouth, and hoped for the best. It felt like bobbing for apples and I had to remind myself to close my eyes. I'm not that good yet, though. We'll just have to keep practicing, simple as that. This thought warms my belly and replaces the bad feelings about the fight tonight. I send these feelings, the good ones, to everybody, as Ringo sings me to sleep.

The rain picks up strength without getting louder. It forgives and forgets. First kisses and playground fights float away. I lean forward to watch St. Patrick Street and its houses, where people wander inside. Lights in windows go on and off in the same gentle time as the strings on the record. I let my eyes go out of focus, and movement on the street synchronizes, like sissy Olympic swimmers. Moms in bathrobes and curlers run out of front doors into the rain, one at a time from left to right, pulling their kids' tricycles from lawns and sidewalks to the covered awnings of their front porches. Up the block, fathers fall sideways out of the streetside door of Paul Donohue's, one at a time, diving into ten-feet-deep Budweiser puddles like skunked swimmers in Jeff hats instead of bathing caps.

I feel nothing but love for them, from them, and lean closer to the window, closer to them, the saints on St. Patrick Street. I rest my forehead on the glass. Beads of rain blink like stars on the tops of two-colored cars. Rain rushes along the curbs and falls into the sewer, washing away beer caps and broken bottles and hearts. Inside houses, people pray to pope pictures, wring their hands, and squirm on plastic-covered sofas. They ask for forgiveness from sin, a Phillies world championship, and salvation in the form of money that will take them from this life, this street, this neighborhood, these houses, which beat like hearts and sink like stones. Fear and frustration float everywhere, covering most everything good, but not all the way. Ringo whispers, *Good night to everybody everywhere.* I slouch back in the chair, asleep, ready like always to dream.

First thing I hear is the door slam downstairs, then the needle scratching the record player I left on, sounding like my throat feels. My neck hurts. The rain stopped. St. Patrick Street is still and quiet. Streetlights look like halos. Muffled voices downstairs. I turn off the stereo and tiptoe to the top of the steps.

"You cut your head *breaking up* a fight? Last I heard, people who come home with forehead gashes were in fights, not stopping them," I hear Francis Junior say.

"Fran, maybe he's telling the truth," Cecilia says.

"There was a fight with Fishtown kids. Bat, knife, gun, assholes," slurs Stephen.

"Fishtown? Bats? Guns? Fran, can you make sense out of what he's saying?"

Stephen mentioning the knife and gun scares me. I didn't see them.

"Course I can't," says Francis Junior. "Drunks don't make any goddamn sense."

"Fran, don't fucking start," scolds Cecilia, her anger rising along with his.

"I'm not starting anything. He cares about no one in this house besides himself."

"Untrue," Stephen says.

"Shut up," says Francis Junior. "I'm this close to punching you in the face."

"That ain't cool, Dad," says Stephen, calm, not mad.

"Fran, calm down before you two start swinging at each other," warns Cecilia.

"Nobody's swinging at me. This is my house. And I'll swing at anybody I want."

"Now you're talking shit, Dad," says Stephen, also getting mad.

"Stephen, stop," begs Cecilia. "Go to bed, both of you."

"I'll go to bed when I want," shouts Francis Junior. "And then I'll get up for work like I do every morning. You wouldn't know anything about work, would you, Stephen?"

"I got a job," Stephen says.

"You go there tonight?" shouts Francis Junior.

"What?" asks Stephen, trying to sound surprised.

"You heard me. Did you go to work tonight?"

"You saw me."

"I saw you walk out my front door in your work clothes. Now I see you walk in the house in plain clothes. Where's your work clothes?"

"I left them at work."

"Liar. You didn't go to work. I called down there. They said you called out sick."

"Ma, tell him to get his finger out of my face," says Stephen, real mad now.

"Francis Toohey, step the fuck away from your son. No need to be in faces."

"I'll stand where I want in my house," he shouts.

"Ma, tell him to take his finger away from my face," says Stephen again.

"Look at his head, Fran," Cecilia pleads. "You're gonna hit him again?"

"Get your fucking finger off my chest or else," barks Stephen.

"Or else what?" yells Francis Junior. "Or else what, tough guy? You want another smack like you got out there tonight? You probably *deserved* it."

"What's that, lover boy?"

Silence. Slap. Somebody gets punched. Something hits the floor. Francis Junior shouts *Fucker.* Stephen says nothing. Cecilia screams. Shit gets knocked over, broken.

"Henry, you a-hole, can we go in my room and play some

records now?" asks Cece, who looks wide awake except for bed-head.

"Hey, truckdriver mouth, you're awake," I say. "What do you want to hear?"

"You pick it," she says. "Something happy, OK?"

The obvious choice, then, is *Good Times,* Sonny and Cher. You can never go wrong with Sonny and Cher. I fish it out of the collection. The cover for this album is nothing special—especially since you can't see Cher's tits—other than that, Sonny Bono's hairstyle here (mental patient bangs in the front, longer in the back) is as bad as it gets. Cussing the lack of tits and the bad hair, I head to Cece's room, where she lays on the bed, arms crossed behind her head. I sit down in a pink plastic chair, the kind fifth-grade gals use for tea parties, its legs bending under me.

"Stephen and Daddy punching the shit out of each other again?" asks Cece.

"What? Nah. They're salsa dancing, which explains the noise. They're honkies."

"Only salsa they like is the kind you dip chips in," she says, smiling. Then, more serious, she asks, "Was Stephen drinking again?"

"Yeah," I say, sad.

"Will you drink when you're older? Box with Daddy? Disturb my beauty sleep?"

"No."

"Stephen probably said the same thing at your age," she says.

"What are you talking about?" I ask. "He was drinking at my age."

"No, he wasn't, dummy."

"Sure he was. He drank beer in class. Opened bottles with the chalk ledge."

"You're crazy. He did not," says Cece, half amused, half annoyed.

The fight keeps up downstairs, but I can't make shit out, since the door is closed and the instrumental "I Got You, Babe" blares in the room. I bet Frannie's here by now.

"Henry, I'm serious," she says. "I don't want you to drink."

"OK, I won't," I tell her.

"Everybody else drinks."

"That ain't true," I say. "Mommy don't drink really."

"But she takes those pills," she reminds me.

"What do you know about those pills?" I ask Cece, who frowns and fidgets with a green bead necklace, yanking it in circles around her neck and chewing it.

"Mr. O'Drain was drinking beer when he crashed his car," says Cece, fast. "That's why Archie can't walk. That's why Megan's dead and in Heaven. That's why Mrs. O'Drain has scars on her face. That's why Stephen's sad and drinks."

"How do you know all that?" I ask, stunned.

"I hear things, homeboy," she says, like Mae West or Grace. "You should tune some shit out."

"Can't help it. Ain't like anybody whispers around here."

Downstairs, something heavy hits the floor. Francis Junior shouts. Stephen shouts back. Cecilia and Frannie shout at Francis Junior and Stephen.

"Why do people drink if it makes them unhappy?" asks Cece.

"I think life makes people unhappy, so they drink to forget," I tell her.

"Does your life make you unhappy?" she asks.

"Nope. I got you, babe," I say, looking right at her, smiling.

"You're corny, kid." She laughs. "But I know. You got me too."

We hug, and I look at the Miss Piggy poster on her wall. Hard to believe just a couple hours ago Phillies Alarm Clock rocked this room like a fucking chair.

"We still gonna live together when we're rich rock stars?" asks Cece.

"Yup," I say.

"On a big farm?"

"Yup."

"Me you Mommy Daddy Stephen Frannie Grace and Archie, right?" she asks.

"I never said anything about Archie," I say, breaking her balls.

"Henry, I'll be *married* to him. He'll *have* to live with us."

"I know. He'll come in handy. We can push him down hills in his chair."

"Cool. I'm in for that. Tell me again what the farm'll be like."

The fight's over. Sonny and Cher sing "Trust Me." Cecilia chokes back sobs and screams, *This fucking bullshit has to stop.* Frannie agrees. He can't understand why people don't get along in this house, why this one drinks and that one throws punches.

It doesn't matter, though. We all left this little house, which is sandwiched between two others that are sandwiched between two others that are sandwiched between two others. Instead, I tell Cece, we live in a farmhouse that sits between a silo and barn. There are no steep lawns with saint statues to tiptoe around, and we can lean our heads against trees that drop peaches. Green grass stretches out in every direction. There are no broads chucking their husbands' clothes out windows, no broken glass, no fights about money, no playground beatings. Mommy and Daddy are back in love, and Stephen's happy, with a new girlfriend maybe, a farm girl a hundred times prettier than Megan. The neighbors are crickets and fruit flies. The ground is covered with wildflowers and dandelions, not bottles and cans. The millions of dollars made by multiplatinum album sales sit earning interest in the bank. Grace loves Henry. Cece loves Archie. Francis loves Cecilia. The parks really are parks, not just basketball courts surrounded by fences and called parks. No Gwen Flaggart or vicious dogs of any kind. Just milk-producing cows.

"What are those things called under cows again, Henry?"

"Udders. They're called udders. You get the milk by squeezing the udders."

"With both hands?"

"Yeah, with both hands. We'll let Archie do that. We'll lower the wheels on his chair so he can glide right under the bovine. Does Archie have a parking brake on that chair? Are there such things as two-seat wheelchairs? Maybe I'll get that for your wedding present. You can ride shotgun. I'll buy you matching helmets too. Stylish ones, like my clothes are stylish."

"Hah! Right."

"What's so funny? Don't you think I dress cool? I have moose on my shirt. How many people do you know with moose on their shirts?"

"None, just you."

"Right, just me."

"Because you're a dork."

"No, that doesn't mean I'm a dork. You're the dork. Falling in love with a kid in a wheelchair is a dork in my book."

"I'm telling Archie you said that."

"You tell Archie I said that. What's he gonna do, run me over? Burn a hole in my head using the sun and his sunglasses? When you buy aviator shades, do they come with a corncob pipe and an army Jeep?"

"I don't know."

"Do you change your last name to Eisenhower? Archie and Cece Eisenhower."

"How should I know? I hope not, though. Yuck."

"You don't like Eisenhower? How about Wisenheimer? Cece Wisenheimer. Because that's what you are, a fucking wisenheimer. I caught that: you yawned and laughed at the same time. That's a bad thing to do to a comedian, the yawn-laugh. I don't know whether to scrap the joke or tell more like it. Now you just yawned that time. Are these jokes not funny? Cece?"

Cece snores softly, sleeping sideways in bed, stretched out across her two pillows, a smile on her face. I kiss her head, pull the needle off the record, and turn off the light. I walk to my own bedroom, put Big Green away in his safe place, strip down to my skivvies, and climb into the bunk above Stephen, who pukes in a bucket while Cecilia, sniffing, holds his head upright. I tell her, *Good night, Ma, Jesus loves you but I don't.*

She laughs through her sniffs. "Hey, you taking care of my records in there?"

"You know it," I say.

"How they doing?"

"They're good. Getting lots of love and attention from me."

"Cece too, right?" she asks.

"Yeah, Cece too," I tell her.

"Cool."

"You could listen to them with us, you know. They're your records."

"I know. I will. Soon as all this bullshit dies down. Tell them I said hello."

"Will do. Good night."

"Good night."

The wind coming in the window is crisp, cold. Stephen pukes and cries. I pull the covers to my neck to stay warm. Then, for the second time tonight, sleep and dreams.

13

Praise the Lord and pass the pickled pumpernickel pistachio nuts. God bless and good morning, all you morons, malcontents, mumblers, mummers, mummies, mothers, brothers, bra burners, church burners, flag burners, flag wavers, florists, arborists, and acrobats. That should cover everybody. Good morning, Smelly Sleeping Stephen and his bucket o' vomit. Good morning, Mike Schmidt. Here's a spitball in your eye, you ugly fuck. Maybe you can reflect upon why you're a fucking asshole as I walk to get a record. I make a quick pick: Charlie Parker, *Jazz at the Philharmonic 1949*. Bop! Bam! Splash! I slap myself with water from the sink faucet. My armpits smell fine. No need to shower. I'll just wet my head, comb, and go. I soak the hair, dance into the bedroom, grab Big Green, and dance back to the bathroom, where Stephen pukes in the hopper.

"Yo, Stephen," I say. "Looking good."

"Yo," he groans. "Thanks."

"How you feeling?"

He pukes. "Never better."

"Could be a connection between puking and drinking," I say.

"Doubtful," he says. "What the fuck are you listening to?"

"Charlie Fucking Parker, peckerhead. Got a problem with that?"

"No, at least there's no vocals for you to sing."

"What's that mean?" I ask. "I got a fine voice. Ask the cats beneath our window."

Stephen grins. I can't imagine finding a reason to smile when I'm close enough to a toilet to see my reflection. "I was proud of you last night, you little dickhead," he says.

"For what?" I ask, worrying he knows I kissed Grace. That would lead to torture.

"For the playground thing," he says. "The tit sermon. That took guts."

"Thanks, pal. All in a day's work," I say. "What happen to those kids?"

"They got released from the hospital last night. Cuts, bruises, broken bones. One of them cracked some ribs. Another broke his wrist."

"You sure?"

"Yeah. I talked to a dude at Donohue's who works at the hospital."

"You hear anything else?"

"Things got fuzzy after that. What happened when I came in? Were you awake?"

"I didn't hear nothing," I lie. "You must've come in and gone to bed."

"How'd the bucket get next to bed?" he asks.

"I did that. You made noises like you were gonna throw up."

"I remember puking. Did I wake up Daddy?"

"No, but you should chill. Your most important drinking years are ahead of you."

"True enough." He laughs, in pain. "I'm gonna quit, Henry," he says, serious.

"When? How? Got a ten-year plan worked out?" I ask, not believing, as I squirt a pound of gel on my palm, then rub it into my fantastic hair.

"Today," he says. "I'm gonna get serious about shit. Straighten up."

"Going to school?" I ask.

"School? Good one. No fucking way. I'll take the fireman and mailman tests."

"Don't be a mailman," I say. "Go to school."

"Henry, I barely passed senior year." Puke.

"You barely tried. You'd make Daddy happy."

"Fuck him," he snarls.

We get quiet. Stephen sprawls on the bowl. I feather my hair and spray like I'm putting out a fire.

"Did somebody have a gun at the playground last night?" I ask, concerned.

"Ralph Cooney threatened me with one," he says.

"I heard him. But did he really have one?"

"Please. Ralph couldn't even shoot a water pistol. He talks shit, Henry."

"I saw him in that crowd last night during the fight. He had a bat, though, right?"

"Yup. Didn't use it. I popped him when I saw that bat. What are you doing?"

"Soaping my pits," I say.

"Jeannie James's wedding's today and you won't even shower?" he asks, stupidly.

"I don't *need* to. Got one earlier in the week. What's with the interrogation?"

"Whatever you say there, Mr. Fragrance," says Stephen.

"Look who's talking," I say. "You don't smell like deodorant come morning."

"Yeah, but I jump in the shower."

"What's it filled with—Budweiser?"

"No. Rolling Rock. I *switched brands.*"

We laugh hard. I fucking love laughing, especially from a Stephen joke.

"So you going to the wedding?" I ask. "I got something special planned."

"What is it?" he says.

"Have to wait and see, handsome."

"Fine. Be mysterious. Will you be preaching?"

"Nah, nothing religious."

"Oh."

"So are you going?" I ask again.

"Don't know if I'll be at the Mass, but I'm scheduled to work the reception," he tells me. "But then I called out again last night. Long as I still got a job I'll be there."

"Cool."

Stephen flushes. We walk back to our room side by side. He crawls into bed while I slip into a brown RUBBER SOUL T-shirt and the same plaid shorts from yesterday. I holster Big Green and head downstairs, which is a fucking mess again, while Birdman swings. I click on the TV in time to see a highlight of prickface Mike Schmidt's game-winning homer last night. He can kiss my ass. I flip for Jesus shows with no luck, then turn off the TV with the remote. Then on. Then off. Hello. Good-bye. Hello. Good-bye.

A note on the dining room table from Cecilia says *Henry, pick up Archie and bring him back to our house. Make sure he has his suit! Also, Jesus loves you, but I don't.* I laugh, pick up a pen, and write AMEN on top of her note—she'll like that—and I grab a pack of Krimpets and open the front door, where Gwen Flaggart attacks Francis Junior.

"Morning, Henry," he says, shaking his leg, trying to smack her on the head.

"Morning, Dad," I answer. "I get anything in the mail today?"

"Couple of guitar catalogs," he says. "You taking up the guitar?"

"Not bloody likely," I answer in a Sherlock Holmes accent.

He looks at me puzzled and maces Flaggart, who rolls away whimpering.

"How is your brother?" he asks, standing there with a sneak on one foot while Flaggart, off to the side, chews on the other.

"Who, Frannie? Same as you. Fighting dogs to the death for Uncle Sam."

"Funny. I meant the other brother."

"He's sleeping," I say, not up for a lie, worrying about going into Archie's house.

"He came in last night talking about a fight," says Francis. "His face was cut."

"I thought you did that."

"He came in like that," he snaps. "Besides, he went after me. Morning, Betty. Yeah, your casino tickets are here. Be right over. You know what happened last night? No workers' comp check yet, Mike. I told you I'd bring it soon as it got here."

"I heard about a fight but that was it," I say. I have to admit this much. You can't be thirteen and not know about a playground fight. "Doubt Stephen had anything to do with it, though. He's a peacenik."

"Please. I'm not saying he was involved on purpose. I figured maybe those Fishtown bastards jumped him because he was drunk. Gimme two minutes, Chalie, I'm talking to my son here. They must've been looking for trouble. Why else are they in our neighborhood? Know what I mean?"

"Not really," I say, turning back into the house to shake off his asshole remark, where the Twelve Apostles painting hangs crooked over the TV, Jesus and His Holy Homeboys looking like thirteen bearded sailors in dresses yelling *Whoa* as they slide to one side of a tilting boat.

"Look," says Francis Junior. "Go up in my closet and grab my new sneaks."

I run for the sneaks right after I turn the TV on and off a couple times, pour myself some orange juice, take Charlie Parker off the stereo, put on the Del-Vetts' 45 "Last Time Around," and dance about the upstairs. Once the song ends, I hit the closet, where Francis Junior has ten blue boxes of new black sneaks stacked neat. I grab a pair, run downstairs, and turn the cable on and off a couple times, then walk to the door and hand him the shoes. Flaggart coughs up the sneak tongue she scored.

"That was quick," he says. "You stop to choke your chicken?"

"I stop to what my what? I don't follow."

"Never mind. You'll know soon enough," he says, chuckling, changing sneaks.

"Dad, is Mrs. Cooney your girlfriend?" I ask.

"What?" he asks, looking up, no longer laughing.

"Is Mrs. Cooney your girlfriend?" I repeat.

"Henry, I love your mom," he says, "nobody else."

"Answer the question," I insist. "Is Mrs. Cooney your girlfriend?"

He stands up and rubs his chin with his fingertip, wheels turning in his head.

"No, she's not," he says. "Who'd you hear that from?"

"I forget," I say, my stomach feeling funny, reeling from his point-blank lie.

"You forget," he sneers. "Right. Gotta go. See you at church."

He leaves. For the first time in my life, after he already spent a year fighting Stephen, ignoring Cece, and hurting Cecilia, I watch him with sadness and something less than complete love. He lied right to my face, and the whole year of him letting me down, letting us down, hits me at once. Now to make matters worse, I have to go to Archie's house, where there are more ghosts than at the cemetery.

I want to cheer myself up, so I walk down the street whistling, strutting, dancing. I call Yo to the Mahons as they laugh and slow-dance to no music on their front lawn. I do the hustle past Mr. Mulligan and Tubby having a catch with gloves and a hard-ball as they sit on bending lawn chairs that beg for mercy. I wink and point to Gerald Wilson and Ralph Cooney as they work on Gerald's no-wheels-having-piece-of-shit car. Gerald calls me a dancing fairy, Ralph asks me to remind Stephen about his dad's gun. Tricycles and Big Wheels zip past me. I dodge them dancing, compliment young moms on their wonderful tits, and ask their fat hairy husbands to put some shirts on. The sunshine reminds me of last night's kiss. I'm lost in a daydream—me singing the Donovan song "Catch the Wind" to Grace on a boat while ten thousand teenage foxes scream from dry land—when I walk to the front steps of the O'Drain house. The good feeling I was forcing and faking, along with the sunshine and warm wind, disappear like they died.

A year ago today, St. Patrick Street held its billionth and last block party. Block parties are a big fucking deal in Philly. Folks plan for it throughout the year, meeting three or four times at somebody's house, drinking beers, eating deli food off an aluminum tray, and watching whatever team's season's in swing. In fall they'll hook up on a Sunday, watch the Eagles, drink Bud cans, and make sandwiches with cold cuts and presliced white rolls. In the winter, it's the Flyers, then Sixers, in that order, along with Bud cans and meatballs sizzling in a Crock-Pot. Spring is the Phils, Bud cans, and deviled eggs. For the block party, each family agrees to make some kind of food, bring its own beers, and pay maybe ten bucks to the block captain. This bread pays for a DJ, who spins bullshit Bob Seger records all night, a clown who gets drunk and pukes on some crying little fucker's shoes, and a couple kiddie rides that shoot sparks and leave burn welts on asses. Shit like that. Cecilia Toohey was the block captain last year, and every year, long as I been alive. She liked doing it. She'd tell people it was fun to have money to manage once a year.

The day of the block party started ugly right off the bat. Cecilia lost the envelope with the money, something like seven hundred bucks. She's the kind of broad who'll chuck her pocketbook through a window if she can't find a quarter she laid in a drawer the night before. In this case, then, she blew her top. It was morning, maybe eleven. Me, Cece, and Stephen were playing chess on the floor, me and her versus him. We whispered to each other before we made a move, never anything about chess but acting like it was. Stephen took the match even less seriously and spent more time making us laugh by spitting the toenails he bit off his toes at us. We lost interest in him and laughing once Cecilia started storming the fuck around, slamming drawers and saying *Motherfucker*. Stephen tried to win us back by standing on his head and farting, and he got us laughing again until Cecilia turned over the kitchen table, which made me jump and Cece cry. Same time, outside, Gwen Flaggart attacked Francis Junior on our porch. Once he maced her proper, he called in to Cecilia, pissed.

"What are you screaming about now?" he asked.

"Nothing," she said. "Leave me alone."

"Stephen, aren't you supposed to be at football practice?" asked Francis.

"Coach gave us today off, sunshine," said Stephen.

"Then take Henry up to Tack Park and throw the ball to him," said Francis. "Henry, run some outs and long patterns. Oh, and do some short shit across the middle. Get the fuck off my ankle, you fat bitch. You want the juice again? Stephen, you throw the ball behind receivers when they come across the middle. Need to work on that."

"Hello?" asked Cecilia, annoyed, loud. "Weren't we talking, Fran?"

"Yeah," said Francis Junior. "You told me to leave you alone. So I did. Stephen, is Coach still talking about you playing d-back?"

"I lost the fucking money, Fran," said Cecilia, matter-of-fact.

"Yeah, you always do that," he answered. "You're a good d-back, Stephen, but you belong at quarterback. I won't let you play d-back just because they got nobody good on defense. That ain't your problem. You got colleges looking at you for quarterback."

Stephen ignored him and made a funny face at me and Cece.

"Fran, I lost the street money for the block party," said Cecilia.

"What?" he asked. "Dog, so help me I'm gonna kick your head in with my heel."

"I lost seven hundred dollars, Fran. What the fuck are we gonna do?"

"First of all, lower your voice," he said. "Where'd you have it last?"

"I don't fucking know. It's lost. You listening?" snapped Cecilia.

"Look, don't talk to me like I'm a goddamn animal."

"Well, you're talking to me like I'm a moron."

"You're acting like one."

"Screw you, Fran."

Stephen watched Cece hold her hands over her ears, then he leapt up.

"Hello, hold on a second, you two lovebirds," he said. "I hate to stop the fun, but the little one here's crying. Cece, if you don't stop crying, so help me, I'll belt Henry."

Cece laughed and shot a booger on the chessboard.

"Oh, that's nice," said Stephen. "I surrender. You guys win."

Me and Cece jumped up shouting, hugging, and singing "We Are the Champions," a song that blows except when it's after a big win. Stephen picked us both up and joined the song for a couple choruses. Francis and Cecilia laughed. Stephen dropped us on top of each other, then held a pretend microphone under his mouth and interviewed us like Howard Cosell, who wears a toupee, in case you didn't know.

"Cecilia Toohey Junior," he said, "you just won the world chess championship with a controversial snot to rook four. Do you feel this in any way taints the victory?"

"What the hell does taint mean?" she asked.

"Gives it less meaning, dear, like you almost cheated to win," he said.

"Hell, no. I'll do it next time. Anything for the win, Howard, you asshole."

"Same to you, boogie queen," said Cosell. "Henry Toohey,

how do you feel about marriage growing up in a family where your mother and father fight like cats and dogs, like mailmen and dogs, like mailmen and sane people?"

"Can't say it looks fun, Howard," I said, "you big-eared rug-wearing cigar-chewing rubber-face fuckhead."

"Bad answer, jerk-off," said Stephen.

"What, like your hair ain't fake, Howard?"

"No, it is, young man, but I am talking here about marriage. Don't let these boobs give you bad ideas. Love is grand," he said, while outside our screen door, a broad yelled *Boo*, followed by a fast laugh, followed by popping gum. It was Megan O'Drain.

"Yo, Frankie. How you doing?" asked Megan, slapping five with Francis Junior, who was real fond of her. "Gwen Flaggart bite you again?"

"Megan, how you doing?" he said. "Yeah, that fleabag bit me again."

"I don't get it. She's always a sweetheart to me," she said, before popping more gum. "Ain't you, Gwen Fwaggart, a wittle old sweetheart? You just have to scratch behind her ears. See, look at that? She's putty in my hands."

"Megan, I swear I'd try if she let me get on the porch, but she don't, so I can't."

"Fair enough, Francis," she said. "Listen, is Stevie Wonder around?"

"Yeah, he's inside," said Francis Junior.

"He look handsome today?" she asked.

"Not as much as me but he looks OK," joked Francis Junior.

"Yeah, you wish, buddy."

"No, I know. Gotta roll."

"All right. Watch out for pooches."

Megan, who always dressed nicely and looked hot, opened the door and walked inside, wearing a purple tank top that fit tight over her nice C cups, along with short denim shorts, white tennis sneaks in perfect condition, and lots of jewelry: big gold earrings, rings on every finger, bracelets on her wrists and one ankle. She had muscular legs and arms but not in a dude way. Her face was her best feature though: real red hair, blue eyes, and a big mouth, in both size and volume. She was pretty and loud and pushy and funny, like Cecilia, like Grace.

"Hello, Tooheys," she said. "How you doing?"

"Hi, Megan," said Cecilia. "Not so hot. I lost the block party money."

"No shit?" asked Megan.

"Yeah, no shit. I don't know what to do."

"Stephen Toohey," said Megan, walking to him, running her long fake nails through his hair. "How can we rectify this problem?"

"Megan O'Drain," he answered, kicking his leg like a dog as she scratched. "That's a good question. I'm not really sure."

"How much dough you got in the bank from your busboy job?" asked Megan.

"Maybe five hundred bucks," he said.

"That's about what I got," said Megan. "Let's go to the bank and make two withdrawals. Five hundred from you, two hundred from me, problem solved."

"Why five hundred from me and two hundred from you?" asked Stephen.

Megan kissed him. Me and Cece shouted WOO WOOO.

"OK, five hundred from me, two hundred from you," said Stephen.

"Kids, I can't take your money," said Cecilia.

"The money'll turn up, Ma," said Stephen. "You can pay us back then."

"Stevie Wonder, let's take them with us," said Megan, pointing to me and Cece.

"Yeah, OK." He smiled. "What do you say, Henry, Cece?"

"I'm in," I answered.

"Me too," said Cece.

"Cool. Hey, Ma, heard the one about the nun, the cantaloupe, and the vibrator?"

She laughed. "You told me that one yesterday. Good stuff."

"See, that's what I love about you most: no class," said Stephen, hugging her, then turning to us. "All right, uglies, last one out the door is Frannie Toohey."

We yelled and ran like loons for the sunshine outside, laughing so hard it hurt.

Frannie and Stephen stuffed their block party beers in a cooler on Frannie's porch next door once Frannie got home from work. Frannie, still in his uniform, sat his stereo speakers on the windowsill and let me DJ with Cecilia's records as they shot shit and drank beers. It was after four. The sun was high, bright, and hot. The beer cans they squeezed left rings on their shorts. Neighbors were either inside houses, fans blowing, lights off, or they were outside sweating, setting up picnic benches, and throwing red meat over black grills. The block was closed off with yellow police barricades, and all the cars were parked around the corner. Kids took advantage, chasing each other all over the place without having to keep eyes and ears peeled for wheels.

Stephen and Frannie chucked empties in a bucket at the same time.

"Stephen, is that your second beer already?" asked Frannie.

"Yup," he said.

"Me too," admitted Frannie. "Gonna be a long day."

They opened new beers and laughed. Down at one end of the block, a couple dads pulled back the barricades to let in a big fucking truck with a ball crawl, dunk tank, and mini Ferris wheel. As the men set shit up on the street, we laughed at all the ass cracks hanging out of shorts, the Malo tune "Suavecito" spinning on the turntable.

"Jesus," said Stephen. "Tucking in shirts should be law around here."

"That'll be you someday," Frannie told him. "Married, living on the street, sun reflecting the sweat off your fat exposed ass as younger wise guys point and laugh."

"That's cool. I'll be married long before my ass gets fat, though," said Stephen, smiling, pulling a box from his pocket, and popping it open. Frannie spit out beer.

"What the fuck is that?" asked Frannie.

"A ring," said Stephen, like Frannie was dumb for asking that.

"An *engagement* ring?"

"Yup."

"Who's it for?" asked Frannie.

"Shut up, asshole. Megan," said Stephen.

"Megan O'Drain?"

"Yeah, genius. Megan, my girlfriend. Sun and beer already getting to you?"

"No, I'm just a little shocked."

"Relax. I'm the one asking," said Stephen.

"Can I hold it?" asked Frannie.

Stephen chucked him the ring without the box.

"Careful, asshole," warned Frannie. "How much did this cost?"

"Hundred bucks," said Stephen.

"Damn. That's cheap," Frannie told him.

"Zirconia."

"Oh. When will you propose? Where? How?"

"Tonight. Right here. I'll sing to her in front of everybody, then ask."

"You serious? Like Daddy asked Mommy?"

Stephen laughed. "Nah. I'm just popping the question, plain and simple."

"The shit'll hit the fan with Daddy," said Frannie. "You should probably elope."

"He'll be fine," scoffed Stephen. "We won't marry anytime soon anyway."

"What?" asked Frannie. "Then why propose? Just wait."

"Can't. I love her. I want her to know, today, now. Ain't waiting for that."

"I never thought a younger brother would propose before I did," said Frannie.

"Frannie, you haven't even had a steady girlfriend," said Stephen.

"Sure, but that don't make my initial statement any less true," answered Frannie, before they both laughed. "Besides, I got my own romantic surprise planned tonight," he confessed, his smile heading south, his face turning nervous.

"You proposing to St. Joan of Arc on the Sullivans' front lawn?" joked Stephen.

"No wedding plans. I'm gonna ask Jeannie James out on a date," said Frannie.

"Jeannie James? Ain't she dating that dude Ace?"

"Yeah, she is."

"And you're asking her out?"

"Why not? She's only dating him."

Stephen laughed. "Fair enough. How many more beers will you need to ask?"

"Ten to fourteen," laughed Frannie, a nervous knee jumping. "What about you?"

"I'd ask right now," answered Stephen.

"Good luck with her, pal," said Frannie, looking down at the ring he still held.

"Yeah, you too," said Stephen, also staring at the ring.

Francis Junior, still in his uniform, stepped out onto the Toohey porch, shoving the door closed on Gwen Flaggart as she attacked him from the living room. His face was happy and nervous at the same time, pleased to see his three boys together, wanting to get in on the action, but not sure we felt the same.

"Yo," he said.

"Yo."

"Yo."

"Yo."

"Early start with the beers, ain't it?" he asked Stephen and Frannie.

"It's a block party," answered Stephen.

"I'm only kidding. So long as you don't miss football tomorrow is all I care about." A weird pause followed. "I'm not walking in on anything, am I?"

"Not really," I said. "Stephen just showed us the ring he bought for Megan."

Frannie spit beer. Stephen laughed.

"Sure, he did, Henry." Francis Junior smiled.

He looked across St. Patrick Street, starting high at the houses on the hills, where fat fucks flipped burgers and yelled at wives for hot sauce and cold beers. Then he looked at the saint statues, all getting green helium balloons to hold from Cece Toohey, who ran across lawns with a bunch in her hands. Finally he checked out the street, where little kids watched impatiently as fellas with tools worked on the rusted, rented rides.

"A ring." Francis Junior laughed. "You'd have to be insane or insanely optimistic to come from my house and get married."

"Daddy," said Cece, back from her mission, "I just taped balloons in all the saints' hands on the street. So now they all look like they're holding balloons."

"I see," said Francis Junior.

"All the balloons are green," she said.

"I know," he said, "they look beautiful."

"Green is my new favorite color," said Cece. "Henry's too. But he always liked it."

"That so?" he asked, picking her up, opening the door, starting inside.

"Henry says green is best because it's the color of grass and trees. Henry says rain and sunshine help make everything green. I like sun better. Rain kind of blows."

The door closed. Us brothers smiled, warmed by Cece and her sunshine.

By the time the sun turned tail and ran from the City of Brotherly Love and its block parties here, there, and everywhere, St. Patrick Street was alive, full of bright lights and shadows. The lights came from the carny rides the kids rode into the ground.

A drunk clown sat in the dunk tank, calling fellas rag arms, begging them to hit the fucking bull's-eye with the beat-up softball and send him swimming in the cold water he wished was beer beneath him. Strobe lights glowed from the DJ table, where a bald fuck spun Motown. On the lawns, parents sat at picnic tables, wives on husbands' laps, talking fast about old tunes and favorite corners where they hung as kids, covered by shadows thrown by their own houses. There weren't any outbursts or bullshit like that, just tables crowded with smiling faces squeezed between balloon-holding saints reaching out for the street, where little kids sat on curbs holding punks and sparklers, wearing neon green necklaces and bracelets, chasing each other in circles to blow off steam.

I played touch football on the street: me, Bobby James, and Harry versus Cece, Archie, and Grace. Stephen steady quarterbacked my team, Megan theirs. The game stayed tied nothing–nothing the whole time because the sun was gone, the street lights blew, and we used traitor Bobby James's blue-silver Cowboys ball. Nobody could catch anything, so the game went like this: Stephen threw the ball off four heads on our team, and Megan did the same with them. It was fun, though, and nobody gave a fuck. We counted steps, ran crisscrosses and buttonhooks, and pushed off whoever covered us.

Bobby James and Archie covered each other. Both claimed to be the fastest man alive, which meant as soon as Stephen or Megan said *Hut,* they sprinted down the street all the way up the Ave, never looking back. Cece and Harry matched up. Cece fixed her ponytails the whole time, and Harry tripped and scuffed his kneepads every ten steps. I played against Grace. She was tough to guard, since I kept getting her cigarette smoke in my eyes. Then on offense she held my shirt and kicked my shins. This didn't do anything for my boner, still a pup at that time.

At one point between two plays, parents at tables cheered. Frannie walked down to Stephen, holding two beers, looking serious. The DJ announced that Jeannie James and her boyfriend

Ace just got engaged. The parents cheered more. The DJ played "Give Me Just a Little More Time" by the Chairmen of the Board. Jeannie and Ace kissed while Frannie watched them, Stephen watched Frannie, and I watched my brothers.

"You all right?" asked Stephen, holding the ball.

"Yeah, it's cool," Frannie said, scuffing the street with a sneak, swigging a beer.

"Frannie, why are you down about Jeannie James?" asked Megan. "Oh. Sorry, pal."

"Look, I'm fine, really," insisted Frannie softly.

"Good," said Megan. "Plenty of hot chicks out there for a handsome dude like you. Stevie Wonder, I hope you propose to me someday."

"Keep hoping, sister. Keep wishing on a star." Stephen laughed.

He grabbed Frannie by the waist and sang "When You Wish Upon a Star" for a quick slow dance. Everybody laughed and grabbed partners: me and Grace; Cece and Archie; Megan, Bobby James, and Harry. After we finished, Megan said, "Archie, let's roll, we have to get to Daddy's thing."

"What thing?" he asked, pouting.

"His union beef and beer," she told him.

"I don't want to go."

"It's only for an hour. C'mon, the trolley'll be at the corner in a couple minutes."

"Aw, man, I hate the fucking trolley."

"We only have to take it there. Daddy's driving us back. Now c'mon," she said.

"One more play, Meg, OK?" begged Archie.

"Fine," said Megan. "Our ball, right? Frannie, you know any last-second plays?"

"Yeah, I got one," said Frannie. "Huddle up."

In the huddle, Frannie whispered and pointed at us a couple times. Before they snapped, Frannie moved down the street and hung half on, half off the curb. Megan shouted *Hut*. Grace kneed me in the nuts. I dropped. Cece snapped Harry's goggles. He fell and cried. Archie ran Jamesy into Frannie, who picked him off the ground upside-down. Megan lobbed the ball to Cece, who ran it ten feet and flipped it to Grace, who ran it five more and flipped it to Archie, who burned for the end zone and the win, then came back, spiked the ball, and did the funky chicken. His teammates jumped on his head to whoop while we bellyached, everybody laughing. The DJ played "Ooh, Baby Baby" by Smokey Robinson and the Miracles. Parents walked down to the street to slow-dance, everybody buzzing about the engagement. Stephen put his arm around Frannie.

"Is it still OK if I ask Megan?" he asked.

"You better," said Frannie, sad but smiling.

They walked back to our picnic table, laughing. The rides were stopped for the night but still glowing with lights. The clown snored drunk in the dunk tank, dreaming of better gigs in smaller shoes. The parents swayed slow as summer trees. Grace tickled Cece by the curb and I felt something warm for her. Megan walked Archie by the hand up the street to the trolley. Archie ran in place, his hand in hers, retelling his racing battles with Bobby James. Megan laughed and popped her gum. She pulled her hand away and chased him up the block. They turned the corner and disappeared into the dark.

By midnight, the block party turned sloppy, and parents moved from picnic tables to porches, closer to their living rooms, where sofas looked better with every sip of suds. Doors opened and shut a lot. The same oldies played by the DJ, who packed up and left (and got booed), now crackled out of transistors on porches. Cars and trolleys hummed and passed left and right up on the Ave. St. Patrick Street was quieter but not quiet.

Us kids stayed near the street after the DJ left, killing the roaches that came out every night. The roaches were big motherfuckers, and it took some balls even to step on one, unless your name's Grace, who stubbed out smokes on their shells and said *See you in hell*. After a while, though, we got bored, gave up on the roaches, and headed for the Toohey porch, where my parents sat with Frannie, Stephen, Mrs. McClain, and the Cooneys. Bombed, they comforted Frannie.

"The important thing was you tried, Frannie," said Mrs. McC, cross-eyed.

"I didn't try. He proposed before I could ask her out," answered Frannie, staring at his can like he was a plant professor looking for fucking molds and spores inside.

"OK, so you almost tried is the important thing," she said.

"Can't even say I almost tried. I was planning on waiting until about now."

"OK, so you got within two hours of almost trying," said Mrs. McClain.

Everybody laughed, even Frannie.

"I hope Jeannie's happy, that's all," he said.

"Wait, did he say Jeannie? Jeannie who?" asked Bobby James.

"Your sister, dummy. Frannie was gonna ask her out tonight," said Cecilia.

Bobby James laughed at Frannie. Stephen jumped off the porch, gave him a wedgie, and attached his underpants to St. Valentine's praying hands. Cecilia grabbed a camera and took a picture while Jamesy flipped her the finger.

"Don't sweat it, you'll be in love again before you know it," said Francis Junior.

"Then you'll hate the bitch, then you'll love her again. Donna, is Bernie asleep over there?" Cecilia asked Mrs. Cooney about her husband, who sat straight in a chair, his head back, his mouth open.

"He's passed out, not asleep," said Mrs. Cooney, disgusted.

"You want Fran and Frannie to carry him home?" asked Cecilia.

"Not really. I'd rather you just left him there," said Mrs. Cooney. "Only problem is our toilet just broke an hour ago. Sounds like it's gonna overflow."

"I can send Fran over to fix it for you," offered Cecilia.

"Right now?" asked Mrs. Cooney.

"Yeah, right now. Fran, you'll go over there and help Donna, won't you?"

"Yeah, sure." He looked over at Mrs. Cooney, who was already watching him.

"Thanks. That'd be nice," said Mrs. Cooney. They walked up the street slowly, talking and laughing, and slipped inside her front door as Mr. Cooney snored.

"Jeannie James is getting married," said Mrs. McC to everybody. "Don't I feel old? I remember her running around in a diaper and no shirt."

"Me too," said Cecilia. "You remember when she was six and went over her bike bars and cracked her front teeth on the curb?"

"I do," said Mrs. McC. "Didn't one boy's bike bang hers from behind?"

"That would have been my bike," said Frannie, embarrassed. Cecilia and Shirley McClain laughed. "I didn't mean to hit her," he said. "I was trying to catch up to her."

"Mission accomplished, kid," said Cecilia, her hand on his face. "So when are they getting married? They mention a date?"

"Somebody said this time next year," Mrs. McClain told her.

"Ace was so nervous asking," said Cecilia. "He shook. You notice that, Shirley?"

"Yeah, I saw that. It was still nice to watch anyway," said Mrs. McClain.

"I know," Cecilia agreed. "I love seeing somebody propose. It always puts me right in a good mood, know what I mean? Reminds me of when Fran proposed. I feel young and in love again. Or almost young and in love again."

"Yeah, me too, same thing. Mr. McClain was even worse than Ace."

"Really?" asked Cecilia. "He always seemed collected."

"He was. Except when he proposed."

"Where'd he do it?" asked Cecilia.

"At a restaurant," said Mrs. McClain.

"Really? Around here?"

"Nah, downtown. A Spanish place called Consuela's on Ninth and Arch."

"Never heard of it," said Cecilia.

"It ain't there no more," said Mrs. McClain. "It's two stores now, a pawn shop and dollar store. It was a big restaurant, real dark except for red candles on tables, with that whole mariachi band deal. Mr. McClain proposed while the band played at our table. He shook and stuttered. I was about to shout over the band for a doctor when he pulled the ring out and dropped it in my cream of broccoli soup."

"Get outta here," gushed Cecilia. "No, he didn't."

"Yes, he did. When he slipped it on my finger it had soup all over it. You couldn't even see the stone. I didn't care, though. It was the most beautiful thing I ever seen, broccoli cream and all. God, that Bernie Cooney can snore. Any way to turn him off?"

"We could kill him," said Cecilia.

"I think Donna'd like that," said Mrs. McClain. "They don't seem to get along."

"Yeah, they bickered all night tonight."

"I noticed," Mrs. McClain agreed. "I heard he treats her bad."

"Does he hit her?" asked Cecilia.

"I just heard that he's bad to her and their son. He yells all the time."

"Ralph's their boy, right?" said Cecilia. "That little guy? He gives me the creeps."

"Yeah," said Mrs. McC, "but it all starts right here with Sleeping Beauty."

"That's a shame. Donna's really cute," said Cecilia. "She could get lots of men."

"I agree," said Mrs. McClain. "How'd yours pop the question?"

"We drove to the river up by New Hope, then he sang 'Beyond the Sea' to me."

"Wow, that must have surprised you."

"Nah, I knew it was coming." Cecilia laughed.

"You knew?" asked Mrs. McClain.

"Yeah. I was pregnant with this jackass right here," she said, pointing to Frannie. "I played dumb, though. He never knew the difference. Quiet, here he comes."

Francis Junior returned, leaned over the railing, and reached into Frannie's cooler.

"Last beer here," he said. "What'd I miss?"

"We were just talking about you, Romeo," said Cecilia.

"What?" he asked, spilling some beer.

"I was telling Shirley here about the night you proposed," said Cecilia.

"Oh. Shirley, she had no idea," he bragged.

The broads laughed. Mrs. McC looked at her house across the street, maybe for her husband. Frannie smiled sadly. Stephen smiled happily. Us kids stupidly laughed, not knowing why, not that we ever do when we laugh with our parents, especially about love.

"Maybe now'd be a good time to let you folks in on a secret," said Stephen, winking at me. He reached into his pocket, pulled out the ring box, and held it in the air.

"That for me?" asked Mrs. McC.

"No, but I didn't know you were interested," he said.

"Holy fucking shit, Stephen," said Cecilia. "How'd you pay for that?"

"Relax, Ma, it's a zirconia," he said. "I'll buy a real one when I got money later."

Francis Junior sat still, staring at the ring as everybody else passed it around.

"What's the problem, Dad?" asked Stephen.

"You're *proposing marriage* to Megan?" asked Francis Junior.

"Yeah," answered Stephen, cheerful but scared.

"So you're getting married?"

"Well not right—"

"You're not getting married," snapped Francis Junior. "You're seventeen."

"That's old enough to ask," said Stephen. "You were—"

"Don't tell me what I was, Stephen," yelled Francis Junior. "Give me the ring. Cecilia, give me that ring right now," he said, yanking it from her and chucking it in the street, now quiet. *Ping-ping-ping*, it went.

Stephen jumped for Francis Junior but Frannie was ready and grabbed him. They flew over the porch railing into the grass, by us kids, who parted fast to let them fall. Stephen tried to get back up the steps to Francis Junior—Frannie held him off—and called him a fucking jerk-off, then turned for the street, where he looked for the ring on his hands and knees, the rest of us scared and silent. Francis Junior launched into a loud speech he couldn't stop, a flood of words that gushed like a sewer drain. *I got married young and dumb. I wished I got the chance to play college ball. But no, I got married without no money. I hate my job and life. I got unpaid pills out my ass, blisters on my hands, arthritis in my knees. You're not gonna fuck up your chance. I never got one.*

Folks came outside of their houses to see who was screaming and tell them to shut the fuck up. Stephen found the ring, blew on it, and held it up in the streetlight. Then the crash happened on the corner. The noise hurt my ears and my hairs stood up. Everybody ran up the block to the Ave, the quiet after the crash making our feet sound like a hailstorm pounding on a tin roof.

Two cars were wrecked and turned over. One was a red muscle car, on fire on the church steps, five feet from the front doors, shooting flames into the sky, looking like a metal bonfire set by God to protect his place. The other car belonged to the O'Drains, a green station wagon with wood panels. It sat on its right side no more than a foot from Paul Donohue's front door. Archie laid on the sidewalk, his legs pinned under the car, his arms stretched like Christ on the Cross. He was out cold, no cuts or blood anywhere, just his little legs under that heavy car. Mrs. O'Drain crawled on the Ave whimpering, her face a bloody mess. Cecilia ran to her as sirens screamed closer. Mr. O'Drain climbed out of the driver-side window, the car still on its side in the air, and fell. He didn't get a scratch besides a scuff on his pants when he fell out the car. When he got up he licked his fingertips to rub out the pants scuff in his knee, not noticing his bloody wife crawling ten feet away or his son under the car. I watched everything excited—not happy excited—but scared like it was a horror movie, until I looked across the street and saw Stephen Toohey, picking up Megan's bloody body. I puked, fell on my ass, and stayed down there, staring at Stephen, who stayed calm, ignored the screaming sirens and neighbors, and laid her down on an old man's Paul Donohue's jacket like a nurse laying a newborn baby in a crib. The ring box fell out of his pocket on the ground by the jacket. He picked it up and put it back, carefully. I don't remember anything that night after that. Next morning, I watched Stephen leave the house in a hurry. He dropped the ring box again, on our steps, picked it up, calm and quick, and walked up the Ave to sell it back to Diviny's jewelry store where he bought it, a couple doors down from Paul Donohue's, fifteen feet from the crash. The ring's still there at Diviny's for a hundred fucking bucks. I figure buying it back from them might bring Stephen back to us. It's worth five fucking Harry Curran twenties to find out.

14

The O'Drain house stands out on St. Patrick Street. Their tall wild grass has no decorations, and St. Sebastian lays on his side like somebody shanked him and left him for dead. The front porch is bare, no welcome mat, no barbecue grill, no Big Wheels. Their plain black mailbox never gets mail, and their plain white door hardly ever opens. I take a breath. Tough stuff, this joint. I knock. No answer. I knock again harder but not impatient. Finally, a hundred locks click. The door swings open: it's Mrs. O'Drain, crisscross scars on her face, deep blue eyes, big lips, red hair, high cheekbones, dancer legs, and perky B cups. Even with the scars, she's a total seafood-Dumpster candidate. Not that she knows it. Since the crash, she only looks at you once quick when she first sees you, then not again.

"Hello," she says, like she's never seen me before.

"Hi, Mrs. O'Drain," I say. "My mom sent me over to get Archie."

"Your mom?" she asks.

"Yeah, my mom. Cecilia," I say, softly.

"Oh, right, Cecilia. I'm sorry. Come in."

The house is musty but not dirty, with closed windows and blinds, the AC running full blast, the only light coming from the

TV. Archie sits in his chair, three inches from the screen, where big-haired politicians argue from chairs with cushions.

"Yo," he says, without looking up from the boob tube.

"Yo," I call back, "you ready to go, handsome?"

"Handsome? You bring a mirror?" he busts.

"I was calling you handsome. It was a joke, though," I say, winking at Mrs. O'Drain, who sits on the sofa's edge and stares at her hands. She was pals with Cecilia before the crash. Summers, they talked together on porch swings, whispering and laughing a lot. Now they just whisper, and it's mostly Cecilia, and they're only together at the O'Drains' front door when Cecilia picks Archie up or drops him off.

"What? Did you say something?" Mrs. O'Drain asks, confused.

"Yeah, to Archie," I say. "My mom told me to make sure he brings his suit."

No answer from Archie's mom.

"Yeah, I need his suit," I tell her.

"What? Oh, right. I'll get it," she says, shivering from the air conditioner's cold wind and moving nervously for the suit, which is wrapped in plastic and draped on a chair.

"I ain't wearing that." Archie pouts.

She leaves the suit, walks back to her seat on the sofa, sits down. I step in to help.

"Yeah, you are," I tell him.

"No, I'm not."

"Yeah, you are."

"No, I'm not."

"No, you're not."

"Can't fool me with that one," says Archie. "I watch Bugs Bunny."

"What if I beg you?" I ask.

"Then maybe. Give it a shot," he says.

I fall to my knees. "Archie, will you please wear that suit? Also I love you and want to have your baby. Will you marry me?"

He laughs. "Now I got two Tooheys asking me to marry them."

"Cece asked you to marry her?" I say.

"Sort of, except Cece don't ask. Cece *tells*," he says.

"That's your fault, you skirt," I say, face-to-face with him, me still on my knees.

"Yeah, well, I'm ready, Henry."

"Cool," I say. "Let's hit the road."

I grab the suit off the chair quickly, looking to get out of there before Mr. O'Drain shows up. Fuck, too late. Here he comes down the stairs. He's a small skinny fella, five-six, a buck forty maybe, with a brown mustache and nice winged hair that went white the week after the crash. Before Megan died, he was a roofing union bigshot. He got on the news sometimes during strike shit, wearing sharp suits, and talking quietly but meaning business. Now he wears blue boxers and white T-shirts, stutters, and never makes sense.

"Hhhhello, Ssstephen," he says to me.

"That's Henry, Dad," Archie tells him.

"You sssstill pppplay fffffootbbbball, Ssstephen?" asks Mr. O'Drain, oblivious.

"This is Henry Toohey, Dad. *Henry*. Tell him, Ma. Ma? Ma!"

A clock on the wall rings the hour. Both of Archie's parents jump.

"What, honey?" she asks.

"Daddy keeps calling Henry Stephen," complains Archie.

"Oh, Archie, behave," she says, like a robot repeating something a TV mom says.

"Anyway, HENRY here is taking me to that wedding," says Archie. "OK?"

No reply. We start for the door.

"A wedding?" asks Mrs. O'Drain. "I didn't hear about a wedding."

"You're going. I'm meeting you there, remember, Ma?" he asks, patiently, not mad.

"Oh, right," she says, frowning, trying to remember.

"OK, 'bye," says Archie. "C'mon, Henry."

"Who's Henry?" asks Mr. O'Drain.

I lift Archie out of his chair and carry him through the door down to the sidewalk, where I sit him on the bottom step. I walk back up to get his chair. Last, I grab his suit from the floor by the door. Inside, Mr. O'Drain pours himself a drink and downs it in one shaky gulp. Mrs. O'Drain looks around and asks, "Where's Archie?" to nobody. I leave the house, stand behind Archie, and wrap my hands around his chair handles, which feel just like a bike's. He leans his head back and looks straight up at the sky.

"The sun's warm today," he says. "It feels good on my face."

"Yeah, it does feel good," I agree.

We walk.

Harry Curran's confused.

"Why would you ask if I'm having trouble breathing?" he asks me.

"Seems like your outfit might be fucking with the flow of circulation," I say, shooting Archie a funny look, both of us laughing. Harry's gym suit today is powder blue and tight: V-neck shirt, short shorts, both trimmed in white; striped tube socks yanked to the kneecaps; goggles dangling at the neck.

"Oh, I get it. The outfit. Shows how little you know about ergonomics."

"Does ergonomics mean 'shows nut sack'?" I ask.

"No," says Archie, "it means 'look at my ass, fellas.'"

"Funny," says Harry. "We should get moving. Jewelry store closes early today."

"We gotta get Bobby James first," I tell him.

"Do we have to?" complains Harry. "Where's he at anyway?"

"Right there on his lawn," I say, "scooping dog shits."

"Oh, yeah."

We laugh and walk the six steps to his lawn. Right off the bat, Jamesy, who gossips like a girl sometimes, starts with whoppers about last night's fight as he holds a Pop-Tart and scoops Beauregard's poops, shoveling shit two ways.

"Ralph Cooney had a rifle up at Tack Park last night," he tells us.

Inside, bridal party broads fly around in panics; the phone rings every ten seconds.

"Who told you that?" I ask, not believing and letting him know that.

"Ralph told me," he says.

Before I reply, Mrs. James, fifty-five, B cups, gold glasses, comes to the door.

"Bobby James," she says. "You scoop all Beauregard's shits yet?"

"I'm scooping them fast as I can, Ma. That OK with you?"

"If Ralph had a rifle, where was it?" I ask.

"How should I know?" answers Bobby. "He mentioned it afterwards."

"You'll never scoop all those shits if you keep talking, Robert," says his mom.

"Gimme a goddamn minute, Ma," he tells her.

"Where did you go after the fight?" I ask.

"We ended up at 7-Eleven," says Bobby, "until my dad chased us away, the fuck."

"Robert James, did you just call your *father* a *fuck?*" asks Mrs. James.

"No, I didn't," he lies. "Maybe you just need a hearing aid."

"Your dad was up at Tack Park last night," I tell him.

"Yeah, he told me he saw you, that you looked like you seen a ghost," says Bobby.

"Felt that way," I admit.

"A hearing aid? I'm still young enough to whip your ass," says Mrs. James.

"Look, I'm losing patience with you, Ma, I really am," says Bobby, biting the Pop-Tart he holds in the same hand as the doody bag. "Henry, those Fishtown fellas are in real bad shape.

Cardinal Krol read them last rites," he lies, dropping a dog bomb in the doody bag, dangerously close to the Pop-Tart.

On the street, beat-up American cars shoot smoke out of tailpipes. Kids on bikes and boards scatter for the sidewalk. Broads point hoses at flowers and yell *Slow down, jerk-off* at the cars, whose drivers flip them the finger. Harry stretches. I comb my hair. Archie stares straight ahead, no interest in fights between punks whose legs work.

"Was Grace at the 7-Eleven?" I ask, trying to sound (and comb) nonchalant.

"Nah, she went in," he tells me.

"Good," I say. "I was worried she left with Burke and Crump."

"Why were you worrying that?" asks Bobby.

"I don't know," I say. "She was all joking with them on the street after Freedom."

"Uh-oh," says Bobby. "Jealousy: not a good habit, Henry. You have to give women some room. You have to know how to handle them and talk to them."

"Robert, check for poopies under the hedge. Beau poos there," says Mrs. James.

"Go back inside and wax your mustache, Ma," says Bobby.

The door flies open. Mrs. James holds a broom like a spear and sprints down the steps for her son. Bobby James, ready, bounces on his toes like a boxer.

"Come on with that broom," he says. "I'll pull all those curlers out of your hair."

Mrs. James swings the broom at him like an ax but misses. Feeling cocky, Bobby dances funny but falls backwards on the grass. Oh, boy, good night. Now cornered, he blows a scared bubble. Mrs. James smiles, moving slow and steady.

"Time to pay the piper," she says, raising the broom for the kill.

Before she swings, Bobby throws the doody bag at her—Jesus H. Christ, I can't believe he just did that; no fucking class—and makes a break for it, slamming facefirst into their St. Aquinas statue and moaning, hurt. There's no escape now. Mrs. James drops the broom, picks up the shit bag, and beats him over the head with it until Francis Junior shows up with the mail.

"Morning, Joan," he says, handing her some letters. "All set for the wedding?"

"Morning, Fran," she answers, taking the letters. "Just about."

He looks at me. "Henry."

"Dad," I say.

"You're not involved in this, are you?" he asks.

"Nope. Just watching," I answer.

"OK, then, see you later."

"Right."

He walks away, head shaking, stuffing letters into boxes to the end of the block, then slipping inside the Cooneys' house as Mrs. Cooney holds the door for him. Mrs. James drops the doody bag on Bobby's chest and walks in the house. Before he moves the bag or gets up, she returns to the door.

"Robert, phone call. I think it's Margie Murphy next door," she says, pointing to Margie three feet away on her porch, twirling gum, a phone on her ear. Jamesy smiles, cocky, still laying on the lawn with the doody bag on his chest.

"I'll take it out here, please—see what I'm saying about broads, Toohey?"

"Hurry up," I say. "Don't forget we're going to the jewelry store, jerk-off."

"Jerk-off? Gimme five minutes. Look, Henry, there's your fiancée," says Bobby, pointing to Grace stepping out on her porch. "Go say hello or something."

He drops the doody bag in his trash can, then takes the phone off his mom to whisper sweet nothings to his girlfriend next door while his sister gets ready for marriage and a house on St. Patrick Street or one just like it.

Grace McClain has stepped out of her house wearing nothing but a big green Eagles T-shirt. Praise His Name! Hair messed, dark circles under her eyes, and yawning, she lights a smoke and walks down her steps to meet us on the sidewalk.

"Handsome Hank Toohey," she says, "how you doing?"

"Gorgeous Grace McClain," I answer. "I'm all right. How you doing?"

"Can't complain. Did Mrs. James just beat Bobby with a bag of dog shits?"

"She sure did," I say, smiling.

"There's a new one," says Grace. "Last week she broke a melon over his head."

"I know, I was there," I say. "You look beautiful today."

"Please, I just woke up," she says. "But fuck it. Why argue with a brainiac?"

"Exactly."

We smile big at each other, happy to be here together, joking under the sun, half a day past kissing under the moon.

"What happened to you last night after the fight, Hank?" she asks.

"Went home," I say.

"You finally leave the bench before the cops came?"

"Nah, I was still up there when the cops and ambulances came."

"Ambulances? More than one? You see the Fishtown dudes afterwards?"

"I don't want to talk about that bullshit," I answer, sounding mean and scared.

"OK, we don't have to," she says, her eyes going soft.

"You have fun before that?" I ask her.

She grins and blows out smoke. "Yeah, Freedom was fun."

"What about between Freedom and the playground?"

"What happened then, sport?"

"We made out behind the Dumpster, dummy," I say.

Harry and Archie shout *Yo* in protest and cover their ears.

"What the fuck, Hank. I was trying to be demure in front of your friends."

"Demure don't suit you," I say.

"Yeah, you're right," answers Grace, flicking her finished smoke at Harry, who shrieks. "How come you never call me?" she asks, pointing to Jamesy and Margie, on their porches and talking to each other on the phone, an arm's length apart.

"I'm more a house call kind of guy," I say.

"House calls," she laughs. "Doctor Toohey. Nurse O'Drain, Nurse Curran."

"Who are you calling a nurse, you mental patient?" answers Archie.

"I'd be a male nurse. They make great money. Oh, Jesus, they're at it again," says Harry, talking about Bobby and Margie, leaning over their porch railings and making out, phones still on their ears, until both their moms come outside at the same time. Mrs. Murphy pulls Margie by the ear into her house. Mrs. James takes the phone from Bobby James and kicks him on the ass down his steps. He walks backwards to us.

"I'm calling child welfare on you," he shouts.

"Do I smell dog shit on your shirt?" asks Grace.

We all crack up, except for Bobby James.

"Up yours, McClain," he says. "Uh-oh. Henry, I think your dad's in the middle of something up the street."

At the Cooney house, Francis Junior points a finger and barks inside their door. Mrs. Cooney comes out, puts her hands on his chest, and pushes him down the steps as he points and talks more. He finally walks away and up to Paul Donohue's. When he's gone, Ralph comes outside and stands stiff as a board. She hisses in his face for a couple minutes, then sends him back in the house and runs up the Ave after Francis Junior.

"Hank, wake up," Grace says, snapping fingers in my face.

"What?" I ask.

"You were staring up the street in a daze."

"I was?"

"Yeah, you were. Like the old man was getting you down."

"Oh. Really?" I say.

"Yeah. Don't let him," she tells me, firm but soft.

"I won't," I answer, meaning it, feeling better, and loving her more.

"Good. Now, what are you doing with yourself before the wedding today?"

"This and that," I say, smiling.

"This and that. Well, don't let me hold you up. Get moving," she says, stubbing out a smoke on her railing, then walking back inside her house, head and ass shaking.

My kingdom for some boner relief.

Francis Toohey and Donna Cooney argue on the corner of the Ave at St. Patrick, as me, Bobby, Harry, and Archie hide behind the wall of Paul Donohue's and watch them. We spotted them on the way to Diviny's jewelry store and ducked back to St. Pat.

"I didn't mean to call him that, Donna," says Francis Junior. "But what do you want me to do? He won't let us alone. He's nuts. What if he tells your husband?"

"He won't tell him nothing, Fran," says Mrs. Cooney.

"What if he does? What if he did?" asks Francis, frantic.

"We'd both be dead already," she says, matter-of-fact.

"Oh, that's a relief. Your crazy son's on our ass and your husband might kill us."

"C'mon, Fran. You got your own problem son. Your wife might kill us first."

"My son's different," says Francis Junior. "Don't even compare them. Mine was happy and going places before his girlfriend died. Yours has always been nuts."

There's a pause here, after that last sentence, which was a slap.

"Donna, I'm sorry," he says. "I didn't mean that."

"He's confused, angry," she says. "We need to come clean, get this out in the open. Everybody besides Bernie knows anyway. Let's do the right thing and admit it."

"What?" he gasps. "You're kidding, right?"

"No. I say we stop sneaking around and tell people how we feel."

"What do you think's going on, Donna? What *are* we feeling?"

"I'm in love with you, Fran," she blurts.

"Oh, Jesus," he says, the prick.

"What the fuck does *that* mean?" she snaps. " 'Oh, Jesus'?"

"Love, Donna? Ain't that dramatic? Look, maybe we should just end this."

"Perfect. You're such a coward. You're scared of that bitch wife you don't love."

"You got it all wrong, Donna. I don't know where you got the impression that—"

"Don't even say it, Fran. I got it. You love your wife. I'm just there to fuck."

"It ain't like—"

"The fuck it isn't," she says. "Don't lie to *me*. You got *Cecilia* for that."

"OK, fine, whatever," he says. "I guess that's it then."

"Yeah, I guess so," she says, tears starting.

"Go take care of your son, Donna," says Francis Junior, gentle now.

"Yeah, you too."

She wheels back to St. Pat fast and almost walks into me. We're face-to-face.

"Hi, Henry, how you doing?" she asks, wiping her wet eyes, trying to sound cheerful, and when she does this, I realize she loves my dad, who just broke her heart.

"Hi, Mrs. Cooney. You all right?" I ask, awkward.

"Never better," she answers, hurrying back to her house, waving me off. We turn the corner. Francis Junior leans against his Jeep, drinking water out of a jug. I walk past him.

"Henry, where you going?" he asks.

"Nowhere that'd interest you," I tell him, angry, turning toward the jewelry store and the ring that'll win me the girl I'll treat right forever. "Least not till tonight," I add, before mumbling, "hopefully."

15

Ron Diviny, seventy-three, slick gray hair, turkey neck, packing heat, jumps at the camera.

"Stop right there," he says, pointing a gun. "Hands up so my wife can frisk you."

His wife, Judith, who looks like him in a wig and muumuu, frisks the camera.

"He's clean," she says.

"Good thing or I'da plugged him. You looking for some jewelry, punk? Then Diviny's is your store for the most divine diamonds on the planet. We got jewelry for every special occasion: engagements, anniversaries, weddings. We also create arrangements for less traditional celebrations such as papal coronations and funerals. So come to Diviny's, on Frankford Ave at St. Patrick Street, but leave the guns and funny business behind, unless you got a death wish, cowboy, because I ain't afraid to die. Are you?" he says before he pulls the pin back on the gun, spins to the side, and shoots off rounds at a black mannequin until the bullets spell out LOWEST PRICES IN TOWN.

"Now that's a commercial," says Mr. Diviny, pointing to the TV on his counter with his gun, which he never puts the fuck down. Doesn't scare us, though. We—me, Harry, Bobby, and Archie—just duck as he waves it and stand when he stops. No big deal. Just have to watch the loony bastard.

"Ronald, be careful with that thing," says Mrs. Diviny, who has raisin tits to go with her prune face. "You shot out the window last week, don't forget."

"Be quiet, we're not supposed to talk about that before the trial. Besides, my gun, my store. People don't like it, they can hit the bricks," he yells, pointing the gun over our heads out the door. We duck. He lowers it—we stand up—and leafs through a Notre Dame clothes catalog, using the gun nose to flip pages.

Harry clears his throat. "We're here to pick up a ring."

"Notre Dame," says Mr. Diviny, still looking at the catalog, not hearing Harry. "The *fighting* Irish. You boys Irish fans?" he asks, pointing the gun at us.

"Hell, yeah," I say.

"You betcha," says Bobby.

"Are we ever," agrees Archie.

"Damn straight," says Harry.

"Good," he says, squinting at us suspiciously. "Judith, why are we still watching the boob tube? My commercial's over. Play a record."

Mrs. Diviny runs to the stereo. High harmonies fill the store.

"The Four Freshmen," I say. "You like the Beach Boys, Mr. Diviny?"

"The Beach Boys were left-wing hippie faggots who sang about commie bullshit like surfing," he says. "Fidel Castro invented surfing to lure our boys in the water to blow them out of it, then storm ashore, the bearded prick. Fidel Castro. I'd love to cut his throat. Now why the hell are you in my store? We don't sell gumdrops and baseball cards."

Harry pulls out his hundred-dollar bill. The needle scratches across the record. Mr. Diviny puts his gun away. His wife offers us iced teas and Tastykakes on a tray.

"OK, I remember now," he says. "You ordered the ring last

week. Said it was for your mom from your dad, right? What did he do, flush her old one down the shitter?" He laughs like nobody ever told a better joke. "She won't even know this one's a zirconia. Joan, do we have that ring ready?"

"Right here, Ronald," she says, bringing over some piece of shit that's not my ring.

"That ain't the one," I tell them.

"What?" he asks. "You picked the hundred-dollar deluxe zirconia."

"I picked *that* one," I say, pointing to Megan's ring, Stephen's ring, my ring, Grace's ring, still under the glass counter.

"Same exact rings, except the one you say you want is used. Are you starting trouble? Trying to be funny?" he asks, his thumb rubbing the gun under the counter.

"I ain't starting shit," I say. "I want that ring. Get it and there's no trouble."

"All right," he says, "but you're not getting any money off because it's used."

"That's fine," I tell him, staring straight in his eyes, in no mood to be fucked with.

"Judith, put this one back, and get the other," he says.

She takes the bum ring away and puts the right one on the clear counter. We move closer. She opens the box with a snap. The ring and its yellow band and brown stone shine brighter than the more expensive bullshit under the glass below it.

"Can I hold it?" I ask.

"Long as your friend with the cash says it's OK," says Mr. Diviny.

"Go ahead, Henry," says Harry. "You like the thing?"

I stare at it, filled with love. I can't answer his question.

"This here's a quality zirconia," babbles Mr. Diviny. "I don't peddle junk jewelry since that investigation in 1981. You could cut glass and rob a jewelry store with this ring, but not mine because I'll blow your head off. The ring also comes with a ten-day warranty to protect your purchase."

I don't give a fuck and tune him out. Here's the ring I'll slip onto Grace's finger to pledge my love. Here's the ring that Stephen sold back when his girlfriend died. Here's the ring I'll hold after singing the song that Francis Junior sang to Cecilia for her love. When I'm done, Stephen'll be happy, they'll fall back in love. Things'll be better, for them, for Cece, for Frannie, for Grace, for me. Tonight I offer all that to all them with a lifetime guarantee. Fuck that ten-day bullshit.

"You know when me and Mrs. Diviny got engaged, I didn't buy a ring," says Mr. Diviny. "I just asked. Worked out for me both times. Didn't buy one then, get to sell them now. Life is beautiful."

"Oh, please," she says. "Spare them the cynic routine. Boys, Mr. Diviny proposed to me on July fourth, 1931, and he spent twice as much on fireworks as he would have on a ring. Ain't that right, Ron?"

"Who knows? I'm old. I can't remember my name most days, dear," he lies.

"Right, Ron," she says, shaking her head at him gently. "He took me out to a field in the middle of nowhere," she tells us. "A couple of his buddies hid in the woods, maybe fifty yards from us, with the fireworks. He told them to light everything at exactly nine P.M., at which point he'd propose. Ringing any bells now, Ron?"

"No, still drawing a blank," he answers, embarrassed by his sweet side.

"Sure you are," she says. "Anyhow, boys, he must've picked his two dumbest friends—not an easy pick—because when he got down on one knee and opened his mouth to ask, all these fireworks flew right at us in the field. Bet you remember now." She laughs as he rolls his eyes.

"OK, already," he admits. "You know I do."

"Those fireworks really came at us, didn't they?" she says, laughing harder now.

"Yes, Judith. It was like Iwo Jima."

She laughs even harder. "Iwo Jima is right. He proposed as we ran into the woods, bottle rockets and Roman candles hitting the trees behind us. I said yes, and we kissed behind a tree until the attack stopped ten minutes later. Here we are, fifty-three years later, still in love. Right, Ron?"

"If you say so, dear," he says.

"I say so."

Harry pays the bill, then puts his hand on my shoulder. Mr. Diviny presses a register button with his gun. The drawer opens. *Ching.* The trolley stops behind us on the Ave. *Squeak, clang.* Archie yawns. Bobby James blows a bubble. Mr. Diviny puts the bill into the cash drawer like a baby into a bassinet, then snaps the register shut. I slide the ring box into my pocket, my hand on top of it, feeling dizzy as we leave the store. Cars whoosh past us slow, like hearts beating, slow and steady.

Back on St. Patrick Street, Archie and Harry prepare for a wheelchair stunt jump using two cinder blocks and the Jameses' broken porch table as a ramp. Grace, still in her Eagles T-shirt, and Margie Murphy, dressed up in a matching summer shirt and shorts set, stand with us on the street for the jump.

The ramp now ready, roller skates, skateboards, and tricycles skid to stops. An excited quiet replaces the noise of play. All you can hear right now are show tunes blaring out of a couple houses, hissing lawn sprinklers, and pulled beer tabs, which signals noontime on St. Patrick Street better than any clock ever could. Harry pushes Archie off the curb into the street.

"How far back should we start?" he asks. "Should I jog or sprint?"

"I need something to jump first," says Archie.

I point to little kids sitting on the curb in organized rows.

"We could lay a few of those little bastards on their backs," I offer.

Margie bitches that using kids is too risky. Grace suggests

Archie's blue suit in the plastic wrap. Everybody agrees the suit'll do. Archie cleans his shades with his shirt.

"Harry," he says, "take me back to the Pinto with the trash bag back windshield."

"Which Pinto," asks Harry, "the yellow or green?"

"The yellow," says Archie. "We'll start from there. I'll need you to sprint."

Harry and Archie reach the Pinto. The rattrap of a ramp waits for them. The plastic wrap covering Archie's suit sparkles in rainbow colors under the sun, like an oil slick at a car shop. Archie licks a finger and raises it above his head, then fires a thumbs-up at Harry. Harry returns a thumb after stretching and retying his shoelaces. The takeoff is strong and clean. The chair's five feet from the ramp when we hear somebody's mom.

"Matthew! Matthew!"

Fuck. It's A-cups Mrs. Melinson, calling her nine-year-old son Matt (crew cut). Harry slows the chair to a stop. It won't do to have a mom catch a wheelchair jump in progress, so we all play it cool. Harry adjusts a wheel like a mechanic. I hide the ramp from Mrs. Melinson, smiling and combing, just like always, see?

"Matthew, it's time for your lunch," she says.

"OK, Ma, I'm coming," says Matt.

"Where's your sister Colleen? There she is. Colleen, you come too," says Mrs. Melinson, before she takes in the scene suspiciously. "You kids behaving out here?"

"Yes, Mrs. Melinson," everybody calls back.

"What's that behind you, Henry?" she asks.

"Nothing special," I tell her. "A tabletop, two cinder blocks."

"What are you doing with it?"

Harry jumps in. "Yo, Gina, how you doing?"

"Fine, Harry, how you doing?"

"Good thanks," he says. "Got a minute to talk about your lawn account?"

"Uh, can we do that later?" she asks, shifty. "I gotta feed these kids."

"No problem, Gina. We'll talk later." He winks at me as she disappears into her house. "She's behind on lawn payments. Now let's get this show going."

Archie and Harry drop back to the Pinto. Archie yells *Punch it.* Harry takes off. A cop car turns off Erdrick on to St. Patrick. I yell *Cop.* Harry stops the chair again. The crowd boos as me and Bobby James drag the table and blocks off the street to let the cop car pass. Mr. James drives the car, on duty two hours before his daughter's wedding. He stops near me.

"Yo, Henry, what's up?" he asks.

"Yo. Work today? You skipping the wedding?" I ask.

He leans toward me. "I wish I could. Where's Bobby James?"

"Hiding behind that car with his girlfriend," I say, pointing.

"His what? How did he get a girlfriend?" asks Mr. James.

"Don't ask me, I wouldn't date the kid," I answer.

"I heard my wife beat him with a doody bag today. We got three 911 calls for it."

"I can neither confirm nor deny that rumor," I say, playing.

Mr. James, a cool customer, laughs without making a sound.

"Fair enough," he says. "I don't wanna know anyway. Is his relationship serious? Maybe I can get rid of two freeloaders in one day."

Now I laugh. I like Mr. James.

"No chance. He has 'Lives with Mom for life' written all over him," I say.

"Henry, I'll shoot him first, I swear it," he says.

"Do it now, save some time and grief," I tell him.

"Maybe tomorrow." He laughs. "Good to see you're feeling better than last night."

"Yeah, I guess so," I say.

"Those boys are all OK," he tells me. "They went home."

"I heard."

"Listen, stay away from the playground for a while, though, all right?"

"Yeah, all right," I say.

"Is Harry wearing an aerobics outfit over there?" he asks, puzzled.

"You gotta ask him," I say. "I don't fucking know."

Mr. James rolls down the passenger-side window.

"Yo, Harry," he calls, "is that an aerobics outfit?"

"Yo, Rob," says Harry. "No."

"Looks like one. All right, kids, see you at the wedding. Oh, and by the way, when Archie cracks his head open, tell the dispatcher to send the paramedics, not me. I'd like to get something to eat before my daughter's wedding."

He pulls away. If he said what he said to make a point, we fucking missed it and reset the ramp before he even turns right on the Ave. The crowd revs up a third time. Harry and Archie sink back, then charge. This time there are no interruptions. Archie stares down the ramp like a navy pilot about to drop a load of lead on Ayatollah Khomeini's head. He'll hit that ramp 100 miles an hour, jump the sun laughing, and show all these pussies with better legs who has the biggest balls on the block.

Crash. Smash.

Life isn't always fair. Sometimes the good get punished while the wicked are rewarded. I don't know about you false-idol-following fools out there but us Catholics have the Pope's word that Big Boy will straighten all that shit out with a flamethrower on Judgment Day. Till then, though, you get the shaft most times, even if you don't deserve it. Like now, when me and Harry take a beating from Father S. Thomas Alminde, OSFS, in the church sacristy. We ran here from our houses wearing altar boy robes over our school uniforms, the standard altar boy outfit, even in summer. We tripped and fell over each other as we went into the sacristy, making a big thump and laughing our asses off.

When the glass door slammed behind us, it shattered. Father, who was counseling a single mom with nice tits, decided physical punishment was required. A priest collar, like a police badge, is a license to bully.

Since I'm smaller and lighter, Father lifts me off the ground by grabbing a tuft of my hair. Tears burn my eyes and I want to cut his throat for fucking with my hair but I keep quiet. You can't win against a priest. The best you can do is let him think he isn't hurting you. Harry isn't so good at this and weeps like a broad as Father slaps the top of his head with a fat ring turned into the palm of his hand.

"How many times must I tell my altar boys to *walk* with *quiet* dignity?" he asks.

The beating now over, Father drapes his arms around us. Harry's sobbing slows.

"Leave the hair be, Mr. Toohey," he says. "Your vanity is a spiritual weakness."

"Yes, Father," I answer.

"That means stop, Mr. Toohey," he says.

"Hold on, Father," I say, "one more time on each side."

"Put the comb away now," he orders.

"All right already, Father," I tell him.

"My two best altar boys," moans Father, "crashing through the sacristy doors like Satan's agents. Don't disappoint me like that again. My heart couldn't take it."

"Yes, Father," we say at the same time.

"Good. I trust you mean that. I hold a higher opinion of you two than most of the other animals. A priest gets to feeling like a zookeeper, not a spiritual leader."

"Good one, Father," says Harry.

"Don't patronize me, Curran. That was mildly funny observational humor at best."

"Amen," I say. Whoops.

"Excuse me, Mr. Toohey?" says Father.

"I'm sorry, Father? What did I say?" I ask, blinking once.

"I thought I heard you say amen," he tells me.

"Oh, that. I did. I was praying. Must have said the amen part out loud."

Father frowns, frustrated, beaten, because he has no choice but to believe me. Priests and nuns are always telling us to pray all the time. Why wouldn't I be praying, right?

"How's Stephen doing?" he asks.

"He's all right, I guess," I say.

"You haven't told your dad he talks to me, have you?"

"No, Father."

"And you haven't told him that your mom talks to me either, have you?"

"No."

"Good. They both resent your dad. What's your take on all that?"

"I don't know, Father," I say, breathing faster, the room hotter.

"Mr. Curran," says Father, "can you step outside a minute?"

"Yes, Father," says Harry, walking through the glass we broke.

"Talk to me, Henry," he says, watching me fidget and frown.

"They all kind of contribute to the mess," I say.

"How so?"

"Cecilia's moods change fast. She can laugh one minute, then scream the next. Francis Junior snaps when she snaps. Stephen can't get over Megan, so he drinks. Also, he hates Francis Junior for porking Mrs. Cooney behind Cecilia's back. Francis Junior porks Mrs. Cooney because he ain't happy to be married. Cecilia ain't happy to be married either, because she's raising four kids plus one in a wheelchair, she has no money to do it, and her husband porks another broad behind her back. Francis Junior says he fights Stephen because it's the only way to wake him up, but he's at least as mad because Stephen quit football, which was something he looked at like he was playing, not Stephen. It's a fucked-up situation, Father, a fucked-up situation, but I have it all under control," I tell him in one long fast blurt that comes out in ten seconds tops.

"It's all right, Mr. Toohey. I'm sure you do. Take a couple of deep breaths," he says, waiting for me to calm. "Mr. Curran, you can come back in now. Let's move to a better topic. How many broads'll be at this wedding today?"

"The head count is two hundred twenty-two, so I'd estimate one hundred eleven females, Father," says Harry.

"One hundred eleven women. I picked the wrong profession."

Father struts back to the rectory from the sacristy through a door. Sweet gig. Every building you need connects to the next by doors, so you never even have to go outside. You work one hour one day a week, then the rest of the time you swill wine, slap kids, squeeze tits, listen to family secrets and sin laundry lists, and zip around town in a red sports car. If there's a difference between Hugh Hefner and a Catholic priest, let me know, because I don't fucking see it. Don't let Father fool you into thinking otherwise.

A thousand-pound oak door separates the sacristy from the vestibule. The closer you get to God, the harder the doors are to open. The vestibule's a cross between an archeological dig, a dungeon, and a haunted house, and smells like incense, dust, and wine. Old creepy Catholic voodoo shit sits everywhere: a ten-inch statue of Jesus driving Satan from the desert; waxy boxes of blue and red candles; buttoned leather prayer books; tall broken crucifixes; kneelers; holy cards taped to walls; old priest vestments; pulpits; long matchboxes; cases of altar wine; and unblessed Communion wafers stacked in plastic packs of fifty. The vestibule surrounds the altar almost like headphones do a head: a dark skinny hallway connecting two rooms on either side. Down the hallway, there's a staircase that leads to a basement full of priest and penguin bones, if you ask Harry Curran, so don't. We never have to go to the hallway or other side anyway. We just stay in the vestibule's first room and fucking wait for Mass, which starts in half an hour.

I peek out of the vestibule door into the pews. The only people here are Frannie, Cece, and Cecilia, who always shows up early for church. Cecilia's into Mass. She makes the Sign of the Cross after Communion, belts out hymns real bad, shit like that. Most neighborhood moms are like that. The dads, on the other hand, fear that Beard Boy hates them as much as they hate Mass, so they wait outside until the last minute, yanking at tight collars on leisure suits, talking sports with all the other dads.

"*Yo, Henry,*" yells Cece, who spotted me.

Cecilia muzzles her. I wave, then go back to the vestibule, where Harry fidgets in his robe and nods toward an altar wine bottle.

"Ever drink that stuff before or after you serve a Mass?" he asks.

"Nope," I say.

"Me neither. You know Greg Kramer? He drank a bottle once before Mass."

"Yeah, he's good people." I laugh. "How close were you to the fight last night?"

"I was right in there," he says.

"So you saw them get beat?" I ask.

"Yeah, saw the whole thing, up close."

"Were you scared?"

"I don't know, really. It scares me today. But last night, I just watched," he says.

"You just watched? Didn't it piss you off?"

"It does now, but last night, no, I guess not. Happened real fast. No time."

"How can you say that? You weren't mad, you just watched. What the fuck. You didn't pull anybody off of them, you didn't run for help, you just stood there," I yell.

"Be quiet," says Harry. "You did the same thing, Henry."

"What? Fuck you I did," I say, quieter.

"Calm down, man. It wasn't your fault. You couldn't have stopped it if you tried," he says. "Look, let's change the subject. Did you kiss Grace last night?"

The beating leaves me, and I take my head off my hand and smile.

"You did," he says. "You must feel good about your chances tonight."

"I felt good about my chances before we kissed," I say.

"Was that your first time?"

"Yeah, that was the first time I kissed Grace."

"What about other girls?"

"Yes. That was the first time I kissed any girl, OK?"

"Was it hard?" he asks.

"Was *what* hard?" I say. "What the fuck does that mean?"

"You know, was kissing difficult?"

"Oh. I don't know. Couldn't tell you. Grace did all the work. Tasted like smokes."

"What's that like? Gross?" asks Harry.

"Nah, but it ain't real tasty either," I say. "I'll help her quit, though. She can't be smoking when she's pregnant."

"Damn right," says Harry.

We high-five, two mature motherfuckers talking knocked-up broads.

"How many people here now, Henry?"

I peek out again. Twenty minutes until Mass, and the joint is starting to jump. Francis Junior joins the other Tooheys in the pew, not counting Stephen. Bobby James stands in the back, wearing a tuxedo, and seating old ladies. He blows a bubble, salutes me, and drags a half-dead old coot beating his arm with a purse for moving too fast to a pew. I don't see Grace yet.

Cece yells again. *Yo, Henry over here.*

The Tooheys leap to shut her up and smile awkward at folks around them. *Sorry to startle you. Our other kids behave better. Look, that altar boy up there's ours.*

"It's crowded now," I tell Harry as I step back inside.

"Damn. Why do I get nerves before Mass?" says Harry.

The groom, Ace, walks into the vestibule, his hair winged and sprayed to my satisfaction, along with his best man and two other fellas in tuxes who got brush cuts and look like bulldogs. Bobby James, who is still in the back pinching retiree asses, rounds out the group as the ring broad.

"'Sup, Henry, Harry," says Ace, shaking our hands too hard and dabbing his forehead with a hanky while his boys pass altar wine back and forth quick till it's finished. Bobby James walks in, and they hand him the empty bottle. Father enters behind him.

"Señorita James, any left in there for me?" asks Father.

"Nah, it's kicked, Father," says Bobby.

"Fetch me another then. I need some fuel before the Mass. Who's the groom here? OK, I can see it's you slouched over that stool like a man with a bullet in his belly. That feeling'll get worse the longer you're married. That's why I became a *priest.* Thanks, Jamesy. Now, I get twenty-five bucks for weddings, and a tip triple that."

"Here you go, Padre," says the best man, forking over five twenties.

"I ain't a padre, hombre. I work north of the border. Listen, the midget's playing the organ out there. That's our cue. I hope the bridal party broads look better than last wedding. That was all heifers and toothpicks, nothing in between, where it belongs. Keep it together, son. No need to be nervous. You'll be divorced before you know it."

"Thank you, Father," says Ace.

"I'm only busting your balls, idiot."

"Oh."

"Speaking of balls," says Father. "I'm sweating mine off in this dress. Let's roll."

Ace gulps. The best man straightens his tie. We walk out. Show time.

Ladies and gentlemen, welcome to cavernous St. Ignatius Church in the heart of Holmesburg in sunny Philadelphia. *Let's get ready to worship.* The temperature outside is 83 degrees and climbing, with high humidity. The temperature inside is 98 degrees, with higher humidity, but it still ain't hot as Hell, so pipe down and keep the top buttons buttoned. And shut up. And buck up. Open your hearts and wallets. Bow down before the three oil paintings behind the altar of St. Julius Erving, St. Robert Clarke, and St. Richard Ashburn. Then light a candle at the statued feet of Jesus and Mary, who slouch and suffer on the altar, their hearts torn from thorns and burning like tire fires set by parishioners one dollar at a time in the name of someone dead.

Up in the back, in the choir loft, a fat midget lady pounds out Dracula's Castle chords on an organ older than the Bible. Fights break out in the pews. Prayer hymnals zip past heads. The hanging lights—which everybody knows are cameras with crosses—tape everything for prosecution purposes on Judgment Day. A fault line runs across the church's high ceiling from earthquakes started by lifetime sinners who reenter the church to find the God they lost. Confession booths in the back sell concessions: cold beer, hot dogs. The congregation stands and sings "The Star Spangled Banner" and the Notre Dame fight song. A bikini broad walks across the front of the church carrying a card that reads BRIDAL PARTY PROCESSION. The announcer introduces the bridal broads like the Sixers' starting five. Then the swimming spotlight hits Grace, only Grace, who looks right at me smiling and wearing a stunning green dress with thin straps and a V-neck that shows off her fake diamond Phillies pendant.

My racing brain and heart slow down. I blink my eyes, and the spotlights are gone and the church looks like it's supposed to again. Grace is sitting with her mom in the middle of a pew that includes the Tooheys and Cooneys. As Grace beams at me, Cecilia glares at Mrs. Cooney, who glares at Francis Junior, who glares at Stephen, who stares at nothing while Ralph Cooney glares at him. Meantime, Mr. Cooney and Frannie sleep in their seats, Archie sleeps in his chair next to the pew, and Cece pulls baseball cards out of her fake fur purse and flings them at Archie until one hits him in the face and he wakes up. Then Mr.

Cooney wakes up and notices the stares and quiet bad blood between families. I'm about to fall from all this until Grace blows me a kiss, then I steady.

Mr. James walks Jeannie to the altar, where he lifts her veil and leaves her with Ace, who cries. Then Bobby James cries, until he catches me and Harry laughing, then he frowns and blows a bubble. Father yanks the gum out of Bobby's mouth without looking up from the prayer book, then recites the prayers from the book—Heavenly Father, we ask you to blah blah blah us as these two yadda yadda yadda—as parishioners close their eyes and catch flies. Finally, Jeannie says *I do,* Ace says *I guess,* they kiss, the crowd erupts, and the wedding party cha-chas out of the church, past rainstorms of rice into the sunshine, where the St. Ignatius billboard, altered probably by Stephen Joseph Toohey, reads NO ANSWERS HERE.

The Mass over, the congregation hangs outside the church in the sunshine. The wedding party poses for pictures on the grass between the church and the rectory, where a St. Jude statue stands under a stone arch, an inscription at his feet that reads DEDICATED BY DAN AND DOROTHY POTTER. A school desk sits next to St. Jude, chained to the arch by a drunken Father Alminde last week so no dirtballs would walk off with it. The priests sell chances and cupcakes from the desk after Mass, whatever brings in a buck. The desk, which came from a second-grade classroom after somebody carved a pentagram in it, causing a huge fucking scandal, is seventy years old and has a −$22.50 street value. Nobody would take the thing even if St. Jude came to life and fucking told them to. But facts like this aren't obvious to men who wear ankle-length dresses, drink altar wine by the wino load, and duel with the devil on a not-for-profit basis.

The Cooneys stand by themselves on the church steps closest to the rectory. Bernie and Donna Cooney argue quiet but hot. Ralph sits on the steps, loosens his tie, and stares at a lighter he flicks on and off, the flame appearing, then disappearing. The O'Drains, who I didn't see in church, stand on the other side of the steps, closer to the cemetery. Not talking, they watch the folks around them and look uncomfortable, out of place, the cemetery tombstones stretching out behind them to mark the endless rows of dead bones. The Tooheys stand half between the church steps and Ave sidewalk. Francis Junior and Cecilia snap at each other like the Cooneys. Cece chucks something at Archie, over with his parents. Frannie watches the wedding party photo shoot. Stephen stands on the Ave, away from the crowd, leans on a mailbox (federal offense), and watches the trolleys passing left or right. Me and Harry stand on either side of Father, who blows off old bats and slides his business card between the big blessed tits of young moms and daughters until he notices the wedding party on the grass.

"Jesus," he says. "I pay a man top dollar to keep that grass spiffy. Mr. Toohey, tell those morons to get off the grass, especially that fat broad with the tennis shoes."

I walk over to where Ace and his men stand like soldiers in a row. Ace, who has color back in his face, rests his hands on the shoulders of Bobby James, standing in front, as Mrs. James takes pictures.

"Bobby James, straighten that tie," she says.

"Bite me, Ma," he tells her.

She runs for him but is restrained by all the groomsmen.

"I hate to break up this party," I say, "but Father wants everybody off the grass."

"Wanna get in the photos?" asks Mrs. James, the only person who doesn't ignore me.

"Yeah, OK, what the fuck," I say, always ready to make a photo prettier.

The best man picks me up by the ankles and holds me like a fisherman would a prize fish with an altar boy robe covering its upper body. Mrs. James snaps the picture. Everybody laughs as I'm dropped to the ground and recomb my hair. For the next picture, I put Jeannie's veil on my head—real gentle—and pose with Ace. Picture after that, Bobby James pretends to beat me with the processional crucifix he stole out of Harry's hands.

Then, since I'm already on the ground, somebody chucks me an empty altar wine bottle, and I pose passed out. After that, all the bridesmaids kiss me and Bobby James. Grace sees this and storms over fighting mad, then me and her pose wearing Ace's jacket and Jeannie's veil. Father sends Harry over to finish the job I started. For the last picture, the wedding party, plus me, Grace, and Harry, configures itself in a cheerleader pyramid. Finally, Father walks over, smiling, and after a picture with him and all the broads, he tells everybody to get off the grass, slaps me and Harry, and pulls us by the ears back to the church steps, where Cecilia drags the family over to say hello.

"Hey, Father, nice service," she says.

"Hello, Cecilia, wasn't it?" He smiles. "Hello, Fran," he says to Francis Junior. "I don't see you much at church."

"That's because I don't go," says Francis Junior, gruff and nervous.

"That explains it then." Father smiles. "Hello, Frannie."

"How you doing, Father?" says Frannie.

"I see you at Mass but you stand in the back and bolt after Communion."

"I sure do, Father," says Frannie. "Nothing personal."

"I'd leave even sooner if I wasn't in charge," says Father. "It's nice to see you both. I know all the other Tooheys and am a big fan," he says, staring at Cecilia's tits.

"Even me, Father?" asks Cece. "I thought you said I was a pain in the nuts."

"I said no such thing, Miss Toohey."

"Sure you did," says Cece. "You said it to Sister Thomas Dorothy last year after you taught us about baptism during religion class. You said unbaptized babies who die can't go to Heaven, that they have to wait in Purgatory. I said that was nonsense. I asked you what kind of God puts babies in a waiting room because they didn't have some priest talk Latin and half drown them? Then I asked what if somebody was talking Latin outside in the rain, and the baby got wet, then the baby died?

Would that count as baptism? Are there nurses on staff in Heaven to care for these babies? If they're up there dead without their moms and dads, ain't that punishment enough? You never answered. You handed the chalk to Sister, called me a pain in the nuts, and left. Remember now?"

"Not like you do," says Father, smiling at my parents. "I remember the class, and your thousand questions, but the rest is up for debate. Your parents should be proud of you Tooheys. You're all bright kids. The sisters tell me Henry's the smartest kid they ever taught. Stephen's sharp too. Where is he today?"

"Stephen?" asks Francis Junior, surprised Father brought him up.

"Yeah, Stephen," says Father. "Has he still been drinking, Cecilia?"

Francis Junior slaps his forehead.

"Yeah," she says. "He came in drunk last night and cut up from a fight."

"Oh, that's right," says Father. "There was a playground fight last night."

"Right," says Cecilia. "So Stephen tried to tell us last night."

"He tried?" asks Father. "What do you mean *tried?*"

"He started to tell us about it," says Cecilia, "but—"

"But he was too drunk to even spit it out," finishes Francis Junior.

"How do you feel about his drinking, Fran?" asks Father.

"It pisses me off, Father," says Francis Junior. "I didn't mean to say pissed."

"It's OK. I curse like a trucker. Do you let him know you're pissed off?"

"Yeah, I do," says Francis, fidgeting now.

"How?"

"I get right up in his face, Father."

"You ever hit him?"

"What if I do? He's grown now."

"Grown? Is he? How does the rest of the family react when you get in his face?"

"Different ways, I suppose," says Francis Junior. "Look, Father, the kid is lost."

"I know he is."

"I'm not the type to look the other way when someone I love needs help."

"I respect that," says Father. "Is your plan working? How are things with Cecilia?"

"Look, Father, I know you got a collar there, but that ain't your business."

"OK, forget I asked about you and Cecilia," says Father, staring hard at Francis Junior, who stares back but not as hard now that Father mentioned the marriage. "Let's talk more about Stephen. I'd like to help you both."

"Oh, you'd like to help, huh? Look, there he is. Call him over," says Francis Junior.

"All right then," says Father. "Stephen Toohey. Come over here, son."

Stephen, standing on the Ave, looks over. Here's what he sees: a priest calling to him. Next to the priest are his asshole dad and older brother, stuffed in suits with moths practically flying out of the pockets. Next to them is his mom, lighting a smoke with one hand and picking his little sister off the ground with the other. Next to all them are me and Harry Curran, swimming in oversized altar boy robes, me combing my hair, Harry doing one-armed pushups. The church looms big and brown behind us all. His reaction doesn't surprise me: he turns around and crosses the Ave, causing car horns to honk.

"Way to go, Father," snorts Francis Junior.

"There's no time for this," says Father. "I like your family. You're good people. But we need to get you all together on this or it will end real bad."

After Stephen crosses the Ave, he starts toward Tack Park, then stops, almost confused. He changes direction and heads home, moving so fast he's two steps ahead of his baggy blue suit, looking at nothing but his scuffed black shoes. From where I stand, it looks like he's letting the wind blow and tell him where to go.

Habib O'Brien, AKA the Lebanese Leprechaun, runs a dance studio called Dance or Die, located next door to Diviny's. Habib had an Irish cop for a dad and a Middle Eastern schoolteacher for a mom, which is how he arrived at such a fun, fucked-up name. I don't know where they lived—it wasn't near here—but Habib's been around ever since he opened the shop at least ten years ago.

Habib lives above the studio in an apartment with his East German wife, Sasha, who has no tits but the best legs ever. Sasha and Habib teach dance to young broads and the odd marriage-proposing stud like me on Tuesday and Thursday nights from seven to ten and Saturday mornings from eight to one. Other than those times, the studio's closed, but their apartment windows are open, and you can hear them in there, screaming each other's names, as they blare Mahler, who is OK as far as fancy-pants music goes.

All this—the name shouting and symphony blaring—happens as me, Harry, Bobby James, and Archie arrive under their open window. We came here after Mass at my request so I could practice my proposal dance steps one more time before the real deal tonight. Me and Harry wear our altar boy robes, Bobby James his tux, Archie his suit with skinny tire marks across the front from today's wheelchair stunt jump.

"What do they do up there?" asks Archie.

Sasha, you trollop, Habib, you bald potent cad, they shout.

"Sounds violent, whatever it is," says Harry as he does some torso twists.

"My parents did the same shit yesterday," I say. "You were there, Arch."

"Oh, right. They were," says Archie. "Must be fighting then."

"Whatever they're doing, I like the sound of it," says Bobby.

"I don't. It scares me," confesses Harry.

"Henry, how should we get their attention?" asks Bobby. "They're closed."

"Gimme some of your gum," I tell him.

He pulls a huge wad from his mouth and holds it out to me.

"Not the chewed shit, asshole," I say.

"Oh," he says. "I don't have any more."

"Look, there's no time," I say. "Gimme four or five pieces."

He reaches in his pockets and pulls out a pile. "Told you I was running low."

I take some pieces and look up at the open window, Mahler blaring, Sasha yelling, *Give it to me, give it to me,* Habib yelling, *I'm giving it, I'm giving it.* I lob a piece through their window to no effect except Sasha calls Habib a dog while he barks. I lob two more pieces in, same deal, no results, except now Habib tells Sasha she's a *bad girl who needs discipline* while she agrees and shouts *Punish me, please.*

"What the fuck," I say, frustrated.

"You're lobbing the shit, Henry. Move back and wing a bunch," says Jamesy.

"No way I'm doing that," I say.

"I'll do it," says Bobby, disgusted. "Gimme the shit."

He takes the gum and steps off the curb into the Ave. A trolley blows by him, inches away, passing with a *whoosh.* Habib and Sasha cry out, *Oh baby* and *I'm coming.* Bobby leans back and wings twenty pieces with all his might at the window. Smash! It breaks the glass. We bolt for the storefront, leaning our backs against the wall.

"Sasha, darling, we broke the window this time. It is usually just the box spring," says Habib, whose deep 7–Eleven clerk accent is more Habib than O'Brien.

"A small price to pay," purrs Sasha.

Habib and Sasha are as close as this neighborhood comes to foreign culture. Which isn't close. Not that I give a fuck. I know all I need to know about foreigners: leisure slacks, discount sneaks, hippo BO, end of story.

"Come back to bed, Bobo," she says. "Let's break some more windows."

"I shall in a minute, love," says Habib. "Let me inspect the damage. Wait. There are four boys beneath the window. One is praying the Hail Mary. Boys, are you all right?"

I pop out smiling and combing my hair.

" Habib, how you doing?" I say. "We didn't have nothing to do with that window."

"Henry, I am excellent," he says. "Who gives two shits about the window?"

Habib is shirtless, bald on top, gray on the sides, beak nose, salon tan, and fat hairy C-cups, which he beats now while making monkey noises.

"Yes, you are Lord of the Jungle," says Sasha. "Is that my Henry Toohey out there?" she asks, looking out the window for me, wrapped in a bedsheet.

"Hi, Sasha," I say.

"Hello, Henry." She smiles, teeth all nasty, eyes all beady, hair short and parted on the side like a fella. Despite that, and the no tits, she's hot as shit with those legs I mentioned, plus she always looks ready to push me up against a seafood Dumpster.

"How you doing?" I ask, smiling, until Bobby throws a piece of gum at my nuts.

"That smile, that face," she says. "I'd leave Habib for you, wouldn't I, Habib?"

"Yes, you would, love," he tells her.

"See, even Habib says so, Henry," she says. "What are we waiting for then?"

"Great. Listen, can I practice my dance routine one more time before tonight?"

"You're proposing tonight?" gasps Sasha. "I thought it was next week."

"No, it's tonight, love," says Habib.

"Tonight? My heart! Habib, fan me. Faster. Not that fast. Perfect."

"Henry," says Habib, fanning Sasha, "you know the routine. Why rehearse again?"

The wedding crowd crosses the Ave from the church into Paul Donohue's to kill time before the reception at Mungiole's, which starts later this afternoon, crossing on each green light in groups. One includes all the Tooheys besides Stephen, but he'll be there soon enough, I bet. I start to think about what Father said about getting our shit together before it ends bad. I think about Stephen seeing the ring tonight and feeling better. I think about Cecilia and Francis Junior hearing that song and falling back in love. I think about me getting Grace. All this rides on tonight, that song, my performance.

"I want it to be perfect," I say. "It needs to be perfect."

Habib sighs. "Fine. I'll be right down."

After a couple minutes, Habib unlocks and opens the door, wearing his usual black tank top, black sweatpants, gray legwarmers, and white DANCE OR DIE headband. Sasha, a head smaller than him, wears a gray bodysuit, black legwarmers, and the same headband. The studio looks like any other: one big room, all wall mirrors and barres. In one corner is a desk with a radio, a TV, a cash box, and a couple stools. Habib motions for us to sit on the stools while he turns on the TV and flips quick past channels until he stops at MTV, where titless Cyndi Lauper dances on a car.

"I filmed a commercial for the studio that should be on the air soon," he says.

"We filmed it," says Sasha. "With my concept."

"Of course, my love," he says, kissing her, his hand on her fine ass. After the smooch, Habib watches the video for five seconds before he erupts.

"Look at this garbage. Who choreographs this?" he shouts.

"Not us," says Sasha.

"Certainly not. These dancers look like swine hoof-hopping on frozen tin roofs."

"Fuck them, let's talk about my dance then," I say.

"What parts do you want to go over once more?" asks Habib.

"Everything," I say. "The whole nine."

"Really? Honestly, you do it well for a straight boy," he says.

"A what boy?" I ask.

"Nothing. Sasha, tell him. He knows the routine."

"You know the routine," says Sasha, smoking now, staring at me.

"One more time," I insist.

"You sure you won't marry me instead of a little girl? Look at these legs, Henry."

Sasha does a couple ballet spins, her calf muscles, like my boner, popping. Wow.

Instead of answering, I gulp.

"These are woman legs, and they could be yours, couldn't they, Habib? Tell him."

"Yes, yes, they could be yours," Habib agrees. "The woman loves you, no question."

"It's tempting," I say, sweating, "but I'm with Grace and you're already married."

"We are not married," says Sasha.

"You live together unmarried?" gasps Archie.

"Yes," says Habib.

"You're going straight to Hell then," says Harry. "No offense."

"Good," laughs Sasha, blowing smoke out her nose. "We hate the cold."

"Why ain't you married?" asks Bobby James.

"Marriage is for other people," says Sasha. "Right, Habib?"

"Yes, my love."

"But why?" demands Bobby.

"We're swingers," says Sasha as Lauper sings "Girls Just Wanna Have Fun."

"You're what?" I ask. We're all real confused at the moment.

"Quiet, everyone," says Habib. "Here comes the commercial." The video ends. The screen goes black for a second. Next thing we see is a close shot of Sasha's wonderful legs, wrapped in legwarmers with her short dinner dress. The camera moves back to show that Sasha is inside a fancy restaurant, where a snooty maître d' refuses to seat her. Violin music starts, and she dances around the maître d', putting her legs on and around him, until he faints. We all cheer, laugh, and yell. Sasha walks to a fat man in a tux at a table.

"Hello, Fedorov," she says. "Give me the plans and there will be no trouble."

"What plans?" he asks, playing dumb, smoking a cigar and staring at Sasha through a monocle as four hot titless dance kittens rub his shoulders. Behind Sasha, five commie fellas grab her. Fat Fedorov laughs.

"Take her away," he bellows, waving his hand.

"Not so fast, Comrade Fedorov," says Habib, stepping out of the shadows wearing a tux and legwarmers. "Unhand the woman."

"So we meet again, Habib O'Brien, so-called Dance or Die instructor," says Fedorov, turning to his soldiers. "Kill him," he orders.

The soldiers shoot their machine guns at Habib, who somersaults and flips across the restaurant. After a final wild flip, Habib lands behind Fedorov, stands him up, and twists his neck. At the same time as he twists, Habib turns his head the same way as Fedorov, in a nice little dance touch. Finally, Fedorov twirls and falls to the ground, dead as a doornail. Habib turns to the soldiers, still holding Sasha.

"Let her go or the same fate awaits you," warns Habib.

They release her. She runs to Habib, and they tango in circles around the soldiers.

"Now we shall leave you with your fallen leader," says Habib.

They tango out the door. The picture freezes with Habib winking at the soldiers, who smile at Sasha, who smiles at them.

A narrator says, *Dance or Die Studios at Frankford and St. Patrick. Are you tough enough?*

The commercial ends, and we clap.

"That turned out perfect," brags Habib. "Now shall we practice Henry's dance?"

"Not yet," says Sasha. "Since this is his last single day, let me dance for him."

"Sasha," says Habib, "the boy has made clear he wants more practice immediately."

"Hold the fuck up, we got time for her dance," I tell Habib, the fucking dope.

"Beautiful," says Sasha, sliding a chair on the dance floor. "Sit here and wait."

Sasha disappears, then comes back in a belly dancer outfit. No shoes, baggy blue genie pants, a half top, and a blue hankie covering her face except the eyes. Oh, Mommy. I need a glass of water and a lap pillow. She snaps her fingers to Habib, who plays a record I can't see but recognize once it starts: "Zorro Is Back" by Oliver Onions, a fast Puerto Rican–type record. Sasha creeps closer to me in the chair. I try to swallow but can't. Forehead sweat stings my eyes. Sasha glides behind me. I stand up to turn and kneel on the chair to watch but she sits me back down by my shoulders. I leap when she touches me like she put phone wires under my wet armpits. Oh, Jesus. She's right in front of me, smiling under the hankie. I think I can hear my buddies cheering behind me but I'm not sure. Yikes. Sasha's all over me, hips shaking, her one leg on my lap, my boner jerking like a fucking jumping bean. I can smell her perfume and sweat. Help me, Jesus. She moves even closer, wiggling, shaking, smiling, straddling me on the chair. I can see the space between her tiny tits, then, again, a darkness. Good night.

I wake up when Bobby James soaks me with a glass of water. Once I stop coughing it up, Habib and Sasha sit me up on the floor.

"I faint again?" I ask.

"Yeah, you did," says Bobby James, laughing. "You faint more than a broad."

"So I do. What fucking time is it?"

"Two-thirty-four," answers Harry.

"Shit. I told my parents I'd be at the bar by two-fifteen."

"Let's go then," says Bobby.

"I can't. I still have to practice my dance."

"Henry, Henry, you just passed out," says Habib. "You should take it easy."

"No," I say, determined. "You guys go to the bar. Tell my parents I'll be there by three. Habib, get the record ready, please. I'm fine."

My buddies leave the studio. The door clicks shut. I move to the floor frozen in the first pose, still in my altar boy robe, holding a banana like a microphone. Habib cues the tune. Him and Sasha watch me from the side like they're chess players and I'm the board. The needle fuzz hisses through the speakers. Habib tells me, *Remember to keep your head up, stay centered, relax and have fun but do not make mistakes that will reflect poorly on this studio,* as the horns start to open the song. I listen to him and the song at the same time, making the first couple of moves, serious as cancer and thinking *I ain't nervous, there's no fucking way in this world I won't do this perfect now, like I did last time, like I will again tonight.*

After walking into Paul Donohue's, under the green shamrock that always sways over the door like the drunks inside, it takes five minutes looking around to know how the place works. You sit down on a stool and put a bill on the counter. The barkeep asks what you want to drink. Say anything but a Fuzzy Navel unless you want to get chucked in a Dumpster. Ask for a Bud. Put your arm around a pal. Sing with him and sway. A chaser is a beer you drink after a shot, a shot's a small glass of straight booze. Knock the shot back in a blast, make a face, and reach for your chaser, which turns your face back to normal. The more shots a fella does, the more drunk he gets, faster. The fellas doing shots talk loud, point clumsy, and drop quarters on the floor meant for the juke. The fellas doing shots want to buy everybody shots. The pool table draws a crowd. Balls on the table crack beneath dark clouds of smoke. A barmaid with tired tits walks around with a tray and looks nothing like the barmaids on posters that line the wood-paneled walls. Chalkboards track stats for shuffleboard, dart leagues, and betting pools. Two TVs sit high where the walls meet the ceiling—Phils baseball on one, Penn State football on the other. The bar's dark, even in daytime.

Everybody is here. On my right as I stand at the door, Cecilia and Cece sit at a table with Archie and his parents, Margie Murphy and her parents, and Grace and Shirley McClain. I can't hear what they're saying, but Cecilia and Grace, both smoking, do all the talking, making frantic gestures while everybody there besides Mr. and Mrs. O'Drain laughs. With the bar packed, the pool tables cracking and covered with smoke, and the juke pumping "Love Me Do," no one even notices me enter.

To my left is the bar, where big asses rest half on, half off creaking stools. Paul Donohue, the huge, curly-white-haired owner and bartender, serves drinks quick while moving slow. At the center of the bar, I spot Francis Junior sitting next to Bernie and Donna Cooney and almost shit my pants. A couple of voices call to me over the noise, snapping me out of my daze. It's Bobby James, Stephen, and Frannie, farther down at the bar to Francis Junior's left. They hang with Johnny Boyle, an older neighborhood fella. I walk down to them, past the shuffleboard, jukebox, and computer slots, relieved to see as I pass Francis Junior that he's not talking with the Cooneys; all three of them stare straight ahead and concentrate on their beers.

"Hey, Henry Toohey, good to see you, buddy," says Johnny Boyle. "Now the whole gang of girls is here." He laughs, motioning to my buddies and brothers. Boyle lives somewhere in the neighborhood but no one knows exactly where. He has bad brown hair, short and feathered on top, long in the back, with a rattail to boot. His eyes are huge, blue, and crazy. He wears a black Members Only jacket with the sleeves rolled up, short brown corduroy shorts, beat-up tube socks, and beat-up white high-tops. He wears this same shit every day; winter, summer, it doesn't matter. Johnny Boyle is a stylish motherfucker not bothered by the elements. He rides everywhere on a pink girl's ten-speed, which he crashes all the time, but always gets up laughing and bleeding. He's probably thirty, but who fucking knows for sure? He's too ugly to be a kid, too jobless and unbothered by life to be an adult.

"Johnny, how you doing?" I say. "When are you getting rid of that fucking rattail?"

"Never. Chicks dig rattails. Chicks dig *me,*" he says, ripping off his jacket and shirt to flex from his seat to make us laugh, and we do, since he has a big gut, B cups, and no muscles.

"Put your shirt back on before I start milking your tits to make White Russians," says Paul Donohue, who has huge hands and faded green navy tattoos on his forearms.

"You would want to touch my tits," says Boyle. "You were a sailor, right? Besides, I got *honey* in these things. Fucking nectar of the gods," he says, squeezing his nipples.

"We used to get new guys like this on the ship all the time, Henry," says Donohue, squinting and laughing, shoulders shaking. "All of them full of piss and vinegar, then we'd take them downstairs and make honest women out of them."

"That's what I'm saying, sailor," says Boyle. "Get me another drink."

"You want an umbrella with that?" asks Paul.

Both fellas, who like each other, laugh and quit with the put-downs. Boyle puts his shirt and jacket back on and tells me to sit down next to my dad, who hasn't noticed me, so he can play a drinking game with me and Bobby James, who is drinking from a Bud bottle. Normal drinking laws go out the window on a wedding day in my neighborhood. At weddings, you want a beer, you got it, no questions.

"What drinking game?" I ask. "How do you play?"

"It's called Quarters. Players take turns bouncing a quarter off the bar into a shot glass. If you make one, I drink, and you go until you miss. If I make one, same deal."

Donohue returns with Johnny's drink, complete with umbrella.

"Here you are, ma'am," he says.

"Fuck you." Boyle laughs, tossing the umbrella.

"I'm in, I'll play," I say.

"You want a Bud like Bobby?" asks Boyle.

"Nah," I say, "just a Coke."

"Pussy. Rear Admiral Donohue, get a pop for the kid in the altar boy dress."

"Which one?" asks Paul, looking at me and Harry.

Harry points to me. "Him. I'm drinking the Virgin Bloody Marys."

"This game's real easy, Henry," spits Bobby, already drunk. "Watch."

He hammers the coin off the bar and it nails the mirror behind rows of colored bottles that shine in the dark bar like jewels in a cave.

"Take a break, let Henry here have a try," says Boyle, handing me a quarter.

I give it a shot but miss, my quarter hardly bouncing. Boyle drinks anyway.

"You came close enough, Henry." He shrugs. "Give it another shot."

I miss four more times, Boyle drinks four more times, orders another drink.

"Look, I'll show you," he says. "When I make it in, you drink."

Boyle bounces one in, then another. I take belts on my Coke. Donohue refills me right away, never missing a beat with the other folks at the bar. Frannie and Stephen watch me and Johnny from behind, Frannie holding a beer and smiling, Stephen holding what looks like a ginger ale and trying to smile through his hangover. Ralph Cooney walks past him twice and bumps him hard enough to spill his drink some both times. Stephen's sober, so he ignores him, but after the second bump, he calls Paul over and points to his drink. Paul takes it from him, pours something pink-looking, and hands it back. Frannie frowns.

"Henry, wake the fuck up, it's your turn," says Boyle.

"What?" I ask. "My bad. Here we go."

I bounce the quarter, expecting to miss, but it drops, and everybody cheers. Next to me, Mr. Cooney asks Francis Junior how long he's been delivering mail on St. Patrick Street, and Francis Junior says fifteen years. I bounce another quarter and drop another shot. Johnny Boyle downs his drink. Frannie asks Stephen why he has to start drinking so soon. He knows it's a wedding and all but it's kind of early to start what with all the recent bullshit. Stephen tells Frannie he'll be fine. Bernie Cooney asks Francis Junior how long he's been married and Francis Junior tells him almost twenty-five years. I miss a quarter shot and Boyle drinks one time for my effort, telling me I tried. Frannie tells Stephen, *You think you'll be fine but you won't. I won't referee any more fights. Then don't*, says Stephen. *Just take it easy today, Tiger*, warns Frannie. That's all he's saying. Stephen finishes his drink, nods to Donohue for another, finishes that in a swallow, and orders another. Bernie Cooney says, *Me I been married to Donna fifteen years and working at Holmesburg Prison for ten. See, my job doesn't require me to stop at people's houses, unless you count the prisoners as people, and the cells as houses. I don't.* Boyle starts showing off, bouncing quarters in the shot glass with both hands, same time. I pound one soda after another. Frannie walks away from Stephen in disgust, stopping once to avoid two six-year-olds sprinting past him toward the poker machines with cartoon pictures of nude broads.

Over at Cecilia's table, she stops a story, looking over upset at Francis Junior, but swallows it to finish her story. Boyle rolls five straight quarters off his nose into a glass. I slam more soda-pop shots, my head spinning; Boyle matches me with whiskey-and-waters. Bernie Cooney tells Francis Junior, *Even if I did work* near *people's houses, I wouldn't stop in anybody's houses for any reason. Would you?* Francis Junior says, *I don't understand what you're getting at.* Donna Cooney says, *Yeah, you're drunk, Bernie. You ain't making sense.* Me and Boyle make every shot now, two fucking pros, and chug our drinks while Bobby James and Harry cheer. Cecilia's gone from her table. Fuck, where did she go? Oh Jesus, she's walking toward Francis Junior. *I'm sorry,* says Bernie Cooney. *I'm not making sense. I guess what I'm driving at is this. Wait, here's your wife. I'll just ask her. Cecilia, you were shooting daggers at Donna here today. Is your* husband *fucking my* wife? Francis Junior buries his head in his hands. Cecilia stares at Donna Cooney with hate, then at Bernie Cooney with calm. She puts her hands on Francis Junior's shoulders.

"Now, why would he do that when he's got me?" she asks.

Bernie Cooney's jaw drops, shocked he got a no, maybe embarrassed. Ralph Cooney bumps Stephen again on another pass. Stephen grabs him by the throat and holds him over the bar. Paul Donohue leaps over it and grabs Stephen and Ralph, whose jacket back is covered with sawdust.

"I'll take care of this, Paul," says Bernie Cooney.

He drags Ralph outside of the bar and beats the shit out of him with the door open, everybody watching. Ralph is crying, *Dad, stop.* Once he does stop, Ralph runs down St. Patrick Street. Bernie Cooney reenters the bar, red-faced, grabs his wife by the arm and takes her to a table. Francis Junior stares at Cecilia.

"Why'd you do that for me?" he asks.

"Fuck you. I did it for them," she says, pointing to us brothers. "And Cece."

She walks back to her table, to Cece and Grace watching her, and picks up joking where she left off, like nothing happened. Francis Junior stays in his seat and stares at himself in the mirror behind the booze bottles, which works with the low lights to shade his face red.

Back at our group, everybody lays low after the bullshit. Bobby James sways and drinks his Bud, and Harry sips his Virgin Bloody Mary, while they play War with a deck of Donohue's nudie cards. Stephen drinks and drops coins in the computer poker. I comb my hair in the mirror, unable to blink from all the soda, which I keep fucking swilling anyhow. Quarters is over. Boyle stands up, wobbly.

"It's way too early to be this drunk," he says, almost falling but grabbing the bar for balance. "See that, Henry?" He smiles. "That's poise."

Boyle heads to the dartboard to throw with some buddies. Shuffleboard pieces pop behind our stools. The jukebox plays "Good Vibrations." On one TV, Mike Schmidt strikes out swinging. A couple of fellas yell. On the other set, Penn State intercepts a pass and runs it back. Folks cheer and bang beer mugs. From behind me, Mrs. McClain puts her hand on my shoulder, then sits on the stool left behind by Boyle.

"So how you doing, Henry?" she asks.

"I'm good, how you doing?" I say.

"I'm all right." She smiles, her mouth cupped on a smoke, which she lights. "You sure? You look down. Don't see you much like that."

"Really, I'm fine," I say. "Just thinking, I guess."

"What about, if you don't mind?"

"Do you still miss Mr. McClain a lot?"

She smiles, looking past me, then at me. "I do."

"Do you miss him worse at weddings?" I ask.

"I miss him the same everywhere, every day. He'll be dead five years Friday."

"Oh," I say, followed by nothing, because I'm not sure what to say next.

"Look at you quiet." She laughs. "It's OK, I don't mind talking about Mr. McClain," she tells me, in a way that seems more request than reassurance.

"Tell me something you loved about him," I say.

"Just one?"

"Tell me as many as you want."

"Oh, we could be here all day. I'll tell you one I just remembered. He always shouted out the wrong answers watching TV quiz shows. Every single time. Didn't matter the show, or the category, or the question. He guessed wrong."

"C'mon," I say, laughing, "he had to get one right, one time."

"Nope, never," she says, really chuckling now.

"What if it was something real simple, like name the first U.S. president?"

"He'd say McClain. He'd say Toohey. Anything but Washington." She laughs.

We grow quiet and serious in a hurry, for no reason really.

"What happened the night he died?" I ask.

"Jesus," she says. "What *didn't* happen that night? You sure you want to hear?"

"Yeah, if you'll tell."

"I'll tell," she says. "A row home fire broke out in Fairhill, where he worked in North Philly. A drug neighborhood. They had like five fires an hour down there. Mr. McClain had enough time on the job to transfer somewhere safer, but he loved to fight fires. He loved to save people. He loved *people*."

"I remember that about him," I say. "He always called us up to your porch when we were little. He used to do that trick where it looked like he pulled his thumb off his left hand with his right. It totally freaked us out but we loved it anyway."

"Yeah, he was a goof like that," she agrees. "Anyhow, he was working on the garden Bobby James trampled the other night and got called in to help with this huge blaze down there. He left right away. Gave me and Grace a big kiss, told us he loved us, and asked me to take care of his flowers until he came back. So I do."

"What happened at the fire?" I ask.

"Getting to that," she tells me. "There was a family inside a house. A mother and her three children. Or her four children. Which was what killed him. They were unconscious and trapped. A neighbor told Mr. McClain and the other firefighters she had four kids. See, she watched a niece a lot too. So Mr. McClain rescued the mother and her three children. I still talk to her and them by the way. They're good people. They live in a nicer place now, too." She smiles, proud. "But like I said, they were under the impression there was another kid in there," she says, smile dropping. "There wasn't. Mr. McClain stayed in there looking, him and his good friend Frankie Pingitore. They were both upstairs when the second floor collapsed. They both died instantly."

"I'm sorry," I say as Neil Young's "Heart of Gold" starts on the juke.

"Don't be," she says, her face more determined than sad. "I'm not."

"Was he good to Grace?" I ask.

"He was golden to her," she tells me. "He really loved her."

"I do too," I blurt, full of caffeine and emotion, calling to Donohue for another soda, my knee jerking up and down, my fingers drumming on the bar.

"I know you do." She smiles. "Me too. She's a special girl."

Grace pops up behind us, slaps the backs of our heads, kicks the smokes machine, and calls it a motherfucker until a pack drops. Then she slaps our heads again and walks back to her table. Somebody spills a drink toward one end of the bar. Couple of fellas shout. A quarter bounces into my drink. Harry fishes it out.

"Something on your mind, Henry?" asks Mrs. McClain.

"I want to marry Grace," I blurt again, still swimming in soda, sadness, and love.

All motion in the bar slows to a crawl. I can't hear anything. Donohue walks to one end of the bar with a booze bottle that glows like lava. He pours the lava into diamond shot glasses, one shot in front of everybody with a seat at the bar. The shots now poured, fellas at the bar drink them down. Their hearts grow and glow. The TVs catch the tail end of Paul Donohue's commercial, where twenty-five fellas, including Stephen and Bobby James, raise their mugs and smile to the camera above. After that the ball games reappear. Hearts stop glowing, at least to the naked eye. Noise returns to the bar.

"You're a good kid, Henry," she says. "I'm sure you'll be a good husband."

I surprise her with a leaping hug.

"Thanks. It means everything to have your blessing. I'll treat Grace like gold. She'll get more love from me than any wife ever got. I won't fight with her. No arguments. None. Zero. I won't cheat on her with the broad up the block either or punch our son ever, not for nothing. No fucking way, not ever. That Bob Seger and the Silver Bullet Band on the jukebox? Yeah, it is. Stay here. I'll be right back."

"Old Time Rock & Roll" blares throughout the bar. I walk to the juke and pull the plug. The song stops. Everybody turns to look at me. The place is quiet except for the TVs. Mike Schmidt hits a home run, the fucking prick, but nobody cheers.

"No more Bob Fucking Seger," I say. "Anybody got a problem with that?"

Nobody says shit back. Good, the fuckers. I plug the juke back in, fish a quarter out of my pocket, pop it in the juke, and punch up Link Wray, "Rumble." Here's a real tune, you fuckheads. I return to Mrs. McClain.

"Sorry," I say. "That had to be done."

She watches me knock back my soda.

"You've had enough of those. Let me get you a beer," she offers, waving to Donohue for beer in a worried hurry as twenty other folks do the same.

Swing and miss once, you're out in stickball. Two foul tips is a strikeout. If you strike out, you're a bitch, unless your name's

Grace. Call her a bitch for striking out, she beats your ass. Grace doesn't strike out, so it doesn't matter anyway. The bat's a broomstick. Nobody runs the bases. Any ground ball that lands in front of the pitcher's feet is fielded clean for an out. Fly outs are fly outs. There are two outs an inning, not three. Hit a line past the pitcher that isn't caught in the air, it's a bingle, which is a single. Over the outfielders' heads, a double. Off the fence, a triple. Over the fence, a home run. Nobody hits stickball homers at Tack Park, which is where we stand, to settle a bet between Stephen and Johnny Boyle. Boyle, who got a walk-on tryout with the Phils twenty years ago, says that in his prime he hit three a day over the fence. Stephen thinks Johnny's full of shit. They bet fifty bucks at the bar that Boyle couldn't hit one out, then another fifty on the game. Here we are, on the playground, under the hot sun, in dress clothes, ready to play.

Boyle and Stephen picked the teams. Ours has me, Stephen, Bobby James, Harry, Grace, and Archie. Boyle's team is him and four fat drunk fellas and the big red beer cooler they dragged to the park. We should win. Unlike them, we're skinny, sweat less, and aren't bothered by wearing dress clothes in the heat. Archie sweats a lot, but that's only because both teams use him as a coat rack for their suit jackets. But sometimes he catches behind the plate and also manages us, flashing signs and shit, when we bat.

We get first ups. Boyle pitches. Hits should be easy, what with his team more interested in drinking suds than shagging flies. Bobby James leads off. He kisses the gold cross on his neck and digs in the dirt that isn't there. Archie tugs his left lobe, grabs his balls, and spits, meaning swing away. Bobby James slaps a bingle to left. I bat second. Archie gives me a green light but I take the first pitch to get a handle on Boyle's shit today. He's chucking waist-high bouncers with no backspin. Boyle bitches, "C'mon, Henry, that pitch was right there." I ignore his ass and whack the second pitch through his legs for another bingle. Grace, who has line-drive power, bats next. She hikes up her skirt and steps to the plate. Yes, boner. Archie pulls both ears, then grabs his balls, meaning bunt. Grace spits at him. The fellas in the field yell, *Chick's up, sink in.* Grace calls them dumb assholes and crushes a double over their heads. 1–0, nobody out, second and third. Stephen, up next, swings for the fences and flies out to center, not shallow, not deep. Harry strikes out. Grace calls him a skirt as she smooths her own. He cries until Bobby James slaps him.

The fat fucks bat. Grace takes the mound wearing her lucky Phils hat, torn and tattered just right. Archie rolls behind the plate. The rest of us stand in the outfield. Grace strikes out the side on two pitches in the first, then does the same in the second and third. We whip the ball around the horn: Archie to me to Harry to Bobby James to Stephen back to Grace. Everybody touches the ball after a strikeout. The game settles into a groove. Nobody scores any more runs. The only people who get hits are me and Bobby James, bingles every time. Harry strikes out. Grace, Stephen, and Boyle swing for the fences and fly out. The other fat fellas strike out. The sun beats down on us. Trolley cars cough sparks past the playground. Grace takes a 10-K no-hitter into the fifth, making the fatsos bellyache about her doctoring pitches. Stephen and Boyle jaw about last night's fight. Harry says he's scared to be at the playground, and Boyle tells him not to fucking worry. Playground brawls are part of growing up. Everybody gets in scraps, what the fuck you gonna do? You should enjoy them. You're only a kid once, you know.

The temperature feels like it's still climbing. On the mound, Boyle wipes his face.

"Damn, it's hot," he says. "Bet that groom today thinks it's even hotter."

His buddies laugh.

"What the fuck you got against marriage?" I ask, annoyed.

"What do I have against marriage?" he asks. "What *don't* I have against marriage? Now, I realize some of you kids probably think I'm single because I'm goofy, unemployed, and drink too much. Not true. Women love me. You know how many times I been engaged? Five times. Yeah, five. First time I was seventeen and got engaged to Danielle, my high school sweetheart. That fell through when I fell off a roof on a roofing job. Took me a year to remember my own name, so of course I forgot who she was, which pissed her off, so she left me, the bitch. Second time was with my therapy nurse, Dot. She was older, and fat, and ugly, if I remember right, but we fell for each other after all those times she fed me soup on a spoon and retaught me to read. Goddamn, she sang the alphabet like an angel. But that ended when the therapy was over. Dame three didn't happen until six or seven months after that, because my guard was up after me and Dot flamed out. I forget this broad's name. She had big jugs, though, and could hump like a chimp. You kids are old enough to hear this, right?" We nod.

"Anyhow, the irony there was she met a guy who worked at the zoo and left me. I hate them both to this day and think I'd kill them if I saw them. But like I said I can't remember her name or face for the life of me, so they should be safe, unless I see those tits. I'd remember the tits. I could pick them out of a pile on a fruit cart. Anyhow, fuck her and those perfect tits. Fiancée four is a big blur, since I moved to Vegas for three years and was drunk the whole time. She was from Texas I think and wore sparkly boots in the sack. I think I got her name tatooed on my ass but I can't be bothered to look or to ask someone else at this point. She didn't mean anything anyway." He takes off his glove and wipes his face again.

"The only fiancée who meant something to me was number five. Christa, the ballet dancer. I loved her. We met at a bar. No, it was a ball game. No, scratch that, it was a bar. We were *watching* a ball game. I proposed to her the night I met her. I was that sure. She said yes. We left wherever the fuck we were to drive to Atlantic City to just do it. We couldn't wait. It was fucking love, man. God, she was beautiful. Black hair, blue eyes, unbelievable legs. But we got in a fight halfway down, after a state trooper pulled us over. I made the mistake of telling her—while we stood on one foot and tried to touch our fingers to our noses—that the ring I gave her was the same one I gave the first four chicks. What? It had sentimental value. If moms can give sons their rings to propose, why can't I use the one I proposed with four times before? You'd love a ring like that too. It wasn't just the proposals that gave it emotional value. I had to sue three of those bitches to get it back. Who wouldn't love a ring like that? Christa didn't, that's who. She threw it back at me and demanded we get taken into custody in separate squad cars, and except for the half second I saw them take her down a hall while I got fingerprinted, I never saw her again. So you want to know what I got against marriage? There you go. Five engagements, one tattoo, one ring, and one loving heart broken five times later, I got a big fucking problem with marriage. Better them than me. I need a minute here."

The story now over, one hour and five innings later, Boyle stands on the mound, holding the ball, about to cry. When he gets our attention, he looks up and laughs.

"Fooled you dumb fucks."

"I can't believe it," says Harry. "So you never were engaged?"

"No, all that shit was true. I just don't give a fuck."

Boyle laughs for about five minutes, then nobody talks. His buddies line up the cooler empties behind home plate. The drunker they get, the more they concentrate on batting. By their ups in the eighth, they're totally serious about tying the score. Boyle hits two blasts—one in the seventh and one in the eighth—that travel far but fall short of the fence. Stephen laughs and catches them both in his back pocket. Archie visits Grace at the mound in the eighth after she gives up a deep fly out and two hits. She spins his chair around, pushes him back to home plate with her foot, and strikes the next chump out.

Bottom of the ninth, the score is still 1–0. Older fellas, on last ups, call for a hat check on Grace, who plays dumb despite the fact she has at least a pound of K-Y under that cap. It's late after-noon now, and folks file into Mungiole's across the Ave for the reception, a couple of drunk dads stopping to sing "Take Me Out to the Ball Game" as they pass us. I still need to run home and change into my suit. I might even shower but fucking doubt it.

"Look: Vaseline," says Boyle, holding up Grace's cap. "She's throwing spitters."

"Give me that hat, fuckhead," she yells, jumping for it.

"No," he says. "I keep it. You pitch the last inning with another ball. OK?"

"Fine," she says. "Keep the fucking hat. I'll strike you sissies out with any ball."

The older fellas toss her a new ball from a can we brought up.

"Yo, Stephen," calls Boyle, "now you ready to watch one go over the fence?"

"Been waiting all afternoon," says Stephen. "Wake me up when it happens."

Boyle laughs and leads off. Grace bounces her first legal pitch of the game. He smokes it. Stephen tears after the thing, backpedaling first, then sprinting. He leaps and catches the ball near the top of the fence. We whoop. Stephen dances a jig. Boyle loses his cool and throws the bat across the playground like a javelin. *Motherfucker*, he screams. *Can you believe that shit?* He tells his buddies *Save my ups, you fat bastards, I want one more shot.* He downs a beer in one gulp to calm his damn self. A buddy retrieves the bat. Somehow they fucking tie the score with four straight singles. Archie rolls to the mound. Grace flicks a ciga-rette at him. Boyle, returning to the plate for another chance, stretches and looks up to the sky.

"Lord," he prays, "I ain't one to ask for much. I know you know I'm lazy and drink. I sleep late. I haven't exactly made a fucking dent as an adult. I blew five engagements and spent time in the pen. If you got a problem with all that we can take it up at a later date. You know I can hit a tennis ball as far as anybody. You saw me hit it over the fence up here as a kid. Now this punk tells me I never hit a ball over this fence. I can't have this. So I'm asking you for one last home run so I can shove *this* bat up *that* ass and never play stickball again. You got that, God?"

He sags at the shoulders, his prayer over.

"Pitch it," he whispers to Grace.

She pitches. He swings. The ball leaps off his bat. It clears the fence, then the Ave. It rockets toward the church and the giant round stained-glass window over the front doors. Smash. Home fucking run. The church window is broken. Holy fucking shit. We stare at each other. The first sound after the window crashing is the stickball bat dropping. Then somebody shouts *Run.* I book for home and a change of clothes. The other assholes bolt toward Mungiole's. I look back once as I run. Grace leads the pack. The fellas push the wheelchair across the Ave in a scared mob. Pissed drivers honk from backfiring cars, but not loud enough to drown out Bobby James shrieking the Hail Mary as he runs. I hit the row-home streets, slow down to a cool-cat walk, and comb my hair calm, not looking anyone in the eye, but not looking away either. Don't mind me, folks. I'm just an ordinary altar boy citizen hurrying home to wear a suit to sing a song, not a church window breaker fleeing a crime scene to stay on the street and out of the joint.

Harry Curran waits, pacing and checking his watch, outside Mungiole's, when I show up wearing an all-white suit and shoes. As soon as he sees me, he smiles.

"Look at you, Toohey," he says. "You look great."

"Thanks," I say. "I feel great."

"You nervous?"

"Hell, no." I smile. "Only good things can come from this. Only *great* things."

I grab the door handle, ready to rock, but he stops me.

"Wait," he says. "I paid the DJ twenty extra bucks to announce your entrance."

"You did?" I laugh.

"I did," he says, proud. "Stay here. I'm supposed to signal to him."

He opens the door, and I can hear the murmur of talk and the dinner music real loud, then the door closes, and the sounds muffle. The dinner music stops.

"Ladies and gentlemen, can I have your attention?" says the DJ, muffled. "If you'll be so kind as to direct your attention to Mungiole's entrance door, I'd like to introduce to you a man who needs no introduction, a man on a mission of love, a man who has better hair than us all, your friend and neighbor, Henry Toohey!"

Harry swings the door open. The lights are off except a spotlight on us.

"I wrote the intro myself," he whispers. "Go ahead in."

Laughing my head off, I walk in waving. It's quiet until Harry starts to clap loud, which gets everybody clapping, loud and friendly. I'm sure they have no idea what the fuck's going on but they like me and they're drunk so they're game. I walk for the dance floor, squinting at the spotlight, not sure where the fuck I'm going, until Harry steers me to my table, which includes the Tooheys, Currans, O'Drains, and McClains, not counting Stephen, who's working here tonight, and Francis Junior, who's God knows where. The applause ends and the lights go up. Everyone at my table stares.

"Nice entrance, Henry," says Cecilia, laughing. "What's the occasion?"

"Oh, I'm all about entrances, doll," I tell her. "It's a big night. Good evening, Grace," I say, kissing her hand.

She laughs and struggles to light a smoke. I sit down next to her.

"What's new, ladies?" I say, to Archie and Cece, staring at me openmouthed.

Cece laughs. "You look like the guy on the cake."

"Fair enough," I answer. "Got something to say, Archibald?"

"It's Archie, asshole," he sneers. "All white, Henry?"

"Yeah, all white. Got a problem with that?"

"No," he says, "but you will if the help brings out chocolate dessert."

"I'll be careful. I guess you can't worry about your suit at this point. The damage is done," I tell him, tracing the wheelchair skid mark on his suit jacket with my finger. Archie has no comeback for this, so he turns to Cece to talk desserts. Grace blows a couple of smoke rings and stares at me, one eyebrow raised.

"Hank, is that a Communion suit?" she asks.

"Honey, we made Communion in third grade," I say.

"So it ain't a Communion suit?"

"Nah, sweetheart, it ain't."

"You selling ice cream then?" she asks. "Can I get a Sno-Kone and a screwball?"

"Don't you like the suit?" I ask, worried now. "Don't I look handsome?"

"I didn't say you didn't look handsome." She smiles.

"Good, because if you did, I'd say you need glasses," I say. "Thick ones."

We look right at each other and laugh. Ceiling chandeliers shine like close-up stars. Light dinner music floats over the room, Henry Mancini or Raymond Scott, one of those two petunias. The people from St. Patrick Street—and other blocks even, but not too many others—talk, laugh, and hold drinks. Everybody looks classy. The place smells like food and drink, cologne and perfume. Smiles shine as bright as bracelets and necklaces. Tonight is perfect. *Henry, I'm thirsty. Hey, asshole, you hear me, I'm thirsty. Snap snap snap. Earth to Toohey.*

"What?" I ask.

Grace, snapping fingers in my face, says, "Your sister wants a drink, Hank."

"Which sister?" I say.

"Me. Cece. You only got one."

"Wait, what is Frannie, male or female?" I joke.

Cece laughs. "You're bad, Henry Toohey. Now get me a chocolate milk."

"They won't have that here," I say. "Give me a second choice."

"Chocolate milk," she smiles, sticking her tongue through the gap in her teeth.

"OK, one soda," I say. "I'm going to the bar, people. Anybody need a drink?"

Everybody needs one, so Harry walks me to the bar, which is a closet, really, where a young fella makes drinks as fast as he can and watches his tip jar overflow. We get in line. Four or five older fellas stand in front of us. On our left, Father Alminde wobbles against the bar with Johnny Boyle, pointing a finger in Boyle's chest.

"Some rat bastards threw a ball right through the window," says Father.

"Fucking bastards," says Boyle. "Sorry, Father. Didn't mean to say bastards."

"No, fuck the bastards. If I catch the little shits I'll cut their balls off."

"Damn right. Cut their balls off," says Boyle, before spotting me and Harry.

"You never know, Father," he says. "The perpetrators could be in this very room."

"We should be so lucky," says Father after looking around. "No window breakers in here. Just Curran and Toohey, two goody-two-shoes."

They laugh. Father scratches his balls through his cassock.

On our right at the bar, Francis Junior talks to Bernie Cooney, both drunk.

"Look, Fran, I'm sorry if I jumped to any conclusions," says Mr. Cooney. "It's just, I'm sitting there in church. Your wife is shooting my wife looks. My wife is shooting her and you looks. My kid hates you and your son Stephen. All the sudden I felt like there was this whole thing happening I was in the dark about. Now don't get me wrong, I can't stand my wife. Can't stand the bitch. She wants to have an affair, more power to her, what do I care? On the same hand, though, I can't be letting some neighbor think he can waltz in my house and hop my wife, know what I'm saying? Anyhow, I just wanted to let you know where I'm coming from."

"Forget about it," says Francis Junior, fidgeting in his seat, staring straight ahead.

"So what's going on between our kids anyway?" says Mr. Cooney.

"Beats me," answers Francis Junior. "Mine don't talk to me."

"I hear you. I hate teenage boys. He gets outta line, you should just punch him."

"What did you say?" asks Francis.

"I said you should beat his ass," says Mr. Cooney. "That's what I do, like I did today. My kid's home right now crying his eyes out, but that'll be the end of that."

"Look, I should get back to my table," says Francis Junior, sick of the conversation, maybe sick of himself, maybe seeing some of himself in Mr. Cooney.

"Yeah, sure. Don't let me hold you up. Sorry again."

Cooney holds his hand out to shake with Francis Junior, who pauses a second, then shakes, only glancing at Cooney's eyes. He walks out of the drinks area without seeing me. Cooney watches Francis Junior almost bump into Mrs. Cooney—neither of them saying a word—and looks down at his drink, rattles the ice cubes, and orders another. *Henry. Henry. Yo.*

"What?" I ask.

"Look over there," says Harry, pointing to Bobby James and Margie Murphy, kissing against a wall behind a tableful of gasping seniors. Jamesy's midget grandma walks up, slaps them hard, wags a finger, and yells. Bobby James reaches in his pocket and throws a smoke pellet—*poof*—and pulls Margie by the arm past a coughing Grammy James. He uses three more pellets on the way to the bar, ducking a drunk one-legged uncle, a cheek-pinching yellow-teethed great-aunt, and a convict second cousin taking marks on pony races in his book. Finally, he and Margie reach us.

"Father, do you think he broke the window?" asks Boyle, pointing at Bobby.

"Who, Bobby James?" asks Father. "I can't rule him out, the little shit. Say, let's bring him over and take turns kicking him in his ass. First one to make him weep wins."

Bobby James reaches in his pocket until he sees Father and Boyle laughing.

"I'm almost out of pellets already," he says. "Henry, get me a Bud bottle."

Mrs. James enters the bar area.

"Bobby, there you are," she says. "We have more pictures to take. Margie, you can come too. No more kissing, though. *Please*, no more kissing."

Poof! Hiss! Another smokescreen retreat. Mrs. James asks nobody in particular where the hell he went. Harry stuffs a five in the tip jar as we order drinks.

"Grace looks beautiful, Henry," he says.

"Doesn't she?" I answer.

"Wouldn't mind marrying her myself."

"Easy, pal," I warn, joking though. "Thanks. I'm a lucky man."

"Are you OK?" he asks.

"What do you mean? Why is everyone asking me that?"

"You seem distracted," he says.

"I'm fine," I tell him. "Everything set with the band and the hearse?"

"Everything's cool. Everybody's ready."

"Beautiful."

For the thousandth time tonight, I check my pockets for tonight's two key items: 1) the ring, and 2) Cecilia's vibrating banana-shaped muscle massager. Got them. I brought the massager in case I start to chicken out about using a real mic. That happens, I'll have the DJ play the record while I lip-sync into the massager, like I do at home. That'll keep me from looking like an asshole by singing off-key.

"Harry, I appreciate all your help," I say, "and money."

"Forget about it," he says. "You're a pal."

"No, you're the fucking pal," I tell him, pointing at his chest.

"Yeah, you're probably right," he says. As we laugh and hug, Bobby James appears from nowhere, calls us skirts, then disappears. "Just make sure to dazzle everybody, Henry. Put all your heart into this."

"You know I will."

The parents, not counting the silent, squirming O'Drains, and Frannie, who isn't married, talk and laugh about love at dinner. Mrs. Curran, who has boring B cups, says her dad chased Mr. Curran, who wears a rug on his dome, around the block twenty times after he proposed. Shirley McClain asks, *How old are Jeannie and Ace, twenty-one, twenty-two? Ain't it amazing how old kids wait today to get married?* I laugh out loud and get looks from everybody. Cecilia says, *We all got married at nineteen because we were all* pregnant *at nineteen.* She blames nuns. They kept guard over contraceptive counters at drugstores. Francis Junior tells her, *Don't blame the nuns because the chicks were all sluts.* All the parents laugh as Cecilia leans over to light her smoke with the tip of Grace's. It's nice to see our parents looking and talking nice, telling stories, laughing.

At the head table, Father Alminde struggles through a prayer and promises to cut the balls off of whoever broke the church window. The best man slobbers through a speech he ends by yelling *Eagles.* Maude James grabs the microphone off him, tells Jeannie she loves her, and calls all men pigs besides her father and new brother-in-law. Ace and Jeannie kiss each time somebody taps a drinking glass. Margie Murphy sits on Bobby James's lap, both of them eating food off of each other's forks.

Jeannie and Ace slow-dance to "Sunshine on My Shoulder."

They hold each other close and move in circles on the floor, tuning out the people who watch them, smiling, pointing, running to them with cameras, flashes going off everywhere every two seconds. The rest of the wedding party joins them. Bobby James and Margie Murphy make out until Mrs. James stops them twice, and then tackles Bobby the third time.

Now, Ace dances with his mom to "We've Only Just Begun." His mom has shoulder pads, A cups, false teeth, and a foot of distance from the top of her bad perm to the bottom of his chin. At one point her teeth get stuck on his jacket lapel. She pulls them off, puts them back in her mouth, and restarts the dance like nothing happened, a fucking pro.

Mr. James dances with Jeannie to an old country song whose name escapes me somehow. Chandelier lights drop sparkling snow that lands and glows on the dance floor at their feet. The music stops coming through the speakers, replaced by a beating heart. Jeannie and her dad dance to this beat. Mr. O'Drain cries right at the table. Mrs. O'Drain pretends nothing is happening, pulls out a compact, and checks the blush she cakes on her face to hide the scars. Grace smokes and forces a fake tough face. I can almost see the arrows in their chests. Cecilia glares at Francis Junior, who ignores her and scans the hall, stopping once at Donna Cooney at her table, then once at Stephen disappearing into the hall kitchen. For a second, the whole sorry scene fucks with my head and heart. People let themselves get frozen in a bad place, lost in space, until they get used to it and can't change. They bury the best of their love beneath a pile of stubborn bullshit, losing chances, wasting time, missing life. But no more, not me, not the people I love. That shit stops today. Tonight I want to show them all that you tell the people you love that you love them now. You can't wait another fucking second. And if they don't get it after tonight, I'll rain pain on their cupcake asses. I'm down in a karate crouch just thinking about it, ready to inflict the Toohey Chop Suey on the hardhearted.

* * *

Get up, get down. Dancing is simple, but it has to be a good song. We don't dance to bad songs, simple as that. To combat bad songs, we drag chairs near the dance floor and chill until something good comes on, then we jump out of the chairs and shake our groove things. The Hokey Pokey's playing right now. Bad, *bad* song, so we sit yawning as adults put their fat asses in, put their fat asses out, put their fat asses in, and shake their fat asses all about. "Thriller" by Michael Jackson comes on next and we jump up to dance. "The Bristol Stomp" by the Dovells sits us down. Next, "This Old Heart of Mine" by the Isley Brothers gets us back up. "Rock This Town" by the Stray Cats: down and groaning. "YMCA" by The Village People: up. "Macho Man" by The Village People: down. "Tears of a Clown" by Smokey Robinson and the Miracles: up.

Archie and Cece are breakdance partners. They hold hands and perform electricity lines. She spins his chair while he does robot shit with his head and arms. Harry Curran concentrates on movements that merge aerobic workout with modern dance. He touches his toes twice, shakes his ass once, karate kicks twice, shakes his ass twice, does two jumping jacks, and follows that with three ass shakes, then repeats this dance, wearing ankle weights under his suit all the while. With his goggles fogging up from the steam he builds, Harry Curran is a grass-cutting, money-loaning, goggles-wearing honky James Brown, or a permless Richard Simmons, take your fucking pick. Bobby James and Margie Murphy do a dance called the French kiss. Ever hear of it? Forget about them; she must be pregnant by now. Me and Grace shake it near each other but not together, respecting each other's need for room to showboat. Grace, who takes ballet at Dance or Die, unleashes her ballerina dragon, even during disco songs. She twirls around, knocks people down, and makes it clear she's a graceful swan who will hurt you if you interrupt her interpretation, so don't.

As for me, I can do it all on the dance floor. I have no formal training. I learned to dance on the streets. My style is a combination of *West Side Story*, *Saturday Night Fever*, Michael Jackson, and Philly Phanatic. I also steal moves from ethnic dance shows on PBS programs. Throwing ass is like fly-fishing: cast it out, reel it in, cast it out, reel it in. Bam bam bam. Here it comes, look out, broads, step back, fellas. Swing it. Work it like a dirty dog. Mix things up with Russian kicks, the Ethiopian Shim Sham, the Flintstone Flop. Whatever the fuck works.

Adults understand none of this. They're not coordinated and concentrate more on not spilling drinks than, yes, getting down. They dance with people other than their marriage partners. Two twenty-year-old broads sandwich Mr. Curran, who dances bad and grins all stupid. Two 20-year-old fellas sandwich Mrs. Curran, who pushes her B cups in their faces. Francis Junior is smart enough to avoid Doona Cooney but dumb enough to shake it with Mrs. Leary, who has small saggy tits—a double fucking no-no—and hikes up her skirt and moves closer, smiling. Cecilia dirty dances with Johnny O'Donnell, who's Stephen's age. Jesus. Watching adults dance at a wedding is ugly business. They're drunk and clumsy and climbing all over people they shouldn't be climbing all over, no fun or love in their moves. They sweat, spill booze, and fake smiles. They check to see what their better half is up to with another fucking someone. It's competition. Only Frannie and Shirley McClain steer clear of the bullshit, sitting at the table, talking, smiling, and shaking their heads at the assholes on the dance floor, not counting us kids, though, because we got it right. We don't give a fuck about adults and their kindergarten games. We dance for fun and stay close to the people we love. We do whatever the fuck we want dancing and don't feel dumb doing it. We laugh and point at each other. The whole thing's a blast and the DJ plays "Glad All Over" by The Dave Clark Five. I'm with all my buddies, and we laugh and shout *I'm feeling glad all over* at the top of our lungs, loving life.

* * *

No two ways about it, my boner's going to blow. Me and Grace are slow-dancing to "Always and Forever," her hands on my ass (fucking swear to God). We grind at each other, and I sweat like I'm trying to lift a car off a kitten. This boner's killing me. It feels like a tree log. Jesus. I'll probably faint again. Maybe I should buy a helmet and padded pants. I check out the dance floor to take my mind off my boner.

A couple of feet away, Cece sits on Archie's lap and sings to him while Archie spins his chair in slow circles. Bobby James and Margie Murphy French-kiss like monkeys, not even pretending to dance. Frannie dances politely with Mrs. McClain, their arms raised all formal, their bodies not touching. Harry Curran dances with his mom the same way, while Mr. Curran saws logs, passed out at the table after three Fuzzy Navels, three more than his usual. Francis Junior and Cecilia dance—not far apart but not close together either. Francis Junior, who looks drunk, holds a bottled beer and talks quick and mad about something, his wet bangs sticking to his forehead. He watches the back of the hall, where Stephen stands with a crowd of older fellas, sipping at a beer. Francis Junior mutters something to Cecilia, who says something back, worried, maybe mad—maybe both. Fifteen feet away, the Cooneys sit at their table near the dance floor. Bernie Cooney stares off into space drunk, Donna Cooney makes puppy dog eyes at Francis Junior when he spins her way. *Yo, Hank Toohey, you fucking in there?*

"Huh?" I ask.

"You seem like you're not into dancing now," says Grace.

"Nah, I'm fine," I say.

"Good, because you seem like you're *thinking* again," she says.

"What, would there be something wrong with that if I was?" I ask.

"Yes, there would," she says. "Thinking is sometimes bad, like all the time. Bogs you down. That's why I ain't a thinker. I leave that shit to losers like you."

"I don't believe you. You got sad during the father-daughter dance, right?"

"Yeah, my dad's dead," she snaps, but not mad. "Good call, Einstein."

"I talked to your mom about him today," I tell her.

"You did?" she asks, surprised. "What did she say about him?"

"That he was funny and brave. That he treated you like gold."

"Yeah, he did," she says, sad and serious, before smiling. "He really did. He could always make me laugh when I felt bad. You do that for people. I see that. You make love seem more real than it is."

"Wait, what?" I ask. "Love *is* real. How can you even question that?"

"OK," says Grace, "it's real, but it don't last, and even when it does, it hurts the whole time. Your parents are miserable together. My mom's miserable without my dad. And I bet if your dad died and mine was alive, your mom would be sad and my parents would fucking fight, know what I'm saying? And look at the O'Drains. How fucked up are they? And what about your dad and Stephen? What's going on there? This whole planet is bizarre. Love is bizarre. Nothing's permanent, especially not love."

"You don't mean that," I say, almost hurt.

"The fuck I don't. Can you prove me wrong?"

"I can and will."

"Look, let's talk less," says Grace. "Put your arms around me tighter."

We squeeze and push harder, my mouth real close to her ear. I think I got a fucking fever, seriously. The music sounds far away, like an echo underwater. People near us streak and blur. Holy shit. My boner ain't aching now. It only feels good. Oh, man, it feels good. I put my hands on Grace's ass. I don't fucking care who sees. I'll take the heat tomorrow. I want to kiss her right here. Something's building in me. I can feel it in my feet first, then it moves up my legs, then it moves above the knees to my thighs, which tingle. Wow. The tingling moves even higher. Grace kisses me soft and wet on the ear. Mayday, the tingling just moved to my underpants. What the fuck's going on? Oh, shit, I know. I pull away from Grace and sprint for the john, knocking over chairs on the way. I charge into a stall and drop my pants. HELLO, I LOVE YOU, OH, MOTHER, I PLEDGE ALLEGIANCE TO THE FLAG OF THE UNITED STATES OF JESUS H CHRIST, THE HILLS ARE ALIVE WITH THE SOUND OF MUSIC. Holy shit. A firework of man stuff. Wow, that was beautiful. I feel like a million bucks. I'm ready to sing, soon as I clean the fuck up. I knew this white suit would come in handy.

Fifteen minutes before showtime, I'm loose as a goose. I could just as soon pass out flowers at an airport as sing to Grace. I stand at the mirror in the john, alone and looking good, my cheeks full of color from the happy accident. My white suit is clean, except for the wet stain, which can't really be seen. Frannie walks in drunk, says *Yo,* and walks to a stall to take a dump. Stephen barges in right after.

"Henry, how you doing?" he asks, also drunk.

"I'm all right," I say, combing. "How you doing?"

"All right."

"Yo, Stephen," Frannie calls from the stall.

"Frannie, that you in there?" asks Stephen.

"Yup."

"Taking a shit or changing a pad?"

Frannie laughs. "Both, so I might be a while. Maybe you can fetch me a drink."

"Can't help you," Stephen tells him. "I no longer work for Fat Matt."

"What?" asks Frannie.

"I got fired," says Stephen.

"Why?"

"Couple minutes ago, for drinking. It's a *frigging wedding*," complains Stephen.

"Oh, Christ," says Frannie. "Daddy don't know, does he?"

"Yeah, I went right over and told him. Of course not."

"What if Matt tells him?" asks Frannie.

"He won't," says Stephen. "He fired me quiet and told me to stay at the wedding."

"When did all this happen?" asks Frannie, flushing, stepping out, moving for the sink.

"Couple minutes ago," says Stephen, "after I helped a band unload their shit."

"They're here?" I ask, pushing the door open to peek out.

"Henry, that band have something to do with you?" asks Stephen.

"Sure as shit does," I answer, smiling, straightening his tie.

"How?"

"They're going to play 'Beyond the Sea' while I sing and propose to Grace with this ring."

I hold the open ring box out to Stephen. He opens his mouth and his eyes widen. I hold my breath and tense up. Stephen tries to say something but can't. His chin shakes and he can't get words out, looking like a fish eating fish food, with a tear running down his face. He looks at Frannie, who I can tell understands what I'm doing and what it means. Just when I'm about to have a fucking heart attack, Stephen smiles and cries harder at the same time. He tries to sit on the trash can but ends up almost falling when it slides from under him. Frannie starts to cry too. I don't cry, because I ain't a broad, plus I planned all this shit to make people happy, not sad.

"You fellas upset with me?" I ask my brothers, worried.

Stephen hugs me hard, shaking. Frannie comes over and does the same. When my two big brothers hug me, I understand why they're crying. We break up the hug. Stephen and Frannie dry their eyes and get their shit together.

"Henry, you can't even sing," Stephen tells me.

"Yeah, I can," I tell him.

"No, you really can't," he says.

"Then I'll go to my backup plan," I say.

"Backup plan? What's that?"

"Lip-syncing with Mommy's muscle massager," I tell him. "Another plus is that it doesn't have any cords, so I won't get tangled dancing."

"Dancing?" asks Stephen. "Wait. Mommy's *what?*"

"Her muscle massager," I say, pulling it out of my pocket.

Stephen's and Frannie's eyes balloon. Stephen says, *Give me that, you fucking moron,* and Frannie says, *Oh, Jesus.* They both grab it off me at the same time. It starts to buzz, both of them still holding it. Father Alminde walks in, spots them and their buzzing buddy, and backs out of the bathroom slowly. Stephen pushes Frannie off the massager and chucks it in the trash, laughing.

"I can't get caught putting that back," he says. "I need another drink now. Henry, looks like you're singing live. Go get her, pal."

He hugs me again, then leaves with Frannie. Five seconds later, Francis Junior, piss drunk, enters, mumbles *Yo,* and heads for a toilet.

"Henry, you talk to Stephen much tonight?" he asks.

"No," I say.

"You see him drinking?"

"No."

"Could have sworn I seen him drinking. It's important you tell me the truth here."

I almost laugh but don't and say nothing.

Francis Junior flushes, zips, and walks to the sink. He stares at me in the mirror and says something like *I need to know when Stephen's up to something that'll hurt him, hurt the family. Me and you gotta be honest with each other, for the family's sake. I ain't the bad guy. One time I get fed up and do something selfish, I'm the bad guy? That's nonsense. Any other man'd do the same thing. She wants selfish, I'll show her selfish. People want me to leave Stephen alone, easy enough. Fuck him then. I'm out for me now. Blah blah fucking blah.*

As he spits and spills, I make a couple of last-second fixes and feathers and smile in the mirror like I will to Grace, to the Tooheys, to everybody, big and open, nothing but love inside me. All this bullshit stops in five minutes, ten tops. I smile bigger at my dad.

"Francis Toohey Junior," I say, "you're a few minutes from feeling better, buddy."

"What?" he asks. "What the hell are you smiling about?"

I hug him. Embarrassed, he lets me, but pulls away quick and asks if I've been drinking. When I laugh, he kicks the trash can by accident. The massager buzzes from the bottom. He tilts his head like a dog recognizing a sound, then lets it go and walks out muttering. The door closes behind him and I'm alone again. I take a last look in the mirror, proud of what I see. With a deep breath, I pull my lapels and say the word *love* out loud. With the trash can still buzzing, I push the bathroom door open, stop at my table to tell a confused Cecilia Toohey that I love her and am proud to be her son and walk straight to the front of the hall, my heart on fire.

16

Harry introduces me to the fellas in the band.

"Henry, this is Dead Freddy on trumpet," says Harry. "He played with Miles Davis's cousin's brother's ex-father-in-law."

"Yo, Henry," says Dead Freddy, "break a leg tonight. It was Buckshot LaFunke's cousin's brother's ex-father-in-law, Har."

"Henry, Bones Mulholic, clarinet. He's here even though his angina's acting up."

"How the fuck you doing?" says Bones. "Henry, knock her socks off, pal, it's hemorrhoids, Har, hemorrhoids, not angina, you got any pillows for these chairs?"

"Henry, Pete Pants Pleat here," says Harry. "The man's as good ironing clothes as he is on standup bass."

"How they hanging, Henry?" says Pete. "You can cut steak with my pants creases."

After we reach the last fella, Fingers Fingherty, I shake my arms and legs to stay loose with my back turned to the crowd. Even without looking, I can tell by the murmurs that folks are buzzing. Which makes sense: the DJ has stopped playing music, the house lights are up, a small jazz band is tuning instruments, the Toohey boy is stretching, and the Curran kid is clapping his hands and running around like a stage director. Something's up, obviously. No flies on them.

Harry slides an aluminum chair, for Grace, a couple feet in front of the DJ. The band's on the right, against the wall. The players blow and tap on their instruments. I roll my neck and jog in place. The murmurs grow louder. Harry stands with the DJ, who flicks a switch—*snap*—and hands the mike to Harry, who taps on its top with his finger. *Pop pop pop. Testing, testing, one, two.* I tell myself, *Stay focused, keep love in your heart, and Grace will be yours. You practiced this routine a thousand times, no big fucking thing. Your mom and dad'll stop fighting and fall back in love. Squat, two, three, four. Arms out. Bend the knees. Again, two, three, four. Grace love, Stephen happy. Stretch the derriere. A big farm. Trees with tires for swings. Love and laughing, no fights. Bees and trees. Roll the arms, two, three, four. Backwards, two, three, four. Inhale, exhale, inhale, exhale. Green. Grass. Grace.*

"Evening," says Harry, "how's everybody doing? As you know, my name's Harry Curran and I cut lawns for a low, low fee. Don't forget there are several weeks of warm weather left. If you need landscaping assistance, please don't hesitate to knock on my door, at the house with the St. David statue. Thank you. Now tonight we got a special performance for you to sit back and enjoy. Ladies and gentlemen, it's my pleasure to introduce to you, for the second time tonight, the one and only Henry Toohey."

I spring from my spot and run toward my buddy Harry Curran. Smile. I take the mike and give him a big hug. He wishes me luck in my left ear, his hand on my shoulder. The crowd cheers loud, having fun. I look for Grace and see her smiling and clapping as the house lights dim and a spotlight opens my heart like flower petals.

"How you folks doing?" I ask. "I feel good. Everybody out there feel good?"

Massive cheers. My eyes adjust to the light. I look quick to my table. Grace laughs. Cecilia and Cece laugh. Frannie laughs. In the back, Bobby James makes out with Margie Murphy. Stephen cheers. Francis Junior pulls Donna Cooney into a coat closet and closes the door. Fuck, maybe I'll start with some jokes, see if that will bring him back out.

"We got any Bible readers out there?" I ask. "The Bible's an interesting book. What's up with the Book of Revelations? Only revelation I got was John the Apostle smoked pot. Seven-headed beasts, plagues, final judgment? I got a judgment for you, John: Lay off the weed and stick with beer. The seven-headed beast'd have six less. OK, maybe five less."

Laughs. Applause.

"And," I continue, "speaking of Fat Matt"—laughs—"did anybody else hear that Fat Matt isn't even Italian? The other day I asked him for an Italian hoagie and he said—"

Fat Matt runs to the front and grabs the mike.

"Don't make me cut the power on you, kid. Sing your song," he says, handing the mike back, waving to the clapping crowd.

"Matt's right," I say. "I'm here tonight to sing a song to the girl I love. In fact, I'd like this girl to come up here right now."

Cece runs to the front of the hall and leaps in my arms. The microphone hits me in the face, not hard, but the sound is loud through the speakers. She jumps on my back and waves to the crowd. I sit her down on the chair.

"I do love you, Cece Toohey," I say, "but I was talking about somebody else. Another girl. You got any idea who that might be?"

"Mommy?" she asks, into the mike.

"No, not Mommy," I answer.

"Frannie?" she asks, grinning.

"Not Frannie either. Who's the comedian here? I'll tell you since you can't guess. Grace McClain, would you come up here, please?"

Grace stands up from her seat at the table. She blushes and smokes, embarrassed.

"Come on up here, Grace," I say. "Come on."

The audience claps. *Go ahead, Grace,* they say. A cheer builds. When it gets real loud she laughs and walks toward me, my feathered hair, my white suit, my outstretched arms, my open heart. She reaches for my hand with hers. I kiss it.

"What are you up to, Hank Toohey?" she asks.

"Sit down in the chair and see," I answer.

Grace sits, puts Cece on her lap, and hugs her tightly. The two of them, these two girls I love, giggle like mental patients.

"Grace McClain," I say, "tonight I'll show you and everybody here my love."

Grace's face shines from red cheeks and white chandelier lights, her green eyes bigger than I've ever seen them, looking almost full of hurt. For one second, I almost forget what I'm doing, but it passes, and I'm ready to rock.

"OK, fellas. 'Beyond the Sea' by Bobby Darin," I say, "let's rip, two, three, four."

The music starts. I grab Grace's hand and start the first verse, remembering the lyrics by remembering the last words of each line: *sea, me, sands, sailing.* Boom. Perfect. I nail the verse better than Bobby Darin ever did, let Grace's hand go, make a spin move, and head to the audience, which is laughing and clapping. I spin, smile, wink, and point. Slide back to Grace. Second verse. Just remember, Toohey: *sea, watching for me.* I cup my hand over my eyes like I'm on a boat looking for land. Cut me some slack; Habib and Sasha choreographed it—go break their balls. Next line, boom, I leap on Cece's lap—I have to, because she's sitting on Grace's lap. *Pop!* go the horns. The band's on time, loud and hot, sounding exactly like "Beyond the Sea" does on Cecilia's 45. I jump off Cece and sidestep to the audience. Bernie Cooney gets up from his seat and moves toward the coat closet. I lock my hands behind my head and, in time to the horn blasts, throw my pelvis three times in front of Grace. *Pop! Pop! Pop!* Her and Cece lean back, shrieking, laughing. Also, some broads in the audience nearly pass out from the move. I do another step and spin toward the crowd to check the back of the hall. Bernie Cooney opens the closet door. He pulls his wife out first and slaps her face. She falls. He pulls Francis Junior out and punches his face. He falls. Stephen, standing in the back ten feet away, runs over to them. Cecilia also sees this and runs back there. Frannie follows.

I soft-shoe to Grace and Cece, my eyes filling, but I refuse to give in to crying. I suck it up and sing the next verse, nailing it, perfect. Me and Grace hold hands. She smiles, not nervous anymore. I want to keep holding her hand but an important part with tricky steps is coming up. *Bump, bump, bump, bump, bump, pop!* The drums kick. I jump in the air like fucking Fred Astaire, moving all the way across the stage to the drums and horns, where a prop scotch bottle full of iced tea waits. I make it to the bottle, open it quick, tilt my head back, and guzzle. The audience laughs. I finish the bottle, stare at the audience all groggy, burp into the microphone (not planned), and collapse (planned). The crowd roars.

As soon as the drums pound, I hop up and glide to Grace, keeping perfect time to band bursts. Stephen punches Bernie Cooney, backing him against the wall. Cecilia takes a wild swing at Mr. Cooney too but misses and goes for Donna Cooney, who is still on the floor, instead. Stephen punches Bernie Cooney again, this time knocking him down, and out. Francis Junior gets up and pulls Cecilia off Donna Cooney. Frannie pleads with everybody without grabbing anybody. I sweat bad. Grace watches me and smiles. Cece, watching me and not the jerk-offs in the back, chants *Henry, Henry.*

I nail the last verse, and I'm done. I kiss Grace's hand, staring deeper at her than I've ever done. She smiles like a queen. I do one last spin and freeze with my legs spread and right arm raised. Grace and Cece beam. The audience, who couldn't hear the fight going on behind them because of the loud music, roars. Francis Junior picks Cecilia up and throws her to the floor, trying to get her away from the fight, not meaning to hurt her. Stephen grabs him by his lapels. Frannie begs. The Cooneys lay on the floor, Donna awake and crying, Bernie on his back, knocked out. Cece screams, *Henry, you were great!* over the roaring crowd. I move toward Grace and fish around for the ring box in my pocket with real panic. A couple of fellas spot Stephen and Francis Junior grabbing each other by the collar and run to break it up. My fingertips find the box, my blood running cold as my fingers hit velvet. I lower myself to one knee and give Cece a wink. She winks back. I propose right into the microphone, so that the whole crowd can share our love.

"Grace McClain, I love you. Will you marry me?"

I open the box and hold the ring toward her. Grace stares at it and starts to cry.

"No," she says, sobbing.

Just then, Cecilia closes her fist and swings at Francis Junior as another fella pulls him away. Her punch lands on Stephen and knocks him down. He gets up quick, choking back tears and touching his bleeding nose, and runs for the door. Cecilia tries to go after him but people stop her. She screams and cries and kicks but can't break their hold. My knees buckle. Half the crowd watches me in the front, the other half watches my family in the back, all of us Tooheys making asses out of ourselves. My chin shakes. Don't cry, I tell myself, don't be a sissy in front of all these people.

"No? Why?" I ask Grace, in a whisper.

"We're kids, Henry," she says. "We're still kids."

Grace looks at me with pity and I hate her for a minute. My shoulders jerk up and down from my breathing. Cece reaches for my arm.

"Henry, what just happened in the back?"

"I don't know. Ask those assholes, not me."

I stare at the crowd, watching me, watching my family. Cece's hand is still holding my arm, and I don't want to be here anymore. I can't help anybody. I want to be with Stephen, the only one who will understand. I pull my arm away from Cece, head for the door, and hit the outside, where the air is cold and the hearse coughs in idle on the corner, Mr. McFadden snoring behind the wheel. A loud pop rings out from Tack Park. I jump, scared, then run across the empty Ave to the sound.

17

Stephen is bleeding. Oh, fuck, I think he's shot. Kids are running away, into a car somewhere close by, peeled wheels squealing as they take off and I run to Stephen and hold him, his head and shoulders on my lap. His stomach is bleeding, the blood spilling out of him to the ground. I have to keep the blood inside his stomach, so I catch it as it falls off of his body and dump it back in the hole in his stomach. Oh, Jesus.

"Stephen, look at me," I say. "Look here. It's your brother Henry. Somebody call an ambulance," I shout. "Please, somebody call a fucking ambulance!"

Oh, shit, I stood up and just moved his head. I almost just dropped him to the ground. I am so stupid. I have to keep it together. Jesus, Stephen's eyes are closing. Fuck.

"Stephen, don't close your eyes. Do not close your eyes, motherfucker. Somebody, please, somebody fucking help me," I shout, the wind blowing hard and biting the back of my neck, sleepy cars passing both ways on the Ave, nobody hearing me, nobody stopping. Where are Mommy and Daddy? Or Frannie? I need them.

He coughs and spits something. Oh, Jesus, is that blood? I

can't tell. Sirens, far off, billions of blocks away, moving too slow, slower than Stephen's belly blood, which feels warm, almost hot, on my hands.

"Stephen, can you hear me?" I shout. "It's Henry. Help is coming, buddy. Listen, buddy. You hear those sirens? They're coming for us. Now keep your eyes open and keep listening to me."

"Henry? Megan?" asks Stephen, coughing.

Oh, Jesus. He's looking at me and the Megan painting behind me, over my back, above my head. Or is he dying and really seeing her? Christ, he spit that shit again. His face is white, and his lips are purple. A car passes fast, crushing a can on the Ave. I can hear the Amtrak train, ten blocks east, running into town next to 95. I breathe the chilly air in hard, like I'm about to choke, like I'm panicking. Don't panic, I tell myself. Hang on for Stephen. Don't cry and look sad or he'll just give up and die.

"Don't you give up and die, Stephen," I tell him. "Say my name again."

"Henry," he says.

"Right," I say, "your brother Henry. I'm right here with you."

Oh, God, look at that blood. It keeps spilling on the pavement. It's all over my white suit. The suit's ruined and Mommy will be mad. I hold his head and hug him but not too hard. I don't want to make the blood come out any faster. The sirens are louder now, screaming.

"Do the sirens have to be so fucking loud?" I shout. "Shut the fuck up, sirens!"

"Stephen, don't leave me here," I beg.

He doesn't answer. His eyes are closed but he's still breathing. He looks like a baby. His hair is soft and feels nice. I hear the door of Mungiole's open, a lighter flicks, a man says, *Oh, shit.* Then *boom*, the door closes, *boom*, it opens, tons of people asking excited questions, running closer to me, their feet flapping on the concrete, a car screeching to a stop, the driver yelling at the mob running this way. People are everywhere now, all around us. I see Frannie first, then Mommy and Daddy.

"Oh, my God, Fran, it's Stephen and Henry," shouts Cecilia, running for us.

"Holy shit," says Francis, standing frozen in place.

"Oh, dear God," someone else says.

People are praying.

"Henry, what happened?" asks Frannie, holding Stephen now with me and Mommy.

"He's shot," says Mommy, matter-of-fact but starting to cry.

"Oh, Jesus," says Daddy, still stuck in his shoes, standing away from us.

"Stephen Toohey is shot," someone yells.

Mommy is crying now. Daddy keeps saying *Oh, Jesus.* Folks in the crowd around us are yelling for help. Cars on the Ave are pulling over now, people getting out, doors slamming shut, somebody asking "what happened?" and somebody saying "the boy is shot" over and over and over as people pray out loud in shriek shouts to God.

"Where's Cece?" asks Mommy, still holding Stephen and looking around frantically.

"Don't bump Stephen hard, Henry," says Frannie sharply, like he's mad.

"I didn't bump him hard," I say, annoyed, ready to fight.

"Is he still breathing?" asks Mommy.

"I think he's still breathing," I say, "I think so."

"Fran!" shouts Mommy, to Daddy.

"Oh, Jesus," he answers.

"Fran, snap out of it," she barks. "We need you here."

He obeys, running over like he never froze, squeezing in with us on our knees.

"Stephen," he says, his face tough and serious, his hand on Stephen's cheek.

Stephen opens his eyes and looks right at him.

"Dad?" he asks.

"Yeah, it's your dad," says Daddy, his eyes moving over Stephen's face.

"I'm sorry," says Stephen, in a whisper.

"No, you're not," says Daddy, whispering back. "I am."

They both smile at each other, much as they can here, now. Then *boom*, intruder.

"All right, get out of the way, kid, get out of the way," says some motherfucker in a white suit, pushing in on the family, on me.

"Don't shove us," I yell. "Who the fuck are you, motherfucker? That's my brother. I'll punch your face if you shove us again, you hear me?"

"Let us do our job," says the motherfucker. "Move out, kid, we're trying to help."

"No, fuck you," I say, swinging.

Frannie and Daddy throw me to the ground.

"You motherfuckers," I yell at the ambulance assholes, while Daddy and Frannie hold me and I kick my legs and throw punches at these assholes putting Stephen on a stretcher and throwing bags of clear bullshit with tubes and cords back and forth. Mommy cries and tells me to calm down but I keep kicking and swinging. In between the words I shout I hear men and women worrying out loud behind me, Stephen wheezing, voices cracking on the ambo radio, more sirens coming closer. Red lights flash on everybody's face every half second. I can see the hole we broke in the big round church window, which, with its sharp glass shards on the top and bottom, makes it look like the mouth of a monster with fangs.

"I'm his father," says Daddy, letting go of me. "I'm going with him."

"I'm going too," sobs Mommy.

"Put him in there, we gotta go," says one ambulance motherfucker to the other.

268

"He's bleeding bad," says the other. "If you're coming we gotta go now, get in."

Mommy and Daddy jump in the back with Stephen.

"Frannie," says Daddy, "get the car and meet us there."

"Henry, get your sister," says Mommy, "and take her home. We'll call."

"Get all the way in, ma'am," says the ambo motherfucker, "we gotta go."

Slam. Vroom. The ambulance flies down the Ave with my mom, dad, and dying brother. Why the fuck are those sirens so loud? Finally, they're quiet. About fucking time. I turn around to look at the assholes talking behind me. The park is packed. Two hundred assholes stand in their Sunday best inside of a bloody playground on a Saturday night. There's something fucking funny about that, and I almost laugh, but before I do, I hear somebody crying. It's Ralph Cooney, sitting on a bench, shaking, holding a gun, his head down. Nobody sees him but me. I run and jump at him, my teeth going for his Adam's apple. *Wham.* The gun slides away, me on top of Ralph. I punch his face and spit at the same time. I open my hands and claw at his face as he cries and kicks at me. Hands pull me off him, people shouting: men shit like "Cool off, Henry," women shit like "Oh, my God, a gun." I get farther from him but keep reaching for his face to pull it off to see his ugly skull beneath the skin.

"I'll pull it right off your face," I shout.

I'm finally totally pulled off Ralph, who lays in a ball, crying, his back to the gun ten feet from him, still on the ground, nobody touching it. Squad cars show up. Doors fly open. Fat cops spill out of the cars and run toward us, their black shoes scuffing the scratchy concrete.

"Take it easy, Henry," says Mr. James, behind me now, holding me by the arms. "There's the weapon over there, fellas." Mr. James nods to the cops, toward the gun. "That boy on the ground there is the shooter."

When I hear the word *shooter*, I lunge again, not saying or hearing anything, until Mr. James holds my arms so tight I get pins and needles in both and notice Bobby James in front of me saying this: *Cece.*

Cece.

The sirens scream in my head as I cross the street, and the faster I move, the slower I go. The street lamps hum loud as the El train. Horn and tire squeals twenty blocks away sound like jet engines. I step inside Mungiole's, where the people there, including Grace and Harry, stare at me, at my suit. Grace moves toward me to say something. I grab her shoulders and sit her ass down in a chair. *Sit down,* I say, *do not bother me.* I take Cece, crying, by the hand, and walk her back to St. Patrick Street. Neither of us says anything except she cries like a baby, her sniffles popping like machine guns. Grace and Mrs. McClain follow behind us, watching over us, but quiet and giving us room. The blood dries on my white suit. Between sobs, Cece whines about how fast we're walking. The McClains keep following us as I pull Cece like a rag doll toward our house. When we arrive, I unlock the door and wheel around to face the McClains.

"Look, Henry," says Mrs. McClain. "I don't want you kids alone tonight."

"We're fine," I say, flatly. "We have each other."

"All right," she says, "but will you call us if you need us?"

I can tell Grace is staring at me but I won't look at her. Instead I nod to Mrs. McClain without saying anything, turn around, open the door, and let Cece go inside. When I walk in behind her, I look first at the phone, hoping for a call from Cecilia about Stephen, hoping his blood stops falling out of his body.

18

The Toohey house is quiet and smells like carpet powder, furniture polish, and glass cleaner. Two end-table lamps glow softly. The dogs snore. Nothing is spilled on the floor. It all calms me so much I could almost fall asleep here standing up. Two or three times a year, Cecilia Toohey cleans the house, really cleans it, top to bottom, before she goes out for special occasions. She says the best part of going out is coming home to a clean house, her clean house, where she raised four kids with her husband, Francis. Francis and Cecilia are at their best when they come home from special nights, dressed up, a good meal and a couple of drinks warming their bellies. They sit down together on the sofa. He loosens his tie and throws his jacket on a chair. She kicks her shoes off and puts her legs on his lap. He rubs her feet. They talk and play cards. Fish, they play. *Gimme all your eights,* says Cecilia. Francis Junior shows her his cards and she changes her request to jacks or nines or whatever he has that she needs. They look around the room and laugh at the pictures of us, their four kids, at different ages, teeth big and as crooked as our collars, arms resting on prop wagon wheels, hair styled stupid, not counting mine. Cecilia says to Fran, *Stephen and Frannie look like you.* He laughs and says *that's because they frown all the time, that's why they look like me.* Cecilia tells him *they ain't frowning, Fran, they're both more serious those two, and more like you.* Fran replies, *now, the second two are more like you, Cecilia. Big smiles. Sense of humor. That's all you, from you, Cecilia. They're more outgoing, should we say? The first two are bug-collector types,* says Cecilia. *The second two are bug-*eater *types,* says Francis, and Cecilia laughs and tells him, *see, you're funny when you choose to be. You hold it in more.* Then they smile at each other and say nothing, staring around at the tiny living room, which is neat and smells nice for now, until tomorrow. The clock ticks on the wall. The dogs fart in their sleep, wake up, and fall back asleep. Francis and Cecilia agree that *everything's OK. We have four good kids. Frannie's a model son. Stephen thinks and feels too much maybe. Henry? Strange but lovable. And Cece, our tough only girl.*

Cece. She stands next to me and sobs carefully and quietly, afraid to set me off, I bet.

"Henry, are you mad at me?" she asks, choking on sobs.

I bend at the knees to get closer. "No, I'm not," I say.

"You seem like you are," she stutters between gasps.

I pull a hankie out of my pocket and check it for blood—none—then wave it at her face like a car wash guy does a windshield.

"Cecilia," I say, "please stop crying before you ruin the shag carpets."

She laughs, because our rugs are nasty.

"Henry, can we listen to records upstairs?" she asks.

"We sure can."

"Cool. Can you fix me a snack?"

"OK. What do you want?"

"Chocolate milk and cheese, please," she says. "Two scoops of powder. Four cheese slices. Skim milk. Thanks, pal." She starts up the stairs in her sundress and fake pearls, the same outfit her mom wore tonight. Stopping at the middle, she looks at me so quick and adult I jump. "Henry, did Stephen get shot with a gun tonight?"

"Yeah," I say, unwilling and unable to lie to her here.

"Did he die?" she asks.

"No," I answer. "Not yet. No."

"Is he gonna die?"

"I don't know."

She stares at my suit, then around the house, then at my suit. "You'll be right up?"

"Yeah, I'll be right up."

"Cool. Hurry, please." She's gone up the stairs.

I hustle to the kitchen. Two scoops of powder in skim milk. Five cheese slices, because she always wants one more after she finishes four. I take the phone to the bottom step, run up the stairs, hand Cece her food, and go to the records. I grab maybe thirty and lug them to Cece's room. The top record is *Album 1700* by Peter, Paul, and Mary. I put it on the turntable, play it, and sit down on the edge of Cece's bed to face her on her tiny chair, to talk. Harmonies fill the room. Cece holds a cheese slice with both hands while she chews, like a squirrel eating a nut.

"This cheese is really good," she says.

"I bet it is," I answer.

"You want some of this cheese?"

"Ain't hungry."

"You should eat more cheese," she says. "You're too skinny. Cheese'd fix that. I got love handles already. I think they're from the cheese."

"Really, I'm not hungry," I insist.

"Are you not eating because of Grace?"

"I don't know. Maybe," I answer, honestly.

"She coming back with her mom?" she asks.

"No."

"Good," she says. "I just want to be with you right now."

"Yeah, same here, kid," I tell her, as we hug and she burps, but quietly.

"What's with the polite belch?" I ask.

"You need to hear the phone when Mommy calls," says Cece.

"Oh, right."

Peter, Paul, and Mary are leaving on a jet plane and don't know when they'll be back again. The room thumps like a headache, a heartbeat, both of us staring in space.

"Henry, do you remember that farm with the cows we talked about last night?"

"Sure I do," I say. "What about it?"

"How many years before we can move there?" she asks.

"I figure seven, maybe six if we get lucky. Why?"

"I can't wait that long. I want to go now."

Cece cries again, so I hug her again. She smells like sugar and wipes her nose on my bloody coat. I hand her my hankie, and she blows her nose loudly, like a foghorn.

"Yes, you can wait that long," I say. "Seven years is nothing. You're already eight. Look how fast that went."

"It did go fast," she agrees. "I still remember kindergarten like it was yesterday."

"Exactly," I say. "The next eight'll go even faster. Look, I'm thirteen. A man."

"Let's not get carried away, pal," she cracks, still crying, but slowing down.

"All I'm saying is you can hang in there. We can hang in there. Together."

"I still wish we were leaving tomorrow," says Cece. "I can't imagine what it's like to live on a farm with all those trees."

"Yeah, you can," I tell her. "Know what? We'll pretend we live in the woods until we get the farm. We'll start tomorrow. How's that sound?"

"I don't know, Henry," she says. "Sometimes I think you left the building."

I leap off the bed, over her head, as she sits in her small chair and shrieks.

"Are you saying I'm insane, Cecilia, is that what you're saying? Because if you are, I agree. *Oooo oooo ahhhh ahhhh ooooo oooo ahhh ahh.*"

I make monkey noises, hop around, and scratch my pits. Cece laughs, which is blood to my joke-telling shark ass.

"Apes. Why'd it take millions of years for us to evolve from apes? All you have to do is slap a Phillies jacket and some work boots on an ape and you got yourself a modern-day dad. Where's the fucking evolution there? Ever see Daddy's back hair? Ever see Daddy naked? Jesus. Anytime he walks around in his white underwear I wait for Elmer Fudd to shoot him with an elephant gun from behind a potted plant. What the hell we listening to? This Peter, Paul, and Mary still? Let's put on something else."

The records change: Iron Butterfly, Conway Twitty, Lightning Hopkins, Little Richard, Ruth Brown, Bruce Springsteen, Chicago, Boston, Kansas, the Isley Brothers, the Five Satins, Ry Cooder, Carole King, Todd Rundgren. Tunes and jokes fly.

The Kinks. "Show me a priest and I'll show you a Swiss bank account and a wife in Utah." The Turtles. "All that ass-patting in pro sports makes me uncomfortable. What's with all these naked Barbie dolls, Cece? Are you running a nudist colony in here?"

Cece laughs at all my jokes, even though she doesn't get half. The whole time I tell jokes and change records, I catch myself looking at the blood on my coat sleeves as my arms flail. I picture Stephen on the operating table, a flat beep filling the room, his spirit leaving his body, his body being put in the ground, covered by dirt, ten rows from Megan, Francis and Cecilia screaming and crying, Cecilia jumping into the grave with the coffin, Francis pulling her out, the two of them sitting across a long table from each other next to lawyers who whisper in their ears, me and Cece living at different houses, Stephen not living at either. Every time I picture this I fight it. I fight the bad feelings because

I got love inside me. Faster jokes, louder songs, a two-armed, two-legged love bomb inside a bloodstained white suit, keeping his sister in stitches as doctors do the same with his dying fucking brother. That's my mission tonight, now, tomorrow, yesterday, every fucking day that Cece needs me as much as I need her to need me.

Cece begs for mercy, finally, holding her gut on the bed as I leap around the room, stepping over records, most of which have been played. Except for one: *Abbey Road* by the Beatles. I have no idea how long we have been home. An hour, maybe two?

"Is that *Abbey Road*, Henry?" she asks as I hold it. "I don't like that one."

"You're kidding me," I say, fucking flabbergasted.

"Nah, I ain't," she says. "I like when they wore matching suits and sang shit like 'she loves you, yeah, yeah, yeah.'"

I laugh, even though I fucking disagree, and lean toward her door, listening for the phone. Please ring. Please don't ring.

"Can you at least play 'Here Comes the Sun'?" she asks. "I like that one."

"OK," I say.

We listen to the song, smile at each other, and sing along real quietly. When the song ends, the phone rings. I leap off the bed and race down the stairs to answer, and when I do, my voice cracks.

"Henry? It's Mommy," says Cecilia, sounding so worn out she might be eighty years old. She gives me the news. I hang up and head back to Cece, who's in bed, with the covers up to her eyes.

"He's alive."

She pulls the covers down and reaches out for a hug. So I hug her, tightly.

"You going to sleep?" I ask.

"Yeah," she says. "Will you sleep on the floor next to my bed?"

"OK. I'll go get a blanket and pillow. I'll be right back."

"Cool. Can you turn the light out too?"

"Sure."

I kiss her forehead, turn the light out. She's almost asleep already. Her baby face looks like Stephen's did when I held him bleeding at the playground. I go downstairs and look out the door, up the street, to the McClain house, where Grace smokes on her porch and stares at my house. I close and lock the door, softly and quietly, and walk upstairs to the bathroom mirror. There are bloodstains all over my suit. My hair is out of place. I pull the shower curtain back and step into the tub for the first time in days. Over and over, I hear Grace say no, see Stephen bleed, and watch my parents fight. They didn't even watch me sing. The water falls in buckets on my bloody white suit. It soaks my shoulders, slides down my legs, and floats into the drain. I turn on the faucet to blanket the sound of my sobs, which make my shoulders heave like I'm fucking coughing.

19

Yo. Good morning. How you doing, asshole?

Ralph Cooney shot my brother Stephen—still asleep and critical—in the belly after two carloads of Fishtown fellas showed up looking for a payback tangle. None of them had anything to do with the dudes who got beaten. They weren't brothers, friends, or cousins. Probably assholes like the assholes who beat the five kids in the first place.

Ralph sat at the playground all night. He didn't tell anybody he had a gun but did say—to kids passing through—he was waiting there in case of trouble. Stephen reached Tack Park at the same time the cars rolled up. He stood between Ralph with his gun and ten fellas with baseball bats. Ralph pulled the trigger. Stephen got shot and fell. The Fishtown fellas ran. Ralph hasn't said a word since and is locked up wherever the fuck they take punks like him. Enough about him, though. I don't have the time to waste.

I'm sitting on my bunk bed above Stephen's bed, in my white underwear looking fucking sexy. I've been awake awhile. I'm sweeping spitballs off the Mike Schmidt poster with a dust brush. Once they're gone I take the poster off the wall and roll and rubber-band it. I don't plan on saving it but I'm not up for crumbling or burning it or anything ceremonial. That'd be the same as shooting more spitballs. I got no beef with Mike Schmidt anymore. Beefs with third basemen are for kids. I'm a man. I shot sperm, got shot down, and held my shot brother all in one night. Can ball hair be far behind? I don't think so.

Mike Schmidt refused to sign an autograph for me, Stephen, and Bobby James when I was seven, in 1978. Back then Francis Junior got season tickets for Sunday giveaway games, drove us down to the Vet, and bought us whatever we wanted. He was different back then, happier. Me, Stephen, and Jamesy insisted on going to games early, afraid we'd miss out on whatever they gave away: batting gloves, helmets, jerseys, wristbands, posters, watches, and sweat socks—always Phillies maroon-and-white, always autographed by our heroes. On this particular game day, like all the rest, we showed up two hours before first pitch, wearing everything the real Phils wore except jock straps. Maybe Bobby James had a jock strap on his head. I forget now. It's been a while.

Schmidt was having a catch with a tanned volleyball-boobed broad, ten feet from us, nobody else in the stadium. We walked over. Stephen called him Mr. Schmidt and asked him to sign our programs. Schmidt never even looked at us. He said no and threw the ball back and forth with the hot broad. Crushed, we sat down and said nothing the whole game. We rode home and didn't say anything then either. I walked upstairs and cried in my pillow, a hard cry, like last night. I swore to hate Schmidt forever. I roped Bobby James into hating him too. No more. Fuck that. I forgive you, Mike Schmidt. Your mustache's still stupid but otherwise you're all right.

I step into the upstairs hallway. Cecilia's decked out in the sunhat and short pretty green dress she wears to church every warm-weather Sunday, looking exhausted but still hot. She looks funny at my underwear-only outfit.

"Yo," she says. "Going to church like that?"

"I might put on a tie. Got a problem with my underwear? You bought them."

She laughs. "Hurry up, whatever you decide. Can't be late for Yahweh."

Cece steps out of her room wearing the same outfit as Cecilia, holding *Abbey Road*.

"I say go to church like that, Henry," she says. "It'll liven things up."

"Hey," complains Cecilia, "I thought you two liked Mass since those young chicks started singing songs with guitars."

"They're better than *Abbey Road*," says Cece, "but I still wouldn't say we like Mass. Still a priest there boring us to death."

"Wait, you don't like *Abbey Road*?" asks Cecilia.

"Not as much as *Meet the Beatles*."

"Yeah, me neither," says Cecilia. "You guys want to hear some of it real quick? It's in here somewhere, right?" she asks, pointing in her bedroom.

"Third row on that wall, left side," I tell her, thrilled.

"Ah, here it is," she says, kissing it. "Want to do a song?"

"What, like as a band, like we do in my room?" asks Cece, delighted.

"Yeah, like that," says Cecilia, as me and Cece whoop. "What song?"

"How's about 'All My Loving'?" I say.

"Fine by me," says Cecilia. "Long as I'm John."

"I'm Paul," I say.

"I'm Ringo. And George!" laughs Cece.

Cecilia cues the tune and picks up a red brush for a micro-phone. I grab a curtain rod guitar. Cece grabs two clothes cata-logs, rolls them up into makeshift drumsticks. The tune starts, and this time, as we sing into the big red microphone, play our instruments, and hop around—me in my white underwear, them in their straw hats and sundresses—we don't pretend we're anybody but us. And we don't pretend we're anywhere but here, in Cecilia Toohey's bedroom, in the Toohey house, 4017 St. Patrick Street, Philadelphia, PA, U.S.A., Planet Fucking Earth. Boom. The song ends fast as it starts. We breathe heavily and clap and hug.

"That was fun." Cecilia smiles. "We'll have to do that more. Get dressed, Henry."

"OK already," I whine. "I have to take a shower."

"A shower? What's going on here?" says Cecilia. "You got five minutes."

She chucks the Beatles record on her bed, and picks Cece up with one arm.

"Out of my way, underwear man," she shouts, stiff-arming me and running downstairs, Cece squealing and tucked under her arm like a blue-eyed football.

I shower, step out, and dry off quickly. With a hand, I part my hair on the side, no gel or hairspray. Damn, I still look good. I grab a collared shirt from Stephen's part of the closet, a green one he outgrew that has no moose on the shirt, or buffalo, bison, or rhinoceri. Just green and clean. I complete the outfit with gray slacks, dark socks, and dark shoes and walk down to the living room.

"Holy shit," says Cecilia.

"Yo, Henry. You look good," says Frannie, who doesn't. "I like your hair."

"Yo, Frannie. Thanks," I say. "You don't, and I don't like yours."

"What?" he asks, checking his reflection in his second-grade school picture.

The phone rings in the kitchen. Me and Frannie race for it. I win.

"Hello?"

"Henry, it's Daddy," says Francis Junior. "How you doing?"

"Yo. All right. How you doing?"

"All right," he says. "Listen, your brother just woke up a couple minutes ago."

"He's awake?" I ask, happy and surprised.

"He fell right back to sleep, but he was up, and the doctor said that was good. So tell your mother he was up."

"Got it. I'll talk to you—"

"Henry, hold on. Tell your mother—tell her I love her too, will you? Can you do that while I'm on the phone? Tell her about Stephen, and that I love her, while I listen."

"OK. Yo, Ma," I call.

"Yo," she answers.

"Stephen was awake this morning. And Daddy says he loves you."

She looks at me, then Cece, then me, then smiles. "Tell him that's good news."

"Mommy says that's good news," I tell Francis Junior.

"Beautiful," he says. "See you at the hospital."

"All right, buddy." I wait and let him get off first, then I turn to the other Tooheys and say, "Now can we get this show on the road?"

We step outside, where St. Patrick Street explodes like a sunshine symphony: squeaky bike wheels, hissing garden sprinklers, humming electric lawnmowers, arguing parents, and cracked cans of beer, all conducted by the dead saints. Cecilia pops a piece of gum in her mouth.

"You see that, Cece? Mommy just ate a piece of gum," I say.

"Say what? What'd she do?"

"She ate gum an hour before Communion. That's a violation of church rules, right?"

"How the fuck should I know?" says Cece, climbing on my back.

We reach the sidewalk, which leads to the church. Outside the church is the trolley stop that leads to the El, which will take us to the hospital, where my big brother Stephen lays, his heart pushing around new good blood that'll replace the old bad shit. Francis Junior sits next to him in a vinyl chair, hugging his knees with his arms, spilling tears on the floor, promising to make things better, to make them good and full of love, like they could and should be, like they will be. Everything's OK. The sun shines, and even when it rains, there's always sun again—except at night, when there are 10,000 suns twinkling in the sky.

Halfway up the block, I see Grace on her porch, smoking, and stop.

"Yo, what's the holdup, homeboy?" Cece asks.

"Hold on a sec," I say, walking up to the McClains' porch.

"Hey, Hank," says Grace, softly. "I heard your brother's hanging on."

"Seems that way," I say, squinting at her, playing it cool.

"You still ain't mad at me about turning down your marriage proposal, are you?"

"Nah, we're cool," I say.

"Maybe you can ask me again in seven or eight years."

"Maybe," I say. "Can't make any guarantees, though. I'll be more in demand."

"Just keep me in mind. Meantime, can we make out more tonight?"

Houston, we have boner liftoff.

"C'mon, Henry, let's go," pouts Cece.

"OK, it's a date," I say.

"A date for who?" asks Grace, confused.

I point at Cece on my back. "Her now, you later. You definitely later."

"Cool," says Grace, stepping on her smoke and smiling. As she walks away, I think, I'll ask again in seven; fuck that eight-year shit.

"Henry, can we pretend we're in the woods outside, like you talked about last night?" Cece asks.

"OK, Cec," I say, pulling her tighter to my back, "you ready?"

"Hell yeah," she says. "I been ready. I was born ready. Let's get it on."

See the row homes on both sides of the street? I tell her. They're cliffs now, not houses. We can dive off them into the river. Yeah, just like Tarzan except nobody's making me wear a loincloth. What do you mean where's the river? The street's the river. Good-bye, St. Patrick Street. Whoa. We almost stepped in it. We have to be careful—the current's fast, and the water's cold. Look, the lawns aren't lawns anymore; they're trees hanging over the riverbanks. There are more than I can count. Their branches dip because of all their apples, which are big as beach balls. C'mon, let's run. Hold onto me real tight. We won't fall in the river. Nah, that isn't a skateboard, it's a raft. We'll hop on that to the other side. Don't worry. We won't fall. Look how beautiful it all is, the river, the trees. You can see it, right? That's because you have love in your heart. Your big heart makes you hard to carry but I still won't drop you. All that love is heavy but I won't let go. Now we're across the river like I said. C'mon, let's keep running. Let's see if we can run as fast as this old river . . .

"Henry Tobias and Cecilia Regina Toohey!" yells Cecilia from behind us. "Slow down! You'll be dirty and sweaty for church!"

We stop.

"Should we listen to her, Cec?" I ask.

"No," she says. "Start your engines, dude."

I make an airplane noise and spin around fast as I can. Cece shrieks.

"Hank, stop spinning your sister and making her laugh. She'll get sick."

And so I do. Stop spinning her that is. I'll never stop making her laugh. My name's Henry Toohey. My heart's twenty feet wide and twenty thousand feet deep. We take off together, me and Cece, in a straight line for the Ave, the church, the hospital, our dad, our brother, our life, faster than a speeding river. The red and green apple trees blur on both sides, like Christmas colors, like happiness, until it seems that they, like love, swallow us happy and whole.

Acknowledgments

I would like to express deep gratitude to Amanda Patten, my editor, and David Dunton, my agent, both of whom are total pros and, even better, good human beings and trusted friends. By extension, I'd also like to thank all the nice people at Touchstone and Harvey Klinger, Inc., especially Harvey Klinger, Elizabeth Bevilacqua, Jenny Bent, and Lisa Dicker. A very special thank you also goes to Johanna Gohmann.

I'd like to further thank the following people for their feedback, encouragement, and advice: Stephanie Diaz, Jim Clark, Heather McCarron, Christa Gersh, Suzanne Toppy, Tracy Price, Jessica Hohmann, Andrew Eastwick, Sean Diviny, Larry Chilnick, Byrd Leavell, Amy Tompkins, Irma Rodela, Dr. Stephen Myers, Pat Brady, and John Aherne.

And special thanks to the following family and friends:

Denise and Buzz McBride; Steve, Fran, and Sarah Bowers; Ida McBride; Charles and Margaret Kilgus; Dede, Kevin, and Aislinn McFadden and the McFadden family; Frankie, Johnna, Alison, and Megan McBride and the Pingitore family; Kevin McBride and Colleen Luberski; Aunt Peggy and Uncle Nick LaForgia; Aunt Susan Meyer; Aunt Arleen McBride; Uncle

Jimmy McBride; Aunts Ann, Fran, Jackie, Jeannie, Kitty, Linda, Pat, Patsy, Susie, and Terry; Uncles Bill, Bill, Chalie, Denis, Jack, John, Thomas, and Timmy; all my cousins, including Barbara Tyndall, Anna and Mario LaForgia, Colleen DiTulio, and Brittany Chatelain; Bob, Bobby, and Joan James and family; Sean, Christie, and Amelia Alminde and family; Jimmy, Tammy, and Oland Clark; Paul, Jen, Emma, and David Donohue and family; Timmy and Shaubie Faia and family; Johnny Walker and family; Chris O'Drain and family; Bridie Tobler and Danielle Walsh and family; Matthew Melinson and family; Matthew Mungiole and family; David Smith and family; Lee, John, Rita, and Michael Ventura; Amy, Kevin, Matthew, Seth, Jake, and Nate Lindner; Larry Berran and family; Michael Spaziano and family; John McGeehan and family; Joanne Revak and family; the Price family; Chris Miller and family; Karen Rae and family; and last but not least, Susan Dilts and family.

GREEN GRASS GRACE

DISCUSSION POINTS

1. In a rapid staccato style salted with curses and slang, Henry Toohey brings his own story to life in *Green Grass Grace*. How would you describe the book's tone and language—and, by association, Henry? Did the writing style or Henry remind you of any other books or characters?

2. Why do you think the author chose to set the novel in 1984? How does this time period shape these characters and their outlook? How might this neighborhood have been different if the story had been set in the present day?

3. In what ways could this Philadelphia neighborhood be seen as a character in its own right? What's the personality of the neighborhood? How are the troubles that Henry's family is experiencing characteristic of—or distinct from—the problems facing the entire community?

4. Even more than most teenagers, Henry is very concerned about his personal style. Describe the image he's crafted for himself. Do you think other characters see him the same way he sees himself?

5. While Henry presents himself as wise beyond his thirteen years, his romantic and idealistic take on the world doesn't always match reality. In what instances does he accidentally reveal his naivete? How has he changed by the story's end? Do you think he'll lose his romantic optimism as he grows up?

6. How does the author use humor—especially in describing Henry and his friends' boys-will-be-boys exploits—to lighten the more serious elements of the story?

7. When his father denies point-blank the question about whether he's having an affair, Henry thinks, "For the first time in my life . . . I watch him with sadness and something less than complete love. He lied right to my face, and the whole year of him letting me down, letting us down, hits me at once" (169). Why does this incident have such an impact on Henry?

8. Why do you think Francis Jr. is having such a hard time being a good husband and father? What expectations did he have for his life, and how have things turned out differently? Why has Stephen's depression hit him so hard?

9. Each time Henry and his friends visit a shop in their neighborhood, they are treated to the shop's brand new TV commercial. What do these commercials add to the color of the novel?

10. All of the action of the story is set in just a few days' time—the last few days of summer vacation. Why is this time frame especially appropriate and meaningful?

11. What role does the Catholic Church play in the story? Does the irreverence with which it is sometimes portrayed—the character of Father S. Thomas Alminde, for instance—undermine its influence, or is the church actually a positive force in these characters' lives?

12. Henry reflects that it "could as easily be 1963" (58) in his neighborhood. He later explains, "People let themselves get frozen in a bad place, lost in space, until they get used to it and can't change. They bury the best of their love beneath a pile of stubborn bullshit, losing chances, wasting time, missing life" (249). For which characters is this description most fitting? How did this neighborhood become so depressed, so trapped in the past? What makes Henry the right person to shake things up?

13. Why do you think the author chose *Green Grass Grace* as the book's title?

14. All of Henry's idealism and optimism coalesces in his plan to propose to Grace, pull Stephen from his blues, and save his parents' marriage. Were you surprised when his elaborate designs fell apart? What was wrong with his plan?

15. Although the events of the wedding reception transpire far differently from the way Henry had imagined, they do point the way to real change for the Toohey family. What challenges does this family still face, and how do you think things might be different for them in the future?

A Conversation with Shawn McBride

Q. Like Henry, you were born and raised in Philadelphia. In what ways has your portrait of Henry's neighborhood drawn on your personal experiences?

A. In every possible way. I grew up in Henry's Holmesburg neighborhood, on a row home block like St. Patrick Street, packed with people, most of whom were extremely crazy and funny and full of fighting-mad conviction about the Catholic Church and Philadelphia pro-sports teams, but not necessarily in that order. You can't live that close to that many people and not learn to survive through beer cans, belly laughs, and fistfights over porch railings. Growing up in my neighborhood, you found in every house you went somebody larger than life, beating some kind of drum, asking you to say hello to your mother and tell your father to go to hell, or vice versa, but either way God Bless and Go Phils.

Q. Likewise, where did the inspiration for Henry, his friends, and their escapades come from? Are there any similarities between Henry and the thirteen-year-old Shawn McBride?

A. I wish. At thirteen I had some of Henry's superficial qualities, minus the ones that make him special. So I combed my hair a lot but was shy and nervous, especially around girls, and lacked his bravery, conviction, and compassion.

As for the inspiration for Henry and his friends, it came from a variety of sources, both good and bad. My daughter Chloe and her friends were a good source. They are much younger than Henry and his crew, but they're such a blast to watch. In any given conversation or game they undertake, all the basics of human drama are covered: love, jealousy, generosity, betrayal, loyalty, competition, name it. They're just plain contagious fun too, full of love and life and energy, open to everything, ready for anything, having no time or taste for bullshit. I wanted Henry and his friends to be all that, and to contrast them against what we become in adulthood, which is assholes really.

Life was fun then. The days stretched out forever, and everything that happened was epic—Dumpster kisses, bike rides, Mob delis, dark dirty bars with open doors, insane neighbors, stickball, basketball, and broken windows. A single day was thrilling.

Q. How did you create Henry's voice? Was it difficult to shape, or did it just flow naturally?

A. It was a little of both. The first couple of drafts, he didn't really have a voice. He told twenty pages of internal jokes in between sitcom-type dialogue exchanges with cardboard neighbor characters. It was one-sided satire, with no love or sympathy for the characters. The pivotal change in his voice came right away though, on whatever draft got me in the right direction. In earlier drafts, I honestly think the opening line was "Hello, my name is Henry Toohey." Finally I thought, What is this crap? and in my great disgust came up with what's there now: "Hellfire, hallelujah, and halitosis. Mike Schmidt sits to pee. How you doing fuckface?" Once I had that, I had his voice and things just rolled from there. But I was still a long way off.

Q. This was your first experience as a novelist. How did the story take shape? What was your creative process?

A. The word "process" implies much more sophistication and expertise than I possess. I initially set out with the mission of playing to my main strength, which is being funny, and staying away from my greatest weakness, which was everything else. I felt no confidence about being able to pull off a plot that built to a climax in structured fashion. So I figured I'd write about a funny city kid in the summertime, because I could lean on jokes and experience and write a narrative that pinballed back and forth—like a city kid's summer day would—for reasons I could later justify. All of which led to an overjokey mess that placed Henry's proposal in no context. The kids just zipped around, he was just proposing to Grace because he was a dreamer, and the story lacked any development of the adult backdrop bullshit hanging over these relatively happy kids. That came later as the story and I got better through nothing more than osmosis and repetitive effort. I was almost disappointed at how much writing came down to the same principles as riding a bike: you can't do it at first, you just keep trying and crashing. Then all of a sudden, you're popping wheelies and have no clue or memory of anything you did that got you from A to B. You just ended up there. Because of this, I attribute nothing to muses, magic, or lightning bolts and smell a fraud anytime I hear somebody talking in such fashion. To me it's all light bulbs, long days, and late nights.

I had no schedule for writing. I work a full-time job and am a weekend father, so I stole time anytime, anywhere. I wrote the story on several different computers, in different houses, at different jobs, on napkins in bars, wherever, whenever.

Q. Henry's story is ultimately deeply optimistic—a tale of love and hope for the future. What message did you hope readers would take away from the novel?

A. I would love for readers to finish this book and run out of their houses to kiss strangers. But maybe most people are too subdued for that, so hopefully they'll take away hope and love, like this question mentions. I can't imagine life without either and feel all my books will include both.

Q. What's next for you as a writer? Will we be seeing more of Henry and the Toohey family?

A. Yeah, sure, if somebody backs the Brinks truck up to my house. I'm kidding. Sort of. We'll see what happens with Henry and the Tooheys. I'm not against writing another Henry Toohey tale, but I need a break from him for now. I don't want to be an author who writes about the same character over and over throughout a career. More power to J. K. Rowling, whose writing is great, but I'd be ready to decapitate Harry Potter by now, then have the bad guys play fricking quiddich with his head, then have them explode it with dynamite after the match. I'd go nuts.

I'm writing a Christmas book—set in Philly (and the North

Pole)—right now. It's about unhappily married homicide detectives, their failing marriage, their explosives-loving delinquent egghead twin son and daughter, record amounts of holiday season snowfall and homicides, bad art, soft rock, AWOL Christmas toys, the Clauses on the rocks, and a toy-tracking bounty hunter elf and his steed, a self-conscious bare-assed reindeer.